MANAS

MANAS

Alfred Döblin

Galileo Publishers

Originally published in German as
Alfred Döblin: *MANAS: epische Dichtung.*
Berlin: S Fischer Verlag, © 1927.

Translation and Introduction © C D Godwin 2021.

This translation © C D Godwin 2021
The translation of this work was supported by a grant from
the Goethe-Institut which is funded by the German
Ministry of Foreign Affairs

First published by Galileo Publishers
16 Woodlands Road, Great Shelford, Cambridge,
UK, CB22 5LW
www.galileopublishing.co.uk
Galileo Publishers is an imprint of Galileo Multimedia Ltd.

USA: SCB Distributors
15608 S. New Century Drive Gardena, CA 90248-2129 | USA

Australia: Peribo Pty Ltd
58 Beaumont Rd, Mount Kuring-Gai, 2080 NSW, | Australia

ISBN: 9781912916214

All rights reserved. This book is sold subject to the
condition that it shall not, by way of trade or otherwise, be lent,
resold, hired out or otherwise circulated in any form of binding
or cover other than that in which it is published and without a similar
condition including this condition being imposed on the
subsequent purchaser.

CONTENTS

A note on the text   vi

Introduction   vii

ONE: THE FIELD OF THE DEAD

[1]	Departure	13
[2]	On the Field	26
[3]	Hijacked	70
[4]	Ekphora	86

TWO: SAVITRI

[1]	To the Mountains	107
[2]	Manas Drifting	197
[3]	To Kailash	210

THREE: THE RETURN OF MANAS

[1]	Down to Earth	253
[2]	Among Humans	319
[3]	Manas and Shiva	355

About Alfred Döblin   401

A NOTE ON THE TEXT

The text used for the translation is the first edition published by S. Fischer Verlag, 1927.

In his earlier epics (i.e. before *Berlin Alexanderplatz*), Döblin made few concessions to his readers. He presented a wall of text, divided at best into a small number of 'Books', and within each Book a number of sections identified only by a single line space and a capitalised word or two. Where he provided a Dedication (as in *Wang Lun*, or *Mountains Oceans Giants*), this was as likely to perplex as to orient the reader. *Manas* does not have a Dedication.

To help orient the reader I have formatted the text:

- 'Chapter' headings are provided within each of the three Books. ('Chapters' in the original are identified by a space and an oversized capital initial.)
- Line spaces are added between major sense-units ('paragraphs').
- Where more than one voice speaks in any scene, indentation differentiates that scene's main speaker from the others.

I have tried to keep close to the original in terms of line lengths and breaks, but have treated the sense-unit, which may be one line or more, as basic, and have aimed to convey the rhythms and assonances, and the emphases and hesitations implied by the break between one line and the next.

INTRODUCTION

This remarkable book – an exciting and intriguing story, told with great verve in a vigorous, direct language of many moods and voices – is the least known of the major fictions Alfred Döblin produced over the forty tumultuous years pre-World War One to post-World War Two. Döblin himself (apart from one title) is the least known of the 20th century's great German writers, though his reputation has grown in Germany since his death in 1957. Smart new editions appear every decade or so, and streams of books, journal articles and scholarly colloquia examine aspects of his art and his thinking.

The Anglophone reader comes to Döblin with little idea what to expect. Maybe a vague knowledge of that one title from his vast output: *Berlin Alexanderplatz – The Story of Franz Biberkopf*. The next novel after *Manas*, it has eclipsed all the rest ever since its publication in 1929.

And with *Manas* you truly are entering virgin territory. Virtually nothing has been written about it in English, and this is the first English translation (maybe the first into *any* language). Even in Germany *Manas* suffers unjustified neglect, which is a puzzle, given that Döblin declared bluntly that Biberkopf is *Manas auf berlinisch* – 'Manas with a Berlin accent'.

There's nothing complicated or 'hard' about the crisp, powerfully dramatic format Döblin chose for *Manas*. (Nothing here of the chaotic noisy word-montage of the Berlin novel!) As I translated *Manas* I imagined it as a graphic novel, a stage play, a film – Bollywood, even! Once I'd finished, I adapted it as a radio play, incorporating about a third of the text along with a synopsis and other navigation aids.

A word about the 'epic'.

Döblin's reputation rests largely on the major fictions he called 'epics'. *Manas* was the fourth[1]. He wanted a new kind of fiction, a break from the bourgeois novel: no more playing with 'plot', 'suspense', 'individuals' with invented 'psychologies', no more cheap eroticism.

Instead Döblin sought to reinvigorate, under the difficult conditions of the modern age, that art with which Homer, Virgil, Chaucer, Dante, Cervantes, for example, enthralled large audiences over long spans of time. These authors, he declared, dealt with themes of universal enduring human concern: life and death, good and evil, power and subjection, fate, meaning; humans acting in and on the world, either in Nature or in defiance of Nature (hubris, nemesis). A daunting task, he knew. The minstrel entertaining with a tale of Troy received immediate feedback: the audience, in a sense, was co-creator. Now the writer in his study produces a book: it may or may not be 'noticed' – often the critic will be ignorant and/or prejudiced; and little feedback from readers will make its way to the writer, who by then has anyway moved on to the next project.

Still, Döblin persevered. His epic fictions cover an astonishing range in space and time – 18th century China; Europe in the Thirty Years War; a hyper-Promethean 27th century; mythical India; Weimar Berlin; modern Europe through the eyes of a Babylonian god; South America pre-Conquest to the present day; the failed German revolution of 1918.

Döblin's fictions – all substantial works: *Wallenstein*, the *Amazonas* trilogy, *November 1918* are each three to four times longer than *Manas* – are best conceived, he said, as symphonies. They proceed not so much by plot-action (though *Manas* does have a very forward-moving plot) as by themes and motifs

---

[1]. The first three were: *The Three Leaps of Wang Lun* (NY Review Books 2015); *Wallenstein* and *Mountains Oceans Giants*.

that swell and fade, appear and reappear in tempi slow or fast, employing an orchestra of voices. And these symphonic fictions in their varied guises do indeed pursue, over forty years, matters of enduring human concern.

The earlier Döblin epics had no clear individual 'hero'. They depicted masses: humans in collective settings (a sect, an army, a townzone), and the massive forces that bear down on them (oppression, war, economics). *Manas* is the first of Döblin's major works in which his enduring and universal concerns are individualised – in Savitri, in Manas the proto-Biberkopf.

To say more would risk manipulating the reader's own reception of this unique work, praised highly by Robert Musil and others when first published, and since ignored. Each reader will, I hope, enjoy something of the same sensation which, in Keats' poem, stunned stout Cortes: 'silent, upon a peak in Darien'.

Cortes, of course, quickly spread word of his discovery. May you do likewise!

Chris Godwin   January 2021
[https://beyond-alexanderplatz.com provides extensive translations and materials about Doeblin's life and works.]

ONE

THE FIELD OF THE DEAD

[1] DEPARTURE

THERE WAS NO MORE RAIN.
Storms shredded the black clouds hither and down
From the eastern iceheads of Himalaya,
Blew them onto mountains and cedar forests,
Onto blooming meadows, southerly slopes,
This bedlam of beasts and trees –
Euphorbia acacia stands of bamboo –
Tossed them, torrents and ice-needles,
Over sheer rockwalls, seething hills and spates,
Over rivers, –
They raced thundering down deep valleys,
Kosi, Alaknanda, Yamuna,
Surged onto the radiant plains of India! –
Storms shredded the black clouds away,
Howled.

And ravines meadows rockwalls awoke to the drumming of
    waters,
Began howling like seas.
And ships rode on the sea.
What sort of ships were they that rode the sea,
Boats bobbing, darting under sail, capsizing, coming aright?
In the pattering of the waters,
Souls, pale misty Souls
Came gliding by nooses of vine, stretched themselves past
    grasping thorns,

Shimmers of silence in the turbulent tumultuous hubbub.
They clumped in white masses,
Waited motionless under the downpour.
Wind whirled them high, breath from the mouth of Shiva,
Three-eyed God on crystal Kailash,
Whirled them high, spun them like a wheel,

Spilled them, mist onto water.

MANAS stood at the window of his garden hall.
In the garden they were singing:

> 'Manas, our jewel!
> When you rode out we knew: you will save us.
> You have returned.
> Come to us, come to us.
> Come to the pool, come into the boats.
> They called out like us, those warriors who fell:
> Manas, our joy.'

They put on shadow-plays, pastoral plays under the palms,
With flutes and tomtoms.

And Manas, helmet flung from him, chain-mail on the floor:
'How long must I stand,
How long must I stand at the window,
How long must I stand here at this window,
How long must I stand at this pale hateful window of glass,
And I have to listen to you,
Listen hour upon hour upon hour…'

> 'Manas, our joy! For two days we shall stay
> And sing out to you.'

'…Listen as you try to befuddle me, enchant me,
You shall enchant me no more.'

Puto, the mighty man, lifted the door-latch.
He had braided his beard, in it little bells tinkled,
His scarf silver-threaded.

The man at the window stretched hands out to him:
'No bowing! No kissing the floor at my feet
Because I command the army. How am I better than you.'

> 'You protected fathers and mothers, they sing it to you,
> You protected children, saved yourself and me.'

'How long must I stand,
How long must I stand here at this window,
And hear myself praised, shamed, goaded, taunted.
Let go my hand! Do not kiss my demented hand:
Its task is finished.
Don't touch my head! It has done wicked deeds.
Tell me, Puto…'

> 'What should I tell you, Manas?
> When will you come to see what they've made ready for you
> In the palace, throughout Udaipur,
> All decked out and never letting up its jubilation?
> When will you see your father's joy,
> How your women yearn for you,
> How Savitri dances, she who holds your heart…'

'Tell me, Puto, what life is ordained for me?'

> '…and touch your hand again, which has saved us.
> But you know the answer, as a tree knows its own sap.
> It is destined: that you shall enjoy your fill of love,
> Delights are there for you in the fields,
> Children are there playing, war-fame is there.
> The Gods look on you with pleasure.'

And Manas on his knees before the mighty man:
'But when in battle they lay down dead and dying beneath
    hooves –

Oh that I can tell it now, and you are listening,
And are with me and accept it and are my friend,
My teacher, and will explain it to me –
In the battle, in the last one, on the Nara River, in the mud, the
    ponds,
I saw their mouths and eyes, their foreheads,
The whimpering faces of my enemies as they stiffened, became
    leaden.
I ripped the souls from out of their bodies!
I broke open the egg: for the first time I saw yolk trickle,
Yellow-white, – I am sickened, I tremble still to think of it.
It was enough almost to slay me.'

    'You saw the horror of a creature facing death, Manas.
    What alarmed you so?'

'Now you at last are here, Puto. They summoned you
Because for three days now I keep to this room.
They are worried because I spurn all food.
At last, Puto my teacher asks me something,
I can lie at last at another's feet.
I wanted nothing more than this the whole day long.
I lay beside my enemy in the sand,
I dropped down at his side,
And lay and gazed at him and prodded him, my brother.
Oh, he is my brother, and really he is me, Puto;
That ghastly twisted face,
It will be mine, it must be mine one day!
And this is me. That is me.
And that is my fate and the truth of now. Of now.'

    'How you tremble, Manas.'

'I'm not trembling. I shall stand up in a minute.
I – am frozen.
I am frozen in the face of the Gods.
Frozen in the face of Death.

Frozen in the face of Now.
And as I swung my sword once more from horseback, on the
   Nara River,
Swung, a – a lameness seized my arm.
Whether I strike, or I am struck, it's all the same.
The sword thrust through the throat just sits there.
Puto, a sea is heaving beneath the land on which I walk!
A fire is burning beneath the land on which I walk.
No victory is of any use.'

> 'And Manas does not see me, Manas speaks to the wall,
> Manas does not turn to the window
> To see that Udaipur exists.'

'And I am lost. And can no longer see the sun.
The lovely sun has been torn away from me.
The elephants I tame are trumpeting in my groves.
Their keepers stand there and I don't come and I don't know
   them.
I cry: Ah, uuih, uuih,
I, Manas, son of the king,
I the victor back from the salty wastes,
I cry: Uuih, I will go to the dead,
I will go from here to let them tear me, grind me,
Will go to sorrow, sorrow, rather than still live, still live.
Rather than still see the sun, see the sweet beloved sun,
The sun so fervently beloved,
Oh Puto, the sun that I have loved so tenderly.'

> 'Oh I know you, my child. Come, Manas, to the King.
> I shall help you, here I am.
> Now take your helmet, here's your armour.'

'Death is real, Puto, dreadful dreadful sorrow.
I must go to where this horror is born,
This deep deep sorrow.
I will not run away from it.

Don't lead me like a donkey to its manger.
You are the mighty Puto, man of powers.
We've been on many a hunt together, bagged much game.
Mount up once more at my side,
And ride with me once more, just once, on this hunt.
Ride with me to the realm of darkness.'

> 'You look for sorrow, Manas.
> Lay aside your princely clothes, throw away your rings.
> Many have done so.
> Scatter ashes on your head.
> Sorrow looms already large, endlessly large
> In our life.
> O Manas, no need to go into the ghastly Beyond
> To find sorrow.'

'Don't hold me back. It is too late now.
I condemn myself for all I failed to see.
The sweetness of this life, I scorn it.
I want no more of its vapidity and softness.
I will take a stand: here I am.'

> 'The Gods have barred the land of darkness,
> The gate is shut and bolted, Manas.'

'You are Puto, man of powers.'

> 'Nothing alive can do what you would do.'

'I am the victor, I am not befuddled!
I am Manas.
Tomorrow early you shall go to the King and say:
"Manas, your son, has returned victorious
From the Nara River, from the wastes of Thar.
The forts have all been taken,
Not one could stand against him and our army.
I crossed the desert, subdued the coast.
I deliver the Rajah to the King.

But Manas, your son, today has sallied forth
In early morning, to conquer a new enemy".'

'That gate is shut and bolted. Nothing alive can shift the bolt.'

Manas' brow flushed with anger. His fists whirled about his head:
'I am the victor! I am not befuddled.
I am not unhinged.
Udaipur does not befuddle me.
I am Manas, and do not go compelled before the King!
Those now singing in the garden, tomorrow early they themselves
Will pile up logs between the banyan trees
Where the Victory Theatre stands.
They must decorate the pyre as befits my station.
Then they must sing as the logs flare up,
And I burn.'

'So, demons infiltrating among the enemy
Have confused you, the wicked things, you the indomitable.'

'And so would you deceive me, mighty man,
And say that I am lying.
You'd grant me still more endless battles,
More endless shouts of laughter from out there,
Like the laughter of this triumph.
See my armband, nephrite with gold and emeralds.
My father gave it me after my first battle.
I was a doughty warrior!
Ever since I've known I cannot win, I have no rest.
So, – fling the armband to the floor. Ten pieces.
Good. See, that is Manas.'

'And see these threads I wear around my neck.
Mighty man you call me. Shiva is my God.
I break these threads.
And shall say no prayers to Shiva
Until I have delivered you to your goal.'

DEEP black sky. Starry sheaves a-sparkle.
Moon drowned in the sea of sky.
Little boat bearing Puto to the King's hall.
Rippling, trickling.

Peacocks screamed in the raintrees,
Flying foxes among the branches.
Forested in darkness, the arc of hills above loud Udaipur.
Thousand temple drums, torchbearers.

Armoured knights on elephants lofted shields, brandished lances,
Jubilant through streets of waving pennants.

Girls with black parted tresses,
Offerings in their hands, flowers and rice,
Gay silk-clad girls jingled as they walked.

At poolside stairs of stone, in the gloom, Puto's foot felt for steps.
Jag Niwas the island.
The Maharajah's palace, pillared halls, domes, galleries.
The old King was not asleep.
He sat beneath a tamarind. From across the pool the water-
    ouzel sang.

And without a word he heard what Puto brought.
The silver gateway, silver gateway lost its sheen.
The glitter on the water, glitter faded.
Ouzel started up again. His voice a breath:
'I shall die, my son will not bury me.
My country shares the fate of Chittor:
There stands the Tower of Victory – now it houses monkeys.'

    'The Merciful Ones are with us and with him.'

'Manas scorns them. He does not know them.
He challenges them, has to challenge them,
And so the Merciful Ones strike at me.'

Jayanta stood, and laid an arm on Puto's shoulder:
'Now you the father, who must bring my son once more into
    the world.
Puto, you were always mine, mine,
Not as a little fish to him who has it hooked,
But as you to – me.
Now you have my son. I give you him, hold me up,
I give you him.'

And rosy morning. Gouts of flame above the forests.
The King drove his son and Puto to a smith.
The smith hammered each a ring about his arm.
And while the chains still glowed, Puto swore an oath
To use no magic to loose the chain that linked Manas and him,
To utter no spell to loose the chain.

There they left the groaning father.

AND Manas felt a stabbing in his breast,
As if a cold blade were cleaving him asunder.
The wooded hills had vanished.
Houses turned to vapour.
Puto and Manas swimming through white clouds,
The quivering air torn open.
Buoyed on thin mist, Puto and Manas,
Impelled by billows,
Air foaming, awash with light,
Ripplerustlerush,
And on, directly on, blown on,
Into the glimmerflitter, into the cooing tugtwitch.

O twitching heart that sings this, whither are you dragging me.
Why bundle me up, bind me and haul me along as if in an
    animal's hide,
And I falter and must follow and am bound and must go along

Even to my dissolution.

Puto, how strange, long lean man wrapped in a grey cloak,
His hood flew after him.

Eyes closed, lips closed they flew, whirled along.
Puto's voice came:

'I am bringing you to people, Manas,
Do not flinch, do not flinch.
You led the army in many a battle,
You have killed many people.
I shall show you people, you shall touch them,
Shall feel them as if they were you, Manas.
Do not flinch, do not flinch.
These are not the beings that danced and sang for you.'

Now his voice fell silent, the storm swallowed it.
Clouds came between him and Manas.
The storm scuttled hail that scoured Manas' skin.
The man was afraid: The chain is breaking, the chain has broken.

But here already was Puto's voice again:

'O Manas, I am your teacher, and I must obey you.
O that I, who helped you grow to manhood
And took care of you, entrusted to me by your mother,
O that I must fly with you.
O my suffering child, my child: now gird yourself.
And if you are a king's son and a warrior,
And your forefathers fought in many a battle
And experienced horrors,
Manas, Manas, summon your blood that it come to you,
Your blood of courage, that it be there when you need it.'

And Puto's sobs swept by on the wind.

'Why weep for me, Puto, flying at your side, held to you by a chain?
What is it I shall find?'

'Not only I was weeping, Manas,
The griffons too, that fly with me.'

'I see no griffons, Puto.'

'They are perching in my hair.
Oh there you are. That I should see you once again.'

The dreadful griffons flew in sight of Manas, bald-headed
vultures,
Sukuni.
Naked their throats, black beaks, the feet blood-red.
Below them raged the storm.
A line of mountains loomed, Himalaya thrust up its first foot-
hills.

Between crags by a whirling spate they came down to land.
And Puto turned, pressed him to his breast, the mighty man,
Blood on his brow from where the griffons had been drinking.

'Take me onwards!' Manas cried.

'And so I kiss you, Manas, to summon all your powers
That they may preserve you, my sweet child.
No monster, no devil shall you see.
You shall feel your blood and blood,
And shall not allow yourself to freeze in fear.
You shall endure all that you have wished for,
And shall extricate yourself, for you are strong.
If, in trusting you to me, your mother blessed me,
So I bless you. And kiss you.'

And they were rising already, tumbled in dreadful clouds,
Whirled in tumbling clouds.
Were they flying or standing still? They could not tell.
Vapour like a solid block lay all about them.

And there was no more rain.
Storms shredded the black clouds hither and down
From the Himalayan peaks,

Onto blooming meadows and slopes, bedlam of beasts and trees –
Euphorbia acacia stands of bamboo –
Tossed them, torrents and ice-needles, onto crags and hills,
Onto swollen rivers thundering down deep valleys,
Kosi, Alaknanda, Yamuna,
Rolling on into the plains of Punjab.
Storms shredded the black clouds away,
Howled.

And hills steppeland savannah awoke to the drumming of waters,
Began howling like seas.
And ships rode on the sea.
What sort of ships were they that rode the sea,
Bobbing like boats, darting under sail, capsizing, coming aright?
Souls, pale misty Souls
In the pattering of waters
Came gliding by nooses of vine, stretched themselves past thorns,
Clumped in white masses.
Wind whirled them high, breath from the mouth of Shiva,
Spun them like a wheel, spilled them, mist onto water.
Puto's voice: 'Now we must part. Go now.'

And Manas went.

SWOOPING down from the mountains, three devils,
Wicked gods suppressed by Shiva.
And when they saw Manas they faltered, clutched one another:

> 'Who is it. Who is it. A human.'

They swished aloft. Alarmed, horribly alarmed,
Coiling flouncing billows.

> 'A human of flesh and bone, with limbs and clothing.
> He's broken through the bounds. Look at him, you.
> Who is it. What shall we do?'

And they saw the griffons flying
Back and forth at the edge of the Field of the Dead,
Puto's Sukuni.
And in the branches, among a plane tree's leaves, Puto himself, stiff as if frozen,
The mighty man, who was known to them.
And they saw the chain that ran from rigid Puto's upper arm
From the tree down across the slope.
As tenuous as air, it stretched like rubber and did not break,
Ran to the arm of the human on the slope.

> 'Ah wretch,' screamed Chanda, 'hey, Puto,
> Call yourself a priest of Shiva?
> What are you up to? Think we cannot see you,
> Sat there in your tree and feigning sleep?
> And full of perfidy you sneak a human here, wretch, onto Shiva's Field.'

Through the branches Puto came alert, fixed on them a hard eye.
They slid away to the side.

> 'Why don't you speak. Why stare so with your goggle eyes.
> Think you'll scare us with your goggle eyes, Puto, wretch,
> Cunning scoundrel, hypocrite.
> Ha, what are you up to in that tree? And your griffons, hey?'

Now his hands touched the ring about his arm,
And even before he moved they quivered, hid among bamboos.
'He's renounced Shiva's service. He's fighting Shiva.'
And with a twitch of the foot they pushed off from the ground,
Like panthers leaping. Whirred elongated aloft.
Puto's voice a blow behind them:

'Don't flee. Have a care, you dogs, jackals.
No doubt the God bade you guard his land,
You, for you are Munda, Chanda, Nishumbha.
The man down there is my child.
Have a care. It is as if I go there.

He is Manas, son of a king, from Udaipur in the land of Rajputana,
   which is my home.
When the cotton tree flaunted its red flowers,
When he had had his fill of victories, he fled the palace.
I shall protect him.
He seeks out sorrow. He would feel horror, and suffer.
You imprisoned monsters, have a care.'

First they flew around Manas in wide arcs, fearful, curious.
Surrounded him like children a giant elephant newly fettered,
And watched every move he made.
By now the demons were huge, and Manas thought them clouds.

Then they burst out laughing.
Pushed off pell-mell, stretched themselves long,
Soared shimmering, bleated yak-yacking:

> 'A human. Wants to feel horror and suffer, hey.
> So he shall, the dwarf, the little toad.'

Darted past crags, through the ravines:

> 'Spirits, oh lovely spirits. Hey, we have a visitor,
> A newcomer, with a body! A human with a body!
> Come and look. Wants to feel horror and suffer.
> A human. Just look at him. Has a body.
> Hey lovely spirits.'

Such a stirring over the ravines.
Stirring in the ravines.

[2] ON THE FIELD

MANAS, a man embodied, clambered over cliffs onto the Field
   of the Dead,
Down to a meadow with red rhododendrons,

And was filled with deep longing.
The rain, the snow receded, the storm receded.
In the distance Api, Nanda Devi, snowpeaks all the way to
 Yamunotri.

This was Nainital,
And there below the lake of Naini, Shiva's goddess.
Shades flitted, flitting mists
Coiled like threads, like snakes about him, glided on.

And he was filled with longing.
Stretched out his arms:
'Why do you not lie in the earth, you dead?
Did the rain wash you out again?
Why do you not lie in the earth but go wandering?
Oh come to me. I have journeyed to you.
I long for you.
I so much long to cry, and melt.'

Not a single voice responded.
They pressed towards him. Lunged close,
Licked at his heels, trailed across his hair.
They clung to his arms.
They fought their way high up his body, to his open mouth,
 his face.

And as Manas clambered over scree and the sky was harsh
 yellow,
There among the broken rocks a hollow came.
In it sat a Shade, sat all bent over, a man, brown,
Mist over it like sacking,
Made no move.
And as the spirits fled in the scatter of stones from Manas' feet
It sat there, did not budge.
Crouching by its side, Manas tried to make out the face.
But the head stayed down between the knees.
Manas whispered: 'You keep your face hidden.

Who are you? May I see you?'
It did not budge.
'Here's my silver scarf. I'll put it here for you.'
Now a snort came.
The man cowered down still lower.

Horde upon horde gathered on the slope,
Pressed down from above all around Manas.
The Souls set up a twittering, twittered: 'Wake him, wake him up, the mole.'
A savage snort from the man, he beat about him,
Was a mere bump on the earth, a clump of mud,
Was suddenly gone, vanished through a puddle into the ground.
The Souls undulated: 'The mole!'

And as Manas flung himself at the puddle
Bubbles came up, and up it came sputtering:

> 'Why come to fetch me. Why come to me.
> Why me. Should I go back to Earth, to Kashmir?
> I was a man whose life was blessed,
> I had everything there was to be had.
> You can ask them:
> They know of me, the princes, the counsellors who rule now.
> I was a strong man. I was handsome.
> I don't know what I did. What I did came flying my way.
> Riches came, landed estates, wives, children,
> And the palace and the slaves and the flocks.
> I was always lucky. The luck was endless.
> And if I had bad luck, it was just the same:
> I never knew how it came to me.'

It splashed from the hole, emerged once more,
Greyblack now, as if head and shoulders were all muddy:
'Maybe it was you who lived my life for me.
Let me look at you. Was it you? Who are you?'

And greedily the empty gaze swept over Manas,
And slid too over the Souls, the slope, the snowpeaks Api, Nanda
    Devi.
Now he clucked, gurgled, Souls shrank back in haste.
He plunged wheezed splashed back into the hole:

> 'Begone from here. I am already dead.
> I was always dead. Let no one fetch me back.
> I shall not go back, not ever.
> I won't go to you deceivers, thieves.'

And he gulped, raged, slurped, sobbed, spat.

MANAS stumbled downwards, to Nainital,
Shook himself, looked about, saw Souls fluttering,
How they followed him and watched him,
And saw his silver scarf at the puddle, and ran on.
He felt his arm, something squeezing it:
The ring of steel.
He thought: What's this, what sort of ring is this.

And like snowflakes thick and wild and frenzied
Souls stormed down upon him,
Arms outstretched, as if with billowing cloaks,
Horde upon horde, and isolates with long piping cries,
Down the craggy slope as if bent on spattering themselves.
Would they spatter?
In restless desperation down a green jagged ravine,
Water spraying aslant across it,
And once more wafted high, spun aloft in slow spirals,
Despite their cries, their deflecting gestures.

Manas stood there frightened, looked at his feet.
Again they swished past, the sound was clearer, more distinct.
At first he heard only humming, twittering,
Now it was a breathing, calling, gentle huffing.

He whispered: I am Manas. I'm not afraid of them,
Not any of them. I want to speak to them.
And spoke: 'Oh all of you, don't flee from me.
I am a king's son from Udaipur.
I have come to you, and all I possessed could not blind me to
    this task.
I want you. I want you.
Oh I want you and only you.
Come, here I am.
Nothing of mine that is not yours, that you may not have.
I give myself to you, I want to keep you.
Ah, how the gods have trodden you down,
How they have cast you out from sunlight,
Just as I suspected.'

And as he stretched his hands out to the awful wall of Souls
Manas started trembling,
Trembled in uncontrollable longing, this Manas,
In soul-dissolving knee-breaking longing, this Manas.
And he stretched out his arms.
And a Shade eluded him.
And another Shade slid away from him,
And another.

And then he held one in his arms, like a veil,
And Manas pressed it to him and closed both arms.
Vapour shimmered cool across his eyes and forehead.
He could not close his mouth, though near to choking.
He would not let the Shade, the cold enveloping Shade, escape
    him,
The Shade in his two arms, at his breast, his mouth,
He would gulp it down and be wide open to it,
As a flue for smoke
Should be filled with it in every corner.

Let the vapour creep forever tickling down his throat,

Let his eyes be dazzled with enlightenment, forever.
Oh how his eyes were brightened,
How white, the terrible ever whiter whiteness,
Ever more glaring glow, ever more piercing glare.

I must kiss it and yet not let it go
And shall for sure not let it go.
And no way and nohow
And never and at no point let it go, let it go.

The glare within him throbbed.
It hammered, boomed, more horribly every minute, and he:
I shall not let it go.
I am here. Manas, you, you are here.
Was he upside down, dangling over the ravine?
Swaying above the green waterfall,
Down over the green splashing water,
Feet scraped raw?
Stop, he tried to cry, it throbbed through him so.

By now the Soul had penetrated deep within him,
He had taken it in, drunk it down.
His head flopped sideways.
He wheezed, hands in the grass,
Knees on the ground, back against the rockwall,
Took off, yawing.

– And flames. And flames. And smoke.
And flames. And choking flames.
And burning. And fire.
And then air, the flames parting,
And air. And a town. A street.

RUMBLE, clomp, zebu hooves,
Rumble, clatter past arcades,
And clomp of hooves, and rattling past all the houses.

Jangle, clatter, water-carriers' cries,
Rumble, clomp.
What kind of baskets there in the bazaars?
Ah, gold-threaded.
And a hundred lamps, crowded bazaars.
And shaven-headed nobles,
And yogis garlanded with flowers.
Clomp, rattle, rumble, clomp.
Jostling pagodas, domes shimmering gold.
A large town, a wonderful town,
Benares.

The river runs below, great holy river,
Holy Ganges.
And laughter, shouting,
Clomp, rumble.
Hooves, clattering hooves and rumbling.
Who sits in the cart, and the zebu run ahead,
And the axle jolts up and down,
And at every bend in the road stones scatter.
Where are the zebu speeding to, through the town, away from the throng?

'I am taking you into the forest, to Dhamek Stupa.
We shall place flowers there, Daksha my friend.
And you shall see the owls, the owl people,
How they sit there by day in the banyan tree, and how they sleep.'

A woman, a slender one.

    'You, Danu, wife of Smirti, you love the banyans so.'

'Don't call me wife of Smirti.
The little leaves of the banyan flutter up and down,
It gives me such a sweet feeling.
And you,
On the box seat is just one black Bhil,

And he is deaf.
And do you not know the owls?
I showed them to you as they flew one night
From a banyan tree.'

    'And you want to see them once again.'

'And I will see them, and you shall see them with me.'

    'Danu, I love to go with you.
    Not just to Dhamek Stupa,
    But I would go with you to the sea, the mountains.
    For you are the loveliest, the jewel of all Benares' women.
    God has blessed your husband,
    Your husband must have great merit to win your hand.'

'I want to show you the owls in the banyan tree
And on the tower of Dhamek Stupa.
Why do you talk so much about my husband.
The servant is deaf, and you may give me your hands.'

And rumble and judder and rattle
And rocking and juddering, dashing over soft ground.

'But you must tell me,
Daksha my friend, as I take you to the banyan tree,
And show you the owls,
And travel with you through the countryside and the bazaars,
That you remember,
That you recall the owls,
Even if they do not screech as they did before,
That you love me.
This you must say to me, Daksha, while I hold your hands,
That you love me, and that you remember.'

How she smiles, takes his hands, lays them about her waist,
How she lifts her eyebrows.

    'I do want to say all that to you.'

'Yes, you must. And more, Daksha:
What you know of the secret of my room,
And how it all went when my husband was with the caravan,
And you stood for the first time at the house door
And watched it, as was your duty,
And then – then you watched only me!'

How she laughs and gazes at him.
And the wheels rumble softly in soft mud, rumble between
    fields of maize.
And jolting and swaying, and rocking and juddering,
And a flutter of curtains,
And smoke again, ever more smoke! And flames, the flames!
Where from? Are the wheels burning, has fire broken out below?
The smoke! The terrible flames!

> 'I will go with you, Danu my sweet, my gazelle,
> As far as you like and take me with you.
> I'll go the whole way with you, and say everything.
> Your throat is sweet to me,
> The flower behind your ear is sweet to me.'

'Go on, Daksha.'

> 'Go on?'

'Yes, Daksha. Go on.
What you saw once, I want to hear it from your own mouth.
It is done, it happened from you, from me,
I must hear it from your own mouth.'

> 'Your room was dark, Danu, you dared not light a lamp.
> And you sat on a carpet in the dark.
> And sat and made not a sound.
> And I: you had led me up the stairs.
> And I was only the watchman of your house,
> And then you disappeared.
> I was afraid, Danu, I might bump into something,

>   I might knock things over. I was afraid.
>   So I lowered myself to the floor,
>   And crawled on all fours, and felt about with my hands,
>   Until I had something in my hand.
>   I touched it without meaning to, and it twitched.'

'What was it, Daksha.'

>   'I can't see it. It's covered up now,
>   The brown twitching thing,
>   Your big toe, the right, the left.'

'Which? The right?'

>   'I don't know. And then –'

'Which toe was it, Daksha? Of course you know.'

>   'You have covered it, Danu. Uncover it, then I shall know.'

'Your mouth must say it.
Your mouth is up there. It knows everything.'

>   'My mouth? And why press me so, Danu?
>   We're going so far, the zebu run so fast.
>   This is it! There's Dhamek Stupa, the ruins.
>   I shall call to the coachman.'

'He cannot hear, he's deaf.'

>   'I shall sign to him.'

'Better to tell what you know. About my room,
My body, my toe and what we did.'

>   'And here is the banyan tree, O Danu, sweet Danu,
>   And we want to stop and sit down beneath the tree.'

And rumble, judder, bump,
Clomp, rumble.

>   'And don't torment me, sweet Danu,
>   And stop and turn around.'

'You don't need to see the banyan tree, Daksha,

Look, we're passing it by.
I shan't waken the owls for you.
And I have something for your mouth,
A fig, a little fig.
It's a little favour for your mouth,
Even if it won't speak to me and won't let me know
What I would so love to hear.'

And he bites into it, they sit embracing, lips to lips,
They bite, eat and kiss,
And tears well from Danu's eyes,
Her eyes swim, tears pour from them.
And she eats, keeps kissing, swallows tearwater.
And he laughs and kisses and gulps.

'Don't worry, Daksha, my tears are not poisoned,
Nor the fig, nor the water of my mouth.
I only wanted to kiss you.
And when I have finished the fig
I shall never kiss you again.'

    'No, you shall kiss me often, ever and again.'

'And shall not offer you my body again,
I just wanted to cleanse your mouth, to kiss it one more time.
Your wicked mouth.'

    'My – ?'

'Yes. You are wicked. And yet I love you,
And I proved it to you.
And if the cart did not skid about so wildly,
And if you did not tremble so,
Could once more gather up your courage,
I could give myself to you once more.
Would feel shame, would tear myself apart,
And for love would be helpless to do otherwise.
When I look upon your face, my body freezes,

And my teeth chatter, so much do I love you.
When you fix your gaze on me
My life is taken out of me,
And I can only wait for what you will do.
When I see your mouth, your lip, your upper lip,
And how the tongue licks it,
I am no longer I.
I kiss your teeth, I must fall into you,
That is what you are to me.
And you did not save yourself from me.'

    'What should I have done, sweet sweet Danu?'

'It is good that you tremble. We tremble together.
I tremble too: a terrible god has hung this over us.
Just let the cart roll on.
We shan't go back to Benares. Nevermore to Benares.'

    'Danu, oh Danu.'

'Oh hold still, Daksha, do stop fidgeting.
I shan't let go of you.
It was not the banyan tree I meant to show you,
Or the owls, or the ruins of Dhamek Stupa.'

    'What have I done to you, Danu,
    What kind of woman are you.'

'A woman like any other, the finest in Benares, Smirti's consort.
Just let the cart roll on.
Once I was created
To be the wife of Smirti, best beloved, most blessed,
And to be happy.
And then again I was created
To go to the window, glance down,
And notice you.
You, by the door, the watchman of the bazaar,
And then I had to carry you around in me,

And long for you, and be enchanted.
And my husband might be here or might be there,
And can never be with me.
And always it is for you I wait, I yearn.
For an hour I stand there, and another hour,
And why for an hour?
And then not an hour and not a moment!
And I must have you, have you always,
And instead of this, you sweet face,
You poisonous beloved mouth–'

> 'Instead of this? O Danu. Say what it is.
> I love you.
> Would I have come with you otherwise,
> Would I have dared?'

And she started keening, sat bolt upright,
Danu, sweet woman, flower behind her ear,
Gold stud at her nostril:

'You pointed me out!
Pointed me out in the bazaar, on the street.
How you pointed me out!
I had to creep along behind you,
Keep you always in my sight.
Follow you out of the house, through the streets, to your room.
Stand outside your room
Dressed as a serving girl, a messenger.
How you talked in there about me, laughing.
There was a man in there with you, or a woman,
It must have been a woman, another victim of your lies.
You talked about my hips, my breasts,
And what I did with you, oh you!
And what you did with me, oh you!
And sometimes silence fell, and then she screamed,
And then you started up again.'

'Woe is me, O Danu, I have been bad.'

'Don't hide your face, Daksha.
Give me your hands. For I love you,
And this evening you will brag about the fig.'

'O Danu, please, stop the cart. I think you mean to harm me.'

'Where will you brag about the fig tonight?'

'Stop the cart!'

'It's not as if I hate you. I can tell you:
We shall brag about the fig at the same place, together.'

'O beloved, do forgive me.'

'And stop your fretting. I can't bear it.
We share our fate, sweet Daksha.
Whatever the one has been, so must the other be.
See now how I weep – but for whom?
For you!
Bend down, feel down there at your foot.
I have clasped my dancing buckle about your foot,
And locked it to the cart,
You can't leave the cart, any more than I!
I have thrown away the key!
O Daksha, quiet now.'

And Daksha roaring, ranting:

'The cart must stop! You mean to murder me!'

And jolting, skidding,
Rumbling,
Mud spattering,
And swaying, crackling.

'Oh see how we fly, Daksha.
Here's a bridge. The forest is coming.
There is no one to hear you. Be quiet just this moment.
Weep with me, do.

Grant me just this one moment.
Just this one more moment, let us live for ourselves.'

    'Stop the cart!'

'Beloved, the coachman is deaf.
Calm yourself, but weep.
There is straw beneath our feet.
The touchwood is down there. Oh be still!'

And the man rises from his seat,
Wrenches himself upright, strikes down at her.
She bends low to the floor.
Fire glimmers between her fingers.
She presses her head to his legs, sobs, begs, grovels:
'Now it is good. Now it is over.
Now beat me, Daksha, just rage at me and beat me!
Hold tight to me, oh lift me up,
One moment more, sweet Daksha, my husband, be good to me.'

And blindly he strikes down at her,
And rages and twists about, foaming.
Embittered blows.
And he cries out and whimpers, tugs at the seat,
She whimpers, eyes fixed on him, begs:
'Oh to me, to me, Daksha!'

And the flames rise.

And she throws herself from him, snivelling, face hidden,
Gulping smoke, despairing,
And moans and moans and begs
And abandons herself to the fire.
And smoke envelops her.
They tumble burning from the cart all tangled,
And are dragged along.
The zebu run on through.
The blazing crackling cart,

And flames, flames, flames.
And tree trunks, roots.
And dust and trees and breaking branches.
And still they coil around each other,
And he cries out and still he coils, and still she coils.
Hot grubbing flames, choking burning flames.

AND Manas, Manas groans as well.
And Manas burrows in the grass,
Kneels, coils about himself.
His hands cannot unclench from the grass,
And then they can.
And out of his gasping breast appears,
Appeared, the Shade,
Wafts, wafted from him, and is far away already –
'Farewell. I am Danu. Farewell, you living man' –
And is gone.

And Manas gasping on the spray-soaked cliff.
He dragged his body away
To where the waterfall sprayed over the cliff.
He threw his body down, tumbled it in the wet, gulped,
Let himself be drenched.
'Water, water. No more fire. Douse it.'
He ground his teeth, gulped, chewed his lips:
'Ah! Not to live! Not to live! And not be born!
And never again be born. Never never never be born.'
And cried, and turned about, cried, gulped:
'And never ever be born. And never never be born.'

LURCHED to his feet, located his body, stood upright.
Such a rush of spirits,
Danu among them, Daksha among them.
And the lush rhododendron meadow stretching down into the distance.
Manas lurching saw his knees walk, his feet climb downward.
Stammered: 'And never never be born.'
And there below the lake of Naini, black expanse,
And still farther downward, snowpeaks
Plunging deep into its mirror.

'It is Manas who goes here.'
And could not find himself, Manas.
'Manas, this is Manas,' loud he cried, flung wide his arms.
He closed his eyes, stood, cried out.
'It is Manas here,' stretched out his arms,
Drew them in, held them out again: 'Manas here.'
Let out a cry, which drew an echo: 'This is Manas.'
Echo came: 'Manas.'

And on he wandered. How lush the rhododendrons.
And as he moved, saw everything.
And now he raced like a horse,
Fell to his knees, and a furious wailing burst from him:
'Ah, it was Benares.
Don't, oh don't forget.
The cart. The axle creaking.
And Danu, Daksha. Them. It was them.
All true. And they are here.'
And talked groaning to himself:
'Oh don't despair, don't give up, Manas.
It's you who had to come here,
Who longed for nothing more than here.
Don't be afraid, Manas.'

And longing was at once lush within him,

He brimmed with longing,
And felt himself filled with longing
That streamed to him like water down from a mountain,
Like a black bourn in a wide gaping bed,
A receptive foaming valley.
'Don't leave me, Danu. I'll not forget you both.'
And it was the old longing flooding into him,
He doting on it, in despair, suffering.
'I want to keep you both. You in Benares. And you others,
I shan't forget you.
Come closer. Come. I'm here. I am not defeated.
I want you. It's you I love, I love,
Love nothing more than you,
More, a thousand times more than my own self.
You poor sweet bleeding lovers, I shall not fail you,
I will have you.'

Manas groaned, stood still, turned about.
Souls wafted close, thronged around him, slipped away.
Numbly he whispered: 'To you. To you,'
And they glided off.
'Don't be afraid. Nothing of me that is not for you.
I want you. I love you. I groan for you.'

Souls danced about him.
And ever more ardently, enticingly:
'Yes. You. Yes. You. It's for you I'm here.'
A Soul lay on him. It climbed away, again sank onto him,
And trembled back like a tendril of vine.
And Manas was open, he stood rigid: 'Yes, yes, you!'
He felt the throbbing and beating in his brain,
The roaring began. His hands grew icy, feet grew icy.
'Yes, you're the one. Don't be shy. I shan't move.'

LIKE a pillar he stood, arms still halfway raised,
Joints rigid, eyes wide open, blind eyes,
The open mouth.
It is a child, he felt it on him, went up on tiptoe, began to shiver.
A child. Oh, it is a child.
Pelle pelle. What is that. *Pelle pelle.*
And felt it deeper in him, in his core:
What does it want.
People after it, chasing. Up steps, down steps.
Why are they after you, dear child, little child.
And you are dead? What harried you up here?

Manas standing: Fine palace, prince's castle.
They're chasing you. They're after the child.
Here's a door. Hide yourself.
They won't hurt you. They are people.
And let them knock, don't be afraid.
It's good that you keep calm.
Pelle pelle. No, don't be afraid.

'Open up, open up, damned dog,
What have you done, you damned wretch.'

The man has a stick, a stick in his hand.
Hide by the wall, hide behind the coat.
He roars: 'Damned dog, damned wretch, damn you, child,
Wait till I catch you, wait till I catch you,
You have robbed me.
You are a dog, I'm coming for you.'

And he bursts open the door, whacks the table, whacks the wall:
'Where are you, dog, where are you, wretch,
Better not let me catch you.'

And the child is caught already.
How he pushes it about. How can you grab at it so,
It's just a child.

'Tell me how it happened.
Girre girre, I'll break all your bones,
Girre girre, you see this: it's a stick, here's a club.
I'll break the fingers from your hands,
I'll break the toes from off your feet, so you can't run,
You nasty wretch, you wretched child,
Girre girre, tell me how it happened.'

> 'What can I say. *Pelle pelle*, good master.
> I found nothing. I found nothing more.
> The gold lay in the ditch, they were snuffling, ruffling around.
> *Pelle pelle*, don't hurt me.
> Oh ow, oh ow, my fingers, my hands.
> Sheep ran up. Look at my hands.
> Let me go home.
> They had it in their mouths, the sheep. I found no more.'

'So sheep swallowed all the gold I lost,
Wrought gold, buckles, rings.
Kri kri, what are you telling me. You dare tell me this.
That's why you run from me up the steps, little child,
Kri kri, damned wretch.
That's why you crawl into this room.
Sha sha, you dare to tell me this.
Tell you what I'll do, I'll lock you up
Next to the pen where the cattle bellow.
Sha sha, I shall let you starve,
I shall tie you up and you'll go thirsty.
Where did you hide my gold?'

> 'The sheep had it in their mouths. I found no more.'

'The sheep had twelve gold buckles in their mouths,
Damned wretch. So I must cut their bellies open?
Where did you hide my gold.'

> '*Pelle pelle*.'

He rips the cloth, he does this to the boy.
He hurls him down the steps, this he does.
The child lies there: will he stand up?
He pulls the child upright by the neck.
There are no parents who can help,
There is no master who can intervene.
He is all alone, a child.
And lies there, sobs and bleeds and cries.
And driven across the dazzling yard,
And into a sty next to the cattle-pen,
Into the sty with kicks.

Oh hush now, hush, it is not over yet,
I know it all too well.
As truly as the sun shines in the sky, so truly,
Mewling bleeding child,
As sure as there are eyes that gaze down on the Earth,
As certain as the soul that bleeds in me and is in you and in us all,
As amply as these tears I shed,
It is not over yet.
The door is only now shut tight.
And what is it. Oh what is it.
And what will happen. How slow it all becomes.
Out there the sunlight fades. No one comes.
Cattle bellow. The night is long.

Morning lightens through the slats.
They have tied you to a slat.
They know you are there.
As truly as the heart beats in my breast, they shall come and set
    you free,
And bring you things to eat.
The day is hot, is dry, is long, unending,
And yet they will come.
So hard, but don't give up.
Our life is hard, our life is odious, but don't give up.

And the night too passes.
And nothing to drink, nothing to drink.
Give him water. The rivers are brim-full of water.
To drink.

And it is night, the second night already,
And it is a child. It stole nothing.
They've locked it in the sty behind the cowshed,
And have forgotten it!

Soon the door will open,
And when time comes for the slats to melt away,
I know it, they will melt,
The floor will grow wheels, you shall ride away from here.
The slats shall become rice and corn and water.

But oppressive heat, flies that bite,
Festering stink, thirst, thirst, thirst
Between the lips, over the gums, on the tongue,
In the throat.
And you cannot drink hot air, even though you gulp it down,
You gulp it down in cheekfuls, but it does no good.
And by the wall, the child.
Festering stink, thirst, thirst, thirst.
I must go there, I can't just wait and wait.
Who's holding me back, I must go there,
I must bring him water.
In every river so much water.
They've locked him in a sty,
Forgotten him.

Licking at slats, nibbling at the slats,
At his own fingers, snuffling his own dung,
And heaving, tries to vomit and cannot.

People in the fields, help, in the houses!
Shiva, help us!
I would give my heart.

Who, who, who is holding me back?

And Manas, rigid as a pillar, gasps and groans, flails about him:
I must go, I will go. You must let me go.
It's just a child. I must bring him water.
And how will this end. How will it end.

Parched. Dried-up tongue.
Don't whimper. See my hands.
What is this? I can't go to him. I can't lift them.
I was made human just so I should see this!

The day is fading. Birds twitter. Now he lies unmoving.
Ah he is dead! He is dead!
He has died of thirst, they gave him no water,
They let him die of thirst, everyone, the gods, I,
And there is his death!

Arms upraised, Manas:
He is not dead. I am still here. It is not yet ended.
Who said his death must be?

Now the little Shade coils out of him away.
Sunken brows, hollow eyes, the drooping head, slack skinny arms.

But it can't be true. That was not his life.
It can surely never never,
Never and not ever have been that.

THE SHADE has vanished now among the others,
And Manas tumbles thunderstruck.
Lies there tumbled on his side, Manas,
Long heavy dark-brown body.

Then he twitches, then he pulls himself upright,
And then again collapses, crushed, struck down by lightning.
Then he sits up.

There are birds around him, scratching at him.
And little tremors travel through him,
And he sits there hours and hours and hours.
It is the mighty yellow sun that moves so silently up there
And sinks down behind Nanda Devi's peaks.

Night-mist comes up condensing from the lake.
Space draws in.
And in the dark of night Manas sits
There where the little Shade left him,
Thin nostrils, drooping head, hollow eyes, slack arms.
And sits there still in the pale light of morning.
Souls came drifting back.
All night they had drifted,
And the wind had wafted them.

Now Manas bent his heavy knees, flexed his arms,
Stood up, stood.
And again he stood and stood, as if hours stood still
Until hot midday. Birds were not alarmed by him.
And see, slowly he pushed on, he went,
Slowly his body went.
Will he not stumble?
Slowly the body descended the stonestrewn slope,
The body's eyes downcast.

He stopped in a meadow.
It was the meadow where the whitethorn grew,
Where boulders lay moss-covered.
There the body halted, turned its head,
And Manas looked about him, turned his head back,
And the rhododendrons were in bloom,
And a little bird, green, flew to a boulder,
Fluttered here and there, pecked at moss,
Pecked at a worm or a beetle or a seed of grass.
Little birds don't eat much, little birds don't drink much,

A little bird gets by on hardly anything.
But what is it there that floats and rises up and sways,
It is mists. Shades in fact.
Spirits, Souls.

And no, Manas did not collapse.
Cramps assailed his belly, tremors passed from his bare feet
Into his shanks, his breast, up to his face.
He danced up and down
And endured it, endured a long while.
Yes, it dreamed within him, I shall go on.
Move a leg, now bend a knee. Go.
He bent the knee, and at the first pine tree
Held fast to it, trembled and did not understand:
A child was with me. Had nothing but its body.
It died of thirst. They forgot about it.

And as the bird twittered,
The tremors passing through him grew more violent,
Cramped him to the ground.
His face twisted across his shoulder. He gulped, suppressed a sob:
Danu was there. The cart, owls, the banyan tree,
Daksha, Danu and Daksha,
Let themselves be burned. Could not live.
None of them could live.

What has happened to Manas here?
Is any weeping more bitter, any weeping more helpless
Than that of the brown man at the pine tree?
An inward whimpering whining, a salty trickling.
This was the man born in Udaipur in Rajputana,
Born to the king's favourite wife, son of a king, lion-strong, wily.
On the Thar river a month ago he chased the enemy
All across the salty desert.
Now his teeth chattered, and not for any chill of fever.
He no longer saw the air for whimpering wheezing.

His head rocked.
His whole body swayed, he spat.
He, who could break the pine tree's trunk with his bare hands,
He held tight to the trunk,
And was like an unweaned infant that has lost its mother.

The Souls who went from me, they should not leave me.
The shepherd boy, Danu, Daksha, it was not, not I, not I who
 chased you away.
It's not my fault I live and you are dead.
You must take me with you. Take me with you!
Take me, Manas, bones and all.
I will not, will not, will not be Manas.

He cried out, his hand felt along his arm:
You must take me!
Puto, let go, you are not my judge,
You are not my guide, I need no guide.
Puto, Puto, man of powers,
Let go my arm.

He had the desire, the deep molten craving, and tore at the
 chain.
He clamped his fist around the ring and kneaded it.
His groans and howls were snatched by the dreadful wind,
Wind from the ice-peaks,
Shiva's storm,
Shiva's raging demons that yacked and yackered and pished and
 slamcrashed.

Puto, slumped down now from the tree, a hill before him,
And Puto far away leaned back, bracing, the chain wound about
 his waist,
His face flushed, cold sweat on his cheeks, knees trembling.
For a long while he could not speak.
He looked over to the griffons:
Oh my Sukuni, the Manas we brought up here,

They are tearing him away. Manas is yielding.

And then: My Sukuni, our child wants to die.
Manas will not stay with us. Will not stay anywhere.
He cannot bear to be with us,
He cannot bear existence.

AROUND the pines, across the meadow Manas climbed.
While the wind swirled Shades, Manas climbed back up the
    slope.
He unclenched his hands.
Flowers gave off a delicate scent.
Faster, faster Manas glided high among the crags.
He stormed on up. His body knew what to do.
Among the rocks and flowers he called out constantly to Puto:
'Puto, I don't blame you.
I want to thank you for bringing me up here.
But I must come to you, you see I'm coming to you,
Just as once I lay before you in the garden hall,
At last I lay there at your feet,
After the desert I had no desire for more long days,
And I could say it out loud,
And you listened and lifted it from me, and were there.
I want you, and you know why,
You, mentor of the old cremated Manas.'

A chasm between two crags he vaulted with one bound.
'There's a chain still on my arm,
From when you brought me here and came with me and
    hauled me up.
I was – you know it, I don't need to say.
Take off the chain!
It's fixed to some other being, was not forged to this one's arm,
Manas not Manas, I am not Manas.

I have no body and no shore, I cannot see the shore,
The dams are broken through, the country washed away.
My face is not my face.
Puto, it is not Manas who comes and calls to you,
Still dragging that old chain, that dead chain.
Take it off!'

He clambered higher up the scree.
There again the green gushing spate, there the ravine
Where spirits tumbled with their drawn-out piping calls.
Slowly the ground-breeze wafted them up high,
Spun them as they moaned.

'Puto, take off the chain. Whatever may come to me, let me
    suffer it.
I don't want to nag, but you must set me free.
Just as you led me here –
I stood at the window, and you could not hold me back –
So now you will say the spell and set me free.
You are the mighty man.
My death is mine, as my life was mine.
No, it was not my life. But my death is mine.
It is my life, Puto, it is me.
And so, Puto, as you have loved me, as always I have loved you,
Set me free.'

And Puto braced himself. Sweat dripped from him.
His eyes strayed to the griffons.
He braced himself.
The plaints wafted over chasms and heights,
Penetrated to him through walls of rock.

    'He wants to leave us. Oh. It has torn him away.
    I must hold him back.'

'My life is mine.
What I speak of is not Death.
And even if you are Puto, are the man of powers,

And can shift bolts:
I am Manas, I am sorrow,
Crushing frantic sorrow, terrible sorrow,
I am dreadful sorrow, Puto,
And am as strong as you, stronger than you and anyone.
I am more terrible than anything there is.
Otherwise it could not have blasted me to bits,
And it has blasted me, as water blasts away a mountain,
And will do the same to you.
Have a care, Puto, when it comes together with me
And falls upon you.
I love you.
Puto, let me go to those where I belong.'

Evening light glowing on the snowfields,
Lower down it was already dusk.
Huge Shades hastened at Manas' side,
Soft greenish lanky giant creatures,
They ran silently alongside, crawled crooked from ravines,
Long bending necks, velvety heads,
Long stringy legs weak as wool.
They slipped hurriedly along, and turned sometimes to show
    wide brows.

Manas clambered, still in light, along the bright cliff
Where first he had looked for Souls,
And held hands out to them:
Would like to kiss the child and shall not leave it,
Shall never and not ever
And never and at no point leave it.

Manas' head bent down over boulders, fists at his brow:
And shall never and not ever and at no point leave you all.
No streets, no houses now, no Danu or Daksha,
No cart.
And rumbling and thudding, zebu hooves,

And Danu sits by Daksha in the cart,
The life taken from her when she looks at him.
And flames, tree-roots.

– Shiva, Bringer of sorrows, Shiva, Scorcher,
You, you, take me. Take me.
Your hundred fingers for my heart, and it is stilled.
You are my God, you the Blazing One,
Who is present, who spares nothing,
Who knows only kindling and the straw in which he burns,
Killer, Terminator, Sorrow-smelter,
Quickener, Ensouler,
You have me. Now you have me.
You raging Sorrow, wandering through the howling of my
    sorrow,
God of torments, my path to you.
To you my path leads through every trial,
You Roarer, Dancer, you God,
You God,
One and only, all-highest God, my God.
I fall or lie or drop away,
Sand or water or flowers beneath my feet,
I am coming to you.
Take me to you as kindling,
I a tree still greening, flesh, with blood in my veins,
Will be straw and kindling for you.
Must come near to you so that you receive me.
Will be taken, destroyed, snuffed out, to be at your side.
Shiva, nothing on this earth that suffers me, nothing anywhere,
By morning nothing and by evening nothing and nothing now.
And I will be gone and will close my eyes.
At your side alone am I suffered and always
And at whatever depth with you.
At your toes, beneath your hands, in your breath, under your
    shoulders,

Where you suffer me to stay with you,
And dismiss me not again, never again,
Oh do not dismiss me again onto the streets of people,
Oh never, never, oh never again
Among the mountains, rivers and in the air,
Never from your side, sweet God of Dying.
Dasher-to-pieces, my God,
God of the Crossing, Crusher God.
Take me to your heart,
Take me,
Forever.
Your fishing hook – here I am, who was once Manas –
Your slingshot, for me.

A THICKET of juniper grew across the path.
Out of it glimmered the Shade, giggling creature,
Climbed out greenish, lifted its head as Manas approached,
Floated crosswise over the path,
Rose breast-high in the twilight in front of Manas.
Trampling, clambering, Manas forced through, looked at it:
'And you. And you. Here I met Danu and Daksha.
Who are you?'

The Shade whirred, swooped over the thicket.

'Good that you have come, Shade.
Come with me, I lie already at Shiva's feet.'

It swooped zigzag, gambolled in the yellow light.

'Come. There is no path but to the feet of Shiva.
I have not weakened, am grown stronger. Made of iron, me.'

The shrill tittering sputtered close to Manas.
A chirping close by in the bushes. The thicket swayed.
The creature dived through branches, over umbels.

'And you. And you. You call so prettily to Shiva.
I heard you shout. You sing. You make me glad.
Sing some more. One hears such awful shouting here.'

'Why are you complaining? Feel me. Come.'

'And you! And you. I'm not complaining.
Is this complaining?'
Exulting: 'Were you at the lake of Naini, with the goddess?
With Kali? Let me look at you.
What did she say?
How strong your body is.'

'I'm going to Shiva.
Embrace me, Shade. Dare to come along!'

'What did Kali say. Tell me about yourself.
You sing so prettily of Shiva.
Such strong arms you have.'

'I - shall take you, and all of you.'

Manas flailed his arms, pushed twigs down all around,
Forced through to the creature.
It hesitated, flitted silver-scaled above the thicket, glinted,
Chirping, chirping.
And struggling Manas, as if a curtain had descended over him,
Without approaching closer, saw, as if he had a second face,
Saw the swaying creature,
Saw, it revealed itself, and he had not even touched it.
As if through a wall he saw,
As if he were already dead.

Came a tittering in the bushes just in front of him,
Where the creature rushed so giddily.
A rushing like a river.
Flowed ecstatic from the creature, streaming.
Rocks clattered, a rivercourse widened.
Green river flowing between banks.

And horrible to see, people, ever more people tumbling in,
Swirling past like fish, drowned people, drowning threshing,
In the green rushing river, down the river,
Swollen river flooding across the land, into trees and scrub.
Manas saw this with eyes wide open.

On the bank, seated on a dais, someone splendid in sunlight,
Rocking on a carpet beneath fanning palms.
Sat splendid on the dais, black-bearded.
Who has such a soughing snickering voice?

It is built along the riverbank, this city,
Ventipura.
The one there on the dais, pearls in his ears,
Plume of feathers and diamond spray,
Blazing eyes,
He has the people driven onto open ground, driven by soldiers
With spears onto open ground down to the great river,
Green tumbling river, the Jhelum.
People cry out,
People wail, leap into the churning current.
And the glee in the blazing eyes.

The green river rushes on, takes the people,
They are swallowed, tumble over, spin, are swallowed.

– And Manas slowly looked away from the river,
With effort pulled his gaze away.
And the creature, greenly vivid in the dark,
Swirled, reared up before him in the juniper,
Leapt giggling in the bushes over umbels, among branches,
Swung its arms among the flowerheads:

> 'Hah, I am handsome, I am strong, am I not strong.
> Is it not a joy to look on me.'

And Manas gasped, he felt for branches, clawed them:
'I thank you now. I know. This is why I broke away from Udaipur.

You are a demon or a man.
No need to go to Hell to find a demon.'

> 'No blood in your lips. Why are your lips so bloodless?
> You are strong.
> I'd like such a body. Or a tiger body.
> Or a vine body.
> Don't be afraid of me.'

'Why afraid? How dare you, wicked demon, say "afraid" to me?'

But the creature had already changed its face,
Could not maintain it.
Its face swelled up, it had to forego speaking,
The terrible surging, rushing, yakking had to come.
That laugh.
The rushing it kept imitating, endlessly.
The avid smacking, the surging rushing.
Its movements were a swirl, it boiled in a roil, a roil of water.
The bleeding female breasts it had sliced off
Floated all around the creature.
The monster grunted rustled in the swirling,
And dragged a carpet along behind. On it was a man:

> 'My name's Unmatti. This is my father.
> He sat in a dungeon, so he couldn't interfere with me.
> He's dead already. Watch now.'

And thrust the dagger out and in, out and in,
His eyes burned into Manas,
Who stood there and did not move,
And pulled himself together, and did not howl,
But struggled for a groan whose tone he could already hear:
'You would cast me down. You're evil.
You imagine who you are.
I can bear you. Come, I want to take you.'
Manas' knees were weak.
What he stammered came only from his lips.

'These my feet. Here's my heart.'

And as Manas bent in cramps, held fast
Like a rock about to topple,
It sprayed forth from the thicket,
Pushed arrogantly towards him, the creature,
Danced gloating and gorgeous,
Spat out people and water, stones, that it loved and relished,
Sucked them back in,
Seething Jhelum, brown-black men,
Breastless women, arms flailing, floating away, away.
They tapped at Manas' lips mouth throat,
Were sucked avidly back in,
Craved by the insatiable creature.

> 'I cannot perish! I shall return a hundred times!
> A hundred times already I've been back,
> Here to the Field, and down to the cities,
> And will return another hundred times!'

It was in Manas' brow, behind his eyes, a thought
In his heavy breast.
He did not flinch: Must I not sob, break down?
But did not sob.
It undulated through his chest.
His gullet could not find a groan,
Numb, numbness closed upon him, emptied him,
Milewide smothering horror over Manas,
Shadowed wallowing horror over Manas,
And dismayed repug-repugnance
And disgust that plugged his throat with ashes.

> 'Hoho! Take me! Take me. Hoho you!
> I shall return.
> Been back a hundred times, to countryside and towns.
> Am I not handsome?'

Launched itself, rose above the flowerheads,

Rattled as if it wielded clappers, straight for Manas.
He sank down in the grass,
Propped himself and could only heave,
And could not vomit the disgust from him.
Lay on his side, chewed grass, wiped his lips with grass:
He wants to break me. I am strong.
Here's my heart. These my feet.
And as he raised himself the creature floated nearer,
Gloated over him, triumphant: 'You, you, strong body!'
And Manas skidding away, rolling head over heels,
Lay hunched on his belly, clutched at grass like a beetle in rain,
Clung tight.
Beside him, all the threshing people
Glided damply past like fish, female breasts floating.
A green-red shimmer.
He hunched, choking, head between his knees,
And the yacking that pursued him:

> 'Your mouth! Your heart! Am I not handsome?'

And Manas flopping like a beached fish to escape it.
Then it was done.
He crawled upright, chased after it like one swimming.
And a second time the tumbling and the spume.
He stood up.
And spun around, thrown down he gibbered,
Lay on his side, curled up.

And when it was over he did not stand, but lay there broken.
Dragged himself up, blinked, felt his legs, sat dumbly.
Braced, braced himself.
And in dull fury, spitting, there he stood,
And rowed his way into the thicket:
'Come, beast, to me! Come, demon, so that I can choke you!'

Along the path, trees spread their branches wide.
A battlefield commander was this Manas,

From the Aravalli hills he rode out to battle,
A giant with mighty limbs.
Prouder he was than any in Rajputana.
Now his limbs quivered,
His knees were bloodied, his arms ruined,
But his brow was proud.

The chain forged around his arm he still dragged with him,
Thought no more of it than a thread.
He stumbled forward, not like a bull to sacrifice,
But like one stunned and helpless.
His gaze like white fire,
Yet his eyes were sunken. Trembling lips.

Again he vomited, crouched on his knees,
Held on to rocks, groaned into the abyss:
I shall go to Puto now.
He must take away the chain. No one shall gloat over me.
Not Unmatti, not that dog, that scoundrel.
Called out babbling into the abyss:
'Child, what's your name, dying of thirst,
You died of thirst. I'm here for you.
This body for you, Manas' inmost being.
It has come for you,
For you I give up all delights.'

And once again his stomach heaved.
He pushed himself up: 'To me, demons!
It never lived! Unmatti never lived!
The Jhelum does not flow! What Ventipura?'
And squeezed himself tight:
I, I! That cannot be conquered.
And felt his way along the path:
'Unmatti never lived. To me! Me, me!'

Twilight fell swiftly. He wanted to find Puto:
I, I! I am no penitent, I atone for nothing.

I do not kneel, scatter no ashes on my head,
I summon them all down to me, every one.
I'll silence them. I shall silence them.
Just let Unmatti come.

He roared across the path where Shades were floating:
'To me! To me, every one of you!
Come all! I have a giant's mouth!
I have a giant's belly, giant muscles.
To me!'

O MANAS, why do you bend like a willow to the ground,
The very top bent to the ground?
You roar.
What do you know of Shiva?
And if you know one face of his, do you know the other?
And how many faces has the Three-eyed One?
As one looks through mist onto water and sees nothing,
So you look upon him and would go to him.

What steps does the great Dancer make, the World-shaker?
And if you burn, what do you think
He means by burning?

The Fount of Ecstasy who dips his feet in rivers,
Scatters a million fish-spawn on the fields,
Turns the universe to dreadful ice, rolls fog.

Who can comprehend
The terrible Magician, Gambler,
When the cobras flick their tongues from out of his black hair,
When he lifts the string of skulls at his blue breast,
Turns his three eyes in this direction,
Whirls the slingshot in his hands?

In the grey of evening, voices swelled to Manas from the valley,
Along the path to Naini's lake.
Confusion of voices, sweet groaning voices,
The yearning of strong men, young men
Who would not die.
It groaned out of the deeps,
Remembering the Earth, and trees in bloom,
And welled up, neverending,
'You, breast of my beloved', 'mouth of my wife';
Was a woman's dizzying ecstasy, unsmotherable, unquenchable,
For her young man, his fingers, thighs,
The proud manhood in its bush of hair,
Was the longing of men for women
As they bend low over the eelsmooth body.
Confusion of laughcries,
Happy giggling in the twilit gloom,
And sorrowful laments, tremulous pleading,
Harried on up by demons, human panthers.
Sharks were swimming.

Manas, arms outstretched, was shaken to the core.
His saliva no longer flowed,
He was adrift on a dreadful sea.
Shudders surged through him.
And as he was giving vent to groans,
Just then on level ground a root curled about his foot.
And Manas stumbled, fell heavily on his hands,
And he wanted only Danu, and Daksha and the child,
And when he stood he fell back down again.
A root had wound itself about his feet.
Good that I lie here, he thought quite suddenly.
Shades sported over him like a hundred crows.
They think me a corpse, he thought.
They flocked near, drew close about him.
But what do those crows want?

They shot up high, then dropped like stones just below him.
I lie here trussed, for them. I know it, and they know it.

And that very moment all went dim before his eyes:
See, ah see, I lay here once.
When did I lie here in the scrub, and could not free my legs,
And high above me crows tumbled,
And Shades?
And did I not once already lie here,
Like this on the rocky path?

He had to watch the crows:
A thousand lifetimes gone.
As if you scoop up water, pour it in the river, scoop again.
The Manas who once walked in Udaipur, for whom Savitri
    danced,
Victor of the wastes of Thar: who was that?
Have I not seen this lemon tree before,
And these wonderfully twisting branches?
How they gesture to me.
And this air, how it thickens all around me.
The voices.
And then what happened?

AND A fear, a wild love swept over Manas.
He did not know from whence it came, or whither it would go.

The crows swept zigzag trails.
Now he raised himself and struggled with his feet.
He was lying on the ground, and was ensnared.
And as he turned to sit upright
To tug the root away and break it,
He saw something to the side, it swayed, it frightened him.
Was it a Shade, a snake?

He had had enough. He thought: I've had enough.
It was dark already.
The solitary Shade just stood there on the darkling path,
Stood and made no move.

The Shade was white in the darkling,
And in it was a sparkling, as of ice and silver.

What kind of Shade is this, thought Manas,
And why does it not move.
Thinks it will scare me if it moves?
I shall control myself and shall keep still,
And see what it will do.
How is it that I so desire this Shade,
And yet cannot place it in my memory.
And it will not mock me, and not say:
Only one of us can be.

Desire rose up in Manas, hot, seething, savage,
And with it shame like pitching waves:
Why does it not come nearer,
And does not want me and will not give itself to me?

Shuffled on his knees towards it,
Had to shuffle nearer, could not stop himself,
Knew that he would cease to be.

The Shade stood silent, motionless.
And Manas raised his hands up to the Shade.
No blessedness surpasses this,
To raise his ruined hands towards the Shade:
'O Shade, are you the sister that I never knew,
Are you Savitri or my mother?
Who are you, Shade?
I feel such love for you, such unbridled love.'

Then Manas saw, close by the silent Shade,
Saw as if he were already dead, and felt his lips go cold –

Do I want this, do I still want this, the thought was in him –
Saw a yellow gleam within the Shade.
Yes, this is it, he thought.
A desert, and in the sand a body lay, alone,
Yellow as sand, all dusty, in a hollow.
And it was a young person, a tender being, almost naked.
His weapons had scattered from him in the fall.
Had big moist eyes,
And gentle features and a big generous mouth,
A lovely flower of humankind.

Close by a horse has halted, a man is on it.
The man jumps down and strides to the fallen body
And is transfixed by it, transfixed.

Who, O Shiva, who is the man that stands transfixed,
Who is the man that lies there?

Ice-cold and trembling, clairvoyant Manas backs away, hovers.
O Shiva, Protector, what will these two do to one another,
The man and the loving flower of humankind?
They will embrace and kiss,
As I would like to kiss the young flower of humankind,
Now, now, this moment I would do it,
If I could only touch them, touch them.

Riders come galloping.
The man who was transfixed now turns to them,
Slow and hesitant, has no idea what to do.

And – that – is Manas!

And the riders gallop nearer.
There is a numbness in his arm.
He trembles, rubs it, shakes it, no strength in his arm: he wants
    none.
And – that – is Manas! Manas, it – is you!
And yet the arm does move,

And he weeps, and is there already.
What, O Shiva, what is Manas doing? –
And he, he did not do this, and does not do it,
Sword in the living breast, in the flower of humankind!
In the sweet flesh,
So that the moist eyes sink back, mouth gapes!
The sword pierces the sweet flesh, the breast,
My own breast.

Cries from Manas, harsh cries No, no.
He screamed a woman's screams,
Balled his fists dumbly overhead, hand clawing hand, tore his hair.
His whole body trembling jolting,
His body thrust back,
Feet jerking in the snaring root,
Eyes white, his mouth a slime, arms threshing.

That is it. And I did not want it.
And I did not do this.
And who did this?
And yet come closer, Shade. And how can I help you.
And take me. Come close to me just once.
Sweet Shade, beloved Shade, my soul,
Most intimate beloved soul, forgive me.
Come! Come closer! And untangle me a little,
Set my feet free. Ah the crows!
I must be dead. I can't touch you, you sweet Shade.
But then I've killed you a thousand times already.
Manas dead! Cursèd Manas!
Your life! What was that cursèd life.
It lives on without end. Lives on in every corner, unreformed!
And can it be reformed?
How can it be wiped clean. And I want an end.
I shall lie down.

Shiva, spare me, Merciful One!
Shiva, All Merciful, take me and not the Shade!
Shiva, Redeemer, Liberator of All!
Shiva, hear my cries, though I be dead.
Who are you, Terrible One, Terrible One?
It was you created this. I am your creature,
Truly no more than a creature of yours,
I can do no more than a creature can, and could do no more.
Take me for the Shade! And already I am burning.
I lie down.

No beast, no tree, Manas no more. Manas defeated.
And stammered: This, this, this.
Crawled, spat beating about him,
Flailed his arms down towards the abyss.
Sweet Shade, sweet Shade, I did not want this.

And Manas, pushing up and still caught fast, rolled
Down to the lip of the ravine.
Beat at his temples.

Insensible, sprawling, Manas lay foaming, head down,
And profound insensibility, black thick insensibility
Swept in on him,
Like a drink into a thirsty mouth.
Heaven-sweet insensibility overwhelmed him entirely
And put to sleep all raging
And took from him all horror and rage.
In deep unconsciousness he lay, curled on the rocky path.

Night advanced.
He saw nothing.
Felt nothing, heard nothing.

[3] HIJACKED

THEY drew near in the black of night, demons,
Sidled along the ravine's floor, drove souls before them.
Up the ravine they snuffled, smelled something warm,
Rare, salty, sweat-steaming.
Was it a living creature there, steaming by the waterfall?
Snuffled about, let droplets loft them, rose with the misting spray.

And there, sprawling, feet in scrub, was a human,
Head down into the ravine.
And as they drifted over him – they could see in darkness –
His breast moved, his breast rose-sank.
They asked not how and why, they snuffled at him,
Found refreshment in the snuffling,
Licked his skin, tried to turn him, lift him,
Huffed dust from his throat.
Five of them together had the strength,
Hauled the head up by the slack neck.

Moon, moon rose over Nanda Devi,
Yellow silent glimmer-rays of moon over mountain peaks.
They worked at Manas' body, thrust aside branches,
Crackling scrabbling in the scrub.
Unmatti's Shade shot up, lofted high and menacing.

They hauled Manas up and on, by arms and legs,
Lengthwise and askew.
Head dangling, body slumped, a deadweight.
Quite naked, Manas. What he had worn of princely gowns robes
Now hung snagged in bushes, ragged.
They hauled him swaying jolting downslope to the west,
Head dangling, body slumped,
Hauled him far along, smacked lewd lips, drooled,
On and on through the night air with its calling Shades.
They hauled the heavy body – it barely cleared the ground –

To the flood-meadows of Martoli Karik, far away,
Down to the smooth soft meadows.

There they had their fun with the body.
Sometimes Manas sat up in the grass,
Stared with stupid eyes, growled, growled dreaming:
Come now, come now, here I am.
Profound insensibility in him,
The draught once more imbibed,
Insensible.
He flung out his arms, lay there in his length and breadth.
The demons took refreshment in his body.

A green long-toothed demon shrouded across the meadow,
It had wash-blue eyes.
Came up to the five, rootled, snuffled like them, licked at Manas.
'Hey, it's him. Look! I know him. Was at the waterfall.
Did you find him? I saw him, waving his arms:
Sorrow and sorrow, o sorrow, o sorrow.'

And mocked, hooted in Manas' ears:
'Heyhey Mister Sorrow! Up now!
*Sat on a throne, was the strongest of warriors in Rajputana,
Flung the enemy back across the Thar River.*
Hey you. You know what sorrow is.
I want to show you something.'

Tugged the hairs in Manas' armpit, stabbed his ear.
Manas groaning, groaning.
'I want to show you something. You'll enjoy it.'
Dragged him by the hair, Manas lurching,
Forced bitter herbs between his lips.

The stumbling man spat them out.
They laughed. On he lurched. He fell and lurched, rolled.

Then, as he went and all about him demons crowed,
There wafted closer a huge Shade, a giant Shade,

A female groaning Shade.
The demons in their merriment did not notice it or hear it.
The Shade seized Manas as he lurched and paced.
And Manas stopped, and as if he were a corpse
Allowed the Shade, the female thing, to lift him up,
Allowed his arms to lie across her shoulders.

Down below the demons tittered, scampered on the ground.
Until one saw this happening, was astonished, its mouth gaped.
Manas clinging to the female in the gusting wind
Let her rock him across the meadow.

She lusted and had his body,
His lolling face, the acrid sweat, the crinkled hair.
And swiftly, swiftly told her story, what she knew, all she knew.
He did not hear the sadness, so savage greedy never to be sated,
He heard nothing.
And as she clutched him closer to herself,
His head pressed to her throat, mouth at her breast,
He snuggled into her,
Must bond to her, and it swelled within him,
Rutting heat and ardour, baneful ardour in him.
In the gusting wind they swayed across the field,
He endured the jolting to and fro across the field,
His seed spurted.

He tore loose with a cry.
With a peal of laughter she let him fall
And fled away with a cry of triumph.

The noisy demons caught him in the grass, drooling.
They carried him past two low lemon trees
To a mighty fig tree.
There they squatted, leaped like cats,
Legs long as stilts, a kangaroo's springy legs.
They made great leaps with them.
Swung Manas in the branches, threw him to each other,

From fig tree to lemon tree, lemon tree, fig tree,
Droned, sang: 'Manas lies in the fig tree,
Battered and bruised, shattered,
Lemon tree, fig tree, fig tree, lemon tree.'

Puto's voice, far off:
'Oh Manas, will you not come, Not come at last?'

They fled in all directions, left him lying.
Hour upon hour Manas at Martoli Karik.
Hours long, the unconscious man alone.
Now and then a stray Shade wafted over him,
Whispered: 'Sweet body, fine body, for me.'
Wafted away.

FROM the Pindar glacier, from its yellow-white dazzle, down
　　black walls of rock
Swept Chanda and Munda
And their master Nishumbha, scanned the landscape, drove
　　shades away.
They scented the human, saw him, flew over him.
'A human. It's a human. It's Manas, sent by Puto.
Now he lies here.'
Darted at him, snuffling: 'Some have lapped at him already, the
　　greedy things.'

All three had humanoid form.
Small and humped, head on his chest,
The one with long hair grey as ice was Chanda.
Fangs grew from his mouth down to his chin.

Munda was blind.
Shiva had cast a glance his way in the heat of battle,
It put out his lights.
A jackal squatted behind him on his hump, and steered him

>   with its paws.

Nishumbha was almost ball-shaped, like a hedgehog, cactus,
Set all over with prickles,
Sometimes he stretched his tiny white head out,
Gave his surly bearded face an airing.

Uneasy passes over Manas, this way and that.
'He still has the chain. Puto's holding on to him.
What do you think, what shall we do.
Puto's far away.'

> 'Take him.' – 'That won't work. He has the chain.'

'When the Asuras fought against Shiva
They had a golden castle in Heaven,
A silver castle in the air,
An iron castle down on the Earth,
And none of these were any help to them.'

> 'You are not Shiva, Chanda.
> See how he breathes. Already gone but still breathing.

'He's dreaming. He must be taken.' – 'But how?'

'It's a body. We can't just leave it here.'

> 'How you lust, Chanda. And how *you* would lust
> If only you could see him!
> A lovely body, strong body.'

'So take him then.'

Nishumba's head poked out through prickles:

> 'I have an idea. Come quietly. Chase away the Shades.
> We'll take him. Puto's far away.
> He's still breathing, but hears nothing, sees nothing.
> He's as good as dead. He's defenceless.
> We'll creep in. We'll creep into him.'

'And Puto?'

'And go back to Puto. He sent him here.
We'll go to him. We'll outwit Puto!'

The demons soared skywards: 'What shall we do?'

'Can't you see. It's a gift from Puto
To us. We accept it. We take that thing and go,
Go into the world. Down to the Earth.'

Whoops and whistles: 'How can Shiva stop us.
Puto shall lead us out. This is our lucky day.
We'll go down to the Earth,
Look around the Ganges, in the temples!
What shall we do?
What shall we do with the holy water?'

Whoops and whistles. How they rocked.

'Shan't drink it. Spray it! And the temples, houses.
Shiva can't stop us. Puto will protect us.
Careful now. First the Shades! Is all quiet?'

And as Manas lay wrecked there, on his face,
The three demons came down to the ground,
The ghastly spirits Chanda, Munda and Nishumbha,
The hunchback, the blind one, and the one all prickles,
Three ancients.

Munda lifted the head. He climbed in through Manas' eyes
Invaded the brain.
Nishumbha entered over the tongue and into the chest,
With each breath he rose and fell.
He sat in there quite still. The breathing was lovely,
He bobbed like a butterfly.

Chanda snuffled at Manas' body.
He went into the guts, bumped around in there.
The others signalled to him: Be quiet!
Afraid that Manas would wake up.

But he slept on. His soul held the veil tight over him,
Helpless, trackless.
Like a board held at both ends
His soul creaked, awaited nothing.

Then Manas stood up in the meadow.
The moon was bright.
The swaying body croaked, groaned, grated.
Prickly Nishumbha swept up and down its throat,
Dug at the throat with his fingers until it yielded something.
It rasped: 'Long must I stand, ha,
Window, glass window, stand, heh, heh.'

The demons burst out laughing,
Snorted, flung their legs about, twisted and turned.
The demons lifted the arms: 'Let's see what we have here.'
One arm stroked the other.
They felt over the breast, lifted the generative organ,
Whooped and kept good hold of it:
'What say we populate the Earth
With children, and such children!'
Chirruped, lurched, fell about.

'Such a chain, such a lovely chain about his arm.
There was a mother in Udaipur
Who was afraid her child would come to harm,
Harm, harm, harm,
Around his arm she tied a woollen thread,
Where is the mother now, and the child harmed?'

The demons set the proud body in motion.
Manas crawled upright from the ground, lurched round about
    himself.
They were too hard on the reins. He stumbled.
Made as if to leap like a demon taking flight.
But could not.
He was too heavy, they had to give in,

Had to see what he wanted.

Now they steered more cautiously,
Steered the body as an elephant is steered from on its back.
And Manas, Manas started off, legs straddled wide,
Irregular jerking steps,
Crashed, crouched, came up again, ran lurching, stumbled.
The arms swung him about.
He was meant to go forward. And turned circles.
Until the demons, circling with him, reined him in,
Constrained the arms, gripped the knees,
And he went slowly on.

Now slow, now faster, on he walked, he ran, this Manas,
Slowly, by jerks, by prods and pushing.
Sometimes the head drooped sideways to the neck.
When the demons became frisky he threshed about.
They cackled at each other, romped in the body.
They were sat in a cart, behind masks,
And steered, steered: 'To Puto.'
And began to amble across the meadows,
The demons, to amble using Manas' body.
They were cocksure, the body's gait was strong,
It obeyed. And in it Manas, sleeping.

On they went the whole night through.
Retraced the path, the long long path
By which the five lewd demons had hauled Manas.

They passed the waterfall.
Manas slept on and did not shudder
When they came to the ravine where Danu and Daksha had
    appeared.
Manas felt no horror going through the clump of juniper
Where Unmatti dwelled.

GREY morning, flashes of white light across the sky.
Black-grey the scrub, the rocks were wet.
Here was the boundary of the Field of the Dead.

At the foot of a hill towered the tree
Beneath which Puto lay.
They approached with trepidation.
But he had already heard their coming.
Puto stood there half awake, peered about,
Chain at his waist and in both hands,
Until he saw the brown wanderer slowly coming closer.

And sudden shock,
And terror, terror,
And wide awake,
And a sharp lookout.

The wanderer came nearer to the tree.

Manas coming! In the blazing light of morning!
And so confused was Puto, breast burdened so with joy,
That he made no move from the spot,
Dumbly went down on his knees, head sank to his breast,
Said nothing.
Above him the Sukuni flapped their wings.
Big brown ants ran about his feet, crawled on his hands.
Across from him they stood, and waited.

'I – I have Manas back. I'll bring him to Jayanta.
When I'm in Udaipur I shall give thanks to Shiva.'

Stood up, sank back to his knees,
Thought of all that bracing, sweat blinding him.
Manas had wanted death, which is available to every human.
When he saw Manas,
Manas at the hill, that dear beloved body, solid, visible,

Naked and torn, but the beloved body,
Strong lordly soul
That he had had to bring here to the Field,
He did not ask: How has he returned,
What will he tell us all, how will he want to live?
He was joyful, thanked his lucky stars,
His whole life for this moment,
The spot where he stood, the tree, the griffons, his sleep,
His waking, the air, this very morning.

'Manas,' he called across, 'it is you, it is you!'

    'Yes,' this much Manas uttered, stood still, made no move.

'They've torn the clothes from you,
But you they could not tear to pieces.
You were stronger than they are.
You are the bravest of us all.
You always were the strongest one among us.
No one has ever beaten you in sport, or defeated you in battle,
And now you see it, have seen it,
For ever, Manas.'

    'Yes,' he mumbled, made no move.
    Hoarsely uttered one more 'Yes'.

Now the demons were alarmed,
Had forgotten, the demons, to practise speaking.
Had leaped and walked, but had not moved the tongue,
And how the lips purse, the throat opens.
Baying and howling was the best they could achieve.

Nervously they came together in Manas' body,
Were unanimous for keeping silent.
But could not keep to it, the way Puto lured them on.
Had to mock him, would play him for a fool,
Began to crow there underneath the tree:

    'You held onto me, Puto, it was a big help.

Now I'm back.'

'Not I who held on, but you yourself.
What use would all my bracing be, if not for you?'

'You sweated. I thought of you.'

'How strange his voice,' thought Puto, 'and what he says.
He is not yet all himself again.
The Field of the Dead is there behind him. –
When you broke through, Manas,
It would not have been enough just for me to pull.
I could protect you only from wild beasts, from Shades and
 demons.'

'Yes, you managed that.'

'And that's why I fixed you to the chain.'

'Yes, you did that.'

And shocking laughter broke out from the demons.
They had to step out with their jerky dance,
The peculiar lurching gait of demons.
Puto was bewildered. What was this Manas leaping there,
What had he brought back from his trip to Hell.
And as he stared incredulous, unhappy, furrowed brow,
He felt for the chain.
And now Manas asked a cunning question:

'You swore, man of powers,
To use no magic, no prayers to Shiva.
You broke the threads around your neck.'

'Yes.'

Manas rocked, crowing, his eyes red-hot, his mouth drooled.
A suspicion drifted into Puto:
'Were there, Manas, any demons
Out there in the Field, who came across you?'

'What? What demons?'

'How horribly you bellow, Manas.'

    'What demons, Puto?'

'Chanda, Munda and Nishumbha, those three.
The blind one, the one all prickles, and the one with fangs.'

    'What are they called?'

'Chanda, Munda, Nishumbha.'

    'Yes, I saw them. Enjoyed their company.'

'The demons?'

    'Yes, good company.'

And Manas rocked clumsily, bold and brazen.
Puto, deeply confused, aghast, stepped nearer.
What horror.
What was it made him stop, and go no further,
Let hang the hand that Manas held out to him.
And then he shook himself and did take one more step.
There in the great tree's shade stood face to face with Manas.

Now Manas sprang back, stood where no leaves shaded,
Sunlight falling bright upon him.
And it – was not – Manas!
That – not – Manas.
It was not Manas. Was he deceived? Not yet awake?
And Puto felt sorrow.
The heart jarred within his breast, because he saw:
Manas has encountered something, he has returned,
But he is no more the old strong golden Manas.

And Puto pulled himself together,
Had to sit down on the ground.
And yet it is still Manas, entrusted to me by his mother,
And however he might have changed,
I will pull him to my breast.

Puto sat there on the ground,

Slowly drew a breath, breathed out, breathed in.
> 'Why do you sit, Puto?
> Since I first saw you it's the second time that you've sat down, old man.
> All that bracing must have taxed your strength,
> Greatly taxed your strength.'

Manas, this is not Manas.
He saw the gleaming in the eyes.
Said not a word when it leaped aside,
The thing called Manas,
When it stared so avidly, drew back the cheeks to grin.

Puto bends down in the grass.
And knows, knows,
Has knowledge fit to set bells swinging: not Manas.
And feels, Puto feels heart-deep,
Breastfeels, mouthfeels, lipfeels:
Manas is dead. Manas has died. My Manas has been laid low.
They could not leave him in peace.
Manas laid low there on the Field, laid low on the Field of the Dead,
As he wandered, laid low.
And is overwhelmed, transfixed:
A deception this. Not Manas. My Manas dead.
And knows, as when one sinks down into deepest night,
And in fathomless sorrow, in the press of sorrow,
Puto crouches low in the grass, breath gone from him.
Killed by sorrow, Manas. Yes, killed,
Our beloved child laid low.
He clutches grass, lets all this run through him.

When the horror fades he crawls upright,
Casts no backward glance at Manas.
Rigid, hands still holding dirt,
Puto steps back from the tree.

Now behind him comes a babbling, squawking,
Leaping this way and that.
He thinks: They leap this way and that.
It is the demons, those wild beasts.
They bellowed, yelped. He walked back from the tree
Where he and Manas had come down to land.
Behind him a squawk:

> 'Puto, teacher, take us with you.
> We want to go with you to Udaipur.'

He paid no heed.

> 'Puto', they roared close at his back,
> 'Take me with you to Udaipur.'

He turned round, head low:

'Take who?' – 'Me.' – 'You?'

Now his eyes scanned Manas' floundering body.
It flickered in him, roped his throat tight.
That mighty chest, those legs,
Manas. It is Manas. What? They've taken his body.
Manas' body. The body of a dead man, brought low by sorrow.
They flounder in it, make it move.
Terrible anger in him, anger of a demon-conqueror, demon-
    hater.
They flounder about in the body of my Manas.

One bound and he was at their side,
They flinched ten paces back.
'You lot!'

> 'Ah, who do you mean?'

'You!' roared Puto.

> 'Me?'

'You lot. Chanda, Munda, Nishumbha.
What other jackals. Who else but you!'

Now they were stung. They tumbled from their hiding places.
On Manas' head Munda squatted.
Out by the mouth and hanging from the lips,
Prickly Nishumbha.
Chanda lurked at the navel, bared his fangs.
They looked around.
They had Manas' body. Just let Puto try to bring it down.

They needed a weapon. Above them was the tree.
Up they jumped, scampered to a branch, broke it.
On all fours to the ground.
Rushing zigzag, coursing round and round, the demons set on
      Puto.

He seethed. He the mighty man.
These the beasts he'd warned Manas against.
They'd taken him, his Manas.
His beard bobbed over his shoulder, gall was in his mouth.

He had no branch. He flung at them the dirt held in his hands.
Their blow connected with his arm.
He felt that it was Manas, but without his strength.
They tittered, scampered back.

'I could put a curse on you, you'd vanish like the air.'

    'We have Manas' body. Fight Manas and you'll feel him.'

'You don't have him, corpse-despoilers, jackals,
You're just worms inside the corpse.'

    'Here's one for you! There!
    Us worms will soon fetch you away.'

'Me?'

    'You. We'll tie you to the tree,
    And set off for that country, the realm of humans,
      Rajputana.
    We can do that. We'll ride in Manas' body. And your body.

They'll welcome us. We'll take you along.'

'Tell me more, hyenas.'

'More southwards, yes. Benares, Madura.
In Manas' body.
In your body. We'll visit Shiva's temple, yes we will!
Puto, come.'

They stood there breast to breast.
Nishumbha's prickles dug into Puto.
Chanda's claws were embedded in his skin.
Munda's fangs scored tracks down his cheeks.

He wrenched the broken branch away from them.
And as they looked around to make a backwards leap,
Stood coiled for action half turned away,
The branch smashed into the left side of the chest,
Cracked open collarbone, ribs,
Slammed into the heart.
The body keeled sideways, body rolled to the ground.
Body lay curled up on the ground.
Lay still, mouth closed.
The ghosts came out whistling, blazing,
Out of the head,
Out of the mouth,
Out of the guts.
Blazed, bleated, whooped.

But out of the shattered chest, look, out of the spurting wound,
    look,
Between the ribs there wafted something long, white, misty –
Puto saw it as he pulled the branch back to him,
And the demons saw it as they huddled in the treetop –
A bewildered human Shade, a thing that gaped,
A human soul awoken from its sleep,
Stretching upward, it stretched out long,
Hung a while above the bloody spurting wound,

Looked at Puto, looked long at Puto.
    'Puto, so it is you. I tried to reach you.'
And hung there without moving.
And seemed to want to come to Puto,
But could not.
And was drawn backwards, lifted up.
And did not understand.
And saw the branch in Puto's fist,
The spurting blood below,
The shattered chest,
And was drawn higher, drawn, borne backwards away.
And looked at Puto, tried to speak,
Opened its mouth to moan, to moan,
And was borne backwards through the treetop
And flew, flew backwards,
Wafted onto the Field of the Dead.

[4] EKPHORA

RAUCOUS riot, the demons' cries of triumph:
'Hooya, Puto, vanquisher of demons, man of powers!
You were raised by Shiva.
How you swing a branch!
Puto, what's that chain about your wrist,
As if you lead a bull to sacrifice!
Puto, who did you sacrifice to this day?
Shiva?
But you swore you wouldn't pray to him.
Come, let's go tell Shiva what you've sacrificed to him.'

Whooshed between branches, through foliage,
Wind, wind, fleeting wind, sighsighsoughing.

Swooped down to the ground, over scrub,
Over cowering wild swine.
Soughsigh.
Up behind Manas wafting on the wind.
Wind moaning, yowling:
Keep hold of me, hold my feet,
My long thin ribbons, my shimmery fluttery.
But don't bite. No clawing.
I'll fall to pieces if you claw me.
Hooey-hoosh-whoosh. Yak-yak-whee.
Fly fast, or you'll be too heavy.

'Hee, hyah, hyah,' the demons' whinnying tiger-cry:
'Woof, aarff.'
Howling away to the east.

AS A PROUD palm, still with its crown and giant leaves –
But it has been turned to char by the forest fire –
Displays black branches, leafribs –
In the crown, birds are all ashes now –
So motionless did Puto sit, his face a blank.
The howling over, birds began once more to twitter.
His hand felt for the ring.
Then worked its way along the chain, to the other's arm
And back again.

Another hour.
And like a mountainside with marble palaces and temples here
    and there,
And an earthquake has seized it by the scruff,
Hurled down slabs of marble, collapsed the towers,
And naked piles of rubble lie exposed and stones trickle, clatter,
Just so did Puto sit.

A wild goat with enormous screws for horns, long beard,
Thick mane of silver-grey down to its knees, stepped from the
    woods.
The goat walked by. Kids sprang after it.

Then a rushing in the air. Leaves shook.
A griffon gyred wide in descending
To where Puto sat, perched on Puto's knee.
He gave a start, recognised the bird,
Looked aside and saw the brown body, pool of blood.
And like children faced with a barking dog,
His eyes flinched away.

The griffon flapped before his breast, clawed at it,
And Puto trembled and let the teeth chatter in his mouth.
His breast rose and fell,
And he struggled and could not find his voice.
And the griffon rose and fell in time with his struggling.
More strange, to Puto even, did his breath sound,
More strange this *ah, ah,*
His body shivering as if chilled.

He pressed the griffon ever closer, it pressed back against his
    pawing
Until he found his cry, griffon clenched against his breast,
And the creature pecked his cheek, blood flowed down,
And he unrolled, raged and screamed and screamed,
A long continuous horrible scream.
This was Puto. A ghastly screamsob.
A wide wound in his chest, brook tumbling from it,
Emerging from a rocky corrie, thundering down its course.
His body shook, arms flailing,
His scream raged in the air.
The air quailed before his scream of pain.
His arms hung limp from him like snakes.

There he stood, a beggar, and scrabbled on the ground, felt his
    way,

And was able to take hold once more of Manas,
Could fling himself upon him, and could kiss his face.
Could press Manas' head against his breast,
As if he were still living.

'*Whoa, whoa, ho*, I called to you, Manas, as you tugged at me.
You did not hear me.
I tugged at you, you did not come.
You took it on yourself, you were a man of strength,
Now you know it all.
No need to call *whoa, whoa* again.
I have you now, my child, my son, beloved,
Now you are with me and will not leave,
And will stay with me, with all of us.
We need you. You are our life, our salvation.
You are our preserver. Without you we cannot live.'

And let go of him again. And again his cry:
'Whoooah! Now we have you, Manas.
We were going to carry you home in triumph
Over the hills, the steppelands, fields.
Mountains will shudder when they see you,
Steppelands, how you've returned from battle.
And bring you to your garden hall:
How long must I stand, stand, stand at this window.'
And grasped hold of him: Come, come. And murmured: Horror.
And tugged at him.

Puto hauled himself up, he tugged at Manas,
Ah, dragged and pulled the corpse behind him,
Ah, lifted it against his chest.
Into the air Puto rose, and flew with Manas, his beloved child.

HE TOWED it behind him by the chain, through the air,
Carried it with him over the slopes of Himalaya.
The body grew heavy, heavier.
Soon no longer hung close by him, at his back,
No longer sailed like a cloak behind him.
The body sank down, sagged, pulled at Puto's legs,
And Puto had to breathe hard.
Down through layers of air the body dragged him,
Heavier by the moment.
Puto heaved himself by bursts aloft and on,
Through billowing swathes of mist over black-green forests.
Crowns of plane trees whipping by.
Who's sat on the body, someone must be sitting there,
A demon, trying to force Puto down.

Puto turned and braced himself and fought,
Surged like a swimmer forward with new thrusts.
Birds whirred high as he flew with Manas over treetops,
Monkeys were alarmed.
But he had to, had to sink down among the trees.
The body came crashing down through branches,
Thudded heavily on soft earth.
And slowly Puto lowered himself down behind it, stood on the
    ground.

His fallen Manas lay on breast and face.
Puto turned him onto his back.
'I can't carry you through the air, Manas, to your father.
Wicked demons are hanging onto you.
Or – I have grown weak.
They want your body as a trophy.
I must take you to Udaipur, to your father.
Come, o come up.
I must carry you in my arms. That's how I must take you.'

And pushed his arms under Manas' torso, fingers, hands, lower
    arms,

He groaned and grubbed until he saw his fingertips.
Manas' body takes my whole armstretch.
Now I must lift him.

He dug his toes into the earth, braced his knees, snatched
     himself up,
Stood erect, carrying Manas, the arms dragging, legs dragging,
The dead man's head hung down and bobbed with every step.

Puto moved one step at a time.
Big black ants bit him on the arms.
Blood pulsed in his eyes, his vision bleared.
He stumbled. Now he saw nothing, only carried, tramped.
He groaned, the man of powers:
How heavy a corpse is.
This hero has such mighty limbs.
He defeated many men.

The body had slipped lower from his breast.
Now he bore the hero at less than navel height.
Sweat made his fingers slippery.
Sweat trickled down his flanks, itching on his nose, his lips,
Puto with his load plodded blind.

Overwhelmed by heat he disengaged his thoughts,
Thought the four sacred words.

Slings of hanging vine brought him up short.
He broke through snorting, from tree to tree broke through.
Held his arms like iron, not seeing them, not feeling them,
They were iron braces, iron gurneys
Out there, down there by his navel.
But he could hear his heavy tread:
Twigs snapping *tump tump* and *crack*.
His hands were nearly level with his knees,
Then it grew cooler.
The forest opened up. A lake must be nearby.
And slowly Puto eased down, cautiously,

Unclenched his hands, flexed fingers,
And slowly stretched arms and fingers
Slowly out.

He had a sense that there was nothing in his arms.
His eyes were blind with sweat, sweat still pouring from him.

He twitched the arms. Now they came higher.
He could bring hands to his eyes, wipe sweat from his brow.
And Puto, trembling, staring at the ground:
Arms empty, nothing down there at his feet.

He turned: nothing to the sides and nothing behind
And nothing at his feet.
And yelled, and ran back, back,
Into the black woods.

They've stolen him, they've stolen Manas
From my very hands. They followed me.
How weak I am, how weak.

But Manas had simply dropped down from his hands.
And as Puto flew along a forest path,
Jackals yelped.
With one bound Puto was across the gullies.
Manas was stranded on a rubber tree's giant root.
Astride the root, which arched high over the ground,
Sat as if riding it. Toppled back his torso, arms up by his head,
Backs of his hands resting on the ground.

He lay as if unseated by the root as he rode by,
His dead body in the gloomy jungle dreaming still
Of his experiences on the Field:
Of Danu, Daksha, they were still with him,
Those two, as they burned and tumbled burning from the cart,
Now he himself hanging from the cart.

Puto chased away a jackal-dog.
He fell on Manas with his head breast arms:

Oh I struck you down. You were proud and I was proud.
You lie dead and I am nothing, and jackals want to eat you.

And Puto, there atop the body,
Fell into a dark despairing dream.
He lay exhausted, drenched in sweat.
Dreamed that he was lifted up, face to dead Manas' face.
He had not secured Manas with a strap,
Something handled them quite casually, as they were nothing.

But both had simply slipped down from the root.
Jackals were taking them,
Jackals, on their backs, six strong jackals,
Light and wind-swift, dodging nimbly between trunks,
Beneath date-palms yucca cypresses,
Past wide ponds where alligators poked their heads out.
Wind-swift through rugged beechwoods.
Monkeys noisy overhead. Mango-birds complaining.
High in the branches squirrels scampered.

Down into the plain the jackals ran, through tall steppe grass.
The Day Star had already set when they went their separate
    ways.
The twined bodies slid to the ground, a village lay nearby.
A river glinted. Cattle lowed,
The jackals away already, lapping at the river,
Rubbing sore backs in the sand, yelping softly to each other,
    digging in.

Puto dreaming, Puto in the grass:
He was eating rice cakes, a hen was pecking at them.
Dreamed a long while, chewed, and swallowed cake,
The beak pecked harder. A cockerel stabbed his finger.
And when the mighty man woke startled, the cockerel flew up,
Sat on Puto's breast, then fled crowing across the meadow.

Blinking, Puto moved his fingers, held up his hands.
Men from the village plodded,

Pushed barrows across the meadow, not far from Puto.
He followed them with his eyes.
And only when they had gone by did they turn to look at him
As he sat there in the grass, the mighty man, and moved his fingers
And followed them with his eyes.

They came closer, recognised the mighty man,
Pressed foreheads to the grass. He did not speak.
Out of the village along with peasants came whitehaired Brahmins,
Shiva's triple threads at the brow,
Bowed down to Puto, who sat and said nothing.
He moved an arm. He parted the grass.
There behind him lay the brown man, strong man, a dead naked corpse,
The saviour, the great victor, beloved by his country,
Laid low by demons.
Puto could only say: 'Laid low by demons.'

NEXT morning humped white oxen hauled the cart
Out of the temple hall, on towards Udaipur.
On the cart, under shrouding cloths, white flowers: Manas.
Drums preceding the train. And waving flags and drumming.
Dum dum, trum. Dum dum, trum.

On the cart, under shrouding cloths, Manas.
And heaped stones, fields of maize,
A stream of peasants joining.
Dum dum, trum. Dum dum, trum.

Under shrouding cloths, Manas.
Saviour of his country, victor,
Laid low by demons.

Dum dum, trum.

Flowering sun, flaming sun,
And love that streamed to him like wind
And raised him up.
Manas under shrouding cloths. But he was dead.
On back to Udaipur, cresting hilltops,
Traversing silent forests.
Dum dum, trum.

Udaipur's white buildings, its bazaars and pools,
But he was dead.
How long must I stand at the window?
But he was dead.
The avenue outside the gate was long, a line of cedars.
The King outside the gate with men in armour,
Jayanta by himself, a slave behind him with a sunshade.
Dum dum, trum. Dum dum, trum.

How did Manas leave? Without a blessing.
With Puto, man of powers.
Trum rum, trum rum.

'Puto, I thought it was you come back to us dead.'

    'And so it is. Your son lives. I am dead.'

'And whose cortège is this?' – 'Mine.'

'So I shall lay you on the funeral pyre.'

He bowed, this Puto, wept before the King who burned with sorrow.

'There lies Manas, my son. Under shrouding cloths, flowers.
Now I have you still, and they all have you, those you saved.
Soon we shall have you no more.
But my child, you took me with you, with you.
My heart, you took me with you.
My flesh, you took me with you.

With you, my blood, my young life.
I bloomed but once, you were my flower,
Now I am barren, and lie before you.
Ah, let me embrace you, my son,
By holding you I hold myself, you are me.
What shall I do when I can no longer feel you,
No longer feel myself.
You are cold to the touch.
How can I live, what is left of me.
And who will pray for me.'

The old man, trembling, grim, stood up:
'Into the city with Manas.
He shall have a roof over him.'
Trum rum.

The great gates, the city opened up.
Into the streets, the bedlam of humanity.
Scorching streets. Humped white oxen, cart,
Manas under shrouding cloths, laid low by demons.

SILENCE in the streets.
Women peeped from latticed windows.
And hundreds thought, as they turned their heads
To the latticed windows where the womenfolk moved,
Of Savitri.

What must she be feeling, Manas' beloved wife,
Manas' calm centre, behind that latticed window?
Tomorrow she would cling to him one last time,
And be burned at his side.

Savitri moved behind the latticed windows,
Stood and looked, as much as weeping eyes allowed,
At the procession trailing behind Manas,

Behind the soul-bereft.

And hundreds thought of how Savitri had found Manas.
She did not seek the one who drew the strongest bow,
Who was best in all the competitions, came first in every race, game, hunt.
'Now, father, grant me this.
If I am to choose a consort – You want me to, and that is good –
Let me seek him in my own way.'

And for three long days she prayed to Shiva,
And went calm and delicate, weak from fasting, to make her choice.
The seven royal scions in the great hall formed a semicircle,
In the hall consecrated to the Soul-bestower, Shiva.
All seven youths were veiled down to their feet,
And Savitri, who came in alone, knew none of them.
Not her father, not her mother, nor her women were allowed to be with her.
Towards the motionless young men in their heavy drapes,
Mute pillar beside mute pillar, this one as nameless as the next,
Savitri tripped light-footed from the door,
Did not even turn her head,
Stood a moment silently among them.

And then she raised her arms, pirouetted up to one,
Laid arms, her smooth ring-decked arms about his shoulders,
Lifted his veil.
And Savitri smiled at Manas for the first time,
Smiled at him as if this were nothing special.
They smiled each to each, like old acquaintances.

For the first time Manas lost the ground beneath his feet,
And yet did not plunge into the depths, but only swayed.
And realised a man cannot only walk and stand robustly,
But can also sway.

She walked side by side with him to the door,

Asked his name, gave hers: Savitri,
As if they were old acquaintances.
And the other princely sons, veils removed,
Felt this, were secretly abashed, and made way.

Through the door Savitri led Manas to her father.
Everyone, even the young loiterers by the fountain in the now silent courtyard,
Praised the Soul-bestower, blue-throated Shiva,
Who is everywhere.

CRUSH of people, silence in the streets,
Trum rum.
Cart behind humped white oxen,
Manas under shrouding cloths, laid low by demons.

The causeway on Pichola Lake, terraced palaces,
Sculpted friezes painted frescoes,
Gardens with fig trees, tamarinds, ginger.
Jayanta on his way to Manas' garden hall,
Dum dum, trum.
But he was dead.

The King, ashes on his face, beneath a tree.
The cart rumbled past close by.
'Who goes there behind the hearse?'
No answer.
'Who goes there behind my son's hearse?
No one shall touch the hearse on which my son is carried.'

Trum rum, but he was dead.
And the cart rumbled on.
The King trembled, looked aside:
'Is that the ghost, the evil demon that laid him low?
Is it here, the thing that laid him low,

Wants to take him, gobble his remains?'

Drums no longer rattled.
In deep silence Jayanta swayed along behind the creaking cart.
Thus Shiva makes a clean sweep of my line.
Are you all afraid?

And stepped closer to what was following behind the cart,
Laid hands on it from behind. They tussled.
The King fell down along with Puto.
They lay atop each other as the cart rolled on.
And the chain was there, the stout steel ring on Puto's arm.

'Ah, Puto, it is Puto! Help me up.
Help me up.'
They raised him to his feet, the old man would not be calmed.
He cried, threshed about, eyes starting from his head:
'What was that? Did you see? I am not dreaming.
It is Puto. He has his chain, the chain unbroken.
Puto has returned.'
And shook himself, spittle on his lips. 'It is Puto.
He has brought my dead son back to me.
The chain intact. How could Manas die.
He swore to keep good hold of him.'

They sat the King down on a bench.
The cart with Manas halted.

'Cut him to pieces. He is the murderer.
Bring him before me. It was no demon.
He must speak.
The men of my court of justice shall come to me.
The murderer shall appear.'

Puto crawled forward on all fours.
The old man clutched the chain, turned his head to right and left,
Took the measure of the chain by eye:

'First take off the chain. I do not want you linked to him.
Are you Puto? Really? Show yourself.'

A groan came from the ground.

'He is dead. But there's no wound on you.'

'Slay me, King! Slay me.'

'All in good time. First loose the chain.'

Puto fumbled for the ring.
And as he fumbled for the ring to say the spell to loose the ring,
The ring – lay – already in his hand,
The ring in his hand,
It was – already loosened, split apart,
Was loosened long ago, eaten up as if with rust.
Trickled like mortar through his hands, crumbled in his hands.
The ring was loosened long ago.

Puto started back in horror, collapsed.
The ring already loosened, but not by him.
Puto on the ground. He swallowed dust,
Screamed, screamed wordlessly.
And *trum rum, trum rum.*
But he was dead.
Cart behind humped white oxen.
But dead, he was dead. Manas was dead.

TOMTOMS, strident fluting in the town that evening.
The people lamented.
The army was assembled.
Hermit thrushes, water ouzels in the gardens sang.
On Jag Niwas island, Puto stood
Naked in a loincloth, long beard, long hair,
Fivefold holy threads about his neck,

Face, limbs smeared with ashes.
Walked silently past the King's guard,
Silently into the palace.

Servants heard the King's cries, the old man's whimpering
    begging,
Dared not go in.

Then it fell quiet in there.
Had they stood nearer, they would have heard
How they wept together, Puto and Jayanta,
For Manas, their beloved. But he was dead.
How one voice would gradually fade and quieten,
And the other would continue sobbing unabated.
And when Puto's crying had subdued the King's,
Jayanta came close to him, touched him on the shoulder:
'Do not cry so, do not cry so.'
And then: 'Do not cry so, do not cry so. I cannot die ten deaths.'

Puto's tears brought home the horrors of the Realm of Death.

'Oh stop now. Do not cry so, Puto.
I cannot die a hundred deaths.'

> 'You not, but he did. He died them,
> There on the Field. And then I laid him low.
> I had to do it.
> I could not go with Manas to the Field.
> And Shiva withdrew himself from me, and loosed the chain,
> And I had to lay him low.'

'Oh do not weep. You are Puto, man of powers.
I cannot bear to see you weeping.'

Puto lowered himself to the mat, raised his ash-smeared face,
And set up a howling howling.
The same howl he had emitted when he fought the demons.
Broken though he was,
Now again the vanquisher of demons, the great yogi.

In a wide swathe around the palace all fell prostrate,
Ghosts scurried from buildings.

'Your scolding cannot take away my powers, Jayanta.
I am Puto.
Your son was not laid low by demons.
I – I laid him low.'

The King tried to raise him up: 'Manas is my son.
Manas was cocksure.
Shiva seeks to punish us.
Man of powers, save me. Don't tear me apart.
Preserve us all.'

'They deceived me, flaunted his body in my face.
But I shall pay them back.'

The King sat at his side.
Puto's gaze was fixed, as if he lived it all once more:

'It was too much for Manas' strength.
But even so he did not break.
Any other surely would have died.
Chanda, Munda and Nishumbha came and saw him there.
Into his body they crawled, he had no defence against them.
Those three crawled in his body
And came tottering to the tree, the hill where I was waiting.
Manas, I cried, you're back,
Now you are safe, you victor, victor.
I'll take you to your father, and I have you back again.
Then I saw the glittering eyes, and how they leaped.
And thought and thought, ah, ah - !'

And lifted his face, set up a howling howling,
And roared so that the empty palace echoed.
Torches outside flickered low, hissed as if water had been
    sprinkled.

'Manas laid low, Manas our beloved,

> Our child, crushed, cast down, by sorrow, so I thought,
> And they have stolen his body,
> And mean to enter the realm of people,
> Those scoundrels, mean to breach the boundary.
> I thought: they have donned the dead body meaning to outwit me,
> Those pestilential creatures
> That drip poison from eyes and throat and navel.'

And Puto groaned again, whirled his arms.

> 'I wanted to destroy their housing,
> The house belonged to us, it was our beloved,
> They had no business dwelling there.
> Their slavering lust for this world of ours must be denied them.
> I struck, I struck, Jayanta: I – struck – him.
> I never would have thought the demons so depraved.
> In a cranny of his body our Manas slept.
> They arranged it all for me.
> I had to strike his chest.
> They crept out fearfully, retreated scattering.
> And there was nothing he could do. He died.
> But this is not the final word.'

The mighty man stood up. Stood rigid:

> 'Have no fear, O King, this is not the final word.
> I came to tell you this.
> Shiva broke the ring from me.
> Have no fear. The demons must not triumph.
> Shiva will not withdraw himself from me.
> I wear nothing now but threads and loincloth.
> I am no longer here for you and Udaipur.
> This is not the final word.'

On the mat the King wept quietly:
'In the morning we shall bear him over betel leaves and fronds of palm

To the funeral pyre, in the garden outside his hall,
Where he would not listen to the songs of victory.
If only he had stayed with us!'

Puto rigid, the man of powers, naked, smeared with ashes,
Fivefold threads around his neck, mark of Shiva on his forehead.

When tomtoms in the town resumed their throbbing, and flutes wailed,
Two mighty birds came flying in the window one by one,
Circled Puto, screamed.
Sukuni, his griffons.

They clawed his hair, perched on his shoulder,
Circled him, Sukuni.
He turned his head, moved so he could see them.

TWO

SAVITRI

[1] TO THE MOUNTAINS

CROWDS packed every street.
Manas to the funeral pyre tomorrow.

Night fell with sudden blackness.
The earth breathed in, breathed out.
Mosquitoes buzzed, thirsty for blood.
Birds safe in their trees.
Panthers creeping.

And there she sat, huddled in her room, Savitri.
No maidservant with her. Door firmly bolted.
Outside they were strewing flowers in the path
To the pyre awaiting Manas and her.

She had put aside all ornament.
The room was dark, moon and stars peeped through the window.
She had passed through every stage of longing,
The young gazelle, those long weeks
While Manas was away at war.

Her thoughts then were like waters rising to the moon:
Face and hands surged towards him.
She had sighed, whispered, shuddered, lain sick for him on the mat.
They had mopped her limbs with icy water,
Hers, who from morn till evening and at night in sleep
Wanted nothing but to see him and to cling to him,
To him who was not here,
Not here in the morning and not at noon and not here in the evening

And not at night.
And had no appetite and could only shiver
And only pout her lips in his direction.
And again, again the pitiless sun came up
Without him,
Went down
Without him.
Until he was here and did not see her
And made no move to meet her,
And she made no move.
Huddled in her room, Savitri.

Outside her room, outside the door a Bo-tree.

'Bo-tree, I come creeping to you.
My father gave you to me,
They planted you outside my room.
I betrothed myself to you when I was small.
Bo-tree, can you hear me?'

Bo-tree loomed silent.

'What a proud strong tree you are.
Protected me, consoled me, gave me comfort,
You my senior consort. Bo-tree, can you hear me?'
The tree loomed silent. Then began to rustle.
She heard a whisper: I hear you.

She clung to its roots: 'I am to die, sweet Bo-tree.
Should I slip into the hall
Where they have laid him out upon the bier?
Guards are watching over him.'

    'Stay.'

'Ah, you want me here with you.
Sweet Bo, I shall stay with you, I am here by you.
I shall always hold fast to you, love you.
But tell me: should I not go to Manas,

To the hall where they have laid him on his bier?
I haven't seen him since he left for the wastes of Thar.'

Thin tinkling bells. What were they saying?
She breathed a tender ah! and wept
And embraced the trunk. Wide branches shivered down at her.

'No kisses, Bo-tree. The moon lies bright on the garden.
They'll see us from the halls.
Speak. I haven't seen him since the wastes of Thar.'

   'Go to him.'

'I should go to him, and you say yes?
And will the guards not see me?'

Again the tree shivered. A green leaf floated down.
She took it in her hand.
She ran, leaf in hollowed hand,
Drew her shawl across her face.
Guards were standing there.
Songbirds throbbed, jackals barked far off.
She dared not enter through the gate,
Torches blazed within.
She ran to a window,
And there she saw, saw.
One look.
And Savitri was already fleeing.
Fleeing, fleeing.
Held the leaf tight in her hand, squeezed it, crushed it, fled,
Wailed softly as she ran.
Ran straight back past the guards, fled back to her hall,
Crying, wailing softly, in bewilderment: 'It is not Manas.
Is not Manas. Bo-tree, it is not Manas.'

   'Who is it then, Savitri?'

'It is not him. I don't know who it is.
A dead man's lying there,

Dreadfully, dreadfully scarred by demons.
Oh what have you done, Bo-tree, sending me to him like that!
I must bathe, I must cleanse myself.
It is not Manas.'

Ran indoors. Appeared among the women.
She danced before the women, jewelled, painted.
And her body, what did her body do?
Her body began to move once more, to yearn, to bloom.
Oh what had come into her.

> 'You'll soon have him back, Savitri,
> You'll soon be in his embrace again.'

And she, swaying: 'Yes, I'll have him back again.'
And outdoors into the darkness, to hug the Bo-tree's roots.

'Bo-tree, sweet Bo-tree, my senior consort,
This for you, this for you:
All the flowers they have heaped on me.
Now you may kiss me.
I think I must take leave of you.
Manas sent the body to me that lies there in the hall,
So that I can know how it goes with him.
He has sent me this sign.
Since the wastes of Thar he's never come to me.'

And overcome, Savitri wept and kissed the tree
And flung her arms around it:
'Because I'm going, Bo-tree,
And because I hate to part from you.
But I can't leave Manas in the lurch.
The town is all laments and shouting,
And I the only one he speaks to,
The only one who hears him.
Maybe he's calling out to others too, and they can't hear him.'
'You're going away, Savitri.'
'Don't grieve, my sweet Bo-tree.'

 'I like to listen to you.'

And now she bared her shoulders:
'See these bite marks on my shoulders,
And the dints of fingernails in my breasts.
With every bite he tried to penetrate my being.
I begged him: bite harder,
It doesn't hurt, it feels sweet to me.
Do you know me now, Bo-tree,
Do you know Manas, and must I not track him down?'

 'I am listening. I am looking at you.'

'I'll be back, Bo, back very soon.
Twenty warriors are stationed in the hall, torches blazing:
An evil spirit has done this.
His father weeps for him.'

 'Stay here.'

'Oh let me go.'

 Branches beat down at her: 'You will be back?'

'Maybe, sweet Bo-tree.'

Ran to the meadow, Savitri at the waterside, loud the frogs'
  croaking:
'How can I cross.
King Jayanta, I cannot come across to you.
I fear your warriors and the priests:
They'll do me a disgrace. You can hear me.
I'm going away. Going to find Manas.
The priests want to keep me under guard
And burn me at the dead man's side.
Jayanta, Manas lives!
It's a false Manas lying in the hall,
Dreadfully, dreadfully scarred by demons.
I shall seek our Manas. I shall bring him back.
He's alive: do you hear me? I shall bring him back!'

Waves crinkled the water, to her delight:
Jayanta hears me. Farewell, Jayanta.
And ran across the meadow.
Frogs hopped between her feet.
Past Manas' hall, *How long must I stand at this window,*
Past her own hall, the long avenue,
Trum rum,
Manas under shrouding cloths, laid low by demons,
Trum rum.
And into the town, crowds packing every street,
And when morning flashed, out of the gate
And out away from Udaipur, on to the sandy heights.

WHAT state was she in, who ran and stood
And gazed about and ran and looked?
A soughing and a whistling in her breast,
As in a forest when a storm is raging.
The forest fills with noise, and then a lull,
A humming long drawn out, playful breezes,
And gentle after-tremors.
She stood like that, skipped a little, rejoiced, was happy:
Manas lives!

Ah then again the dark and snarling storm.
She faded, sank down, stretched out her arms,
Covered her head, rubbed her face:
I must go on. I must go to him.
I cannot live.
And running against trees, ran,
Oblivious of time,
To the heights, the heights, the heights.
Until she fell down in a faint, slept,
Resisted sleep, was seized by sleep,

And lay, swooned away in sleep.

Wild beasts from the forest could have sniffed around and eaten
    her,
Or poisonous snakes attacked her.
Sleep took her in
The whole night through and half the day,
Little Savitri.

In hot sunlight she came awake again:
Oh, I fell asleep outdoors, no beasts attacked me.
Thought of Manas. Her life was back.
And happiness, yearning joy were back,
Lip-twisting, smile-beguiling,
Breath-forcing, limb-quickening joy.

Luck luck, a hen strutted past.
A hut by a mud wall. A woman stood outside:

> 'Such a fine lady, you look so weary.
> Come in, be our welcome guest.'

'I fell asleep in the forest. Snakes left me alone.
I'm not weary.'

> 'Now sit by us in the shade.
> Such a fine lady. You're of a noble caste.
> You mustn't drink from our jug.'

They sat under the shady roof.
And without a word spoken, tears poured from Savitri.

> 'What's troubling you? They've driven you away.'

Her back bent lower, tears fell into her lap.

> 'You needn't cry because they drove you away,
> And you have no home.
> The high-ups have strict customs
> And stricter than a person can endure,
> Or a woman can endure.'

Savitri's head hung down.

> 'But we are poor, we look about, take what we find.
> Many call us thieves.
> With us everything is easy, with us you'll be quite safe.'

'No one drove me away. I have to find my husband.'

> 'Then he's abandoned you,
> Abandoned you?' The old woman shook herself:
> 'Just like men.
> But you're a child. And you cry for this?
> You shouldn't lift a finger for him.
> Listen:
> If you want him back, then go home again,
> Must act as if you'd no idea he was gone.
> Must act the same as yesterday, the day before,
> And it will all be fine, and much better even than before.'

'I must look for Manas. But he is dead.'

> 'What's that you say?'

'He's not dead. They just say he is.'

And gave herself up to tears, wept bent over herself
With silent sobs.
'They laid him on the funeral pyre
And now they've burned him.
But it was not him they did this to.
It was the wrong body laid out there.
He's gone, and I don't know where to find him.'

> 'He wanted to come back to you?'

'I shall look for him throughout the land,
In the mountains, among the army, where men go hunting.
And if I don't find him
I shall go to Shiva up into the mountains,
Into the ice.'

The old woman had embraced Savitri, now she let go the girl.

'What have I done that you step away from me?
I shall go to Shiva and fetch Manas back.
And if Shiva has him and will not give him,
Then Shiva can have me as well.'

She sat crouched over her knees, forehead rested on a knee:
'No god can steal my Manas from me.
I am not Puto, who can bend Shiva to his will.
I have no power, we women are weak.
I shall fetch Manas, who is mine.
Dare tell me, woman, that he is not mine.'

In her hand the woman held a jug:

> 'Don't drink with me. It means perdition.'

And Savitri, gulping water: 'I drink, it's water. It refreshes me.'

And her hand shakes, the jug falls from her hand.

> 'Let it fall, sweet child.'

'I shall look for Manas, I shall find Manas. Say yes, say yes.'

> 'Yes, yes.'

'You'll see, I shall find him.
It is decided and proclaimed, for him and me.'

And prepared to move off again, Savitri,
And ate and laughed, Savitri,
And ran about and helped the old woman.

AND at evening once more into the forest,
Into the great dense forest where wild beasts prowled.
Where else but in the forest can she feel at home,
There where the wild beasts prowl and it is endless
With its trees and thickets and lakes.
And Manas must be somewhere.
Where could he be lying, where be hunting,

If not in the vast boundless forest
Where wild beasts prowl,
Daytime beasts and those that come out at night,
And snakes slither high into the branches
And strike at birds' nests.

The trees she saw were unknown to her,
And when she asked them they ignored her.
And when she asked animals, they ran right past
Not understanding.
But this did not pain her,
For Manas was in here somewhere,
Far behind it all.
Animals and trees said nothing of him
Yet all knew as much about him as she did.

She would set her ear down gently at a spring, and listen:
From where? A sound of him from somewhere.

The wind, when wind slides smoothly through the trees,
Who faces, quivering, into it? Savitri.
And quivered and her mouth was open:
Not in my mouth, wind, but in my ears.
I want to listen, you have travelled far and wide.
Who have you seen?
You've seen houses, villages and towns,
And seen forests, and now you feel me
And carry my words onwards.
Now people and souls can hear me,
If they want to hear me, miles away.

Come, wind, into my ear.
No whistling, please, come gently,
So I can listen and check out every voice.
I know a certain tone, can know it in a thousand.
It is a human, his name is Manas.
Take my words, take my breath, my scent with you.

Here is my body. Take it to him, so he knows I'm coming.
My name's Savitri.
It will do him good to know I'm coming.

But at night time in dense undergrowth
She woke up. A crashing in the forest.
She was startled.
And listened, listened, listened,
Into the endless forest where wild beasts prowled,
Where animals snarled and hissed, and screamed from time to
    time
And birds fluttered in alarm
And everywhere a crackling, droning, breathing.

There's nothing human behind all this, she thought, sat up,
Listened to the forest.
A thousand voices out there,
A thousand noises swelled around her:
There's nothing human behind all this.
She sat quite still.
A thousand voices there, a thousand noises swelling,
And I do not hear him.
He's not here. Has been lured away, confused,
Something holds him fast.
There's nothing human behind all this.
It's not my Manas who hides away,
Him I know so well, my sweet life.
He'd have come back to me long ago.

Turned her eyes to right and left:
I shouldn't have run away.
I should have taken hold of Puto,
And shaken him and asked: what have you done with him?
There's nothing human behind all this.

And lay back down.
Her heart beat wildly,

And a thousand voices were out there, noises.
No more laughter, no sleep for Savitri.

When the storm broke loose next morning
She ran into a village,
Hired herself out, did hard labour, threshed rice, ground spices.
A profound reflectiveness came over her.
She sighed no sighs while grinding seeds,
Was tireless on the threshing-floor.
The other women watched her:
She so delicate, so refined, she never wearied.
And spoke little and was always thinking:
There's nothing human behind all this,
And pressed on.

The forests were uncanny, no voice in there.

Savitri traversed steppelands, endless grass.
And wastes of sand with thorny plants.
Grey hares sped past, jackals slunk around.
She went hungry, and lay down heedless of her hunger.
There's nothing human behind all this.

Sometimes she spoke to herdsmen, joined a caravan,
Grew scruffy as a dog.

IT WAS in a sweltering thicket, she lay wilting,
Not asleep, not awake.
Something grabbed her from behind, pulled her by the throat,
A human hand turned her to face the sun.
She stammered: 'Oh, I want nothing here,
I mean no harm. I'll be on my way.'

    'I believe it. But stay put.'

It was a blackbrown man, a steppeland man, his body naked.

He pulled her by the hands:

> 'What are you looking for?'

'I am Savitri.'

> 'And what are you up to here?'

'I'm not up to anything.'

> 'Lazing about, not up to anything and lurking around.'

'No, good man.'

> 'Stand up now.
> Why won't you stand, are you so weak,
> Why don't you come to our huts?'

'I didn't see them.'

There in the scrub, huts of branches and brushwood,
Very low, some dug into the ground,
They were creeper-covered, all overgrown,
You really could not see them.

The man laughed:

> 'Oh, it's you, the one they tell of, running about
> Looking for her sweetheart.'

'My husband.'

> 'Yes, I know, you idle loitering creature.
> He should have beaten you more often,
> Then you would have stayed at home.'

He grasped Savitri by the shoulder:

> 'Come off the path. You'll give us away.'

And pushed her on ahead,
Gagged her mouth when she tried to scream,
Pushed her into a dark hut.

> 'I shan't hurt you.
> So slim and fine. You'll help us.

> We're poor people, we have no time for sweethearts.
> We must look to it that us and the kids don't starve.
> You'll stay and help us. Will you?'

'I don't know you. I've never seen you.
Why did you drag me in here?'

> 'Such burrows are all we have. Will you?'

'Don't be so rough with me, good man.'

> 'We're not good people.'

Urchins playing in the scrub around the huts
Fled when they saw Savitri,
Head over heels into the scrub, into burrows, disappeared.
The man's face did not change.

'Why are they hiding?'

> 'They're afraid.'

'Not of me…?'

> 'Of everyone.'

She lowered her head. She took the man's hand.
She did not look at him. 'I – shall stay.'
Sat in the scrub with men and women.
Her breathing calmed. She slept long and soundly.

They sent her to caravans, herdsmen, who had lost their way.
She had to behave like a native woman.
And when the slender lady came by singing, with her high-
    born grace,
They followed her gladly along paths through untamed scrub,
To where robbers lay in wait with slings and bows
To plunder them.

Savitri stood, went somewhat to the side when the screaming
    started,
Stood, one hand at her hip, the other slack,
Looked this way that way, felt no emotion,

Hauled spoils.
She had to go with other women around the villages
And sell the goods discreetly,
And look lively in darkness and by day, and never rest.

One night they carried in a dying man, a robber: 'They shot him.'
They pulled the arrow from his throat.

> 'Why did you not guide them better, you Savitri,
> But you let them see us, so they could shoot at us?'

The man hit her, shoved her at the dead man:

> 'Could have all been killed. And nothing gained.
> All vanished with their dromedaries and carts.
> You betrayed us.'

She whimpered: 'You must not say such things.'

> He hit her with his fist: 'Say again, I must not.
> Betrayed us, those were your people,
> You still always thinking of your sweetheart.
> Look at him, this was a man worth more than your beloved,
> You loitering creature.'

She whimpering: 'Not betrayed. I did not betray you.'
And could not be dragged back from the corpse,
Cried, wept beside it until morning.
'You must not say such things.'
And pursued the man the whole long day through scrub,
Tearstained Savitri.

He pushed her away, could not look at her.
Children aped her, the women grinned.
They would not let her attend the burning
However much she howled.
And he must not drive her away, of course she'd stay with them,
He should forgive her for her failings.

On till evening, when he went into his hut,

She still could not let him be.
Had to leave her bed as the night-storm thundered:
And did I really kill him?
I him. And I him. I him – And do I bear the guilt.
But what guilt should I bear. And what fault have I incurred.

She ran through hissing rain to the hut next door,
Woke the man up. Lay down at his side, arms around him:
'I may lie with you, and you may not push me away,
And I did not kill him; say it to me, believe it of me.
How can I put things right.
I want to lie with you, I want to feel you,
And nothing will happen to you, and I shall stay with you always,
So that nothing happens to you.'

She wound herself tight around him:
'Nothing will happen to you, and I'll do everything for you.'

And when the man embraced her:
'Tell me true, I did not kill him?
You'll say it, and you'll help me, you will lift this from me.'

    'You did not kill him.'

'And you're not just saying that, you do believe it?'

    'I believe it.'

'Say it: I did not kill him.'

    'You did not kill him.'

'Not not not!'

    'Not not!'

She clutched at him, kissed him on the mouth,
Wildly wildly on the eyes, forehead, cheeks:
'Not not! And I'm still here!
And I'm alive. Oh how good, how infinitely good!'
And lay entwined about the man
And pressed her body to him, and gave herself to him.

Never in Manas' arms had Savitri trembled so,
Never entwined herself in such blissful agitation,
As now in this tribesman's arms.
And had to throw back her head and howl for joy,
So the man must press his hard hand to her mouth:

    'Savitri, what is this howling, why do you wake them up?'

And when he fell asleep,
She sat watching next to him in the straw, remembered:
She had sat like this in the forest,
Voices and noises all around.
There were crackling sounds, but nothing came, no voice came
    to her.
And now, now!
She kissed the straw she lay on, straw under the man's back,
And gently kissed his bare sweaty back,
Crouched at his feet, her breathing calm and happy
Only when at last she found the spot she sought
At his feet,
Lay furtively at the man's feet without waking him,
His feet on her hair and between her hands.
And sometimes his feet twitched in sleep and fidgeted.
Then she shivered with joy, and had to curl her body up.

WEEKS passed, months passed,
She did not change,
Savitri, happy girl, ensnared by scrub, swallowed by dense bush.

One hot day she walked beside him through the scrub,
Gazed into the steppelands:
'There's something I must say.'
Looked radiantly at him, searched his face:
'How long, tell me, how long have I been here?'

'Ten weeks.'

'I've been looking at you ten whole weeks.
Do you know what? Have you never noticed?
Not once, not once have I asked you for your name.
Often I hear them call a name,
They call a name out, and then you turn around to them.'

'Yes, and so?'

'I don't know it. I've never heard it.
I shall never speak it.
I know better what your name is. From today I know it.'

'Why from today?'

'Yes, from today. Your name – oh I cannot find your name.
I cannot name you, but I feel that you are he.'
And gazed steadfast at him, searching:
'How strange. It's on the tip of my tongue.'
And flung her arms around him:
'All my life is at your side, my soul alongside yours.'
And laughed again: 'You've grown more handsome, you are richer.
I could easily have spent my life with you.
In the scrub. Yes, in the scrub with you.'

That night the black-brown man, her husband, took her in his arms,
Held her about the waist.
The hut door he had wedged half open,
Sumptuous moonlight poured in through it.

'Why did you run away from home?
Where did you live,
Who was your first sweetheart,
And what children do you have?'

'I have no children, as my body shows.
I come from beyond the mountains, far away.'

> 'And who was your sweetheart?'

'My sweetheart had always the same name as you.
My sweetheart was always you.'

> 'But what was his name?
> What was it called, the city you came from?'

'There was a city, yes,
And I had a full life, yes,
But always the same, yes.
Actually nothing ever happened.
The only thing that happened was you.'

Night came in through the open door.
Savitri, without moving, rested her eyes on his face,
And felt herself into his face, into the corner of his eye,
The lines on his broad nose.
She held his head in her hands.

> 'Three months you've been with us, Savitri.
> I like you very much, you are my woman,
> But you were looking for a sweetheart,
> So you told us all, – your husband, you were married.
> And I saw, you had bite marks on your shoulders
> And the dints of fingernails in your breasts.'

'You have no idea how you made those?
You don't know, but I know.
Attend now, I'll tell you something.
And when you hear it, then you'll know.
The moon is shining in and you can look into my face.
You'll know it all again.

Then you were not so sweet, then as now.
Some fruit tastes bitter straight from the tree,
But after it has fallen is less bitter,
Yet is the same fruit.
It was in a hall by a lake, a pool, you were not the same as now.

You were strong and happy, now you are more handsome,
And I too have grown more beautiful.'

    'Savitri, I have always been a poor man,
      I've never lived in a hall, never travelled beyond the scrub.'

'You don't know that. Just look at me, dear husband.
You must only find the right memories.
I searched for you in forests, in the steppelands,
Trum rum it went in the avenue of cedars,
They bore someone on a cart, under white shrouding cloths,
Trum rum to a hall, I recall it well.
It was theatre, I knew it right away.
You were gone from there like a fleeting scent.
And then I ran away and it was enough.'

He held firm beneath her radiant gaze.
Her eyes were fixed on him, and how they shone now!
He wanted to be puzzled, but was not.

'In our new nest, dear husband, in our new nest, you and I.
You were rousted out, and so was I,
Do you know me? I am Savitri.'

There was a buzzing in him.
He held his hands beneath her armpits,
Had to say 'Yes', could not pull away from her,
As her face drew close to his.

A trepidation, sorrow rose up in him,
A sorrow from afar, but from where,
Out of the scrub,
Out of the steppelands,
Out of the mountains.

Savitri smiling: 'Our new nest, our new nest, husband dear.'

What had wafted in the door and held him.
Near to tears he was, what had come over him, he must lie down.
He breathed, she held his hand. He slept.

IT WAS on this night, the first rain showers were falling,
On this night Savitri woke from her warmest most welcome of
    sleeps
And sat up in the dark, as every night,
But this night did not move, as every night,
To lay her head at the man's feet, delighting in their every twitch.

She sat and sat and sat
And sat and sat,
Her eyes wide open, looked around
And glanced around and her eyes were open,
And glanced behind her and above her
Up to the roof and to the floor and through the door,
Then clapped a hand to her mouth.
Because because because
That groaning, roaring: it is Manas.
Manas roaring. Dying Manas.
Because because
His cry for help, they are killing Manas.
And he is struggling and no one comes to help him.
Roaring out across the darkness, into the darkness his cries.
A mass of dark clouds rolled the roars along,
A swathe of gloom streamed through the night as through a
    funnel,
Poured from a funnel on through the night to her,
Dreadful laments of the beloved, dying,
Inexorable laments, surging fading,
Of the inexorably dying man.

She sat up in the straw, clutched at straw.
And as the cries resounded through the air,
Her trembling resonated with each change of tone,
Squeezed her, choked her.

And then the man awoke: he could hear nothing.
And only when she jerked erect a fourth frowning time
And a searching came into her eyes, and groans and inability to
 groan,
And only when she clutched at him,
Trembling, a dark distant trembling streaming through her body,
Then the cries streamed through her body into him.

 'O sweet flower, why are you crying?'

'O my husband, he's dying. My beloved, my heart is dying.'

 'Yes, I hear it.'

They endured this for a long hour. Then Savitri lay back down.

When morning came she lay deep asleep beside him in the straw.
All was quiet outside in the scrub.
The man took her in his arms, carried her, she did not waken.
She grew too heavy for him. He lifted her across his shoulders.
Her arms dangled down his back.
She did not waken.

Towards noon there was a mountain.
He had wandered northwards.
He laid her down, tore a strip from her shawl,
Tucked it in his loincloth.
Prayed to Shiva on the ground, prayed humbly and at length,
Checked that she was comfortable, and was away.

SHIVA, she dreamed, there on the ground,
Do you know I'm on my way to you?
Great God of Worlds, Savitri has a big request of you.
When I was told to choose a consort,
Shiva, you stood at my side,
And have stood a long time at my side.
Shiva, I have lain with a good man in the scrub.

He helped me, as no one has since I was born.
I was near to dying.
Help me not to cause him sorrow. I must go from him.

And Shiva's voice spoke: 'Give him your body one more time.'

Savitri spoke: If it is your will.
But she felt shame, wrestled with herself.
Thought: I must give my body to him.
Dragged herself sadly across to where he lay,
And wanted him to drink her to the full,
Like a mother her infant, and then wean him.

Then something dug her in the breast as she bent down to him,
A log or plank, or a stanchion from the door,
Or what was it, she couldn't push it free.
It had been so dark inside the hut, and now was light.
The door must have sprung open, and it was day already,
And she had to go now, close the door behind her.

And as she turned, pain shot through her breast.
She opened her eyes, sat up.
She was awake, had shifted in her sleep to lie across a root.
Sat up, Savitri. Unknown hilly landscape all around.
How had she come here.
In the night she had dreamed of Manas.
Manas calling in the night,
Dying Manas, roaring through the night,
A swathe of gloom had streamed out through the night,
The roaring poured towards her as through a funnel,
Manas calling, dying Manas.
Oh – there beneath the tree– Manas is calling me, I must go.
Her teeth chattered, despite the heat:
I must go to him.

And thought of nothing and was up and away,
Smallsmall human in a giant landscape,
Over hills, some high, some low,

Over levels filled with blowing sand,
And ever onward, never resting, past cacti big as trees.
She did not feel the sun that hurled its heat down on her,
Savitri did not feel the sun,
Rather the sun must feel Savitri as she clambered over sandy
    levels
Straining towards Manas.

How straining?
In such a way that hours and hours went by unnoticed,
And when evening came there she still was
Where she had been that morning:
Manas groaning roaring
Because because because
His cries for help, rolling through the night,
A gloomy mass of clouds rolled through the night.
So there Savitri was at evening still.
And the landscape with its hills and sandy levels
Had not changed.

Just one drink of water from a spring, one mouthful of tough
    grass,
Then she lay down in the gloom, meant to watch and wait all
    night.
But when the stars came out above the vasty levels,
Savitri was asleep on hard ground in a hollow,
Dreaming of the blackbrown man once more,
With whom she had been living.

Now he was far away, but she needed to take proper leave of him,
A proper parting, Shiva had told her so.
And in her dream she opened his hut door once again
And sought him in the shadows there inside.
He sat up, asked her: 'Do you really mean to go away, Savitri?'
She had to bend down over him.
'Go away, I from you, dear husband? Why do you ask?

I've never gone away from anyone.'

He pulled her by the neck: 'I just had a feeling.'
She embraced him.

> 'I only want to lie with you and hold you tight to me, Savitri.
> And hear the blood beating in your breast.
> I was lying here all alone.'

And as they lay in their embrace,
She was able to take sweet leave of him,
Silent wafting sweetness,
So that he had no sense at all that she had left him, and was far away,
Rather she was looking back, watching him:
He was walking through the scrub, away from her,
And he felt that she was with him.
This was such a lovely feeling
That she woke up, lay released and blissful in the hollow
With no thought at all of Manas.

She thought: This is Shiva's gift, that I lie here.
This he has granted me and granted him,
And everything is fulfilled.

And suddenly she thought: how did it come about
That in the morning she was gone from his hut
To lie beneath this tree.

A profound assurance permeated her.
She gazed up at the stars: everything is fulfilled.
She stretched: Everything fulfils itself,
Just as the sky itself is filled with stars
And the night with darkness, so everything is fulfilled for me.
And so he comes, surging, with the sound of bells.
Ah, I feel like singing.

AND in the dark,
While only stars sparkled over her and the moon was far away,
Savitri in the hollow started singing:

'I do not sing of flowers, I do not sing of trees,
Nor of birds.
I sing of the moon.
Where is the moon? He has fled far away.
He flees behind the blackness, the big white moon
In his white coat.
He flees behind the stars, small as a bee,
And flies around, he likes to buzz around in the dark.
But whenever he can he shows himself
And looks down.'

And she began to cajole, lying there in the hollow,
Hands behind her head:
'Aya, can you hear me? Aya, can you hear me?
Once there was a big pond where rushes and lotus grew,
This was long ago.
In the pond there lived a Snake God,
And he had a lovely sister,
Her name was Nila, Nila was her name.
Oh Nila was so beautiful.
I want to sing of Nila, because one day she saw the king
As she was playing in the pond.
He wanted to talk to her, but she would not,
He wanted to marry her, but she would not.
"When can I talk to you, lovely Nila,
When can I marry you? I am the king.
What are your terms?"
She only said "I have none", and swam away.'

Savitri paused her song and gazed up at the sky,
All the stars were there still. She smiled.
She smiled and resumed her song:

'That's what she told the king, what Nila told the king.
How will the king respond, what will he do, the king?
Such a great king. What will he do?
King Baz thought and thought
And stationed two men at the pond.
They were to catch Nila when she came to harvest rushes,
When she came to pluck lotus flowers along the bank.
How lovely Nila was as she went along the bank
With no clothes on.
I do not sing of trees, I do not sing of flowers, I sing of Nila.

The men could not lay hands on her,
They chased her. She turned around
And pulled them after her into the pond,
And they became two fishes.
Then the king sent twenty men,
And all of them were pulled in too, and all swam in the pond.

A simple task for Nila, Nila lived in water,
She swims in water as I swim in sand, in air,
Swimming is nice, and twisting and turning,
Oh how good it is to live, oh, I do like living.

She laughed and waited in delight, there in the pond,
She splashed about and waited
While the king walked along the bank
And had no idea what to do, or how to come to her.

Moon, I want to ask you something,
Stars, it's your turn to tell.
What did Baz do to catch Nila, and did he catch her?'

Sawitri gazed smiling at the stars.
They stood there sparkling merrily,

Fingers to their lips, and listening.
And the moon hung behind clouds with a pallid gleam, winked,
And then hid away.

'Oh, you don't know, you stars.
Not one of you knows what happened, but you're all agog!
King Baz put on his armour.
And when he spotted Nila in the rushes
She swam and would not come closer,
Just swam farther out, where it was really deep and still,
And then he took – then the king took –
What did King Baz take?'

The full moon, white and full,
Shot out from behind the clouds above Savitri.
The stars shrank back and spluttered:

> 'I know, I can tell, Savitri, hoho, let me!
> King Baz took his sword,
> He'd waited so long, he was angry, he saw no way out.
> He took his sword, hoho, and pointed it at his heart.'

'Not his sword, he didn't take his sword.'
Savitri's smile was merry: 'You guessed wrong!'
Savitri merry: 'Moon, moon, hello lovely face!
Moon, eye so bright! Gentle man in white!
Now there you are and I can watch you, gentle weaver man.
A ribbon for me, a little bow for me,
A camisole for me.'

> 'But tell us, tell us, what he did, this King Baz?'

'What do you want with Baz?'

> 'Did you not tell how he stood on the bank, hoho,
> And stood there confounded, no idea what to do.'

'A camisole, moon, a little skirt.'

> 'What he took, King Baz, a sword, hoho, say it was a sword.'

'Not a sword, he didn't take his sword,
Man in white, weaver man.' – Savitri with her merry smile:
'He took, he took a running leap, King Baz –
I want a little skirt, a camisole, you –
And jumped into the pond.

"Who plays so rough so suddenly, King Baz,
What are you thinking of?"
And she wiped the anger from his face.
"Now you'll turn me into a little fish
Like my two men, and my twenty men." –
"But why would I not fall in love with you, King Baz?
I shall come with you to land, right now,
And stay with you your whole life long."

And swam with him to shore, and loved him,
And lived with him – well, why not –
And maybe I'm their daughter.'

And the moon's eyes opened wide, and he grew pale, paler.
Savitri laughed and sang and gazed up at him,
Savitri on her back there in the hollow.
The moon, abashed, looked down on Savitri.
And when he had observed her for a while
He too smiled, a broad tender smile.
He pulled clouds across his face
And spoke with the stars to left and right,
Kept glancing at Savitri as she still sang:

'I do not sing of trees, I do not sing of flowers,
I sing of the moon.'
Then she fell asleep again.

AND NEXT morning, at heavy break of day,
After she had passed so sweet a night,

Savitri clambered heavily from the hollow,
Trudged over sand, swayed right and left.
And in the middle of the day lay down for hours
In the waters of a rivulet.

I'm going to Manas. He cried out so horribly.
I shall take it from him. I shall stroke it away.
He should not cry out, I shall wash it all away.
And from this day on, ever since this night,
She had no more fears, Savitri, was no longer driven.

And when the roaring reached her
As she walked across the steppeland and came to high mountains,
When the roaring came to her across the mountains,
Then she crouched low to the ground,
And her arms came up all by themselves,
As if an ailing creature, ailing child came running to her.
Took it on her lap, held it, suffered with it, comforted.
Wait just a little longer, three days, four days,
And I shall be with you.
Let it go to run across the ground, ailing creature, away from her.
I am no nursemaid, I am not a girlfriend,
I am Savitri, coming to Manas.
It's not Manas who cries out,
But Savitri, coming to Manas,
Savitri to Manas.

NEAR Hardiwar an ogre blocked her way.
Lal Gulam was his name.
He dwelled high on a sheer cliff, and meant to eat her up
As he ate horses and oxen and herders and hunters,
Whose bones lay mouldering all around.

He was no timid sneaking desperado,
But a howler and a growler, Lal Gulam, a rager, a ranter.

In the mountains for miles around they knew
If he was sleeping or awake, if he was guzzling or already sated,
The grinder, hooligan, sorehead, guzzler,
Lal Gulam, ogre on the sheer cliff near Hardiwar.

He had lived two hundred years,
Clinker grinding in his belly.
For days he had been uttering groans,
His snarls and hissing, wheezing *hurr-hah, hurr-hah*.
He did this when his hunger grew, and no one came along.
Savitri came climbing up from Hardiwar.
She had gathered willow switches on the slope.
Along the way the groaning reached to her again,
Dying Manas, to her.
And in a flash she sat right down,
Said Shoo, shoo!, chased the groans away: Go, go, begone from me.
Back to your corner, back into your nook,
Shoo, begone now.
And brushed them aside with her switches.

Hurr-hah, hurr-hah. That groan, that snarling wheezing,
Lal Gulam looked down from high above,
Saw her coming, a colourful thing,
A tender calf, how good it would taste.
His greed kept him furtive.
He dragged himself from his lair, crouched and quivered with greed.
She was only small, just a morsel,
She was a fly, but his belly was a yawning void.
There she was walking up the slope,
The path up the cliffside where he crouched and skulked
And held himself quite still,
And his eyes bulged, and his glances darted.

But when she came and was there right by him
His lungs let loose,
And *hurr-hah, hurr-hah* screeched and whistled from him.

The hairy lumpish human beast that grunted and groaned and
    roared:
  'You'll taste sweet, my mouth is sour.
  Hurr -hah, I need to eat.'
The switches dropped from Savitri's arms,
She wanted to turn back, but he dragged himself towards her
Over the path: *hurr-hah,* and she could not move.

The hairy ancient human brute approached her,
The wheezing monster,
Its jaws blew out a horrid fetid stench across the path,
It dragged itself on all fours, its legs were stony.
She wanted to throw herself in the ravine.
He stood still, bent back his head:
  '*Hurr-hah*, if you tumble down I'll crawl after you,
  And catch you just the same.'
She didn't heed him, didn't understand,
And swayed, frozen to the spot.
  'Don't move. Drop the switches.
  I shan't eat you. You're too small. Just a puppy, or a fly.
  I shan't hurt you. *Hurr-hah.*'
She had to sit down on the ground, frail Savitri.
He leered from a distance:
  '*Hurr-hah*, now now. Ask me something.'
'What should I ask.'
  'Who I am. What my name is.'
'What's your name?'
  'Lal Gulam. I'm hungry. I have to eat you.
  No one ever comes along.'
'My name's Savitri. I have to go to Manas. Let me pass.'
  'Who is Manas. Does he want to eat you?'

'He is my husband. He's lost. Or dead already.
He calls to me day and night.'

    'He's hungry. Why him, not me?'

'Because you're an ogre, he's my husband.'

    'You are small, you are light, there's no weight on you.
    What can you provide?
    You'll die today or in the morning.'

'I shall not die.'

    'What? Haha!'

'I shall not die.'

    '*Hurr-hah, hurr-hah.* You're trying to make me cross.
    A little thing. A speck of dirt. A lump in rags.
    A few bones dressed in skin.'

'All that. And yet. You shall not eat me.'

    Why not?'

'Because I know it.'

And he roared and grunted, whinnied, bit the air around,
He bellowed, Lal Gulam,
And the mountains sent back ghastly echoes:

    'Come closer! I shall let you through! Hoho!
    Walk on by me!'

He crawled backwards to his lair.
Savitri had gazed into his face,
Had got to know his eyes, his mouth,
And his stony legs.

I'm going to Manas, on the Field of the Dead.
A sight like this won't scare me.
And she sauntered past – he all ready to pounce –
And turned to face him:

'Lal Gulam, you've lived here many years,

Your legs are already stone, you cannot run so fast,
Come with me down the mountainside,
Show me the path.'

Rage dizzied him, words failed him, he huffed:

> 'You speck of dirt.
> You little dog. Puppy, what can I say.
> Run off. I shan't snap at you. I don't snap at dirt.'

'The path, Lal Gulam, of course you know it.
You came along it once to live up here.'

> He roared, beat about him: 'Keep going.
> Run away. You'd better run.
> I shan't eat you. Go away.'

But once more she drew him on.
And from his lair out crept the ancient shaggy man-beast,
Roaring as if speared, and crept along behind,
Greedy still to snap at her.

And when the path grew wider she let him by.
He crawled on past, ahead,
And at a bend pointed howling to the path.
But she did not let him go just yet,
Not yet, however much he howled and chomped
And turned about and turned in circles.

'Lal Gulam, up here you have nice weather and good air,
Where you live beside the path.
But why must you waste away up here
A hundred years, two hundred years.
Come with me.'

Now he broke out in such wheezing fury that Savitri grew
    alarmed,
As if his neck were being sliced open.
Three times he turned right round,
Drew himself up, showed his paunchy midriff,

The fiery eyes in the rumpled bushy face,
And set off at a gallop, on all fours
Legs clattering, back up the path,
Howling, groaning, slurping strings of drool
And spitting them through his teeth onto rocks,
Tossing his head.

But in the morning,
Savitri still sleeping in the thicket where he had left her,
He dragged himself down the path,
Suppressed his snarls, his asthmatic panting, grunts of hunger,
Waited at the thicket, thought: I'll eat her, I'll eat her not.
And drearily, as if still in his lair,
Set up his old tune as she began to stir,
The howler, growler, ranter and rager,
The grinder, the hooligan.

'What do you want, Lal Gulam.'

   'I'm hungry. My belly aches.'

'Come.'

And so he crawled with her the whole long way
That he had crawled two hundred years before.
People fled from them.
First he devoured two calves he found trussed up on a cart.
The people had run away.
And he grew calmer.
Then he found water and she with him.

It seemed to him that he was bolder now,
He could pounce on Savitri, or run away,
But for three days did not find the courage.
Until on the fourth he bellowed out: He does not know this
      place,
These are unfamiliar mountains,
He wants to go back now to Hardiwar and the cliffside.

And does he want to waste away up there,
And who will burn his body.

Burn? He's not near dead yet.

Savitri calmed him down beside a stream,
Took his head in her hands, his neck,
And asked: What did it all mean, two hundred years,
Or three hundred, or two thousand,
And always guzzling, always hungry
And bellowing and going without.
'Yes, yes,' he cried, Lal Gulam, as if she stabbed him in the mouth,
And he made to bite her hand.

'And no one there to burn your body,
You rotting away with all those bones you leave lying around.'

And again he howled and bawled, Lal Gulam,
And flung himself in circles and chewed his nails.
Then when she moved on he trailed after her,
Steppelands, boggy forests.
Hurr-hah, hurr-hah a constant low refrain.
People steered well clear of them.

Mouldering carcasses of game relieved his hunger.
And when night came he bawled and howled alone.
And she didn't notice how he gazed at her with leering eyes,
And wanted to snap at her but only bawled
And grumbled, chewed his claws.

And he crawled behind her, glowering,
From Hardiwar to Pauri, Pauri to Rudraprayag,
Long days, long weeks, uphill, downhill,
And never spoke a word to her.

And only when sounds echoed to them from the Field –

Here already were the giant peaks,
Puto fighting the three demons,
Chanda Munda and Nishumbha,

Who had taken up position at the Field's edge –
Only then did he, Lal Gulam, cringe,
The crawling thing, the ogre:

> 'Savitri, I want to go home. Back to Hardiwar, to my lair.'

'Whyever go back to your lair,
Over a hundred mountains, through a hundred forests.
People will not let you by.'

> 'That's not your concern. I will go home. I must go home.'

'Run along then. Run along.'

And off he clattered, Lal Gulam, with a roar of rage,
And on the way ate several humans,
And could not make it through the wastes and forests,
And three days later turned up again.

Savitri was already at one of Trisul's passes.
She evaded him, climbed up a tree.
He stood below and yackered: *hurr-hah, hurr-hah.*
For a day and night he stood there:

> 'Come down, Savitri, I have to eat you.
> Come down. I must eat you.'

And when she would not, he gnawed the treetrunk,
And driven by his rage and pangs of hunger,
Rage horrible to see, turned round in circles.
Up in her tree Savitri wailed, but he did not hear her.

He wheezed and grunted.
A panther took it for a wild boar's grunting,
Crept up, crunching crackling over brushwood,
And then *graugh-argh!*
Its throaty baying at the woodland edge,
Crept and crawled towards old Gulam and his *hurr-hah.*

The panther rubbed its head against a tree,
Then leapt straight for Gulam,

Who bit it, squeezed it, tore at it and crushed it.
They tumbled and twisted, knocked each other down,
Baying and snarling, wheezing and snorting.
Lal Gulam tore the panther to pieces,
Shredded it, devoured it.

Then he spat and vomited around
All the blood and scraps of meat inside him.
And the tree, the giant tree in which Savitri sat,
He butted with his head and chest,
Each charge ferocious.
At every shock Savitri screamed and whimpered,
Until he fell flat, groaning in mid-charge.

Savitri saw in horror
How in the grass his eyes rolled, rolled up,
How his arms flopped back past his head,
And he wheezed *hurr-hah*, face fierce and bloody,
Long greasy tongue licking at the grass.

And when he lay unmoving and stretched out,
Savitri came down from the tree.
Lal Gulam with his fierce and bloody face, long greasy tongue,
Lay stretched out on the grass, a corpse.
Woe! welled up in her, and her body clenched.
Woe! she crouched down by him, silently,
And held his eyes open and then closed them.
Ah, she paced about and groaned, found no peace.
And sat down and had to pace again.
Who will burn his body? He can't just rot.

Piled brushwood high, rubbed long sticks
Until they flamed, and Lal Gulam lay in smoke.

EVER since she had Lal Gulam's company
The groaning had not even once reached her,
Manas dying, and still it did not.
Her face was hard, but in her was an obscure urge
To hear the awful cries and groans despite herself.
And when they came she did not kneel to take them on her lap,
Did not repel them,
Walked on with the groaning, groans and Savitri,
Hard face, hands ravaged from collecting twigs, rubbing firesticks.
She descended from the pass into tumultuous din,
Into battle-tumult: Puto fighting with the demons.
Why not into the tumult, into the clash of arms,
Into the slashing storm,
She and the groaning, together into the tumult and the storm.

What state was she in, as she stood and lay and plodded on
Away from Udaipur?
A soughing and a fluting in her breast, as in a forest
Where the night wind howls and scatters leaves,
The forest moans and fills with noise.
But no lull this time, no humming long drawn out,
No playful breezes.
Assailed instead by unremitting sinister snorting gusts of wind,
Carried, jostled, pawed by blasts from baleful jaws,
Blown back, bowled over by the wind,
By the wheezing *graugh-argh* and *hurr-hah, hurr-hah*.

I must keep on, I must keep on. And why not keep on.

Mountains had closed in about her.
The flowery meadows were far behind already,
The southern slopes, bedlam of beasts and trees,
Euphorbia acacia stands of bamboo,
Behind and below her the rivers in their deep valleys,
Thundering Alaknanda, Kosi, Yamuna,
Ravines meadows rockwalls.

The mountains gathered round her. The mountains boomed:

> 'Here we have stood since Time began,
> We enclose the Field of the Dead.
> Rivers stream out from us, little clouds fly over us,
> Stones splinter and slide down from us,
> Nanda Kot, Trisul, Yamunotri, Badrinath.
> We buttress Kailash, Nanda Devi,
> Our ravines are filled with ice, our summits are ice-bound.
> Shiva's breath is on us,
> Shiva enthroned in the sea of mist.
> Here is night, and storms and snow,
> Leopards, ibex, blackhaired dogs.
> Take care, stars, to shine the whole night through,
> Take care, take care, vagrant mists,
> When we tremble, when Shiva's tread is on us,
> Boisterous giant dancer, his heels upon us.
> Take care, take care!'

Crags and bushy thickets all about Savitri.
Lal Gulam dead, Manas dead.
Only booming, unremitting booming, and so much booming.
Lal Gulam gone, Manas gone,
Not I who booms this – I cannot boom,
I just breathe it – cannot even breathe,
I just feel it – cannot even feel,
I just think it – cannot even think,
It's simply true, simply true, somewhere in the air ahead of me.

Summits booming, Trisul, Yamunotri, Badrinath,
I cannot even make a start for something that is simply true
Somewhere, in the air.

The battle-din of Puto and the demons drowned out the
 booming
As a smithy drowns street-cries and the creak of carts.
Leaping panthers surged down from the passes.

Down from the heights a holy pilgrim neared,
Shiva's white stripes on his forehead.
Savitri stood still on the path and bowed to him.
An antelope behind him.

'Say prayers for me, pious man.'

> 'Not this path, woman!
> Hearken to the mountains' booming, the battle-din.
> It is Puto fighting there, Puto and the demons.
> The man of powers has to fight with them.
> Do you know him?'

'I – have heard of him.'

> 'Puto is up there in the mountains.
> No one can know him, but can only hear his voice.
> And the voice of those three,
> Shumba Munda and Nishumbha.
> Puto will not yield, the demons will not yield.
> They want to go to the land of humans.
> They laid low a friend of his,
> Puto laid low his friend, the demons tricked him.'

'It was Manas, say it was Manas.'

> 'Come away from here.'

She inclined her head: 'Thank you, pious pilgrim.'

The mountains, mountains boomed. He stood, arms raised:

> 'Little person, woman, not the mountains.
> Do not press on into the mountains, saucy mouse.'

Her voice was louder:
I do not feel it, only think it –
Do not think it, it is simply true –
Simply true, somewhere in the air ahead of me.
Haul in the truth, there in the air ahead of me.

> 'You dare show your face here, woman.

> Do you not press it to the dirt?
> Saucy mouse, your face here, here?'

'My face, what has my face done to him?'

And as she went, the little thing Savitri, she wept:
My heart, they torment you – go your own way.
When a knot comes to your hands, take it up, unravel it.
Don't let yourself become unravelled.
How good, how good it will be for you
To do what I tell you.
I talk to you out loud.
Nothing, dear heart, will do you so much good
As to do just what I tell you.
I you. I you. I you.

SAVITRI followed a broad trail that led up to a hill.
And by the hill along the trail a tree stood, a mighty tree,
Which was the tree where Puto took up his station
Many months ago.
Where his griffons, the Sukuni, perched and flew about,
While Manas on the Field of the Dead snared souls.

Against this tree, this hill, Puto had braced himself,
Chain wound about his waist,
Face flushed, cold sweat on his cheeks, knees trembling:
O my Sukuni! had resounded through the air,
*I led Manas here, and they are tearing him away from us.
Manas is brought down.*
And then: *Sukuni, my Sukuni, our child wants to die.
Manas does not want to stay with us. Will not stay anywhere,
Cannot bear the world of people, cannot bear existence.*

And one day, early, Manas had appeared among the tree-roots,
A dreaming sleeping Manas, made senseless by Unmatti,

Manas numbed and drowned by sorrow,
In the sparkling morning.
A mighty brown body moved there beneath the tree,
And in it sat three things,
Steered it like a great grey elephant,
Bellowed out at him, at Puto.

And then over these roots, in these leafy shadows,
The screeching, capering of the demons.
Manas' chest clubbed open.

But from the wound, the spurting chest,
Wafted something long, pale, a mist,
A bewildered human Shade, human soul awoken from its sleep,
Beneath these branches, above these roots.
And looked at Puto, not shifting from its spot
Above that spurting wound.

And drawn backwards, lifted up,
Not understanding.
And saw the branch in Puto's fist, the shattered chest below,
And was lifted ever higher, drawn
Through the buoyant swimming air,
Drawn backwards, bewildered human Shade,
Manas' soul.

Tried to speak, opened its mouth to moan,
Drawn backwards through the topmost branches of the tree,
And flying backwards, wafting into distance.

This was the tree, brown earth, roots
That writhed like worms, black ants crawling.
Savitri stood beneath it, aside now from the broad trail,
Released from the broad trail,
Turned round, turned round,
And it began to speak.

She looked up, looked behind,

And did not know what to see or hear.
And saw the creeping ants
And felt the monstrous barky trunk,
And could not stand up straight.

And turned and turned,
Was surrounded by a close-held secret,
O what secret was it that surrounded her,
Then as she knelt down on the ground
To know it, to scoop up air –
She tried to catch an ant, make it run across her hand –
Her head was turned aside, pulled back by the neck.
Her hands could not support her, her eyes grew wide.
She was surrounded by a secret.

Her staring eyes looked to the treetop, through the leaf-gap.
And – she – felt – it – all.
This is where it – happened.
Leaves fluttered, looked down to see what she would do.
The tree stood quite still. It knew everything,
Waited for what she would do.
Air was there, wafting around the tree
This way and that, fanning, calm again.
What will happen.

And Savitri, enveloped in the secret,
Felt Manas dying, dying endlessly,
Endlessly dying Manas, somewhere through the branches.
Who, Manas? Manas and something else,
Something alien, not human is there too.

And laid her arms along the ground,
Stretched out her freezing body.
What happened to him. I must fetch him.
Her head rested on the ground,
Wild hair, bare arms, clothes in tatters.

Ants crawled in columns.

A breeze disturbed the leaves: *graugh-graugh, hurr-hah.*
It shook her,
Shook Savitri hour by hour there on the ground.
Leaves, branches, trunk, air all waited, watched.
This too happened here.

When she clambered upright in the light of evening,
And her eyes, attracted by the leaf-gap, were drawn always to
    the leaf-gap,
Questing harkening impelled by longing,
There where his soul had brushed the leaves,
Leaves she could not touch –
She started to breathe in, breathe out again.

She breathed it all and became quite weightless.
It slipped from her as if from an egg, a shell.
Manas slipped away there, Manas went there on his way.
What path for the beloved?

Through the leaves, over the tree, the high way.
Going higher, ever higher, the beloved.
Now quite flown, farther than the wastes of Thar.
But he was here, this his way, through the leaves.
Precious holy ground, surrounded by a secret!

And she wanted to go after him, went after him,
This much is certain.
Just as she had found him that one other time,
So now.

I have come this far,
Now lie beneath the tree from where he ebbed away.
No one else has come this far,
No one has looked for him.
And I am here, and I know which way he went.
And it is not over yet.

As if she had to seep into this place,

She wandered, trailed around the tree, over roots,
Breathed in, breathed out,
Felt herself in and out by hand,
Her upraised fingertips, knees, toes, searching eyes,
Harkening ears, her skull,
Gave and took,
Was one with the air, the leaves, the ground beneath her feet,
Absorbing, giving out.
It had no power now over her.
Now no longer on the ground, among the leaves.
Savitri breathed, and smiled.
The trunk unmoving, leaves, branches, air:
Savitri was happening below.
From below came a gentle light,
On the ground were suns and moons.
They suffused the tree.

When Savitri was already long since gone,
Then everything started twittering, treetop, leaves,
Grains of sand, roots, ants: *Who was that?*
Something to do with Puto, Manas and the demons,
But maybe not. She had vanquished them.
And everything began to fidget as if grown stiff,
Feet all gone to sleep.

Air, air burgeoned and swelled around,
Rose like a flock of birds,
Blew gusts, subsided, played in circles.

Ah! the tree pulled aside its branches,
Closed the leaf-gap, opened it and closed it.
And then the treetop leaned across,
Offered itself to the sinking sun,
Let light and colour tumble, soak all through it.
Sand, sand flowed, rolled towards the roots,
To the black columns of ants.

The ants did what they had long neglected:
Tended their little homes, fungus gardens,
Bedded their white eggs looser and more snugly under roots
    and stones.

AND SO Savitri entered the Field of the Dead.
Yes, she had set foot on the Field, beyond the hill,
Streamed onto the Field like a beam of evening light.
As if a town lay barricaded behind walls ramparts earthworks,
And no gap where anything could penetrate, only thuds and
    echoes,
Like that she wafted in: a thud, an echo.

From the hill she climbed a cone-shaped mountain,
Saw nothing, did not bow thanks. Darkness gathered.
In gathering darkness she had slipped onto the Field,
Like a soft morsel into a mouth that does not notice it.

The Field ascended slowly. Mountains rose higher.
They were clad in gentle green.
Their booming faded in the twilight.
The din of Puto's battle faded.

Not realising where she was, Savitri,
Her eyes still saw the tree, the leaf-gap,
The dark hill, its secret.
Manas flew away here, far away, in confusion.

Then she fell asleep on grass.
All about her as she slept, a playing calling whimpering chasing.
In half-sleep, deepest darkness she heard something, felt:
Is this a sea I swim in,
Are those ships sailing on the sea, capsizing.
Are those sails, what kind of sails.
Are waves. I the swimmer.

It was Savitri lying there, tender girl,
Gone from Udaipur across the Aravalli hills,
Up into mountains, onto the Field,
Smallsmall past the clash of battle,
Onto the Field of the Dead.

And now before her that monstrous icebound region, Shiva's
    realm:
Field of the Dead.
Horror sorrow craving, yacking demons, night upon the Field.

In the early morning she was sitting
On a little boulder, Savitri,
And a mist came swimming up and did not race away again.
She sat there troubled
And thought: what am I thinking of,
What am I doing and where am I.
Among high mountains?

When she stood, the mist, the Shade did not go ahead of her.
She turned around, went aside, gestured with her hands,
She clapped her hands: It wants something from me.
But before she even spoke,
Her eyes had closed, her hands fell slack,
And thus, a house without a door, without desire,
She stood and granted access to the Shade,
That slipped and glided all about her.
How it glides about, she breathed, is it someone?
What do you want?

It groaned.
She blinked, her eyes refused to open,
Was spellbound: It's saying something.
It flitted all about her, slippery damp, glided high, came closer.
Her eyelids fluttered.

'My hands are down.
Who are you, will you not tell me?

Are you mist, or what?'

It swam up to her mouth. Sank dully to the ground,
Spread itself wide and smooth like water,
And lay there undulating.
Savitri bent down cautiously. And as she bent down
She knew now where she was and what this was,
That lay there at her feet:
A poor dead thing, a soul,
And she – on the Field of the Dead!

And Savitri staggered, thunderstruck!
Her goal attained, and what a goal!
First she stood up, then lay down,
Had to lie down beside the Shade. It swirled high.
Her lips still closed, she turned over where she lay.
Her goal attained, and what a goal!

And the Bo-tree:
Bo-tree, should I slip into the hall,
Guards are watching over him?
And fleeing from the bier, leaf in hand,
It is not Manas. Not Manas.
And sorrow and joy and Yes, Yes to everything
And lying down, standing tall, seeing everything and being
    there.
– It passed. She sat up. The Shade still floated round about her.

'Shade,' she whispered, 'don't be frightened of me,
I am a stranger.
I shall just sit here, shan't chase you, touch you.
Will you speak to me.'

'Yes,' and the eager Shade flitted closer.

Savitri turned her head, looked about,
At the cliffs, the gorges – Field of the Dead,
Field of the Dead – Yes to everything –.

Everywhere mists in motion, veils,
White flitting hordes, uttering cries.

'You are all dead here? You are souls.'

    'Yes.'

She shuddered. Her eyes filled with tears.
And Manas was here, and so he had no body,
A Shade, a vapour, no more his strong handsome body,
Lacking eyes, and arms, and mouth.

'You have no body.
Your bodies have been burned, or lie in the earth.
What are you all doing here?'

    'Waiting.'

'For what?'

    'We don't know.'

'And what will happen to you. Will you stay here always?'

    'We shall disappear. I don't know where.'

'Can you not come back to us again?'

    'I don't know.'

She stared hard at the Shade as it flitted, dived at her, swung away:
'You are all still human, and have cast off your bodies.
Are you still human, if you have cast off your bodies,
Feel no hunger, don't eat, don't procreate?'

The Shade dived eagerly at her, and every time recoiled:

    'We're not dead, are still avid to return.
    There are many worlds,
    But we hanker most for this one,
    For a while.'

'A while?' – 'Yes.'

'And then?' – 'I don't know.'

'And then you hanker no more for us?'

'I don't know, I don't know anything!'

Savitri stood up, dreaming.
Maybe you'll simply be snuffed out.
Dreamed, smiled, walked on.
The Shade flew at her side, ahead,
She followed dreaming, head down,
And always smiling.

'Well, Shade, it's strange to look at you.
You talk and feel and you're like air, you're mist, lacking eyes, arms, feet.'

'We have no body. It's been torn from us.
We did not give it willingly. Where is it now.
But we shall find one, a different one.
In this world, in another world.'

SAVITRI followed on behind it, dreaming,
Her eye on the rockwalls now closing in.
Yes to everything, touching, questioning, contented.
Whichever way she turned, she was everywhere.
A winding path led upwards.
Then she was parted from the Shade.
The misty horde whistled overhead.

Savitri did not go like Manas,
Who offered himself for laceration, and seized Shades
Trembling, in knee-breaking soul-slumping longing,
Arms outstretched.
He pressed the Shade to him, could not close his mouth,
Even when near to choking,
As a cave fills with smoke, so would he be filled by it.

The sun had come up in the east.
I seek nothing, Savitri stood silent, I am here, expecting nothing.
And looked about her in delight.
Turned her body this way that way.

The mountains thundered at the rising of the sun,
Souls fluttering darting whimpering,
A shimmering about her, like sunshine on fallen leaves.
Ruffles on the surface of a sea, glimmer of waves,
A measureless ruffling sliding ebbing.

A glance through a narrow latticed window
Into a street bazaar,
And a thousand people are in motion, keep changing places,
And always the same ones anew,
Their clothes swirl, they show shoulders, lift their arms.
And now a colour lies upon them, and now ten colours all at once.

I seek nothing, expect nothing, Savitri shivered, looked about.
And had to slowly raise her arms
And let laughter bubble in her closed mouth,
Despite the swimming swirling all around her.
Hummed in her mouth so tightly closed.

Ah, if only I still had a voice!
And what a voice it would be: *graugh-graugh, hurr-hah!*
I'd like to roar, they're inside me,
With their voices, – shout for joy,
Let their voices out, my dear voices,
Tree, ants, path, the dusky man I lived with.

It was impossible, she must give in, her mouth must open.
And a gobbling poured from it,
While her body shook, her throat swelled,
Blood rushed to her face,
The groaning rose out of her, the grumbling
Hurr and the drawling *hah*.
And again the grumbling and snapping

As she raised herself on tiptoe and her enraptured body danced:
Hurr-hah to mountain peaks,
To rockwalls, the enormous sky, away to right and left.

And on she wandered, lithe and languid.
The cry came back to her from every side.
Every cliff, the sky, the ground
Was kissed by the cry.

SHE turned her frame this way and that,
Her enraptured body danced with excitement:
If now a gravedigger were to come and bury me,
I would say nothing.
If flames were to come and turn me to ashes,
I would say nothing.
If the peak of Nanda Devi were to topple and engulf me,
I would just stand there.
She stood, looked around, a Shade was on her arm, she rocked it.
And held one, cradled it, let it breathe on her,
And looked with longing now, with mournful joy at others,
At the two or three she did not have.
I love too much, she laughed. So insatiable, Savitri.
I love too much.

'Why hold your head so low?' she breathed to a Shade.
'Breathe together with me.'

 'Let me go.'

'You press so hard at my breast, you.
Are you an infant, do you want to suck?
Ah, I'm still so young, have not yet borne a child.'

 'No no.' And it slid back to her knee.

'You're sinking down. Do you want my body, are you a man?'

'No no.'

'You're a woman.' – 'Yes.'

'I too. My name's Savitri.
I was just complaining to the tamarind:
"Dear shadows, I am so alone," now here you are.'

Shade on her arm, Shade pale twitching darting,
Rocking on her arm, Savitri trod a long long path,
Leading almost on the level to the mountain,
Went slowly beneath the lovely close-set tamarinds,
So that they walked in half-darkness, nothing strayed towards them.

And in the half-dark Savitri noticed that the Shade had eyes,
Saw eyeglint from the darting thing, light not yet snuffed out,
A gentle calming sight.
It came with her, a tender soft-eyed thing,
Began to speak with longing, as Savitri led it on:

> 'Oh how you lead me on, Savitri.
> I never walked like this with my beloved.'

'And now you walk with me.'

> 'To walk like this, free of sorrow, lovely avenues,
> Huts and houses tucked away behind the trees,
> To see sun and shadows, and be gladdened by it.'

'What are you remembering?'

> 'Always someone goes beside you, and there's pressure.
> And others go ahead, squeeze hands tenderly, their faces
>   open.
> Ah, with you beside me now, you living, you so lovely,
> All the feeling comes straight back into me.'

'Look up.' – 'Later.'

And after a stretch in silence, the Shade began again to speak,
Its head still low:

> 'So we went deep into the jungle, my husband and I,

> There we are, our feet step from the cart, one glance tells me:
> How marvellous would the jungle be without that pressure.
> Without the pressure.
> Fan-palms, drowned forests, aerial roots and vines, peacocks, all that,
> Plumed fronds of bamboo, tender lovecalls of wild creatures,
> All that,
> And at your side the man whose children you have borne,
> Whom you lie beside at night and walk with by day.
> You see how he's torn it all all all away from you.
> The bamboo fronds stand waiting,
> It's not for you the flowers flaunt their colours,
> The whole world torn from you hour by hour, your life, your self.'

Now welled up in Savitri: *And I am lost.*
And I can no longer see the sun,
The dear sun has been torn from me.
And knew: this was death.

'Oh Shade, what was it happened to you?'

> 'They drummed into me: a woman must serve her man.
> But what can a woman do who languishes for love.
> I can't believe that women are condemned to this.
> Are they, are they.'

And Savitri straight away: 'No, sister, we are not condemned to this.'

> 'Now I'll tell you more.
> Pen a young tiger in a stall and it will nuzzle, scrabble,
> Until it finds the weak point, the rotting slat,
> And will go hungry, lie there and worry away
> Until the slat grows soft, and crumbles,
> And it can make the blessed leap.
> Oh you, here we are as if I were still alive.
> You, what is death against the blessed possibility of that leap.

> Death is nothing. If only you'd believe that.'

'I believe. You found the weak point.'

> 'Yes, the weak point.'

'And death.'

> 'I don't think of that.'

How radiant those gentle eyes.

> 'You lead me on, Savitri.
> You are good to me, let's sit here on this root.'

And the Shade itself, as if still alive,
Draped itself across a root, and Savitri sat beside it.
The Shade was radiant:

> 'Who says that I am dead. I shall sing to you.
> – There was a long room.
> There was a little garden. A low fence.
> There was a gold pendant at my temple,
> A painted bird of paradise on my other temple.
> A glance from two eyes, from two eyes in return,
> Two hands that clasp and don't let go.
> None saw who had the gold pendant now.
> And every day over the fence to me,
> And every day the room kept silent,
> Kept silent many a night.'

It fluttered up, the Shade, beat around, flew off, came back,
And fluttered again, stammered, lay back down:

> 'A knock came at the door,
> What was it to me.
> A rough voice called: open up!
> What was it to me.
> An axe shattered the door,
> What was it to me.
> An axe split open a skull, ah ah.'

Squeaking fluttering: 'Not my skull split.
He tied me to the bedposts, two ropes for arms and legs
And one more for my breast.
My sweetheart lay murdered on the bed. And I still living.
The night passed. My heart, I had no heart.
And yet I was glad, oh woman,
Can you understand:
Now I could hate him, the wicked man
Who tied me up and lunged out with an axe.
Now I was allowed to hate him.
The night was mine, the floor was mine, the air was mine,
All confederates of mine, do you see?
What has he done to you, there on the bed?
You were my lover, I can say it now out loud.
I sing it out the whole night long.
So many lights down there on Earth, night smothers them all.
So many homes and mountains on the Earth, night shrouds
   them all.
I sing it to black night.
And every mountain, every home shall know it:
My lover lies there on the bed,
Though I can't go to him, that is what he is still.
So carry it onward, night, and tell them all, all –
Dark and almighty as you are,
And by day the sun is almighty –
To every home and roof and tree and mountain and
   sleeping beast.
All the streets I hid myself away from, they shall know it:
My lover, my lover, ten times my lover.
And what if he be dead, he has only been laid low,
And is still my lover.
And if I weren't tied up, I'd jump across and sit by him,
And feel good, good, good, good forever!
I sing the whole night through.

Let all the relations hear it,
Let all the servants and acquaintances hear it,
Let the neighbours hear it:
Here I am at my sweetheart's side,
Whether he's dead or living is no one's business.
I'm with him in the room, we are lovers,
And the wicked are still wicked.
I sang the whole night through, ropes tight around me.
At noon there was music in the house.
I thought, I don't mind.
They've invited guests, they're coming to the house,
They want to drown my singing: go ahead.
And I called out even louder, would not lie still,
I had to sing for both of us.
While he lived we had to meet so furtively.
For him too I sang.
I could feel how happy he became with me.'

Lay at Savitri's side, the Shade, in Savitri's arms, head low.
And 'Thank you, thank you' Savitri breathed,
'You need say no more, now I know it all.'

'Ah, so you're afraid? Don't be afraid. You can listen to the end.
I shan't flutter. I'll lie still, see how still I lie.
— The wicked man stooped over my lover's body, in my room.
I couldn't see what he was doing to him, there on the bed.
He loosed the ropes, I wouldn't look at him,
I the righteous, he the wicked one.
His Shade better not fall across my path!
He took me from the room, unclothed and battered as I was,
He took me through the splintered door, along the passage, through halls
Where musicians stood with lutes and pipes, which suited me.

Then the wicked man put in my hand a little box,
And told me to be quiet. For I still sang
To let the whole day hear what I'd kept secret for so long,
Shamefully secret, to my shame.
He took me to the great red hall, for he was rich, and I an ornament,
In sight of all the relatives, his and mine, and all the neighbours.
I stood there quietly and was glad to listen
As he told them what had happened,
And told me to open the little box, show them all what lay in it.
I opened the box, I'd no idea what was in it,
I thought, it's all the same to me what's in the box.
How I screamed, you, when I saw what it contained.
Though he lay dead back there, I held a part of him,
I had not expected this.
Something, something that he meant to shame me with.
His organ of generation, with which he and I and the God Shiva
Had engendered so much bliss.
He meant to shame me.
Yes, it grieved me that my lover lay there murdered,
He who was so kind and tender and merry,
And this one can take a knife and mutilate him so.
It was the last straw: how I screamed down on my knees and wept
And cried out to them all and showed them what was in the box
And how he spat upon my life.
Then his fat cruel face beside me, his dreadful eyes, his foaming mouth,
His sabre at my neck.'

Savitri squealed: 'Stop, don't go on.' Curled up.

The Shade swung this way and that, Shade rocked on Savitri's
 shoulder,
Floated at Savitri's mouth: 'Don't be afraid.'
The Shade enveloped her:
These must be Shade-kisses, this gentle tapping at brow and chin.

   'And I want to tell you more, I can't go on.'

'Why not.' – 'I can't say it.'

'Why not?' – 'Are you my sister?'

'Your sister, come what may.'

   'Come what may?' – 'Yes.'

   'And it is not done yet, you. The sabre did nothing to me,
   The Field of the Dead leaves me unchanged.
   I loved him so very much.
   I loved to gaze, gaze at his beautiful form.
   I couldn't wait to gaze upon him.
   And then I had to have him: his body, his chest, his loins.
   And that will never cease.
   The sabre did nothing to me.
   You look away, there are tears. Are you still my sister?'

'Yes.'

   'I'm ashamed. I can't go on.'

'No, no shame, don't be ashamed.'

   'And you see, Savitri, it's still all so sweet, unfading.
   I always held and kissed and hugged him.
   We could never have enough.
   When my husband came, he disgusted me.
   Every embrace of his disgusted me.
   When I saw my children, I didn't know
   How they could have come from me.
   And I didn't want him, but only this other one.
   And there is no end to it, and it is always there in me.

How I embraced and loved him, how he embraced me:
It was no longer a merely human act.'

'Then what was it?'

The Shade at Savitri's breast raised its head,
The brown living orbs were there,
The seeing radiant eyes, human lights,
And pressed itself tight against Savitri, spoke in a deep decisive tone:

'It was divine!'

And Savitri's jubilant: 'You see!'
And kissed the Shade, the misty dampness of the Shade,
It slipped away, floated high among the branches,
Laughed, sang softly like a bird:

'I want him.
I will go back to him. I shall find him.'

And in the roaring of the open Field
Savitri ran towards the black rock walls: You see! You see!
The woman, the Shade was floating there.
Which one of many was it? Thousands there.
And Savitri stood and raised her hands.
Every cliff teeming –
There, black gigantic cloven walls of rock,
And gorges and green-tinged slopes, side valleys –
All teemed with misty hordes.
It was not mist, but Shades in their masses.

And this is a vast prodigious world,
That dies and does not want to die,
And yearns and wants to go Beyond.
Fingers clinging hand to hand, these fingers loosed by violence,
And they must leave.
All floating about the mountain slopes,
One single knocking, begging at a door slammed shut,

Why shut,
Severed heads, young arms.
Gathered here all about the icebound peaks,
The faded with the blooming, and those not yet budded.

'COME back,' Savitri cried, 'you Shade,
Woman, don't flee from me.'
In black anger she, eyebrows bristling, Savitri aroused:
'Go back! Stop drifting around, stop singing, laughing!'

A soughing sound behind her.
Savitri not alone here on the Field.
There were the booming mountains,
Shiva's breath upon the Shades and the swarming demons.
On she ran, Savitri.

If a flame were to come and turn me to ashes,
I would say nothing.
If the mountain were to topple and engulf me,
I would just stand there.

A drumming came from bushy thickets.
She thought: It's war, and I'm going into it.
The thickets lay at the foot of a crag.
Something white assailed her,
It had followed her all along the winding path.
Had to duck her head and duck her head, Savitri.
What was it?
Was pressed so hard she had to twist aside.
Slipped into a little cave below the crag.

It was not a drumming,
But a strange, deep, intermittent swirling.
She would rather be outside.
Where was light? She turned round, hunched over.

She wore no shoes, no clothes,
A rag hung loosely from her shoulders, wound about her hips.
Her breasts were bare, no longer proud as in Udaipur.
She went taut and lanky on her long legs,
Her buttocks were not rounded now.

In this frame lived not Savitri only,
Savitri and Manas too,
The dusky tribesman calling out,
The bare endless steppeland, tree full of secrets,
Magical sleep beneath the moon.

'Who are you?' Savitri bridled in the entrance to the cave.

The white thing did not speak,
Snorted, flapped, swerved towards her,
Assailed her without letup, never touched Savitri,
As if Savitri were a plunging glacier.
But the white thing was so unruly,
Besieging her, surrounding her,
Leaping at her like a wild beast from a tree.

Ah, she sighed exhausted, leaned against the wall,
What, what should I do?
But it came growling at her, like a dog reunited with its master,
No imperious drumming now.
And when it next came at her, all growls and snorting,
She listened, shuddered:
Hurr-hah, Lal Gulam's call, it is Lal Gulam.
Oh be off with you, she shuddered, you slink after me,
And it never ends.
He forgot to eat me up, and cannot let it go.

And darted from the cave into the scrub.
There again it came at her.
Ah, she shuddered, her lips grew paler, eyes dry and blinking.
It's you! You slink after me.
Do you still know how I climbed your path
And had no idea you were lurking there,

And had willow switches in my hand to chase away the shouting.
I wish I had some now.

And ran deeper into scrub, his *hurr-hah* at her back:
I don't want you, what is it you want with me.
His growls crescendoed to a drumming.
He was a warrior,
Why can't he be one again, or a drummer.
And all the time the swirling.

Savitri ran until she was alone again, stood on a mountainside.
And all the ravines and green-tinged slopes,
Side-valleys, all teemed with misty hordes.
The mountains boomed:

> 'Rivers surge out of us. Little clouds above us,
> Nanda Kot, Trisul, Yamunotri, Badrinath,
> We hold up Shiva's throne.
> The Bluethroated One roams on Kailash.'

Out of the chasms rose a booming clattering.
Souls were lofted high, the myriad humans.
All this she saw, the little thing, the speck upon the mountainside,
    Savitri.

Dreadful booming! Let them boom away.
Let the mountains strike me down.
I don't like any of them, don't like the Shades,
I do not like them.

Hid face in her hands, threw back her head:
Yes, yes, I – detest them!
I know I do. I can't help it. I don't want them.
And screamed, incandescent in the mountains' booming:
I do not want you, not not not.
I have no sympathy. I do not want. I cannot.
If I had whips, I'd chase you all away.
Ha, the God and the evil spirits are right to harry you.
I hate you.
Wish an evil spirit would devour you all, so that you'd be gone.

Mulish tears as she sat there hunched:
Why come all this way to see this,
Let them pester me like this. I must go on.

More Shades wafted near to her.
She plucked a shrub up by the roots, flourished it at the mist.
She picked up stones,
Still crying, gulped back salt water.
And because she could not gather stones enough,
Scooped sand up in both hollowed hands,
Flung it at the swirling mists.
The sand blew back onto her.
I don't care. Just so I don't see you.

SEPARATING, then not separate, a pair,
They darted like a single Shade, hung in the air suspended.
They swung around Savitri in an arc.
Such cries of sorrow from them,
As from a creature borne off in an eagle's talons.
They closed in on Savitri. They were a pair, inseparable.
As if encouraging Savitri they did not float away.
Swerved about her shoulders, lowered themselves towards her lap,
As if she meant to pick them up and walk away with them.
She heard their moaning, groaned: 'What do you want.
What do you want. Aah.'

They crowded in on her.

'Go away. I'm not here for you.
You must be lovers, so what, lovers snared in sorrow.'

 'They thought us lovers, even when we lived.'

'And you were not? So let go of one another. Go away.'

 'We shall not let go.
 If there's a spark of soul in you, you'll grieve with us.'

'And if I grieve (I won't) what happened to you?'

    'Grieve with us and ask no questions.
    If you have to ask why you should wail at sorrow,
    Then where is your soul.'

'You'd better not ask me who I am.'

    'Ah, wail with us. Help us to cry out.
    Ah Survasu, cry out, you.'

        'You cry out, Aisya.'

And circling about Savitri ever closer they cried out, moaned.

    'Moharma destroyed, hometown wiped from the face of the earth,
    Houses destroyed by rocks, by fire,
    Temples, streets, the home where I grew up.
    Aah, fire fire all across my town. No ground now for my feet.'

        'Aah, ashes underfoot,
        They broke open the dikes, a swamp now beneath my feet.'

Savitri curled up, blocked her ears: 'Wailing. What good is wailing.'

    'Aisya, you're a woman, you talk to her.'

    'Survasu, you're a man, you speak.'

'Let each other go. It's not the worst.
Home lost, thrown in among slaves. That is not the worst.'

    'Hold on to me, brother, don't let her deceive you.
    It's a demon.'

    'I'm a man. My name's Survasu.
    We survived, and were driven away.
    They lay under shattered roofs, those who gave birth to us and nurtured us.
    I was young, was I a man already?

There was air to breathe still, and sun and moon,
But nothing else. I just my body. I without a life.'

> 'Survasu, closer, do not leave me.
> You without a life, I too without a life.
> But you and I, were I to find you,
> Then I would have a life.'

'But where did I find you, Aisya my sister,
Breath of my hometown,
Eyes of my father, you, hand of my mother.'

> 'Cry with me, weep your fill, brother.
> I without you and no father and no mother and no home.
> Don't let it fade, what happened to us, brother.
> Children of a prince we were, rich,
> Harried through forests, and the whips and cudgels,
> The kicks, our enemies' insulting words.
> I fell down.
> And always farther from Moharma.'

'I cannot see you, sister, are you weeping?
If I could only see you, Aisya,
The shape of your body, the look in your eyes.'

> 'But I'm here, just hold on to me.
> Though I lack a body I'm still here.
> And no one tore the body from me.
> You know why I dissolved: for you.'

'Yes, and I for you.'

> 'Ah, say out loud, Survasu, why you dissolved.'

And Savitri trembling: 'Don't say it!
Stop whizzing around me!'

> 'For sure, around you and around everyone.
> Sorrow should not sink into the abyss,
> Should be sown with ample seed.
> And if you are a human or a beast, you will take it in.'

Trembling Savitri: 'Don't say it!'
And weaving about Savitri:

> 'I homeless, fatherless, motherless, brotherless,
> And I still young, unmarried, I Aisya, trodden down.
> Until my limbs caught the master's eye,
> And he summoned me – but not to beat me.'

'And I Survasu, lacking home and joy and lacking you,
Only laments and longing,
And summoned by the master from the corn mill I was treading.
What possible new torments can he heap on me.'

> 'A dark room, Survasu.'

'I know, Aisya.'

> 'A dark room. Why did they put you in this room, Survasu?'

'I shall not say it, Aisya, sister, my sister.'

> 'A dark room, a long night.'

'The whole night long I heard breathing across from me, Aisya.'

> 'You heard me, did not come to me.'

'I heard you, as I trembled in the corner.
I stayed in my corner, Aisya, trembling.'

> 'I was supposed to mate with him, was supposed to bear his children,
> Him I couldn't see in the dark room, who had limbs as fine as mine,
> And stood there in the corner, would not come closer.'

'I had become an animal, Aisya, treading the corn mill,
Circling round and round from morn till night.
Now I was to be a stud, nothing but a brute beast.'

> 'Survasu, I thought about Moharma,

>How I rode a snow-white elephant.
>The Pox Goddess had struck our town.
>I held flowers of offering in my hand.
>We made our way through the gloomy town.
>That was another night.'

And Savitri curled up on the ground:
And I too knew such a night. And survived it.
Trum rum through the streets, Manas laid low,
And I helpless in the streets.
Who will save me. Who me.

>'Why should he come closer, Survasu,
>The one there in the corner sniffling.
>He was as scared as I was, a prisoner like me.
>He wept the whole night through, I heard him.
>What home was he weeping for, hopeless like me,
>>abused like me,
>Was supposed to throw himself on me,
>And was a human being.'

'Aisya, after the longest night comes the morning.
Maybe you trembled: at some point your limbs lay still.
Morning came.'

>'I was in the corner.'

'I stood across from you, Aisya.'

>'Looked at you.'

'And we looked at one another.'

>'I saw your shoulders, throat, your head, your hair.
>Morning came, it grew light and lighter.
>Whose shoulders there, whose throat, Survasu? I asked.'

'Shall I come closer? I asked you, Aisya.

Whose head, mouth, whose eyes?'

>'When I returned your glance, Survasu, say, what
>happened?'

'I cannot say it.'

> 'You fell to the floor, brother. Took not one step, just fell right down.
> It is my brother, I had thought him dead,
> Crushed with my parents beneath a roofbeam.
> Not crushed. There he is. It's him.'

'And there my sister, she knows me, she's beside me on the floor.'

> 'My brother alive. And everything is not yet over,
> And he's here with me in this room.'

'Right by your side, Aisya.
For a whole night we had trembled in our separate corners,
Had stood and kept our distance.
In a flash I was at your side,
In the corner where you'd been trembling, breathing.
I raised you up, and couldn't lift you. You had fainted.'

> 'No thought of Moharma in my mind, brother,
> Nor of slavery.
> Just night and darkness.
> In that moment, brother, that was all I found.'

'Come, take a turn with me, Aisya.
The woman down there is trembling.
She doesn't know what sorrow is.
For our sorrow's sake, let's not keep silent, but sow the seed.'

'Not on me,' Savitri groaning.

> 'On you, and on everything that lives.
> We're of one blood. Why not on you.
> Survasu, tell what happened.
> Come down with me to the ground.'

'With you, sister.'

'Not on me,' Savitri groaning.

> 'Brother, when the night was over, and you raised me
> up –'

'When I held you, Aisya, I would not believe it,
Not yet, by no means yet.
Could not, even though I saw you. It was barred to me.
Until I succumbed,
And warmth flooded back and I was holding you,
It was really you I held, Aisya, from Moharma, from my
  father's house,
Here with me in this room.
Side by side with me in a big empty room,
On mats, in sunlight.'

> 'In what life was that, Survasu?'

'Life with you, of course, always with you.
Moments can't be measured, sister.
I was happy, and wept.'

> 'Until, brother, we – you know what happened –
> Until we looked out through the window.
> It was morning now.
> A bird was sitting on a branch outside the window.
> We looked at it, couldn't miss it, head to head,
> As it pecked insects from the bark.
> Then it started up within me. And in you.
> I thought of what had happened to us, what was
>   happening now.
> The pecking bird. My eyes filled with tears.
> A welling in me. Terrible welling in you.
> And so defiled, I Aisya from Moharma,
> And you, brother.'

'An animal, me, my sister – an animal, you!'

> 'Said nothing more, Survasu.'

'Nor you, Aisya.'
    'Gazed and wept. Gazed and wept.'
'Whimpered, sobbed.'
    'Lay, arms outstretched, floor streaked with tears.'
'Weeping, such weeping!
It grew dark in you and me. The earth sank from us.'
    'Don't leave me, Survasu.'
And they fell silent. 'Go on,' whimpered Savitri.
They fluttered, pulled away, shivered, were silent, silent.
Savitri whimpering: 'What happened then?'
Aisya breathed: 'Nothing.' Were silent, silent.
Savitri whimpering: 'You're on the Field of the Dead. You're both dead.'
Aisya breathed: 'Nothing.'
'The earth has sunk away. You died. How?' – 'Nothing.'
'Died, died, weeping in the room, what for?' – 'Nothing.'
Savitri wrung her hands, cried: 'Speak to me!'
The pair kept whirring, silent, twined about each other,
On the ground, above her head,
And it came surging into Savitri:

    'Nothing happened. Died one by one
    In grief, in a strange place.
    Breaths mingled side by side endlessly, in sorrow.'

One groaned: *Ah!* *Ah* groaned the other.
Aah groaned the first one, *Aah* the other.
Oh oh moaned the one, moaned the other.
Dropped to the ground, onto stones. Voices taken from them.
Fled cawing away, away,
Flapped lame-wing over the bouldered hillside,
Split up, torn apart, pulled together, merged, and were gone.
Oh not to lose each other.

OAH OAH! Savitri, and stretched her arms out to them,
Turned around and around and was swept away.
And in her it burgeoned – yearning,
And like a tree she was filled with sorrow and yearning:
Don't go from me. I want you, I love you.
Love nothing but you. More, a thousand times more than myself,
I, Manas, king's son from Udaipur, I want you and nothing but you.
And had to stand, stretch out her arms, turn around and around:
Don't go away from me, you two!
Gave up everything for your sakes, all other love renounced!
Stay with me, you two! Into my heart, you!
I Manas from Udaipur.

And as she struggled and braced herself,
Crushed greenery beneath her breast,
A thought floated past above her,
– What sorrowthought itself above her, burrowed,
Cut into her breast, bubbled up in her,
Torment, yet another torment, and such a torment,
One that chirruped, pining yearning,
Dragged wispily like an endless endless thread,
Like thread,
A chirruping sorrow, a highpitched hum –
Her hands icy, head lay at the crag's edge:

O what, o what,
It's taking me, lifting me up,
Carrying me over the vortex.
There are flames, flames, and rumble clomp, zebu hooves,
And Danu in the cart, flowers behind her ear,
And Dakscha. And flames.

– Begone, begone from my breast.
Begone, I am Savitri,

Begone, even if my heart goes with you.
I am Savitri, forever Savitri,
Begone from my mouth, I, Savitri.
Away with you, why won't you go.

Stood up, Savitri, shook herself, flapped frozen hands,
Gulped, sobbed: I am Savitri, you should not come at me.
Stood and trudged away, sobbed anger into empty air,
Chin quivering:
It's not true. You aren't here.
You won't let this place grind you down.
It's not true, you don't deserve this,
No one would dare to trample you like this,
You the radiant, you the sunkissed.

Like a lioness' her fierce face, her gait:
Only me here. No other humans.
All too cowardly, sitting far away and praying,
And burning their dead or burying them.
And that is all, and dead is dead.

Eyes glowing: Dead is not dead. Manas not Manas.
It is I who have been robbed.
Growled: If a mountain were to topple and engulf me,
It would do nothing to me.

White cloud-masses drifted past up from the valleys,
Closed in on the rockwall, closed in on Savitri,
Cows with dewlaps and udders, bringing damp,
Fine rain, grey whiteness and rain.

On Savitri went, her cries no longer jubilant:
Hurr-hah, hurr-hah to the mountains.
Every rockwall, the ground, the sky kissed by her cry.

Her only wish now a mountain in her way that she could
    overturn,

A sled at her heels to drag it along behind her.
She looked back to see if she was followed.
Mist everywhere, things floating in it, groaning, groaning.

Somewhere nearby the thundering of a river,
Where was it churning.
Then the mist lifted, she could see about her,
Which one should she snatch at.
If anyone is there, stay!

They float around like mist and rain, and are no more like mist
    and rain.
If only they wouldn't melt away, I'd give all of them a shaking!
Shoo shoo, away from me!
If only one were there that could not escape my grasp!
And if only I were an evil spirit, and could rip it to pieces!

NOW she had found her way down into a corrie,
Shaking with cold.
Broken walls of rock reared up, black walls,
The ground was grass-greened, sheltered from the wind.
Low ferns, dripping cacti grew side by side,
Tangles of wild raspberry vine trailed away.
An oak tree had been split by lightning.
In a swamp mosquitoes droned.
Savitri, damp, freezing, continued on.

Somewhere nearby a furtive noise,
Rustling as of reeds in ponds.
A quiet-calm human song was singing.
Tall gouts of vapour rising among the ferns,
A spout shot up amid the green, sprayed, fell back.

Two spirits at play there, in a carefree heaven,
In the hollow between palms and raspberry vines,

Climbed high, laughed, dropped back, laughed,
Whipped up a gentle spraying, sprayed and turned,
Did not drift away.

Two spirits holding pitchers. They were bailing out a well,
Hurling it to the wind, which carried it away.
They were singing.

How Savitri lowered her head, stood, gentle mouth, drooping head.
What now flowed obscurely through her,
Welled bubbling through her?
She had passed through every stage of longing,
Take hold of him, hold him in her hands.
Hands, face surging to him like waters to the moon,
Want nothing but him only, and only turn herself towards him.

They laughed, sprayed, laughed, sprayed.
The singing was a monotone, a breath no louder than a glance.
And always *ai, ayah, oh, oah*. And the giggling.

> 'The well, the well is deep.
> Oh if it were still deeper, our work would not be too hard.
> Tell me, Garut, could it be deeper?'

'Down to the bottom of the world!
I am bailing just for you,
Bailing just so I can see you, and go always at your side.
Ai, ayah. Oh, oah.'

> 'Garut, fly away with me, into the green, into the thickets.'

> '*Ai, ayah. Oh, oah.*
> Our bodies lie at the bottom, you and I, yours and mine.'

> 'Why do you bail here at the well
> And fling it to the wind? Always it fills up again.'

'If I fly off with you, I'll fade away, and you'll fade, Marut.'

Darted from fern to fern, sweet singing of their voices.
Sudden glitter, dustmotes.
Braided gouts of water, braided voices.
And as they swooped down swerving, like swallows twittering,
Their clothing brushed Savitri, Marut's clothing – she was startled,
Swelled up, stretched out long like a worm.

As she fell back she froze, gentle Marut, and Garut with her.
The pitchers rolled across the grass.
Garut held up swooning Marut.
They swayed trembled over the ground, and could not flee or fly.
They faltered past Savitri this way and that.

Her head was lowered, Savitri, her mouth gentle.
She had passed through every stage of longing,
Had sighed, whispered, waited for him,
Had suffered, frozen.
All the flowers they heap on me, for him.

They faltered, two butterflies above a flower, net poised over them.
And Garut fluttered as he sang *ai, ayah*. And came no closer,
And Garut back at Marut's side, holding her,
She silent, nothing to hold on to:

'Who are you, who who are you, *ai ai ayah*, who are you?'

And he again fluttering across the grass with swooning Marut:

'*Oh oh oah*. Must stand up, stand up again.
Who are you, are you, strange being?
Up again, Marut.'

'Who is it, is it?'

Savitri voiceless, head low, hands open,
A dream upon Savitri, slack lips, slack arms,

Arms dangling down before her knees.

> 'Did the Gods send you to destroy us, hunt us down?
> Are we not bailing fast enough?'

Marut, the little thing, to Savitri:

>> '*Ai, ayah*. Beat me. Not him. Don't seize him, seize me.
>> The passion was mine, the guilt was mine.
>> I shall give him up to no one, shall hold him tight for
>>   evermore.'

A dream upon Savitri:
And stand once more, and you adore,
And cannot lift a hand.

> 'She's a timid thing, the one I lead, *ayah*.
> Her name is Marut.
> Some plants are too tender to touch even with a finger.
> Let us flutter.'

>> 'Nothing has happened. Let's flutter.'

They clasped hands, gripped each other by the waist,
Flew around Savitri,
Lifted the rag from her shoulders, blew onto her. They could
      blow warm.
Savitri sank down in the grass. They blew and blew to warm her,
They felt her arms all over, and her throat and neck,
And dried her off.
Garut's lips touched Savitri's:

> 'You sit still, you let us fan you, you are not hard.
> My name is Garut, you dear thing. And who are you?'

'Once I was called Savitri.
I don't know what I'm called now.
Or how I shall soon be called.'

And Garut's lips rested on Savitri's,
And their eyes rested on each other,

And she absorbed his voice:

> 'You're a human. I was a blessed spirit,
> Yonder where Mount Kailash looms.
> All around Shiva's crystal throne we flew,
> Thousands flying around his throne, waiting on his glance.
> I was once a blessed spirit at Shiva's throne,
> And then became still more blessed.
> He sent me – I shall not say where –
> I'd be swallowed up by joy were I to name it.'

'Go on.'

> 'I went into this country.
> Bright green ita-grass, the ground soft,
> Tall the gamboya trees, their leaves so shiny.
> They were a wanton people.
> I went as a human, I was to be pious, save the people.
> But among them –'

'Go on. Don't lift your lips from my mouth.
Some things can be spoken, some can only be felt,
And some can be seen only eye to eye.'

> 'What was in the people? I needn't say it.
> You have eyes, you can see.
> On your lips, next to mine.'

And a scent of hyacinths came to Savitri,
And Marut reached out for her mouth.
Savitri offered her lips to her:
'But don't touch, Marut, you so mild, so happy,
Just feel once more what happiness is.
Here. Scent of hyacinths!
Here I sit in rags. What jewels I once had!
I don't know what you once wore, I had it all, all.
Many women were my friends.
I had a consort.'

'Where is he?'

'My name's Savitri. I left home long ago.
Ah, scent of hyacinths.'

'Your limbs are flailing.'

'So long since I ran away from home, wandering, searching.'

'For whom?'

'Don't speak. Don't ask. You see I'm trembling.
Tell me who you are. Be good to me.'

And Marut's lips lay on Savitri's, which were cold,
So close, and ever closer, as if they wanted to grow into hers.
Their eyes rested on each other, black light in black light.

'I walked there, you Savitri, beneath the shiny leaves.
Someone was praying in a temple, a sago palm stood outside.
He was so pious.
Are you listening, and do you want to listen?
This is no new song.
Songs always start in different ways,
A little bit different, and always end the same.
My name is Marut,
And he no longer wanted the name he had before.
Wanted the same name as me.
His name was a proud one, I can't recall it.
He called himself "Marut" like me, Marut, and Garut too,
And when we held each other and he stroked me,
He breathed "Marut" and I breathed "Marut" back at him,
Another I, and he is I, and I am he.'

'I know. I know. Go on.'

'It's hard to explain.
Hold me close to your lips, or I must flutter and be at his side.

> But how you breathe yourself so full, Savitri.
> How it comes out from your mouth.
> With you I can breathe in time, and full!
> Oh don't make me talk just yet.
> Let us breathe together.'

And eye to eye they breathed together, Savitri and ethereal Marut.
A slow breath in, and Marut was lifted up
And let herself back down.
Savitri filled herself, and breathed it out.

'Oh Marut, it does me good to breathe with you, in and out
    like this.
Now don't leave.
There are mountains, they can't crush me,
But there were times when they almost buried me in sand.
Breathe with me once more, give me some of your breath.'

And Marut was lifted by another inhalation
And let herself back down,
And Savitri swelled, and gave herself out again.
Marut's eyes began to smile:

> 'Once there were two who called themselves "Marut",
> Now I know another one.'

Savitri, she did not smile:
'What, oh what happened to you?'

Now Marut parted from her lips,
Flew off to Garut, this gentle Marut,
Scent of hyacinths about her: *ai ayah, oh, oah*.
Took up pitchers from the grass, swung them through the air,
They scooped water from the well.
And soughing reeds, quiet-calm human singing,
Two spirits at play, in a carefree heaven.

> 'Can you hear me? I was a blessed spirit.
> I was summoned back to Kailash, Shiva's seat.

> I was meant to leave her, and once again
> Be a blessed spirit among the Blessed.'

Water sprayed among the ferns. They flung it to the wind.

> > 'There was a well outside my house,
> > I often sat with Garut there, you know this.
> > And when he was supposed to go to Shiva's throne,
> > We sat there on the well's rim, looked down into it
> >   as usual.
> > Two figures rose to meet us,
> > Ever clearer the closer we came, and if we drew back,
> >   they faded.
> > *Ai, ayah*, didn't we want to go right in and meet them?
> > It is you, it is I,
> > The water-mirror keeps us apart.
> > Or do you want to go to Kailash?'

'Don't ask, don't ask, Marut,
If I want to go to Shiva on crystal Kailash.
I am where you are.
And whoever goes to Kailash will no longer be me.
Here's a well, Marut, I am so drawn to it.
Crouch down with me and gaze into it.
Let's sink our bodies in the water.
I no longer want to be a blessed spirit!
I shall stay with you.'

> > 'Into the water, *ayah*, into the water, Garut, with you!
> > And I on your neck: down into it!'

Giggling and tall gouts of vapour amid the ferns.
In the hollow between ferns and raspberry vines
They climbed high, laughed, dropped back, laughed,
And sprayed.

> 'Shiva called out: "Your body lies in the well
> Together with a human female.

You shall be dead, just like a human, it's what you wanted.
I shall carry your bodies to the Field of the Dead,
I shall throw them into my well.
There you shall play with her, you and her together,
For all the time it takes to empty the well and your bodies
   lie exposed.
Then you shall go wandering."
That's what Shiva called out, "On Earth or back to Kailash,
As you will."
Oh, Shiva's punishment was mild.'

Two spirits at play, in a carefree heaven,
Climbed high, laughed, dropped back, laughed,
Whipped up a spraying,
Turning swooping in the green ferns, between ferns and
   raspberry vines.
Tall gouts of vapour in the air.
They swung pitchers in their hands to bail,
And giggling splashing.

> 'The well, the well is deep.
> Ah, if only it were deeper.
> I want to play with you forever.
> Tell me, my love, could it be deeper?'

'Oh Marut, it could be so much deeper!
Down to the bottom of the world!
I bail just to keep you in my sight.
My time on Kailash now is through,
I shall not visit Earth anew,
I only want to go with you.'

And glowering, Savitri, ever blacker, Savitri's face blacker by the
   moment,
As black as smoke that writhes around a flame.

'Some whimper, others giggle
Until they moulder and are blown away.

Oh why must I come to the Field of the Dead.
There is a spirit, blessed,
One of the mighty, so he says, up on Shiva's mountain.
Sunk to the bottom of the well he plays and giggles. –
You, Garut, come here, stop flying about. Come.'

    '*Ai, ayah*, I'm here with you.'

'This playing, why the playing?
Chattering, laughing, why this and this, nothing more?
Field of the Dead, why the Field, I don't like it!
And then the other thing, I mean Evil, Life,
Food taken from my very lips.
And stop giggling! And let Marut go!
Throw away your pitcher!'

    'We shan't splash you, we'll dry you off.'

'Throw it away.
You say you're of the Blessed, a power on Shiva's mountain.
It is only right you lie in the well.'

    'We play and have delights.'

'And could have a thousand delights, if you'd just stop your
    giggling.
Ghastly giggling.
Giggling and splashing: shame on you!
You could have real hands, could go down to the well,
Fetch your body that lies down there, and hers.
And you would not have to stay here,
You two would have to wander like me –
Look at me now – away from here, away from the Field of the
    Dead!'

    'Shiva called out.'

'And Shiva called out! Let him call.
You really should have stayed.
You should not have dashed yourselves to pieces.

And stop your giggling, do stop your giggling.'

    '*Oh, oh, oah.*'

The spirits let go the bailing-jugs,
Garut dropped wordless to the ground,
Pale Marut floated over Savitri's face:

    'Aren't you Marut too, like me?'

'I am not Marut. You heard me, my name's Savitri.
Or was Savitri. Soon it won't be any more.
I do not want to be Savitri.
Yes, shrink back, flutter, buzz, because I cry out.
Two souls were weeping: Aisya, Survasu,
Twining over the ground, such twining, braided together,
They whimpered, and I was meant to whimper with them,
And scatter seeds of sorrow over everyone.
I, I have no sorrow! One stone's as bad as any other!'

And Garut Marut fleeing into ferns:

    'Careful, my Garut, it's a demon,
    It breathed with me. I'm already poisoned!'

Savitri hunched, arms on knees, hard,
– Is not Manas who cries out,
Savitri is no girlfriend, nursemaid,
Savitri going to Manas, Savitri to Manas -
'Garut, what are you called? What is your name?'

    'Don't say it, don't tell her, my Garut.'

'Garut, your name.'

    'Who are you to ask me what I'm called.
    Why do you slink into our valley and ask me all these
       questions?'

'You should take a look around you.
For I cannot look at you when you sing and flutter and coo
And are so pathetic, you sweet, feeble, frisky thing.'

'Who are you?'

'Yes, be all defensive, *who are you*.
If I were a midge from that oak, or a frog from the ground,
It would be all the same to you.
They could ask you, and what would you say,
You great blessed spirit from Shiva's Kailash Mountain,
Would you sing ditties, *ai, ayah*, and dance and splash water?'

'I never want to see you again.
I breathed with you.
I'm here of my own free will, I sing and am happy.'

Hunched Savitri, she raised her fists:
'Shade in which you have concealed yourself,
How can you speak of *free will*?
The word tumbles from your mouth, you can't bite it.
You writhe like a snake, but I shan't let you go,
I shall catch you by the head, because you are bad and wretched,
Like all those that float around here twittering.
You shall say your name, you shall utter it, it shall resound in
 your ears,
And guard yourself against it if you can!'

Garut pleading: 'Will you fall away if I say my name, my
 Marut?'

'Don't tell her. Look at her: a demon, it has poisoned me.'

'Your name, Garut!'

'What are you asking?
And what if she falls, she that I pulled away from everything?'

'Your name, come along. And don't go near my mouth!'
– Not Manas who cries out, not Manas,
Savitri, she is going to Manas, Savitri to Manas. –

'I – ah – I am called – Parikshi.'

And Marut fallen from him! And he groaning!

And Marut wafting back across the grass,
Impelled by a breeze:

    'She knows your name!'

'And now, Parikshi, ask me anything you want.
Anything you want to know, you must ask me.'

    'I don't want to ask, I shall flee from you.'

'You will not flee from me.
You will ask me, you must ask, you shall ask,
You have it in you, now you have it in you.'

    'Not in me.'

'In you!'

    'Who are you, why so forceful?'

'Speak!'

    'How – did you come to the Field of the Dead?'

'That's one of your questions. Ask another.'

    'I hate you.'

'I know. You hate me as you hate yourself.
You're afraid of me as well as you, *Parikshi*.'

    'Damn you, woman!'

Not Manas who cries out,
Savitri, going to Manas, Savitri to Manas.
'Am I dead, ask that.'

    'Shiva will kill you.'

'He's not my enemy. He was yours.
You condemned yourself. You spattered him
When you threw yourself down the well.'

And Parikshi groaning, he looked about him, searching.
There she was, floating in the wind, the wind.

    'Come, Marut, my sweet, my sweet life.

    Now she's insulting us. Come to me.'
And sighing, pleading by the oak tree:
    'Garut, help me, Garut.'
He swayed, glided, hung suspended among ferns.
Savitri hunched, not moving, arms on her knees,
Savitri mocking: 'Off you go.'
    'Oh Marut! I want to go to Marut, demon.'
'So fetch her. You must fetch her.
You must fetch her in a different way, Parikshi.
What word will you utter, Parikshi?'
He swayed, Parikshi,
Swelled up among the ferns, trembled: 'I don't know.'
'Do you want a beating, will you just hang there,
Or will you – speak to Shiva?'
    'I – don't know. Don't know. O shut up you!
    Marut, help me!'
'The word, Parikshi. You know the one.'
And he dragged it from himself, the blessed spirit,
Trembling, with no trace of giggling in his voice:
    'POWER!'
And Savitri jubilant at his side: 'That's what you will say!
Power! That's the word. Power!'
And raised her arms amid the green: 'Power. Say it with me.'
And the spirit groaning, sobbing, roaring: 'Power!'
Together: 'Power!' The black bowl of the corrie rang.
'Take up weapons, Parikshi! For yourself!'
    'Weapons.'
'Pick up stones. For yourself!'
    'How can I pick up stones.'

'Tear a limb from the oak tree. For yourself.'

    'I have no arms. I am dead, killed.'

'You have arms.' – 'I can't see them.'

'You have arms.'

    'What are you saying. What are you shouting.'

'You have arms, Parikshi.'

    'No.' – '*Yes!*' – 'No.'

'You will stop hiding yourself away.'

    'What!'

'An end now to your hiding, Parikshi, you know this.'

    'No.'

'Take up weapons!' – 'Oh.'

'Pick up stones.'

    'I, I have arms.
    Ha! I shall move my arms, I shall move them.'

He darted, flung himself about. A flame was over him.
Dark in the bowl of the corrie,
Night thrust in, lighting flashed around him.
Groaning in delight, Savitri, flashes dazzling from her eyes:

'Support him, Marut, come to me!'

    'I'm afraid.'

'He's of the Blessed, he won't abandon you.
He dares to do it. He's going to Shiva.'

    'Shiva the Terrible, Shiva will tear him to pieces.'

'Tear to pieces. And why not tear to pieces!
Hold him, Marut, if you love him, hold him so he won't break
    down.'

Parikshi enveloped now in flickering,

And muttering and booming all about him,
And a rhythmic drumming.
This was the blessed spirit's heartbeat.
Mighty the flames upon him, high as the corrie wall.

'It's burning us up, Marut! Speak to him.'

> Marut sobbing: 'Let him burn me.'

And the tender creature comforting, beckoning through the flames:

> '*Ai ayah, oh oah*, oh Garut.
> There was a well outside my house.
> You sat beside it with me.
> Two figures, they came to meet us, *ai, ayah*.'

And Parikshi raging, towering over the corrie:

> 'To me, my voice! To me, my life!'

He shot up from the corrie, sombre shining, dark-red glow,
Moon over the black Field.

At the well among the ferns, Marut dragged herself across the ground:

> 'Save me, Savitri. I'm all alone. Savitri!'

> 'To me, my life! To me, my life!'

See how he shines. I want to follow him.
Ah, I, I, I shall not be Savitri for much longer.

[2] MANAS DRIFTING

MANAS floated this way and that.
At first had lamented the Shades, even lay down in the road, a beggar.
Carried by breezes, nothing to cling on to
From Trisul to Yamunotri.
Forests appeared. He drifted between treetrunks,
Thought he could descend to the tangled floor.
But the draughts blew crosswise, and he could not reach the ground.
The ground was not for him.

Gentle endless drifting in the depths of valleys,
Along flanks of mountains white with settled snow.
Up above, day followed uneventful day,
Every evening the sun sank, fiery blaze behind the mountains.

All at once the fire was gone,
The sky black velvet, monstrous glittering of giant stars.
These kept silent half the night.
But towards the middle of the night,
As if their lungs must first be pumped full of air,
They began to speak. A massive murmuring.
They spoke among themselves.
Though they were motionless and only slowly wheeled away,
Like folk who lie abed,
And are trundled slowly together with their beds,
They conversed with one another,
Now softly, now in angry agitation,
Only to fall silent, minutes at a time, and then start up again.

Meanwhile the mountains seemed to cower,
All the colossal peaks of Himalaya: Api, Nanda Kot,
Nanda Devi, Trisul, Yamunotri,
That spread themselves so mightily below with snow and glaciers,

And boomed all day.

But beneath the murmuring and celestial back-and-forth
They kept silent.
It was soundless in the high mountains
While the stars spoke, streaked and wheeled away.

In grey dawn the mountains once more eyed each other.
They stood alert in the sudden flashing light,
Squeezed mist back from their feet,
Pulled salvos of cloud towards them,
Boomed what they had to boom.

Down near the ground, Shades fluttered,
Brushed against Manas.
He had been carried off to Martoli Karak,
Where mocking spirits had sported with his body,
At the foot of Pindari glacier.

He saw the black fractured corrie, and remembered:
Something had dragged him by the armpit hairs,
It was here that something took him, an enormous female Shade,
It was wonderful,
He had clung to the female thing in the thrumming wind,
His seed had scattered.

Now nothing tried to cling to him.
Who is this passing by with a soft high-pitched moan?
Oh of all the multitude of moaning voices,
Does he not know this one? So who is it?
Was it not she who sat jolting
Beside the man, she pert slender thing?
And she could not leave him,
She burned, burned, Danu and Daksha together.
Moaning she passed him by, like hunted game
That is allowed no rest and is harried on, and harried on.
But she did not notice him.
None in the valley noticed him.

He was dead.
He loomed among a thousand Shades,
Could find no footing on the ground,
A king's son, mighty – now could only moan like them,
Wait for the wind to drop so he could sink at last down to the
 ground.

Oh, this flying on the wind,
Restless incessant seething and tumbling,
Tossed upward, buffeted down.
Not knowing now, and then what.

I float beside them.
Perhaps some of them I bested,
Now I'm like them all. All.

Whipped across the crevasses of Pindari glacier.
A breath blew from the crevasses.
We are worse than gnawed bones, not even a jackal to snuffle at us.
That is me.

He was blown upward,
Told himself to hunker down.
The tempest, gouts of rain, harrying demons.
And behind it all, the finality of dying.

How Manas' thoughts were torn away.
Shades came with the gusting waters
And the pattering hissing of the blizzard.
Just now they had whimpered, and already they were silent,
Losing themselves – to where?
Carried off one by one, to other worlds,
The finality of dying.

Lightning flashed.
Now they vanished, those driven towards dissolution,
Who still clung on and would not offer themselves up quietly.
They raged, curled tight.

Demons appeared, tore into them,
The ghoulish tiger-screams of demons rang out over avalanches.
Awful expiring caterwaul of those finally, finally dying,
In their caterwaul a human voice still audible,
And now nothing but wafting air.
Behind it the demons' braying, braying, and their huffing clacking fury,
And wafting air.

Where the Panchagori fell away from Milam glacier,
A thumping sounded through the sharp shrilling of the blizzard,
Rhythmic thumps.
Something lying on a crag.
A rocky pulpit thrust out over the glacier,
Something lying on a crag, a human Shade.
Demons assailing it, as though it were a log of wood.

And as they hurled stones through its Shade-body,
The thumping came, *thump, thump.*
And it, it did not move. Did not dissipate.
Did not shatter. It lay as if extinguished, but not yet cleared away.
Maybe it was itself a demon
That had changed its shape, meant to tease them.
What they did had no effect. They could not rouse it.

They hurled stones to kill, cut it to bits.
It appalled them and they threw stones, threw blindly,
It would not waft away or melt away.

They hurled stones in a fury, braying, sobbing,
Still it did not wake.
It was a dead thing, but stubborn, hopeless,
And would not go quietly,
Terrible in defiance, in its stark terror curled up in itself.
Only Shiva could unlock it.
They stood and stood and their stones thumped,
And they could not, would not believe their eyes.

Manas drifted past, below the rocky pulpit:
I, betrayed.
They sit there in their houses,
Beyond the steppeland, behind the Aravalli hills.
My father lives, knows that I am dead.
He lives and I am dead. That's my father.
Puto, where is Puto, the man of powers.
And how, how I fought for all their sakes.
They still living: and thanks to whom.

He let himself be blown along the Panchagori:
I was Manas. I defeated every army
That marched against us.
No fortress could withstand me.
Then, then, then:
How long, how long must I stand at this window?
And would not turn around
And would not listen to their singing,
And had to come to this place, to Sorrow.

And groaned, and sifted through his thoughts,
And at first did not heed, and then did heed,
As he looked about, the other Shades.

But I am not like these. I am Manas.
Not one among them dared to do what I have done.

And wild fear in the face of transformation,
And suddenly they were hurled down from the rocky wall,
Were tumbled valleywards, on their own, abandoned.
There were powers they had no chance against.
The Milam glacier creaked.
Demons, harriers of souls, went hunting in among them.
An avalanche thundered down from Mangraon onto the Shade-hordes,
They were crushed, buried, smashed to smithereens.
Were fluid, airy, picked themselves back up.

Manas called out to himself in the billowing snow:
Defy them, Manas, stand up, show yourself.
Let them smash you! Do it.
They had tumbled into a riverbed. It was dry,
The river had been diverted by big boulders,
Flowed now around the mountains under settled snow.

And as the Shades drifted in the riverbed,
Prurana, local mountain demon, thought to snack on them.
Manas saw the mountain demon's face, slate-coloured,
As it came down towards them up above the boulders,
Saw how it shoved the boulders, Prurana,
Grunting shoved aside the boulders.

And a raging spate of water.
And the Shades, remnants of once human beings,
Threshing, swallowed up,
Disgorged with gouts of snow onto the valley floor.

Manas, swept aside behind a boulder that held firm,
Pulled himself groaning from the water,
Looked for traces of the others, saw none.

Prurana, mountain demon, watched him furtively,
Looked right at him.
At first Manas tried to sneak away.
Then he saw the dreadful odious creature creep along,
All nonchalant,
Like a hunter making sure the prey won't scent him.

Already the mountain demon was reaching out its arm.
Manas felt such huge revulsion.
The slatey monster's skin crawled with scorpions and spiders.
In Manas a fatal swooning moment:
It'll catch me, and devour me.
He was seized by the demon's paw, the ancient stony face came
    near,
And Manas, Manas held firm, his head kept steady:

He unleashed the river on the Shades!
Pushed boulders aside, the Shades had no chance.
Let him show his face!

And Manas, though a Shade, began to smoulder,
To smoulder in a frenzy:
Let him crush and swallow me, just let him.
His Shade-body opened like a flower, ruddy radiance suffused it.
Prurana drew back his paw,
Saw snow melting from the arms and shoulders.
Around the feet of the tiny Shade the snow was melting.
The dreadful monster retreated behind boulders, clear of the
    flooded bank.
Thought a bit, looked round at the Shades, the valley,
And climbed into the water.

And Manas stood stock-still beside the boulder
Where he had held firm.
He was smouldering still.
And as he stood there, tears ran from him.
For hours he stood and wept for grief,
For what he must endure, and that they dared do it.

He turned again, looked for traces of the others in the valley.
When he saw them his tears dried up.
He watched them from behind: a herd of cattle, driven.
They were driven back and forth, absurdly,
Tipped up, tripped,
Tried to climb upright again like humans,
Could only manage it when the breeze abated.

Then down across the glacier,
Down from Milam, guided by Prurana,
Came the Mother of Pestilence, astride a panther.
Durga, Kali is her name.
Black and marl-daubed her giant body,
She had four busy hands of bone,

Carried drums, and slings to strangle with.

Behind her, riding donkeys, the Mothers of Terror,
Yellow-fanged fire-red naked women,
A pack before which every living thing falls sick.
They urged their skittish mounts down the glacier with switches.
Manas stepped from behind the stony rubble as they neared:

'Take me with you, great Mother of Pestilence.
Make me a demon. What are your demons.'

The awful Mother saw him. 'A dead, a human dead.'
A black spirit draped itself across her shoulder from behind,
Sputtered at him. She shoved it back:

> 'You are Manas, who came up to the Field?
> I saw you at the waterfall, and at Martoli Karak.
> Ganesha and I had to laugh to see you lying there.
> We laughed when the demons set you lurching.'

'You laughed.'

> 'They are no friends of ours.
> And sometime we'll seize hold of them again,
> And do with them what must be done.
> But they handled you so marvellously.
> All of us who saw you laughed.
> How they lurched inside your body, how they leapt.
> And when Puto saw you at his tree, on the hill,
> And they gave themselves away, -
> Ganesha, what was it there?'

He, grey on his rat's legs, beat the snow with his trunk:

> 'You asked me something?'

'Yes, and?'

'Who is this standing here?'

> 'It is Manas, his soul.'

Ganesha swung his trunk, trumpeted:

'His soul!
Just look at his soul! It's past its best. Haha!'

'Ganesha, he'd like to know why we laughed,
You and I and all of us, when he came onto the Field.
"Sorrow, sorrow, I want sorrow."
And the demons took him when enough was enough.
And he lay there and Puto came.'

'Yes, Puto.'

Ganesha crept around Manas, swept clouds of snow about him
 with his trunk:

> 'That was their master stroke.
> I fell in love with those three.
> I thought to myself,
> They are so lovely, those three, they leap so jauntily,
> They really should be gods again.'

'Why did you laugh at me.'

'At you?' The gods exchanged a glance:
'What's your problem? Are you complaining?'

Ganesha leaped towards him on his rat's legs.
And Manas fled.
Ganesha all around him: 'Moaning, you're complaining!'
Bellowed out his trumpet-laugh, laughed, laughed,
Ran rings around Manas, hemmed him in.
Other spirits, attracted by the guffaws, came along,
Encircled them, asked questions, queried ghastly Durga.
Ganesha rolled in merriment on his back.

> Durga cried: 'We must get on! Ganesha!
> Come, Ganesha! Humans are waiting.'

He was wheezing himself breathless laughing.

Down the glacier went the Goddess of Pestilence.
She drummed her fingers on the drum.

Ganesha floundered upright:

> 'He comes into the Realm of the Dead
> And asks himself how dead someone is
> When he is dead.'

And leaped along in Durga's wake.
The fire-red Mothers surrounded Manas:

> 'Puto brought him up here,
> Puto stayed back, far back at the tree.'

And laughing with sweet sentiments, they flounced along in
    Durga's train:

> 'Those three played a cunning trick.
> Puto himself was forced to crack his ribs.'

And as they laughed, the demonic swarm slapped their thighs.

Ice cold fell on Manas, lifted by the wind.
And I can no longer see the sun,
The lovely sun has been torn from me.
I Manas, the prince's son, I cry out: *uih, uuih.*
I shall no longer see the sun,
The sun so tenderly beloved,
The sun that I have loved so tenderly.
The burning done, and prayers said over me,
They all went back home.

He whirled up, tried to follow Durga,
Hold onto her cart, sell himself dearly.
Was glued to the spot, snow all around him,
And he smouldered:
I nothing to them. Shame, oh shame. What am I to them.

And whimpering he turned around in circles,
And those he had not seen since Durga came riding by,
The Shades, came now in one vast wave,
As if driven by a windmill, through the air up from below.

Came from the surface of the glacier,
Dropped onto him from the sky among the snowflakes,
Singly at first, then in heaps as if shaken from a sieve,
In heaps, dense thronging hordes.

Manas hated them. Disgust fermented in him,
But he had to bob along with the tripping stumbling Shades.
He wafted with them over the peak of Mangraon,
No use twisting turning, no use crying: shame, shame.

Chirruping, chirruping all around him:

> 'Goes for one, goes for all.
> Flying, rippling.
> Air is vast, has space enough.
> We are forlorn.
> Dissolve us, soon we shall be water.'

Chirruping beside him:

> 'We'll be gone soon.
> Snow turns to water: we are gone in spray.
> Turned to ice. Why not.
> Gone. Gone.'

Kept chirruping, none listening to any other,
Each chirruping for itself alone.

> 'To be snow, be wind,
> Dripping through the air,
> Seeping into earth.
> Who invented death?
> Dissolve, disappear,
> Not know yesterday, tomorrow,
> Not know myself, not know, not know.'

A mighty voice booming through the blizzard,
A bell resounding, fading –
Manas thought: What is this bell that rings out so, and fades? –
It came from himself: Shiva-o, Shiva-o, Shiva-o,

Long-drawn calling, pealing:

Shiva-o,
You Raging Sorrow, Terminator,
Shiva your works, what are your works.
How great your works.
You are almighty, Shiva. You shake worlds near and far.
End, end your work.
I flake in snow, I, I call out no more.
My hands are open, my arms hang slack.
I tremble, I am here, Shiva-o,
For you, your work, your finger, your glance,
Shiva, Shiva, I call to your hands, your holy work, Shiva-o.

This resounded out of Manas,
As he tripped and stumbled with the myriads.
And in parallel there swelled in him:
I do not want to end. They've torn me away.

And bent double
In rueful recollection of his cry that time on the Field
As he clambered over rocks:

Only to be with you, Shiva.
I fall or lie or drop away,
Sand or water or flowers beneath my feet.
I come to you as kindling,
I a tree still greening, flesh, with blood in my veins,
I will be straw and kindling for you.
Want to be taken, to be nothing.
Oh nevermore in the streets of humankind,
God of the Crossing, Dasher-to-pieces,
Away with me, away to your heart.

And sped headlong with the myriads
That chirruped, or were already silent.

He wafted with them over gorges

To the peak of ice-extruding Mangraon.
And no shuffling, no twisting turning was of any use.
Only the cry: Shame on me, shame.

They were driven against a long rocky ridge, as if against a dam,
Piled up, snagged, tried to find a way around.
Manas, Manas. Shame on you!
But it was just a logjam.
Their thoughts vanished.
In a heave, like a horse leaping, they were carried over the ridge.

Flying again, dreaming, pensive,
Manas embraced a Shade that was jostled close against him,
Held fast to a Shade: 'O how goes it with you. Let's keep
    together.'
He couldn't see its eyes,
Did it have eyes, was it not snuffed out already,
Letting him embrace and hold it, as if nothing.
No groaning from it, just a huff of breath.

    'How goes it with you: just what I was thinking.
    How goes it with you, goes with you.
    Who I? Who you?'

And huffed, a wordless voiceless breathing.
And in disgust Manas let it go,
It was coming to an end, resigned to seep away.

Tears on Manas. And gasping and twisting turning.
Nanda Devi reared up through the storm.
And out of Manas' tears and weeping came a trembling,
And from the trembling a swooning,
And this aroused more trembling, and yet more weeping, tears,
And blindness, darkening imprisoning blindness.
To see no mountains, light, no day or night.
The wind, as it will, snow, as it will,
Imprisoning blindness.

Blind beggary deep within him,
And calling, calling, how long now, calling from a closed
    mouth,
Move on, calling without moving.

[3] TO KAILASH

RESPLENDENT, Mount Kailash.
Every hall of the crystalline palaces resplendent,
And every hall deserted.

The three-eyed God, the Dancer, Archer, the World-shaker,
Had descended from Mount Kailash.
The Blue-throated One
Sailed on black clouds alone through rain and hail
Across the Field of the Dead to the south,
Came down by Cho Mafam,
To the Green Lake peeping out among the peaks.

At Cho Mafam he stayed put on a stony waste –
No customary trip across the lake, a white swan,
For conversation with the Lake God.

At Cho Mafam he stayed put on a stony waste.
The heavenly minstrels and the lovely sirens who lead
    penitents astray
Hung far back on the slopes of Kailash,
A ragged fringe of the black clouds that had carried Shiva here.

Four fires Shiva built around him on the stony margins of Cho
    Mafam,
Two to the sides, one before and one behind him.
He sat, legs folded, on a tigerskin, his gaze directed downwards
His thoughts he channelled to the chambers of his heart.

And so he let the fierce flames on all four sides start roasting,
  charring
His breast, face, back, limbs,
For many days, he never stirring.
Then the terrible God stood up,
With a lump of rock he heaped the fires together.
He hung there in the huge undying flames,
He himself.
For many days allowed himself to burn,
Allowed himself to burn,
Not stirring.

And while he mortified himself and smouldered, all alone,
There came a ragged stream slowly down the slopes of Kailash:
His timorous entourage.
The minstrels and their lovers and the lovely youths,
Eleven Rudras, those curly-heads who howl in storms.
On clouds, owls, oxen they came riding, floated from peak to peak
Towards the thick smoke, the billowing glare of flames
That rose up from Cho Mafam.

A long while they ranged themselves around the mountain and
  the lake.
Listened a long while to the roar and crackle of the fire,
From hour to hour more horrified.
Saw: the terrible three-eyed God suspended in the flames.
Could dimly see the outline of his strong beloved body
When the wind, which he himself had summoned, blew fiercer
  on the fire,
And he was lifted up together with the flames.

And he kept silent in the smoke,
And took no notice of them. They withdrew.
On the slopes of Kailash they sat in snow.
Then they scattered: 'What is it?'
'Why does Shiva mortify himself, keep silent?'

'Are the worlds about to perish?'

They made a circuit around Kailash – nothing revealed itself.
He silent, splendid.
The Field lay there below,
The usual flow of Shades, demons busy at their work.
The booming from the mountains reached them
Just like every other day.

They sneaked invisibly, those who were like the wind,
Into the verdant land of humans.
Upturned many a leaf to check that trees were growing normally,
Felt over various grasses,
Watched peasants ploughing in the fields, same fields as always,
    same crops,
Same tread of peasants behind oxen.
Eagles swooped on doves as usual.
Eavesdropped on priests conducting holy ceremonies,
Bathing, sacrificing, praying.
Nothing anywhere revealed itself. Nothing.
But something monstrous and mysterious was brewing:
They could feel it.

Softly they slipped back up from of the land of people.
They thronged the mountainside
Where Shiva, World-shaker, did silent penance in the flames,
Suspended in the huge fire, not stirring.

MOUNT Kailash resplendent.
Resplendent the halls of crystal Kailash,
And every hall deserted.

Drawing near to crystal Kailash,
Rising from the black bowl of the corrie,
Parikshi,

Blessed spirit sent packing by Savitri.
No music around Kailash, no rosy clouds bringing scented
   breezes.
The airy swings had ceased their swinging.
And when Parikshi came to Shiva's palace, the gates were open
   wide.
Lutes timbals lay along the path.
Flowers veils salve-pots powders,
As if all had fled.

And when he stepped into the broad vestibule,
It smelled of sandalwood,
But was empty, empty in its gilded splendour.

Parikshi stood stock still, cringed,
Felt the fearpump of his blood in lips and fingers.
From the next hall he could hear a wheezing.
At first he was afraid, then pulled himself together,
Then felt afraid again.
Peeped through a gap in the silver door,
Saw, lying on the marble paving, Nandi,
Guardian of Shiva's gate, monstrous ox,
Head tucked to its chest, sleeping.

Slowly Parikshi, blessed spirit, still glowing red,
Pushed open the silver door.
The sound aroused the beast. It raised its head, glared at him,
Lowed once, let its head fall back.

'Ah,' sighed Parikshi, 'Nandi, let me see Shiva.'
The ox closed its eyes.
'Oh Nandi, do you know me? Let me see Shiva.'
Nandi yawned, bellowed with his wide soft mouth.
And again Parikshi begged.
And the ox yawned, bellowed, head raised high, louder, louder,
Roared so the whole palace thundered.
Never had such a frightful bellowing come from Nandi.

He never once glanced at Parikshi,
Closed his jaws, chomped, dropped his heavy horned head to
   the ground,
Rubbed his dewlaps, grumbled, licked his chops,
Slept.

Parikshi slipped past.
Wandered through the halls and chambers of the splendid
   palace,
Saw things he recognised. But nothing stirred.
Yet Shiva's power over Kailash must still come from somewhere,
For icy air from the ravines did not penetrate the palace.
And down below was night, but the palace lay in steady
   brightness.
What had happened here. And there was nobody.
The heavenly musicians had swarmed away,
Their lovers with them, and all the palace denizens.
Had humans ceased to pray, were evil spirits on the march again,
The Asuras, hideous ones?
Why had everyone fled the palace?
And he crept on with foreboding:
What happened while I flew around and played with Marut?
Oh, playing in water.

Anxious roaming, listening, searching,
Door after door, room after room,
Empty halls, open doors, lutes left lying.
Oh such trepidation, and no more pride or urgings.
Why does no one come to welcome me.
And I'm alone. Oh so alone.
Sat in a doorway, wept: 'Oh how hard it is, all so hard'.

When a warm gust blew on him through an open window,
Almost floored him, he stumbled to his feet,
Went back through the empty halls to the muffled snoring's
   source.

Saw Nandi lying, lingered at the door.
Though Nandi lay quite still he was such a fearsome sight,
The huge beast, sleeping, his dull grumbling.

Then something darted from a corner,
One of those that served as lamps in Shiva's room
With the jewels in their heads.
Parikshi flew after it through the gate.
This thing, it's on its way to Shiva: After it!
They flew down from Kailash,
Southwards, over bristling mountains.

IN THE billowing clouds, the storm, he lost it.
Oh, I the outcast, Parikshi wept.
But in the glow that never faded, night or day,
Parikshi, as he wandered through the air,
Spotted the valley where Shiva paced, his penance over now.

In bitterness Parikshi neared the fissured floor of Cho Mafam,
Came down to the ground:
Why did that woman send me packing.
I was so happy, flying around in my valley.
Ai, ayah, with Marut by the water, *ai, ayah*.

And so he stood, overcome, completely passive, at the entrance
    to the valley.
No trees grew here, no grass,
In the black dreadful fire-scorched valley where the World-shaker
    paced.
'What do you want?'
One of Shiva's praise-singers had come up to him.
    'Oh nothing.' And wept.
The heavenly musician: 'Who are you, Why do you stand here?'

'Ah, leave me alone.'

So the musician went back to the others
Milling about at the valley's edge, whispered.

They reported to Shiva: Someone standing at the entrance to
 the valley
Weeps, and will not say his name or what he wants.
They thought: Maybe he can throw some light on Shiva's actions.

But Shiva overheard what they were saying,
As they moved away across the stony ground.
The Three-eyed One paced onwards, silent.
And Parikshi too made no response.

He flayed his soul
To think how he had flown up from the corrie, abandoned
 Marut.
What had he done, to her and to himself.
Oh bitterness, what sorrow, unbearable affliction, darkness.
And ever and again began to weep.
And as he wept – out there day succeeded night, day and night –
He had a revelation: This is punishment.
I was supposed to bail water from the well. I fled away.

The tenth day he stood there, weeping endlessly,
There came clad in raffia skirt, strewn with ashes, penitent's braids:
 Shiva.
The Three-eyed God came alone, moved in profound contem-
 plation.
His gaze fell on the blessed spirit
Who stood unmoving at the entrance to the valley,
Eyes downcast, weeping.

Shiva stood a long time to one side, observing.
The minstrels and the sirens gathered in the distance,
Watched as Shiva stood, not moving from the spot,
His glance fixed sidelong on the weeping stranger.

Shiva angled his head, looked towards the sun,
Turned his head back towards his followers.
They drifted nearer. Shiva whispered:

'Who is this?'

    'He won't say.'

'He's been here long?'

    'A long time.'

'Wandered here?'

    'Yes.'

Then no questions.
They stood silent around Shiva and the oblivious stranger.
Beyond them the morning grew high.
Then they noticed a change in the unknown spirit.
He still wept, but all light was fading from him.
They felt: he wants to snuff out his existence.
As a human wants to be snuffed out,
So he too, the blessed spirit.
And this terrible instance of the urge to disappear,
To be no more,
Kept them rooted to the spot.

And they saw: Shiva too stood rooted there.
At first they stayed back, circled from a distance
The World-shaker and the unknown spirit.
Then could hold back no longer,
Thronged forward, pressed close about,
And the spirit's groaning, his insensate groaning
Was taken up by them, repeated as an echo.

He groaned softly, the soul sinking from him groaned,
But their groans were in horror at this sinking.
He must not give up his being, the world,
Not turn his face from it and condemn them all.

And the softer his breathing,
The more wildly they thronged about him.

And when he was almost languishing
They had to cry out all the louder: *Oh, oh, oah*!
From him the merest breath, from them a wail of misery, an urging.
It billowed from the black burnt valley to the pass,
All around Shiva and the blessed spirit.

'Oh' they cried out, beside themselves,
'Shall we too be extinguished?
He is a blessed spirit, he should not be extinguished.'

So overcome were these tender beings
That they started up their piping music,
There by Shiva, and Parikshi fading,
To sustain him, for themselves, to give him all they had.

Now he made a move, the World-shaker,
Took a step towards Parikshi.
The spirits huddled back.
And again he angled his blue throat,
Looked to the sun, slowly turned the ash-smeared three-eyed face,
The fleshy face towards the fading spirit here,
Opened his mouth, and Shiva spoke at last:

'Oh Parikshi.'

And when the whimpering, the deep soft helpless sobbing did not stop,
A second time from Shiva:

'Parikshi, oh Parikshi.'

Through the sobbing: 'Yes.'

'Parikshi.'

'Yes.' The spirit opened its eyes.

'Are you Parikshi?'

And again Shiva angled his blue throat, gazed at the sun.

> 'Yes, I am Parikshi, Lord, great Lord. Still Parikshi.
> I am coming to the end.
> I cannot stay here longer.
> I am glad there is an ending. An end is granted to us.'

'You were once on Kailash, were in my crystal palace once?'

> 'Yes.'

'And are weeping, why? And will be extinguished, why?'

> 'I… don't know.'

'Because you are alone? Because you do what you don't want to do?'

A smile about Shiva's mouth.
His upper lip with its black stringy whiskers twitched.
This was the mouth that kissed Uma, daughter of the mountain,
And as he bit her lips
Her fingers shook with pain, to his delight.

How blissful now the look on Shiva's white-smeared face,
As he gazed upon Parikshi and his tears, then up to the sun,
Such a strange gesture.

Then all of them heard his voice.
Which voice?
The World-shaker had many voices.
When he and the other gods whooped and cheered,
Whipping up the ocean –
They pulled on a line, the whirlpool was a mountain,
Beauty, joy, intoxication arose from the roaring ocean –
When he whooped like that, he had a voice.

When he broke out in his chariot against the Asuras, enemies of the Gods,
And they stormed from their three fortresses to meet him,

He raged so, that his chariot began to founder, the world swayed,
Another God had to heave the chariot upright,
And there he had a voice.

When he spoke to Uma in the mountain grove of Gandhamadana:
'O beloved, o beauteous, you are sulking.
With my fingers I would like to pluck some of the moonlight
That slips through the leaves, and wind it in your hair,
So you forget that you are cross,' —
There he had a voice.

The voice that Shiva came in with now enlivened, beguiled,
  seduced,
With the sweetness which is what one lives for.
Now the voice that he came in with swelled,
The mating call of every songbird —
In his voice was an astonishment —
He spoke, the thought spoke from him:

'Here is Parikshi, a blessed spirit from my mountain,
Whom once I sent down to Earth to bring improvement to
  humanity.
He was diverted from his path by love,
No longer heeded when I summoned him.
He threw himself into a well, rather than heed me and improve
  the world.
I brought him to the Field of the Dead
And put him with the one he loved, by a well.
They were to scoop water, endless water, until they found
  their bodies again.
I imposed the mildest punishment, on him and her.'

Parikshi, gushing tears: 'I, it was I, great Lord! An ending now!'

'And you weep. And here you are, Garut.
In the black corrie you and Marut sang:
"*Ai ayah, oh, oah. The well, the well is deep.*
Ah, if it were deeper the work would not be too hard."

I often heard your singing on the Field.
I called you the mango-birds of the Field of the Dead.
"O Marut, Marut, it could be deeper,
Down to the bottom of the world.
I scoop for you alone, for you, so that I can see you,
Splash with you and flit here and there.
Oh, oah, ah, oah!"
And then you fled away from Marut, Parikshi,
To Kailash, to prostrate yourself before me?
And say: I repent, great Lord Shiva,
I was the mango-bird of your Field,
Now I am here, receive me again among your blessed spirits?'

> 'No, no, not prostrate myself. Not repent.
> Repent of one thing only: that I abandoned Marut.'

The spirits around Shiva jostled nervously.
Shiva touched a finger to his mouth: Don't be afraid, don't be afraid.
And the smile on his face did not fade, only broadened in greater bliss.

'Did you come here of your own accord?'

> 'I came here.'

'Of your own accord?'

> 'I… was forced up here.'

'And who forced you? Don't be sad, Parikshi.'

> 'A woman who appeared.'

'A woman, living, with a body, on my Field?'

Shiva, the penitent, lifted up his arms, his toes pointed,
Began to dance a dance: 'Singers, sirens, my minstrels all.'
They stood behind him, lacking lutes, lacking flutes or drums,
Unprepared to accompany Shiva in his dance,
No makeup, no ornaments in ear or nose,

Brows, cheeks unpainted.
They were not cold, for heat still radiated from Lord Shiva,
But haggard their faces, from grief and fear,
From searching, wandering in the land of humans,
Hands scratched, fingernails torn.
Still, they could find their voices,

And now they exchanged glances, thronged around:
What should they sing for Shiva? What did he want to hear?
Some began to follow him in the dance.

Rambha, beloved of the minstrels, tentatively raised her voice,
Wordless, just a trill to set the beat.
But Shiva had stopped already, his arms bent back:

'No time for delay, not one, not one moment.'

And already he was flying up,
Slowly like the opening eyelid of a sleepy eye,
Then faster as if only now he felt that he was flying,
That he could fly
After his terrible penance.
Minstrels, praise-singers, dancing girls swirled after him.

BLESSED valley of Cho Mafam,
Which bore Shiva's weight, location of his penance
And the first steps of his dance.
Within the black walls of the valley, living flowers began to
    glimmer.
As the radiance of his horde vanished towards the north,
Fernshoots rising from the stony soil
Looked towards him, fed on his disappearing light.
They pushed up high, earth pushed them,
To worship Shiva in green red and brown.

Away Shiva flew with the praise-singers, dancing girls

And with stupefied Parikshi.
How the musicians caressed him as they flew on blue-black
    clouds.
They headed north towards sparkling icy Kailash.
How they held him, clung to him.

> 'What did Shiva say to you, how did you cheer him up?
> Who were you before, what happened to you?'

But he stayed silent.
The word 'ending' still lay on his lips,
He was astonished: what was going on.
It had been so hard for him in the corrie,
The woman chasing him away, tearing him away.
What did they intend, these and Shiva?
They pursued Shiva through a raging storm,
Flew over Kailash.

Shiva let one pleat of his raffia skirt brush against the radiant
    palace.
He wanted to be gone already from the mountain.
But then the mountain's murmur reached his ears, as it yearned
    for him,
And a low groan as Nandi, guardian of his gate, felt his nearness.

He came down.
His feet trod the ground, which arched beneath him
Like the soft pelt of a beast, the back of a stroked cat,
So that Shiva, the penitent, swayed and smiled,
Bent down to the ground.

He stood still, stretched himself upright.
Minstrels and dancing girls swarmed about the halls
Where they were at home.
They gathered flowers, laughed, made themselves beautiful.

At the side of Nandi, the white bull, Shiva crouched,
One arm about the burly neck.

They spoke secret tender words to one another.

Shiva came in penitent's garb to his palace,
As a great God he went away.

The lovers of the minstrels, sirens, dancing girls,
Saw his unchanged wonderful smile.
They led him off, away from Nandi, who growled in bliss,
To take a holy bath in the central chamber of the palace,
Where a spring flowed from the mountain's core.
Three times he submerged himself in the silver basin.
Then dancing girls wiped remnants of white ash from his body,
Which dripped and dazzled.

Oh the longing for him when they touched him.
And when a glance from his three-eyed face met them one by one,
Their rapture was complete.

He smiled as he left them.
He wore an elephant's skin for a smock,
His brown body sleek and shining.
Four arms grew from his shoulders.
The cobras that he wore in his hair
Played in the warm air to dry after the bath,
Writhed about Shiva's voluptuous silent mouth.

The lovely youths, the Rudras, scattered petals over him.
In the first chamber he gazed about:
Heavenly minstrels, singers and dancing girls all were there,
Rambha and Manaka, lithe, enchanting, irresistible to every
	penitent,
All there, awaiting his signal.
But his only signal at the doorway was: Open up!

Crouched to say farewell to Nandi.
And they swarmed airily aloft,
Gods, blessed spirits, alluring youngsters,
A thin mist leaving Kailash in its wake.

INVISIBLE against the blue of sky they swept along,
A warm airstream above icecold Himalaya,
Only now and then showed greenish in a flash of sun,
Like the lustre on the wings of butterflies.
Jagged glaciers, massed peaks down below.
When day came, the mountains boomed.
When it was night, the stars emerged,
A mighty murmuring.
Though unmoving they conversed among themselves,
Now softly, now in angry agitation.
The peaks lurked. Silence in the high mountains
While the stars talked, argued and wheeled slowly away.

Now it was midday.
But above the crowding mountains, jagged glaciers something
    floated
That was not day and night.
The mountains' booming now was out of place,
Their silence out of place.
Above them was a humming, whirring, a whir that faded and
    then swelled again,
Like ten thousand birds of passage overhead,
Flying from the south.

The black icebound mountains had no song.
They were heavy massive mountains, age-old beings, deeply
    bedded,
But their flanks thrummed like strings that cooed bass notes.
They felt that they were happy, Trisul, Yamunotri:

'We are fixed and heavy,
And something has come over us that turns us into sounding
    strings.'

They purred, cooed,
Amplified ten-thousandfold the welling wafting that swept
 over them.

Through the azure, shimmering greenly,
Moved the World-shaker, Dancer, Penitent.
With him the curlyheaded lovely youths, Rudras with their
 crescent horns.
They swept over Badrinath.
Parikshi, the blessed spirit, swept on before them,
Transparent blue, and often glancing round.
He must show Shiva
Where he had left the woman who had flushed him from his den.

Parikshi, still faint with sorrow but no longer fading,
They had salved his body in the halls of Kailash,
Had soaked him in song.
He had no idea, nor the minstrels, Rudras thronging all around,
What had restored Shiva to his shining self,
When he stood at the threshold of Cho Mafam valley, weeping,
And spoke of the woman who had chased him off.

Melancholy, yearning, Parikshi swept on ahead.
He must find the corrie with the playing water:
Ai, ayah, oh, oah, Marut, most beloved, most blessed.
They shimmered greenly in the blue, the horde with Shiva.

And here it is, black corrie dropping away.
At Dung Pani Shiva laid himself across the mountain crests,
Minstrels Rudras sirens at his side.
Shiva laid his bare breast on boulders slabs of stone,
And on clumps of mosses, bushes, dwarf-tamarisks.
His head loomed free over the ravines.
None saw any movement down below
In the corrie, or on the snowfields,
On the endless soaring snowy peaks, basins of old snow,
Or farther west on the bald summits,

Like rumbling thunder Shiva's grumbling over the ravines:

'How could this happen.
Long time.
A grief, there was a grief.
How did it come. Something missing,
Suddenly something of me missing.
Who took something from me.
Who can take something from me?
And what.
It was the shadow of a thing that stepped out of me.'

The God angled his snake-squirming head: 'Look there!
It's not a Shade. No Shade. Look.'
And pointed to Dung Pani,
Where rockwalls reached towards the clouds.
On a dreadful wall, surrounded by dead human Shades,
Pursued by countless Shades, a woman, brown.
She was climbing. Shades pursued her.

The crests where Shiva lay began to shake.
The tender ones around him saw his agitation:
They sang. He boomed: 'No singing.'
So they hummed, cooed deep notes just like the mountains,
Which seemed to please him.
And for a long time, while Shiva lay across the crests,
Which softened under him and made a hollow,
They cooed, cooed.

'See, I was lacking her,' he breathed, sang in a child's voice:
'I weep, I can no longer be with you. Ah, Shiva, let me go.'
And then a deeper voice: 'She weeps, she can no longer be with me.
She wants to go.'

And Shiva singing in a child's voice:
'Ah Shiva, what has become of me.
You are good to me, you shine, you are full of joy,

What has become of me? What have you done?
Have you tied threads about me
That pull me down, away from Kailash?'

And he, deeper: 'I have tied no threads about her.
She wants to wander, she will leave.'

And like a child: '*I give light*
From my fingertips, light from my hair-ends,
And my hands are frozen.
You cannot stop it happening
That everything on Kailash is bright and lovely, and I have no peace.'

And he, deeper: 'I know she has no peace.
She shivers, she is freezing.
Where will you wander to, what worlds will you enter,
A thousand worlds of sorrow and joy?'

And humming: *'To Earth.'*

And he, deeper: 'She is at the door.
Vanished already. To Earth.
And is gone. And yet we live.
For I am Shiva. I live beyond all this.'

A black look as he turned back his head:
'Why do you not sing?
I thought you'd disappeared.'

    'You forbade it.'

'When?'

    'Just now, great Lord.'

He smiled: 'Ah!' Looked ahead, pointed to the dreadful rock
    wall:

'There! there! And you don't sing.
Sing, my minstrels, sing I tell you!
I am mouth and there is wine.
I am vat and there is wine.

I yearn, and there is the beloved.'

And as always when he felt a yearning,
Shiva made gestures,
Drew himself long, and undulated like the creeping roots of
    giant trees,
Knotty roots that dive into the earth
And after a long interval come up again, thick-swelling.

In growing delight Shiva stretched and undulated.
He was the God who in his grief
Had hung suspended in the dreary fires of Cho Mafam
And now felt the joy he had drawn near to.

The dreaming minstrels, sirens clinging yearning to him
Had never seen Shiva so besotted.
His chest heaved up and down.
He cast off the clubs and snarelines at his belt,
Too heavy for him, everything too heavy.
The Rudras, youths, crescent moons in their hair,
Leaped over him, pulled open his elephant smock.
The grateful God breathed easier.

He was unsettled, overcome with lethargy and restlessness,
Like a round water droplet on a heating plate:
The droplet jumps, rolls, jumps, wants to become steam.
So rapt, so full of longing they had never seen him,
Those there on the mountain crest
Who had been created in this World Age,
The young and slim of body, joyful,
Whom he kept by him until their souls were all sung out,
And then he created them anew – he would not let them go to
    waste,–
They had never seen him toss and turn like this,
Breathe like this, breast-deep.

He lay half on his right side,
Head on outstretched arm, whispered:

'Do any of you know what a lover does, who loves his beloved?
He does not rush to the beloved,
But circles round her at a distance,
Observes her while she can't see him.
He grazes on her, his eyes graze.
Nothing compares with eyes for sensitivity.
The eyes hold all the senses in their hand,
Are linked to all the senses, all the limbs
Of the strong body, the great soul,
As the sun is linked to everything on Earth.
Just one opening in a wineskin,
And wine can fill the whole skin to the brim.
What hands can touch as delicately as the eyes.
What mouth can kiss so blissfully,
Kiss and suckle with such hidden intimacy
As the eyes.
What can deliver such smiles and wiles
And do such good and make all well
As the eyes, a glance,
A long lingering landing well-embedded
Quite weightless glance,
Which is a double of the one that does the glancing,
A doubled 'I', without weight, floating,
And with one eyeblink there I am with the beloved.
Ah, what sensuousness penetrates as deep within the soul
As that which streams in through the eye.
I won't go just yet.
Look, gaze at her who goes with human Shades across the snow.
You should see her.
It should happen twice, the same thing twice, three times:
Happen over there and here and where we are,
You should see it with me,
And I want to speak it out as well.
Words spoken should deliver it to every ear,

It should live as sound, a third time.'

In his exuberance Shiva flung himself on his front.
His hand twitched, snatched at a cloud.
There came thunder, hail slanted scattering down.
Shiva laughed, was startled, jumped in fright:
'I don't want thunder. Hah, no thunder. Hold my hands.'

Three youths held tight to his hand.
Then again the twitching started.
Shiva pulled free, and grabbed: a raging blizzard.
He was startled: 'What -? You're supposed to hold tight to my hand.'

   'We are not so strong, great Lord.'

Already he was murmuring again,
The glance directed at the snowfield from his three-eyed face
Was rapt: 'Hold it anyway.'
Now ten of them on his hand, hand held tight at knuckles, fingers.
They called softly to each other, braced against the rocky ground.

Now the murmuring enraptured God,
Spellbound by the snowfield, felt pain from his hand.
He turned: 'My hand! Who's hurting me,
Who holds my hand so tight, so tight?'
He pulled free. Thunder crashed across the peaks,
Flash upon flash of lightning, clouds stampeding.
He blew on his hand, stroked it, glaring: 'Leave my hand alone.'
They had to let him get away with it.

HE IMMOBILE still along the mountain crest.
Silent, he who revels in the boom and howl of storms,
In the twittering of birds, the roar of tigers fighting,
Among noisy monkeys, flamboyant parakeets,

Golden mango-birds.

He gazed out over the ravines, chin in folded arms,
Only a greenish gleam in the air between him and snowfield.
Shiva spoke in his thoughts to the woman wandering there,
And Savitri, trudging through snow,
Stood still in confusion, stood in a dream, asleep.
Turned her back to the mountain,
Did not know why.

The voice came from over her shoulder, soft and ever softer.
She pulled a face. Turned this way, that way,
Crouched over the ground.
Picked up snow in her fingers, rubbed it between her hands.
A speaking came to her, softly.

She let herself down on her knees,
Had to sink down even lower, had to bend her head way down,
Kneel all bent over, and kneel and wait and receive it, let it speak,
Wet hands at her throat, eyes open wide.
The Shades had all slipped away.

Shiva's first word made contact,
A sound, a sound, ever and again a droplet of sound,
Droplet sinking in sand, evaporating.
A droplet, then nothing.
Droplet, nothing.

'*Lak, lak.*' Shiva huffed: '*Lak.*' And again: '*Lak.*'

Until Savitri knelt, bent double, repeated it: 'Lak.'

'*Om.*' – Savitri: 'Om.'

'*Tami.*' – 'Tami.'

And Shiva: 'Who are you?'

    And Savitri: 'Who are you.'

'I am asking, who are you?'

    'Are you.'

'Yes you. Who are you, do you know?'

'I?' – 'Yes.'

'I… know.'

'Who are you?'

'I am… Savitri.'

'Look at me.'

'I am looking at you.'

'Do you know me?' – 'Yes.'

'So who am I.'

'Don't ask.'

'Who am I.'

'I… don't want to talk.'

'Am I Savitri?' – 'No.'

'Am I a swan?' – 'No.'

'Am I… Shiva?'

Savitri's arms clutched tight at her breast: 'I won't say it.'

'Am I Shiva?'

'Ah, I won't say it.'

'Am I Shiva?'

Absorbed in her dream, she began to weep:

'But you should know.'

'Yes, I am Shiva. You have come to us again.'

'I am coming. I shall come to you, really.'

'We long for you, we thirst for you. You've been on the way so long.'

'I am at the end now. I know it.'

'Come, Savitri, don't delay. Don't withhold yourself from us.'

'But I am here. You see me. I am coming.'

'Savitri, sweetness, child of sunshine, stand up now, and move.
See how I lie across the mountains.
The Rudras, you know them, my dancing girls, my singers
All are gathered here,
Flown here from Cho Mafam, flown here from Kailash.
How Kailash will rejoice when you set foot there once again.'

'I am coming, and… and… and I do not want to. Oh.'

'Don't keep us waiting.'

'I don't want this. Don't. Oh.'

'Will you come to us again, Savitri?'

'I want to come to you, come to Kailash, yes.'

'Come!'

'Ah don't shout. Don't shout so. I am coming to you.'

'You are coming.'

'Grant me one plea, Shiva.'

'What is it you want, Savitri, sweetness, child of sunshine?'

'Yes, call me that. Say it to me often, say it.'

'Savitri child of sunshine.'

'And the sweetness!'

'Savitri sweetness, golden radiance, joy-bringer, woman of smiles.'

'Yes that's good. Say that you will grant my plea.'

'I shall grant it.'

'Grant it me. I want to die among people.
I want to take one more step among people.
I want to have travelled every step of the way.'

'Yes, Savitri.'

'Will you grant this plea, Shiva?
I must search for one thing more.
There's one more thing I have to seek.
I must keep on. Let me keep on.'

'You blessed one, our boon. Go as you will.'

'Only a little way, Shiva.'

'As you will, you blessed one.' Then Shiva fell silent.

The dream, the voice fell from Savitri.
Her cold arms hung down, head lifted from her breast.
On the mountain crest, among the silent Rudras,
Among the silent resting minstrels, the silent dancing girls
Shiva turned over, silent himself and in command of his four arms,
The mighty body, the stamping legs.
Turned over and leaned forward from the hollowed crest,
Leaned his chest out over the ravines, and their rising mists.
Stretched his giant arms out across ravines,
And with one hand, one hand
Felt across ravines, the snowfield with its rising mists
Towards Savitri.

With the index finger of one hand
Shiva made silent contact with her face,
The finger, daubed with paint from his own face,
Moved across Savitri's brow,
And with paint from his own face
Shiva painted on Savitri's brow the wedding mark.
Her head, turned to him as if she felt him,
Her icy brow, face drawn taut with sorrow, received the wedding mark.

SKIDDING down in snow, Savitri, set free now.
Savitri on the Field of the Dead,
Opened her eyes, closed, opened her eyes,
Stood up, turned around, brushed snow from her knees:
I must have been sleeping. Sleeping.

White mountain crests, snowflakes drifting, swirling Shades.
Onward, onward, like every other day.
Not give up, not freeze – she did not freeze –
Not give up, not starve away – she did not starve away –
And strode and stood and strode and stood.

She looked about her.
The words she wanted to say and did say were not hers.
Still she called out to the dead:
'If only I could send you down to the land of humans,
Across the mountains, into steppelands, plains.
Break in, take my body, take me.
Destroy whatever you want,
Show what is real,
What is happening to you, and to us and all of us!
Onward to bridges roofs crags rivers!
You can do it. You can do it.'

Shades rustling around her:

> 'See how we flutter, how we are harried.'
> 'Look at me. I am here.'
> 'We are dead. We are dissolving.'
> 'None have died. None have died, ever!
> All were murdered!'

And suddenly the word stuck in her mouth,
Swelled over her face and breast like dough,
And as she raised her arms and her mouth became wide,
She felt like one who jumps into a river, believing she can swim,
Now sees the banks slip by so fast, so fast,
The forest slips by so fast, and sees:

She is in a current, the current carries her.

She felt, Savitri, the current surging up within her,
A melting, urgent, knee-trembling longing – for what?
It is what streamed through Marut and Parikshi,
Had not let go the hands of Aisya and Survasu.

No conjurer of the dead, Savitri,
Ever a wanderer, from Udaipur through steppelands,
Yearning, seeking:
I wander, seek, have forgotten nothing.
There's one more step that I must take.

Ah what stern surging longing welled up over her.
Flaming love, terrible lacerating love.
A shore, a coastline must be nearby, surf crashing so.
Yearning, for what, – blessed body-melting knee-trembling yearning,
Its breath all about her skin.

Shiva's wedding mark flamed upon her forehead.
Her fertile days were on her.
In her breast and arms she carried blood of magic.

And as she looked about her, walked, dug into snow to cool herself,
Up from the ravines came whirling Shades, demons, errant gods,
Shivering in the mist the wind blew to them,
Mist of her blood.
It was the mist that lures saints from their caves, frisky after being reborn.

Savitri's bosom stood proud, her face glared,
Hair billowing smoke and fire. Eyes hands feet streaming heat.

What force does the fire of love possess?
Mild it is, tender and ensnaring,
Sweet, never to be sated.
Four arms has Shiva, the fire of love a thousand!

It takes hold of all that lives, cradles it, draws it to itself,
Meekly, tenderly.

And Shiva flung himself down upon the mountain,
When he saw his fire wandering on the Field,
So near to him the magic, the power of miracles.

BUT among the Shades, unobserved by Savitri,
Among those drawn in by the love-mist
Came drifting –
Flew –
Was drawn in –
One Shade in particular.
Silent cryptic thing
That no longer made lament, was driven, drawn along,
A bundle, a long oval,
One Shade among the many, no eyes, no limbs,
A Shade that flew, and sought,
And called out in its closed mouth.
She held the Shade embraced in both her arms.
She took the Shade to her.
She slid on with the Shade, through the snow,
And did not know what what what was happening.

As if a blade had struck home in her breast and cleaved it,
Savitri fell down with the Shade in the snow.
Did not speak to it, said nothing, felt it over with her hands.
No snowy mountain there, no Field of the Dead.

She rocked it this way, rocked it that way,
And suddenly brought out of it an *ah, ah*, a groan of agony,
Lay there, trembled,
And slowly raised her head, saw it standing there.
Still standing there. And Savitri whimpered, cried out:

'Who are you? Who is it?'
And dragged herself closer, arms held out to the Shade.

Her hair billowed flames and smoke, her eyes glowed.
From the snow she lifted herself up to it,
And howls, awareness, and laments, such lamenting,
Rasping, wheezing, *oh*.
And dragged herself away: Oh corpse, corpse, oh dead, a dead
    thing.

And now Shiva stood up from his mountain,
The Blue-throated One, World-shaker;
Like a war-elephant over flowers in a meadow,
Loomed over the peaks,
Looked around to where the Rudras lay,
Beckoned them with his arm.
He rattled the chains he carried at his belt,
Fastened his smock,
Swung slings and snarelines through the air,
Whistling, shrilling all around him.

Those howlers the Rudras raised their voices,
Stormed over to him, around his shoulders.
He whooped. The wide evening sky thundered.
Then silence.
The Rudras hurtled about him.

He lowered himself to the snowfield on his knees,
A long way from Savitri and the Shade.
Stretched his arms out across the snowfield,
To where they stood, embracing, speechless,
Savitri, and a Shade.

Threads hung from his fingers, slender coloured threads.
His hands, as if constructing something, moved across the Field.
He huffed his warm breath over the Field,
And smiled, huffed.
And Savitri, in her arms the Shade,

Knew who it was she had, and felt herself transported.

Such long paths. A tree by a hill.
Mysterious gaps between the branches,
Steppelands, dark man, a hut,
And plains, ricefields, a city.
She held the shade, the bundle, in her arms,
Carried it, such long paths.
Not leave you, you so mauled, suffocated.
She blew breath into it, squeezed it.
Not leave you, you will live, now I shall live.

Its eyes looked at her, dreaming staring eyes,
Lamenting eyes.
Why lament, you should not lament.
I can: I'm the one lamenting.
A city, city, yes, this is the one.
Udaipur.
*Trum rum, trum rum a*long the streets.
Cart with shrouding cloths.

Hold you tighter, tighter to me.

She looked the Shade in the eyes,
Looked aside, looked up.
There was a garden hall, a pool and boats and palms.
And she shuddered suddenly, clutched at it:
This – was Death! She was already dying!
But if she died she could at least hold him
And die with him, and want to die.

Oh just to die with you.
You've come back at last from the wastes of Thar.
Now it's all forgotten, what happened to you.
Now you no longer think of what has been.

And his arms snaked around her.
Who was she holding? She knew who.

He had come back from the wastes of Thar,
Back from the wastes of Thar to her,
Back from the wastes of Thar, back, back,
From the wastes.

And again she let go of him who clung to her,
And swayed.

The jubilant Thunderer went all around the Field,
Strewed black dust of sandalwood down on her,
Draped her with pearls and silks,
Stuck green barley shoots behind her ear.
She bloomed, trembling, extended herself wide.
About the Shade's neck – it was growing, growing –
She twined the tendrils of her young arms,
She pushed her toes close up to his.
She huffed breaths on him, the Shade huffed breaths.

And he should do more, do more than breathe,
Encompass her whole body, feel, enclose her,
Give her his mouth, his mouth, its wetness,
The fullness of his hair, his flesh,
The folds of his ears, give it all,
The hardness of his head and the supple skin that covers it,
Strong knees, the heavy breast,
The belly that moves in and out in breathing,
The striding legs, give it all.

A dark garden hall was over them.
Singing drifted from the pool, endless singing:

> *Many the barques*
> *That sail on the round pool*
> *With their pale blue awnings*
> *Past the fan palms.*
> *Calling out, calling each to each, ayee, ayee!*
> *Calling from the shore out to the barques, ayee, ayee!*

- Girl with shining hair,
Hair streaming in the wind,
Do not glide past in your boat,
Like a windblown leaf in the water, ayee, ayee! –

On the shore you, proud man,
Enticing, signalling with your eyebrows,
My finger, more I cannot hold out to you across the bow,
The water kisses it,
You disappear behind the palms.

They lay on the mat,
And now she began to tussle with the unspeaking thing.
It grabbed the back of her head.
Ah, he can do this.
He kissed her mouth and eyes,
Pushed her lips up with his lips,
Kissed her exposed teeth.
Her round cheeks he kissed.
Dug his nails into her shoulders,
Filled his hands with her two breasts,
His knees and ankles pressed against hers.

She felt it and pushed back and breathed, felt it.
It came from her, she yielded it.
Was Manas that she bore from out of her,
Bore out of her in love's tussle.
And yielded up herself and did not yield.

He held her by her narrow hips,
And braced himself.
In the shadowed hall, eye plunging into eye,
In the shadowed hall her loins,
She turned aside, thrust back,
Their loins were joined.

A chinking, they did not hear the chink,
The tinkling of Shiva's little bells,

As he made his dance about the Field,
Rudras and singers following him.

BLISS to the point of swooning that fell upon Savitri.
And like a plank that someone puts across his knee,
He bends it, it deforms,
And now a will is there: it must be broken, it will break.
And as a mouth can open
So casually and say Yes into the air and it is good,
Thus was Savitri's mind made up,
Savitri consummated, and everything at its goal.

They lay there on the mat.
And Savitri felt the deepdeep truth about their touching,
The deep reality of their touching touched Savitri,
Boundless, strong-walled, marble-hard reality,
Devoid of dreams and language,
The point of origin for every landscape, every people,
Every chance encounter.

They did not see Shiva, the great Dancer,
Sorcerer, the Vanquisher, Rope-swinger,
Whose noises filled the air as he circled over them.
But she heard his tinkling bells, Savitri, louder by the moment.
And louder the tinkling,
Clearer, shriller the rushing, the surf's roar.
Something there calling her, she must go to it.
She heard, stood up. Broke through the hall's roof.
Stood tall, like a cork bobbing to the surface,
Like a swimmer climbing from water onto land,
Dripping, feeling the way, eyes bleared, blindly swallowing
She stood, broke through the roof,
Pregnant with reality, gasping, spitting,
Lowing like a ruminating cow in grass:

What is…*oh*. What is… *oh*.
Oh, where am I?

And gulping, gasping still, she climbed, Savitri,
Up into the icy Himalayan air,
Whimpering, clinging on downslope,
A trailing vine trying for a foothold,
Climbed into the rosy evening,
Herself shimmering red, glowing, clouded.

A human lay below her in the snow.
Savitri was borne higher, sobbing,
Her feet skidding still in snow:
Oh, I don't want this, I don't.
But she grew and climbed inexorably.
Her wailing whimpering was a rush of wind at craggy edges.
Wailed more wildly, stretched, fought, tensed herself,
Beat about her, waves and surf about her.
And floated, showered with tears, and flew,
A bellowing bellowing wail from her,
Deep wheezing of an organ, breast-welling,
Raging groans, groaning across the mountain peaks,
As a giant roars when dragged by chains of ice out from his cave,
And those who drag him, all the thousand, hide themselves.

And the alarm of the Rudras,
Alarm of Shiva's minstrels dancing-girls.
The Three-eyed One had in his hand a spear,
He was dancing on the glaciers by himself.
They played their lutes, blew flutes, beat drums,
Twilight had come.

Over all the mountaintops he danced his jaunty giant steps.
At first the peaks had kept their silence, now they boomed
    with him.
With every step upon the mountain, ice cracked.
That was Shiva's heels, setting the beat.

Savitri turned: Where am I? Oh do help me.
The blessed ones thronging: Who is it, is it?

With a spring Shiva launched himself into the air,
Sent his spear ahead to announce to Kailash his approach:
Savitri, Savitri's with us! Savitri is with us again!

And carried her over the roaring cracking mountains,
In his arms Savitri, smouldering, she spellbound in his arms.
Her eyes were open wide, she tried to kick herself away from
    him.

Shiva hauled her, his chest upon her,
The chain of skulls rattling along behind.
She stared up at his blue throat.
The Fearsome One bore her through the icy air,
Enveloped in the scent of sandalwood, blaze of stars.
The howling still slipped in little waves out across her lips,
The howling ringing in her ears still.
She closed her mouth,
Looked, sought, looked below.
The Blissful One, the Three-eyed God carried her.
It was strange to look up at the blue throat, the great three-eyed
    face.
The glow streamed far out behind: gouts of flame.

The glow was still upon the mountain crests
When Savitri was already over Kailash.
The Rudras gathered up the flames,
Hurled them high, carried them along behind Savitri
From crest to crest.
Flung them to each other until the mountains lay in darkness.

AND Kailash resplendent, loud with jubilation,
Its crystalline shimmer in the Himalayan night.

Savitri, heavenly woman, had been bathed,
Salved, clothed, adorned.
She went with dancing buckles at her ankles,
Fine gold pin at her nostril,
She bade them hush their jubilant uproar,
Let them lead her through the scented halls.
She knew them of old.

– *'Ah Shiva, I cannot be with you.'*
His deeper voice: *'She weeps, she cannot be with me.'*
'Ah Shiva, what has become of me?
You have laid threads that pull me down from Kailash.'
He deeper: *'I have laid no threads.'* –

She stood at the door of Shiva's room,
Rested an arm on fawning Nandi's horns.
The Blessed Ones went past with adoring eyes,
Minstrels, dancing-girls, one after the next,
And the heavenly spirits, their servants.
She glanced at them all, head low.

Then one came along, gaze averted, not looking at her,
And not adoring.
She took it by the hand, drew it to her, closed her eyes:
'I know you.'

The spirit breathing: 'Yes.'

'You are Parikshi.' – 'Yes.'

'You know that I know you?' – 'Yes.'

'And from where?' – 'Yes.'

'Say it.' – 'I… I cannot say it.'

She let go his hand: So it is real? It is all real!
And stood. Adoring spirits wandered past.

And then: 'You Parikshi, what are you up to?'

    'I serve. I serve the Great Lord.'

'And you want to stay? I chased you off up here.'

He turned away his head, lay down at her feet,
She stroked his back: 'Go, Parikshi.
Shiva will not scold you.
There's a dark ravine, a tree stands in a corrie,
Water's gushing, there's a well.
Two mango-birds are singing.
Go, Garut. Don't forget me. Greet Marut for me.'
And turned away.

She sat with heavenly ones on a mat,
The fleshy Three-eyed God on a tigerskin before her.
Down his bare sleek breast a chain of skulls hung like pearls,
In his locks cobras darted out their tongues.
And the Three-eyed God kept bowing to Savitri.
He himself strummed a lyre.
They drank the intoxicating potion, soma.
Head low, rings on her fingers, hands folded, Savitri sat.

    'And how long will you sit like this, Savitri, love?'

'Have patience, great Lord. We flew so fast.'

    'You went away from us, Savitri.
    I had forgotten, in the vasts of time forgot:
    You were once with us.
    Then I felt: I am withering.
    In Madhura I walked by lotus pools,
    They brought me fruits, honey, sacrificed, cleansed my
        precious stones.
    As I walked I saw: I am withering, all is withering,
    Gods, the Blessed, and what will become of the world?
    Shall we again be cast down, shall we be devoured?
    I hung myself in fire, did penance, penance at Cho Mafam.
    You felt us, and your messenger came.
    You always send a messenger when you're on your way.
    I came to meet you,

  You fount of loving, who plunge into every world,
  And sit before me.'

'I am with you, Shiva.'

  'And you, who are our light?'

Savitri raised her eyes: 'What should I say?
I'm still dusty from the long long path.
I was bathed, and still it covers me.'

  'Naughty dust. We bloom when you're with us.
  Minstrels, dancers,
  All of us feel like cheering because you're back with us.'

'Cheering! And I, Shiva? Am I nothing?'

She raised her slender hands above her head,
Fresh ashoka blossoms fell from her lap.
She shook herself. Her gentle eyes glistened:

'Threads that pull me lower!
Threads that drag me higher!
And I, I!'

  'There are no threads, Savitri.'

'Snowfields I traversed, horrid ravines, cliffs,
And storms, and everything real.
They swirl, they are harried,
Shades, how many Shades, a thousand Shades,
I held one of them.'

  'You're here now, Savitri. You were among people.
  Do you not see?'

'I held it. And no longer hold it.
What am I myself? Am dissevered, a Shade.
Must search like them. And wail, and search.'

  'Now you would plunge into the well, Savitri,
  Like Garut and Marut.'

'Ah, if I could. I cannot.'

   'You can.'

'I… don't want to. I… don't want to go down the well.'

And with a smile the Three-eyed, Mighty,
Blissful, Blue-throated
Shiva gazed across at her from his tigerskin.
He let his foot slide from thigh down onto skin.

> 'You have come back again, Savitri.
> What would we be, would Kailash be, without you?
> Everything flourishes where you have been.
> Look around.
> You won't abandon us.
> Now you are with us, encumbered, pregnant,
> At our side, you child of sunshine,
> You spice, you diver into every world.'

And as the minstrels sang, Savitri brought fresh ashoka blossoms
And laid them at his feet:
'Yes, tell me Shiva,
I come back here, go there and thither,
And have never been away.'

   'You lover, diver into every world.'

'So sing, dear dancing girls and minstrels.
I shan't keep you waiting,
I'm coming.
I shall find new names for you and me.
My hands in yours, my lips on yours.'

Kailash seethed.

THREE

THE RETURN OF MANAS

[1] DOWN TO EARTH

AND there was no more rain.
Storms shredded the blue-black ragged clouds hither and down,
Hurled them with thunderclaps over glaciers snowfields ravines.

Through the thunderclaps the Rudras flew,
Eleven of them, Shiva's curly-head companions, moonhorns at their brow,
Bearing the man on their backs.

Over sombre Nanda Devi they flew.
Its double summit flashed blue in the storm's flickering.
The mountains, unsettled by Shiva's dance,
Now started their booming.

Gori brook surged white from Milam glacier,
Tumbled southward.
Rushing Pindar cascaded down from Nanda Kot.
To the west, Ganges had set out on its course,
Foaming through the mountains.

Such crepitating across the night.
Moon and stars hid from the boisterous Rudras.
Forests on the southern slopes awoke,
Euphorbia acacia stands of bamboo,
Howled along like dogs in the night,
One dog here, another there responding with a long-drawn howl.

Eleven Rudras, on their backs the sleeping man,
Headlong through the dripping night, southward,
Swooping to flick snowcaps from rocky ridges,

Shake them from their arms down into valleys.
They spat sprayed hail as they hurtled on.

By morning they were roaring over mountain jungle,
The flame-headed ones. Their eyes flashed green.
Here was the boundary of the Field of the Dead.
They snuggled wearily into snow that steamed.
They laid the man down.
Fell asleep beside him until the sun flashed.

Then they let winds whirl them aloft
Light as air, stretched flat, they rode high, flickering
Whenever a ridge, as they passed over,
Brushed a back or a drooping arm
And grazed them.
Were giddy, called to one another, sang out over distances.

LAY there, sleeping, sleeping, Manas,
Manas sleeping in a fig tree.
The branches spread wide, the fig tree held him up.
And when Manas stirred, the branches thrashed and bent.

Manas rolled tumbled onto softened ground,
Curled himself up, his face bespattered, feet in a puddle.
He wiped his mouth, gulped air.
The branches whipped high again,
He saw them.

Suddenly he jumped up.
Stood, stood, wiped his mouth,
Saw: a tree, icy peaks behind it, glimmering,
Ground beetles at his feet, brown body, his body.
Muddy all over.
Toes that splayed in mud,
Beetles piling onto one another, biting, feeding.

A tongue in his mouth, scent of sandalwood in his nose.

He turned around,
Started running through dense cedars spruces rhododendrons.
And suddenly as he ran gave out a roar.
And heard his roar, stood still to hear his roaring,
Stamped, heaved out his roar with a lungful of air,
Pulled it back in,
Heaved it out, sucked it back,
Until his chest stood proud and he could again give out his roar.
He called out until he coughed, bent double.

Then, bulging bloodshot eyes, full lips,
He knelt panting, looked about him,
Waited for his breathing to come easier,
Listened to the forest:
Nothing moving on the breeze, no creatures creeping.

He was alone, he had roared.
When the mouth closed the roaring stopped.
These were the ears that heard it.

Weeds growing on the ground, with prickly leaves:
They were here, he could grab them.
And he stood up, uttered random yawps,
The forest acknowledged them.
He seized a weedy plant by the head,
Uprooted it, swung it,
Then flung the thing into the mire:
It was his seal, there it lay.
Just now its roots were in soil,
Now they lay bare, this was a proof.
This had happened, two different things, before and after.

And whooping trumpeting Manas stood among the giant trunks,
Looked about him – what was it all –
Splashed, laid claim.
Then he ran on.

He clambered down a rocky gully
Overgrown with orchids everywhere, red yellow,
Black water splashing down.
He had to go down, clamber across the rushing brook,
Back up beside the brook.
Then he fell.
And as he felt himself falling he wanted more,
No grabbing hold as he yelped and plummeted.
He had to see what would happen,
Fall and then what. A bush caught him.

He hauled himself up, his head lay downslope,
Head bleeding, hands and arms raw.
There was blood. He had blood in him.
And joyfully he licked his arms, rubbed his cheeks.
Blood, lovely blood.

He clambered over landslips, his eyes flickered
When he leaped high over a rubbled riverbed.

He wore no clothes, had no cloth of any kind,
Not like the Manas who came up from Udaipur
To seek out the dead on Nanda Devi.

He laughed in the dry riverbed, on a limestone boulder.
Stood, stretched,
His hair stood on end in ecstasy,
Spittle dribbled from his lips,
Mosquitoes and bees buzzed around him.
The riverbed was overgrown with thistles, stinging nettles.

He flicked rainwater into the buzzing insect swarms.
Why did I waste my time up there in the ice!
I could have caught my death of cold.

He beat about him at the insects
That flew up in buzzing clouds:
You think I'm carrion? Am I a corpse?

Those days… are over, my lovelies.

And leaped from boulder onto stony bed,
Beat about him, strode into the strident swarms.
They cleared no path for him,
So he cleared one for himself,
Whirled, spun, ran, leaped away,
Left them behind and laughed:
Am I a corpse? Can a corpse run away?
Well then! Well then!
And uttered a few more *well thens* to himself.

Clambered in pathless clefts,
Hand over hand around rocky spurs, everywhere dense with
 growth.
Marvelled, marvelled: Can it ever end,
These mountains trees stones leaves,
A million leaves, air.
Ah, I was dead, was dead, really dead, I,
There with the Shades on Shiva's Field!

And then he shouted out,
No thoughts came unless he murmured, spoke,
Eyes flitting, hands exploring:
Was dead! Alive again!
Threw stone after stone into the black cascading water
That dragged massive loads of scree down to a corrie:
Alive again! One!
Alive again two!
Alive again ten!
Alive again a hundred!
Alive again ten thousand!
Alive again a hundred million and a hundred thousand million
 and three!

Water splashed.
Its roar drowned out the clacking of his stones.

He kept throwing until he heard it and, satisfied, marched on.

The mountainsides were lush with stands of bamboo,
Thistles grew among them man-high,
The sky above even bluer.
Manas sucked the pith of a wild thistle.
His mouth sucked as he strolled and strode.

SQUAWKING overhead.
A bird shot over him, a grey flying creature,
A parakeet with curved beak, yellow tail feathers,
A ragu, kiru,
It flew squawking over the thicket.

His heart rose into his mouth, Manas had to gulp.
A bird flying there: was it he? He himself? Who was it?
He sat down, Manas.

The creature stopped its flitting,
Settled into the thicket,
Came strutting out from the shady thicket,
Little kiru, throat black with a touch of pink,
Sky blue its collar.

In his hand Manas held a slender bamboo cane.
The kiru strutted between his feet.

'Little Kiru, how good to see you.
How long it's been since I saw you last.
Little Kiru, tell me your name.'

The kiru hopped around the tree.

'Kiru, your name.
Or mine, if you won't tell me yours.
Do you know mine?'

In his excitement Manas crouched, laid his arms on the ground,

The green parrot hopped between his arms.

'Mine or yours? Am I called Manas or are you?
I think, Kiru, that you are Manas? Say it.'

It hopped this way and that.
Now Manas took the cane and tapped the kiru on the feet,
It pecked. Manas tapped it on the head.

'My name, Kiru. Manas, say it, am I Manas?
Say it, say it.'

He nagged, his voice rose, the creature flapped its wings.
He shouted at it, whispered, spoke, dropped to the ground,
Held the kiru:
'This is a bird, this is a Kiru.
In the towns it hangs from rooftops,
Hangs there by the dozen, idles all day long.
It goes into fields when the corn is ripe,
Steals, screams all day until evening,
The green robber, screams like ten monkeys.
Now it won't talk, pretends to be dumb.
Look at me, Kiru. My name, now.'

It ruffled its feathers, stretched its green feet.

'It's all right to speak, Kiru.
Because there are no humans here to talk to me.
You won't get away.
Your neck is sleek, you're a little female.
Maybe I'm blocking the way to your tree-hole,
And you have young waiting for you there.
Be quick now, then I'll go.
What I ask of you, dear green Kiru,
Dear little woman, little mother,
Is the simplest thing in the world.
Every one of your children has a name.
Give one to me.

Is my name Manas, or something else?'

He started to cajole:
'A long time ago there was a Manas,
Dear Kiru, little green mother,
Don't be afraid.
I shan't hurt you, but don't you hurt me either.
This Manas was a mighty warrior, what they called a mighty warrior,
Went at the head of an army, had a shield,
And a sword, and a club
And a bow and arrows, and shot and slashed and swung,
And sat on a horse.
Such a man was this Manas.
He lived in Udaipur, which is... I don't know where.
All I'd like to know is whether I am he or are you,
Or how it goes with him.'

The kiru's beak stayed closed.

'Say Manas. My name is Manas.'

The kiru squawked: 'Manas.'

'Again.' – 'Manas.'

'And again.' – 'Manas.'

'Good, good. You wouldn't have escaped alive.
Now I'll be on my way.
But that was forced from you.
You must say it of your own free will, Kiru.
I shan't prod you. Now jump between my arms.
What's my name?'

    'Manas.'

'Good Kiru.' – 'Manas.'

'Good Kiru. Good green mother.'

He opened his arms. The bird sped away across the grass.

Manas in pursuit, whispering:
'What's my name, quick.'

    'Manas, Manas.'

Manas threw away the cane,
Mother Curvybeak whirled high.

'Now you're free. My name, Kiru!'

And the little bird, cawing over the shady thicket,
Wheeled in the air, squawked, screeched,
Then shrilled: 'Savitri.'

'Who?'

    'Savitri, Savitri.'

And Manas, silent for a moment, sat on the ground.
Let loose a laugh, fell back against the trunk,
Threshed about in laughter:
Savitri! I'm a woman!
Savitri! Me, a woman.

THE kiru climbed, disappeared over the treetops,
Manas following with his eyes.
Like a wild horse Manas stamped his feet:
I, Savitri! I have no name.
I must call myself Kiru or what else.
What difference does it make?
Who, who will give me rice to eat?
Leaves a million, air a million, world a million!

He walked on, a wild horse, feet stamping:
There was a wander-wanderer.
A long time since he'd eaten, eaten, eaten.
Who gives him rice to eat
Because he's hungry?

Who gives him linen and silk
Because he has none?
Who gives him a roof for the night
Beacause he likes to wander in the open but not sleep there,
With all the beetles and the clammy worms,
And the bright tiger and the huge long cobra snakes.

And he sang and chewed on thistle pith:
Who'll give me something to eat,
Who'll give me something baked, boiled, fried?
So who is he, what does this fellow call himself,
Wandering here and making such a racket?
It'll be revealed soon enough,
Revealed in ten days,
Revealed in thirty-five years, or in half an hour.
Someone should look into it.
The kirus have no idea. Kirus think that I'm a woman.
That's not in the Vedas and not in the Upanishads,
The priests don't know it, and I don't know it either.
So it would be a sign of feeble-mindedness,
But one easily overcome.
No need to ask a doctor,
All will be revealed, soon enough.

And sang and chewed on thistle-pith
And spat and broke a new stem:
Pleasant life! Life a thousand miles across!
And would be even nicer if I had something to eat,
Something solid but not woody.
Something boiled, or baked, or fried.
Lots of parrots flying through the air,
I shan't eat them,
They can fly about without a care and lay their eggs.
But a pheasant might well come along
And take pity on me, after my long time of fasting.

Shiva, your world is lovely, if only I weren't so cold
And the pheasants did not always fly
Where they are no use to me.
Shiva, you are lovely to have made all this,
And I really do rejoice in it, despite my hunger
And the big misunderstanding between me and the noble tribe
    of pheasants.

All is lovely, Shiva,
And I myself, hungry wet creature,
Constantly plucking thistles and ita-grass,
Why am I lovely?
Because I have everything that you have made,
As if I had made it myself,
And because I'm marching through the mountain forest.
Really I'd rather call myself Shiva,
Everything is so lovely.
And then every creature, when it calls to him,
Would mean me, mean me every time.
But I'd better keep this to myself,
Even though it hits the nail on the head.
It leaves an opening for switched identities,
Let's keep it secret, between me and Shiva.

He laughed, spat, sought for something he could chew on,
Pushed through the tangled vegetation.
And roared again, whooped and beat the ground,
Strong brown Manas, mud-spattered, smeared with blood.
Heaved a roar from him, pulled it back.
He could never have enough of shoving, scraping, bumping into
    things.

Green walls roared about him,
Tendrils creepers treetrunks leaves
Called to each other: Who is it, is it?
And always the respectful soughing salutation:
'Savitri.'

BUT through the green walls, from far away
Rang out a clashing and smashing,
Slamming and hitting.
It rang out *rum*
Rum dum.
Rum and *rum.*
Manas took it in with open ears.
Dreadful menacing slamming hitting,
Crashing and then silence and more crashing.
He had legs, had to run as fast as he could into the crashing,
Slamming hitting smashing pelting,
Clattering, *rum dum, rum dum.*

Out of the forest.
An exposed rocky ridge.
Such clattering cracking.
And over it blue sky, thin white clouds
And a blooming silence on the ground,
Big butterflies bobbing, bright-dappled.

But on the high slope, wilderness of scree,
Wide rubblefield, there moved
Among boulders and scrawny cacti
An ash-smeared scrawny man
With club and slings and shield.
Facing him, above him, at his side three demons,
Little darting storming figures twisting as they leaped,
Came crashing up against his shield,
Tripped him, came aiming for his mouth.

Already he had spun around, lifted his club against them.
They stood, leaped apart, man and demons.
The demons, trailing smoke, darted high above him,

Pelted stones down.

And Manas stood and stood there on the ridge.
Behind him pine trees raised green candelabra arms.
The power of speech had left him.
They were fighting in bright sunshine.
His face screwed up in glee, in glee,
As they lashed out and huffed and crashed.
Manas laughed. Glee and craving gleamed in his eyes.
He flared his nostrils like a beast. He trembled with desire.
His breast did not want to rise,
And he giggled, his throat, his breast, glee-craving.
He emitted grunting happy groans, soft cooing laughter,
Like the clink and clang of tin when lightly tapped.
His face was twisted
As he stood there, Manas, and his legs stepped out,
His mouth bliss-blessèd.

Have I not seen this before?
Rum, rum dum.

Both sides were pelting stones
And staggering, oh ye gods, staggering,
Head over heels among the rocks,
Came up again, ye gods,
Stretched long, dived down, clashed,
Head over heels, four heads together.

Was he thinking this, was he seeing it?
Chuckling cooing breathless Manas,
And laughing, laughing
Full-throated, from his deepest breath,
As he watched the demons leaping, and the ash-smeared man.

And the demons as they swooped heard the laughter,
Were offended, exchanged glances as they flew.
What was amiss: 'What's the rascal laughing at?'

They thought it was Puto laughing.
Then the laughter kept on coming, and it came from the
   pine-wood,
Where something living stood, skin gleaming, and shook its fists
   at them.
   'Why are you laughing, wretch?' screamed Chanda, the one
      with fangs.
   'You're risking your skin.
   Watch out, we'll come after you.'

He called across: 'But who are you lot?
Why are you fighting,
What's all the noise about? How you leap!
I can't keep my eyes off you. I'm looking at you.'

And shouted as he made his slow way down:
'Get on with it, you lot, set to! Set to!'

   'Who is it? Ask him who he is.'

      'A human? Maybe Puto brought him
      While we were resting, sneaked him out of the forest
      With his magic, to fall on us from behind?'

   'But Puto hasn't left his spot.'

      'You weren't watching all the time, you don't know
         Puto.'

   'He's one of us, Chanda, I tell you, one of us.
   Why mention Puto?
   He's from the Field of the Dead, or my name's not
      Nishumbha.
   He's come to help us.
   His body's a decoy, just look at him, stout well-freighted
      belly,
   How he gleams and glistens!
   Why does he giggle at us, laugh so gleefully?

He gives himself away.'

And they gurgled their language,
Secret speech of demons on the stony slopes:

> 'Say, brother, who you are.
> We know you! *Kirr-kirr-kirr.*

Manas roared: 'Yes, come closer, so I can see you better.
How you cackle! Fight on!'

> 'Who you are, brother, *krr-krr*? Quick!
> We must guard ourselves from Puto.'

'Keep fighting!'

They flapped about: he wasn't one of them.
Nishumbha, the one with prickles, fluted:

> 'We are. We certainly will.
> But you should show yourself.
> Come closer, get a good look at us.'

And Manas was already down off the ridge.
He was happy, laughing, approached
Over the tricky stones, past thorny clumps,
Stumbling, crawling over the scree slope.
And as he clambered, gawping smirking down at them from
  boulders,
Human for sure, a splendid human,
A stray, a juicy morsel,
They signalled with their eyes,
Chanda Munda Nishumbha, those three.
They stood all three together on boulders, facing Puto.

First Chanda let fall his club,
He hopped at Puto, landed short as if by accident,
Lay between boulders, whimpered.
But Puto made no move.

Then Munda, jackal on his hump, threw away his shield,

Stood shieldless.
And Puto made no move.

Nishumbha stared long and hard at Puto,
Saw how out of breath he was, gulping air,
And hopped away like a wagtail.

And Munda, as if sleepwalking, crawled slowly towards his
    shield,
Pulled it to him, ambled backwards across the slope.
And Chanda climbed out from his hollow, club behind his
    back.
They shuffled steadily across the scree, casting cautious
    backward glances.
But Puto made no move.

And then, ten steps away from Puto, they turned their gaze
    from him,
And went for Manas in a frenzy,
For Manas, who saw them coming.
They struck at him with shields and clubs.
Down from his boulder Manas tumbled.

Puto stood there, not moving from his spot.
Manas, fallen backwards, wedged between boulders,
Shouldered his way out, arms guarding his face.
He spluttered rumbled: 'What's this about?
What are you playing at?'

They swung their clubs shields slings at him.
He clambered onto a flat-topped rock.
Their screams as they attacked were horrible.
He whirled and pumped his arms.
The demons enveloped him in fog,
Impossible to see through it. Such anger in him:
'Anyone there? I can't see for fog!
Foggers, damned foggers!'

How they came at him again, stabbed him, bit him,
Rage flaming over Manas.

He crouched low, concentrated.
From the rock, propelled by toes and knees,
Shot straight at them,
Straight at Munda,
Who was knotting his sling to fit around Manas' neck.
He grabbed the damp sticky demon.
It chirped and stretched out long like a salamander,
And became slender as a willow wand in the air.
Manas held it by the hips, pulled it to the scree.
And as it grew thin, squeaking,
He bent it in the middle like a hairpin.

Now the demon swelled again, stretched out.
Manas shoved it with a kick among the rocks.
Trod the protesting snarling writhing thing with his heels,
Squeezed Munda flat, snatched away the sling.

Now pointy-head Nishumbha made a dive at Manas,
Who glanced around, saw him coming,
Dived at Manas, meant to slit his belly open.
He slammed into Manas' hand, the left,
Pincered the palm as tightly as a crab
And twisted round, boring with the spindle on his head.

With a cry Manas flung him off, one shake, like a burr,
Straight onto the rocky ledge before him.
Blood spurted from his hand.
One of Manas' feet held Munda down,
The other was in front of him on the ledge.
Pointy-head Nishumbha had landed with a crash by Manas' foot,
Lay there, rolled limp into the cleft.
Manas kept his foot on Munda.
Nishumbha lay stunned, stretched out.

Now Manas scraped and shoved him down with the other one,
Sucked at his wounded hand.

Rocking, rocking in the hot air, bright sun, Chanda rocked himself,
Saw them both vanish, waited.
They did not reappear.
He spiralled up. Bent his neck to see
Where they both were, what they were doing.
Like a giraffe he stretched his neck long, longer, over his shield,
Swaying flying came slowly close to Manas, who stood,
One leg in the cleft, sucking at his left hand.
Chanda saw: the other two weren't there.
Swayed closer, stretched out longer.

Now the thrum of Manas' sling: crack! against the shield,
Caught a corner, knocked away the shield.
And Chanda floated long-necked, empty-handed,
Stared after the shield as it fell to Manas' feet.

As the helpless demon flew and floated,
Manas cried: 'You! You! Who are you.'
Chanda was so stunned he couldn't give his name.

'Chanda, don't be scared, I'll give you back your shield.
The other two are here as well!'

    'Where are they?'

'Your two friends. Down here, in the cleft!
You can see them, they're waiting for you.
Let me show you.'

Chanda stretched out his long neck.
Manas did not whirl his sling.
Slowly he enticed the demon nearer.
Then, as Chanda hovered close by above the rocks,
Manas grew impatient.

The demon pretended to be stupid,
Looked under his shield instead of in the cleft at Manas' feet.
Manas gripped it by the long probing neck,
Stuffed it in the cleft as if into a pot,
Removed his foot from the first two.

He used Munda's sling to bind all three,
And dragged them,
Slowly dragged them scrambling across the scree behind him.
Dragged them like a sack behind him.

Soon they started stirring, soon they cawed,
Fell down.
Across the hot scree he hauled the gabbling demons.
Beneath the fissures of Manas' arm they fell silent.

RADIANT Manas, demon-bundle at his heels, went up to Puto.
Sling-cloth circling his right arm, he halted,
Wounded hand at his mouth, he sucked blood.

'And you, you stand there. And what will you do to me.'

Puto behind a protecting slab of rock,
Shield slanted over him, waited.

'Will you attack me like these did, the ones I have here?'

    'Who – who – who are you?'

This bloodstained face, this face,
Puto knew this face.
Was it not, he leaned back to look,
Was it not, oh chilling horror,
The face of Manas, Manas back again?
Whom he laid low, who had flown up to the Field,
Whose body the deceiving demons had brought to him.

Now here again, the body. Was burned long ago,
Was a pretend-body, not even a corpse.
They were trying the same trick, because they knew
What suffering this body had caused him.
It was mockery. A wicked trick.
Breathless beneath his shield, Puto, the merest whisper:

> 'Just let them go.'

'What did you say?'

> 'Just let them go, those you're dragging there,
> That bundle. No need for such games.
> Just set them free.
> You can come at me all together.'

'So you too will attack me.'

> 'Just let them go, stop pretending.
> You can come at me as many as you like. Ten more.'

Avert his eyes.
If only he did not have to look at him, this Manas,
The beloved face, his body. But, but, how it paralysed him.

Manas stammered: 'I won't let them go.
We'll soon be done with one another, anyway.'

And it struck Manas, as he drew near:
It is Puto standing there!
He and his Sukunis carried me up here through the air!
And then he stood beneath a tree, held a club,
And he himself, Manas – above a shattered breast,
Spurting blood below him – was drawn higher, pulled away,
Carried backwards through an opening in the leaves,
Through the tree's branches,
And flew away.

'He laid me low.
He did it, this is Puto. He wants to lay me low again.'

Screamed: 'You'll lay me low again.'
Menaced with a furious roar: 'I was on the Field of the Dead.
All that is over. I have returned.'

And sling-cloth on his arm, he hurled a shot at Puto.

'One death I already died, because of you.
A horrible dying, as you know,
A dreadful dying in the snow, you know it.'

With a roar he threw himself on Puto,
Beat him, he sank down, shield above him.
'I'll kill you! But for you there's no returning.'

A groan from under the shield.
A whimper: 'Stop squashing me. Leave me alone. Mercy.'

'I'll kill you.'

> 'You, let me look at you. I beg you.
> Let me up. I want to talk to you.'

Manas moved away, sat gasping, his eyes rolled.
Puto, ash-smeared, long beard, picked himself up,
Mighty man, coercer of demons, stood up straight,
Laid the shield before him on the ground,
Stared breathing hard at Manas,
As the trussed demons hissed down at him.

> 'You are Manas! Manas, you, Manas!'

'And who are you.'

> 'It is you. It is you!'

And Puto quite bewildered.
He lifted up his arms, his face twisted, quivering.
No laughter from him, nor any tears.
And monstrous monstrous joy,
Tempestuous joy, it forced a titter from him
That sounded like a painful whimpering.
And then wild sobs.

He dropped facedown to the scree:

    'You, you! It is you! Returned!'
No thoughts, stammersobs, let it surge through him,
Laughed.
He felt for Manas' legs, embraced them:

    'My child, my child.
    It was not meant to be the end.
    With a club I laid you low.
    It was not the end.'

'What are you saying.'

    'Shiva has fulfilled it for me, more than I prayed for.
    I have done penance. He has released you.
    Shiva is just, Shiva is kind.
    Shiva is the fount of mercy.'

'No one sent me. I came here by myself.
I fought my way across the Field of the Dead.
I came close to dissolution.
I had no body, you took it from me.'

The old man overwhelmed: 'Thanks be to Shiva.'

'Let go my legs.
Why am I still here with you.
What has that old stuff to do with me.
Nishumbha, come!'

And he pulled the bundle with the demons to him.
From the sling he loosed Nishumbha, who had stabbed him.
Nishumbha struck like lightning at prostrate Puto,
Stabbed him in the neck, the arms.
The two bound demons howled in envy when they saw this.

    They piped: 'Stab him! Stab him, Nishumbha,
    In the belly, in the heart.
    Bite him. Spear him in the jaws!'

Manas kicked them, tugged Nishumbha back,
Swung him like a chicken through the air.
He squawked, trussed up with the others.
Manas bundled them together.

'Go away, don't stand around, you Puto.
Be on your way, go home.'

Puto lying there stared at him, groaned, yet still laughed:

>'Manas. Manas. You are Manas?'

'Be off with you. Stop snivelling.
I won't let you escort me back.'

And stepped past him, full of scorn:
'Look at him, you lot. My teacher!
Taught me, and struck me dead, all at once.'

And the demons strained and tottered.
Suddenly he threw them like a flock of doves into the air,
They whirred, rushed back, rushed down again.

> Nishumbha howled: 'You lord, great lord,
> Set us free, we mustn't go beyond this point.
> We must not go into the land of humans.'

'Must not?'

> 'We belong to Ganesha, lord with the elephant's head.
> We are his servants.'

Manas dashed them onto stones, swung them high, dashed them down:
'Whose servants, Ganesha? Say again, who do you belong to?'

They howled.

'Say again, Ganesha.'

> 'You, you.'

'What about me?'

> 'We belong to you.'

He stumbled lurched behind them,
They fluttered whirred over the hot stony slope.
There was no end to the slope.
It led into a ravine. Manas would have to scale its walls.
And he stood sweating, stared at the massive mountainside.
'No more walking. You lot must carry me.'

He untied them, looped the leash around their necks.
And in a flash they transformed themselves
Into Kalongs, flying foxes,
With strong bodies, canine muzzles,
Pointed hairless ears.
Their cries as they flapped up from the ground
Were like cocks crowing.
Brownblack their thick fur,
Brownblack the mighty flight membranes enfolded in their arms.

They waggled yelped could barely leave the ground.
Manas threw himself on Nishumbha's soft back:
'Why do you shiver, Nishumbha?
Did I tie the leash too tight?'

  'The leash is not too tight, lord.
  We can't see by daylight.'

'Why not?'

  'We are blind by day.'

'Don't worry, Nishumbha, you Chanda, Munda.
I shall steer you.'

  'We'll break our heads. You'll fall with us.'

'I'll steer you. Mush! On!
Out of the sun. Even I am burning.
Into the woods now, over snow.'

And the three flying foxes rose blind into the sky,
Nishumbha leading.

He carried Manas, who steered him,
Munda and Chanda behind, on the leash.
Over the ravine, high above the slope
Where Puto stood gazing after them.

Puto there alone, Puto fell to his knees,
Pressed forehead to the ground, and prayed to Shiva:

> 'You shall not let me fall, great lord.
> And if ever I have served you badly,
> You know that I have served you.
> And you shall continue to protect the one who flies there,
> You shall continue to protect my child.'

Stumbled swayed climbed across the hot slope.
Blood dripped from Nishumbha's bite-wounds
Down the bony ash-smeared back.
He fell often, gulped smiled shivered:

> 'He has returned, our beloved child!
> I shall go to Jayanta.
> Our dear child returned!'

THROUGH white clouds and lashing wetness Manas flew.
The mountains down below receded.
Lush foothills came. He could not see them in the lashing clouds.
The cold refreshed him.

The lumbering Kalongs were dazzled.
Their clawed feet stretched out behind them as they flew,
Munda and Chanda willingly towed along.
Nishumbha gave a squawk, the other two yowled behind him.

> 'You lie heavy on my back, great master,
> You weigh on me like a giant.
> Strong Shiva, when he goes away from Kailash

> Riding on his ox
> Could not be heavier.'

Manas heard this, kept silent.

> 'You lie heavy on my back, great master.
>
> When night comes, lovely night,
> And covers the terrible sun,
> Wait until nightfall, then fly on with us.'

Whirling through the lashing clouds.
No thought in Manas
Of how he and Puto came here in the howling storm
Chained together, the dread Sukuni speeding on ahead,
Wooded hills already faded, air foaming, awash with light,
Ripplerustlerush,
And on, directly on, blown on
Into the glimmerflitter, into the cooing tugtwitch.

Nishumbha's back fidgeted and arched:

> 'Go no further. Turn around.
> Become a demon like us.
> You'd be the strongest of us all.'

Manas laughed, snorted: 'Go lower, so we come out of the rain.'

> 'Back, master, come to us on the Field of the Dead,
> Harry the dead, tear souls apart.
> And if gods come along, Ganesha or Kali,
> Then, then – '

The three Kalongs yelped and bleated in their craving,
Sailed on side by side:

> 'Yes, come, turn back, what do you want with humans!
> Fill your mouth whenever the fancy takes you!
> We'll bring you as much as you want.
> Go with us!
> And if Ganesha comes, or Kali…

Help us.'

Rocking keeling tossing up and down through the air.
He thought: I have to see the Earth again. Have to see it in its
    blooming.
It's not like harrying the dead.
How they grow among trees rivers animals,
The people in their cities – I have to see it.
How elephants roam the forests,
Stand at ponds, suck water with their trunks,
Buffalo, white deer, geckos, the langur Hanuman,
Leopards, marbled cats,
And then palm trees, banyans, tua trees.
None of those on the Field of the Dead.

They swung over a broad sandy plain,
A great tawny waste of steppeland stretched below them,
And then rounded hills, forested, quite high, many side by side,
Lines of steep hills.

  'You lie heavy on my back, great master.
  Oh we are hungry.'

'It'll soon be dark, Nishumbha.
This is the lovely great Earth. We'll go down onto it.
What do you eat?'

  'From trees. Bring us to a dark wood, great master.'

'Not people?'

  'To a dark wood, great master.'

Fluttering flying across a chain of hills.
Glowing air.
Poplars grew far up the slopes, acacia in thick stands.
The huge flying foxes perched dangling in strong branches,
Hung quietly by their claws, heads down,
Slept, though it was night.

MANAS tumbled blissful onto an acacia, a springy bed.
First he roared with delight, as he had that morning in the
 mountains.
The kiru went through his thoughts,
The tumble in the ravine,
Wandering through the mountain forest.

Fiercely, fiercely he roared out from his tree-couch, rocked.
The Kalongs were frightened.
Creatures rustled away, scolded nervously from a distance.
Then he lay quiet, sated. He stretched out,
Went to sleep like the flying foxes.

A big bear lumbered through his dreams.
The sea of grass was man-high.
The black bear ambled through the sea of grass,
Looking for Manas, rose on its hind legs,
To sniff above the grass-heads.
Did not see him.
Paws raised, it passed once quite close to him.
Manas shivered inwardly in delight, the bear ambled past.
And with lustful feelings, but unsated, he woke up,
Found himself sleeping in his acacia bed.
Black night still.
And again the whooping joy, enormous,
Thrusting through him, urging, banishing all sleep:
Returned! Kiru, I, I!

The whole night long he roared out in the forest.
Pounced on a collared bear that came out from its tree-hole,
Fought with it a while,
Flung it by the throat away through the air.
Waited for it to reappear.
But off it went puffing, squeaking.

The Kalongs woke up, moved about,
Wanted to carry him,
Plundered trees, walnuts, mulberries,
Stuffed themselves sleepy.

IN THE morning came a *trum rum*. Drums beating *trum rum*.
Men among the trees, clad in white garments,
Men going down into the river.
The sun had risen clear and bright,
Their arms lifted to it.

Manas watched tenderly from the hill by the black woods,
Licked his lips,
Kept tight hold of the tawny foxes.
They wanted to tear loose at the scent of humans.

'Stop yowling, stop squealing. Those are people, they'll hear us.'

The foxes strained. He kicked them, they fell silent.
The foxes were blind in daylight,
Were avid to hurl themselves on humans.

And Manas, ready to shout out in delight,
Clambered with them along the forest edge, hesitant, happy,
Stepped out at a gap
Into harsh light, slowly through the tall grass.
Climbed down the hill towards the river.
The Kalongs balked and braced,
They clamoured struggled, tugged by Manas' leash,
They tugged back, stalled, yelped protests,
Foamed clawed crowed in the grass.

That harsh light! They were forced out into blazing light.
Manas ahead whistled as he pulled at them:
'One two, those are people, little manikins
Paddling splashing in the water, ducking in the water.

One two, little manikins,
Hope they don't drown in the riverkins.
If you could only see them.
Hope the fishikins don't bitikins,
And their feetikins don't get wet,
Or their bellies. Or their shoulders.
But the sun will quickly dry them off,
Little people all together, nice and dry,
Lovely sunikins up there for them.'

He turned, urged the Kalongs on:
'Come come, little beasties, little devils, Kalongs, quiet now.
Just take a look, one two, one two,
How they splash.
Clothed in white, a hundred manikins!
A whole forest of them.
How they all run about, unafraid of one another.'

He let out a laugh, smacked his mouth to stop it.
Squatted down beside the slavering Kalongs:

'If only you could see them! A hundred manikins,
Jumping about, exchanging greetings, making gestures.
Tigers, they're scared of them,
They're scared of tigers, Kalongs.
But not of manikins.'

He threshed on through the grass towards them,
Tottered on tiptoe, pulled faces, dragged the Kalongs:
'None of them fears the others.'
Laughed, smacked his mouth.

Suddenly the tall grass ended,
The riverbank was there, short grass and stones,
And with a howl the Kalongs broke loose, raced ahead,
Snapping at air: demons on the scent of humans.
Manas racing up behind.
They tugged flapped flew on blindly

To the river, in among the people.

Screams, cries from all the people,
They hurled themselves in the river, dug into sand.
Protests, senseless headlong flight, and howling,
And falling, lying there.
The demons in amongst them, after them, their claws in some,
Teeth embedded in them. They licked hot blood.

Manas kicked them, beat them, tugged at them.
He cried out behind the people, hooted:
'Hah haha! Why d'you run away, why run away!'

He forced the Kalongs to the ground, laughing.
And when the people kept running away
He urged the Kalongs on behind.
'Catch them. Why do they run!'
He let some be brought down.
They cried piteously under the Kalongs' claws,
He shoved the foxes back,
Prodded the people, had a good look,
Ran fingers through human blood.

'But why did you run away?'

The Kalongs licked his fingers. He choked them.
Then he stood still.
People whimpering around him.
He dragged the Kalongs back into the grass,
Ignored their bracing squealing rearing on hind legs.

In the forest he picked up a lump of root,
Beat the three of them on backs and heads:
'What is it you want?
That's for the blood!
You're supposed to eat leaves, or what I give you.
You're supposed to eat leaves.'

And sat for an hour with the Kalongs in the forest,

Thought how small and ludicrous those people were
And how they had run away from him.
Tied up the Kalongs as they lay there snarling,
Tied the Kalongs to a tree,
The tawny lumbering flying foxes, still blood-savage,
Straining at the leash and jumping up behind him.

And went to the forest edge, went alone,
Stood peering over the tall grass for another glimpse of people.
Saw some still lying down there, young and old,
And others coming to their aid, carrying them away.

His little thoughtful eyes squinted at the scene:
'How ludicrous they are.
They help each other, pick each other up.
They don't hurt each other.
And to me they're so hostile.'

His thoughts were friendly, he was happy:
'Such funny creatures. Funny creatures.
I could fall in love with them. But they're too timid.
I shall see that the Kalongs don't hurt them.'
And stared in fascination as down below a man was comforted,
White-haired, bleeding just a little,
How they kissed his hands, massaged his knees
And everything they did. Their weeping.

He slept.

BUT behind him in the forest the Kalongs were not asleep.
Manas had beaten them with a lump of root.
Their ribs hurt.
He would not take them to humans.
They wanted to be gone.
They bit rasped nibbled at their leashes.

While he moved about the forest they kept quiet,
In fear.

But Nishumbha was possessed by his thirst for blood.
He would huff and puff, come what may.
Nibbled gnawed tore,
His claws tore constantly at the leash
Until the leash lay loose about his neck.

Then he dropped down, spat, waddled to one side.
The other two cackled, aghast, in fear.
But he ignored them, waddled on,
Blindly towards the light.

On he waddled, heedless of bumps and scratches.
The other two crowed grunted, would not quieten down.
What was happening.
They dangled from their branches, horrified.

Nishumbha crawled out of the forest,
He was dazzled.
Sniffed right and left, the demon, his long tongue lolled.
Then off he flew towards the scent
Where they were gathering bodies.

His aim was good. Flying and leaping he brought two down.
The others fled.
One he covered with his flight membrane, held him, squashed him,
Sucked him dry.
The other he scrabbled with a paw to one side.
The man screamed, until he too was taken.

And on he went, the lumbering brownblack Kalong.
Clawed down another human,
A female running to one of the dead.
Covered her. But was already vomiting. He'd had enough.

Then he didn't know what was up with him.

Was drunk. Flapped low
Along the riverbank, blinking, groping for a tree to perch in.
He lay on misty ground near the village, in grass, flat on his belly.
Began to wheeze. Snored.
In sleep his feet clawed for a branch he could not find.
Drums beating in the village.
Out they came hasting with sticks for a basting,
Surrounded him, knocked him about,
Arrows impaled him, cudgels assailed him,
He flapped up crowing, waggled his wings, yawned.
He spat blood, scratched, and lay flat on his belly,
Head under his flight membrane,
And snored on.

Ropes ropes from every side thrown over him,
So he could not lash out, and they could roll him along.
He snored and yawned.
Ropes around the feet, and up and around the chest.
And tugged tight, tug tug.

> Nishumbha thought: 'It's Manas.
> What will he do to me?
> Because I got drunk. He'll beat me.
> I can take it.'

He let them drag him over the ground,
The fat monster, sated Kalong.
They hauled two corpses along behind.
The Kalong sniffed about him at their scent.
The people wailed.

BY NOW it was already noon across the steppeland, hills.
Manas, escaped from the Field of the Dead, Manas thought:
I'm hungry. But it's hot. I'll rest a while.

When the sun, the sun goes down
Then I'll go to them and find something to eat.

He strolled back into the forest, lay in grass,
Looked up to see if any monkeys were about.
The Kalongs were dangling there. Whining, rocking.
Why were they rocking?
He asked: 'Why are you whining?
You're hungry. So am I. Wait till the sun has gone.'

They kept whining. He jumped up.
They had never whined like this.
Only two were dangling in the tree, two ponderous rocking
     creatures.
'And where's Nishumbha. You're not asleep.'
They whined, would not show their heads.
Manas thought: He's hiding from me, stupid thing,
Or someone has come and taken Nishumbha away.

'Where is he? Where's he hiding?'

    'No, not hiding.'

'Who took him? Why didn't you help him.
Come down here!'

They flapped down, leaped waddled crowed:

    'Who took him? Come come, great master,
    We are not to blame.
    He wouldn't listen. Nishumbha has no sense.'

'And now? What's going on?'

    'He chewed through the leash, is gone.'

Manas darted to the leash. Chewed through.
Stood snarling, beat the Kalongs with his fists,
Squeezed their throats, hit them on the nose and in the eyes,
And with the leash tied feet and wings together.

They had to hang there on the tree, let him beat them,

They wailed and whimpered.
Hung there tightly bound. Could not come down
Unless he would untie them.
They had no defence against birds and snakes that came at them.

Then Manas stormed out of the forest,
Peered down from the hill, saw nothing. The valley empty.
But there were huts. He stormed off to them.
He wants to steal humans, that beast Nishumbha.
He won't listen. Has to stuff his belly.
The big brown thing lying there, that must be him.
There by the huts,
He must have lumbered there to scoff and scoff and drink his fill.

Manas ran closer.
And people all around the Kalong.

Why was he stretched out so still, and ropes around him?
Manas saw this from a distance, groaned.
Ropes around Nishumbha, the lumbering motionless flying fox.
They've struck him down! He, he's dead!
He's paid the price. He's caught it.
They tied him up and dragged him here,
And beat him to death. My demon.

And dumbfounded Manas at the huts,
He came to a halt, panting.
Dumbfounded, knew not what's what.

They all standing, not moving.
After a while men came forward from those standing there.
Came with spears and bows, slings and sticks,
In a row, a curved line, uttering harsh cries,
In a line behind him.

He was surrounded. They danced this way and that.
Manas thought: This is my dream. That's the bear.
They're crazy.

They've struck down my Kalong.
First they strike him down, now they want to capture me.

When he moved he showed no trace of fear.
They hurled spears
That he waved aside as if brushing flies away.
Stark naked Manas,
He had lost his loincloth careening from the forest.

Now they ceased their shouting.
A big dark fellow with a shield came forward,
Called out: 'Hey, hey! You!'
Behind him they were drumming, dancing.
Manas thought: Let him come a little closer.
These are semi-savages, Bhils.
I've never killed a single one of them.
I couldn't tame the Kalongs,
And so I gave them a good thrashing.
I've done nothing to these here. Just let him come.

Again the man called out: 'Hey you, hey you.'
Then threw his spear: 'Hey you, you deaf?'

Manas grabbed the spear, weighed it in his hand.
Instead of throwing it, walked,
Walked calmly towards the man,
Grasped him by the topknot,
Hit him with the spear about the head
And on his back.

At once the man fell down in the grass,
His shield dropped at his side.
A shower of spears rained down on Manas.
He batted them aside.

What were these little people thinking? Kill him?
Come at him with spears and arrows,
At him who had been on the Field of the Dead?

At first Manas was merely angry,
Then all at once felt sad, why he did not know.
Why did he grow sad? Why was his heart so heavy all at once,
As if a black spring were welling up in him,
Had been blocked by sand and now suddenly broke gushing
    through?
As when you hold a steel blade to a flame
And a sombre bluish shimmer overruns it.

'Why am I sad?' thought Manas.
He sat in the sand, let his head droop,
Sighed and waved his hand as arrows flew: 'Oh do stop it.'
His sadness, dismal sadness grew.
No one spoke a kindly word, no one wanted to be kind to him,
Out of all these hundreds who all knew and nodded to each
    other.
He was alone.
They planned to finish him off
Like they had Nishumbha, still snoring over there.

Quietly they began to throw ropes over Manas.
And then howls, tugging: Manas leashed!
They've put me on a leash, he thought,
So heavy had his sadness grown.
Ah, ropes, on him.

Now they tightened the ropes about him.
He couldn't shrug the ropes off.
They tugged at him, howling.
He stood up. Could only go along.
Such sorrow. What had he ever done to them?
He was ready enough to go with them.
Maybe they would talk to him,
Maybe his black grief would then flow away,
But anyway, it was good to go with them.

Off to a wretched village:

They pulled him past miserable huts of wood.
Drums were beating.
They halted. Manas thought: I'll sit down.
The Bhils were happy to see him sit.
They thronged about him in a circle.
More and more of them laid hold of the ropes,
Manas saw even children pulling on the ropes.
And was happy happy,
It was good that he'd come with them.

Three men stepped into the circle, stepped close to Manas,
Were dressed in white cloth. The village priests.
Sat facing Manas amongst the ropes,
Placed little vessels, flowers, offering bowls before them.
The oldest turned his gaze on sorrowing Manas:

>'You understand our language?'

Manas squinted at them, nodded.

>'You know what we are saying to you,
>And you can answer in a way that we can understand?'

Manas was happy they were speaking to him.
'I understand you.
You are Bhils, you speak the Bhil language.
What is your village called?'

A tremor ran through the men, loud buzzing in the crowd.
The elder pulled himself together:

>'So you are human like us?
>You have bones limbs and a face like ours,
>You are brown.
>Your face has the lines of a nobleman from Rajputana.'

'And that's what I am. Or was.
You know me well. I come from Rajputana.'

>'No, you have not come from Rajputana.

>Tell the truth.
>We are the judges of this village.
>You must respect our laws. You must not lie.'

'I come from Rajputana.
But I haven't come from there just now.
I've come from farther off, far off.'

>'From where?'

'Yes, from where. Don't ask.'

>'You must say, from where.'

'Just leave it. I won't say.
I mean you no harm. I'm glad you're speaking with me.'

>'But we cannot release you from this obligation.'

'What obligation?'

>'To tell us where you have just come from.'

'And why not?'

The priest turned to the others, exchanged glances with them:

>'Because... because we don't believe you.
>You come here from the North,
>Out of the forest, maybe from the mountains.
>Your face is that of a nobleman from Rajputana.
>But you have no clothes, no jewels.
>We do not know – '

The old man fell silent, held hands up to his face.

'What don't you know?'

>'You can imagine.
>When a prince goes on foot, is naked,
>Comes out of the forest, alone,
>And monstrous beasts are with him,
>Then... no one can believe he is a prince.
>And when he – '

'Go on.'

> 'I shall go on.
> You see how everyone here is trembling.
> We are peaceful people. Our lives are hard.
> We pray to the gods as best we can.
> We can think of nothing we have left undone.
> But there must be something.'

Wailing behind him. 'What is it then? Tell me.'

'We…'

And now the elder and the two priests came to his side,
Pressed foreheads to the dirt.
His voice was low and husky:

> '…We do not believe that you are human.
> That anything that looks like you could be a human,
> Even though it has the face of a Rajput noble.
> You bring with you evil creatures.
> They are Kalongs, but Kalongs are small and placid,
> They live beside us, we protect them.
> Yours, though, are monsters, the one back there included.
> He has drunk our blood. Now he is sleeping.'

'You did right to beat him. He won't listen.'

> > 'We thought him a demon,
> > The other two Kalongs as well.
> > And you, you… also seem to us to be a demon.'

They bent low again, rubbed foreheads in the dirt.
Loud bitter wailing at Manas' back.
He turned his head to them, then chewed his lips.
Behind him they were pounding drums.
Masked men with clappers
Danced into the circle around Manas, stood still,
Observed Manas,
Who looked at them, and felt drained.

He thought: They drain my energy.
Instead of being nice to me, they make me faint.
I feel quite limp.
His knees were hurting, he stood up with a groan.
The judges scrambled to their feet.

'I am no demon. You do me an injustice.
You have laid my Kalong low, and now you dare to call me demon.'

They drummed harder.

'Stop that drumming. I am no demon,
Did you not hear me? What's the drumming for?
My ears are bursting.'

    'Where have you come from, you must tell us.'

'From the Field of the Dead. Where else.'

    'So you say.'

'Yes, yes, the Field of the Dead. Now what?
Stupid Bhils.
Stop the blasted drumming!
And what has happened
If I say I come from the Field of the Dead?
Were you ever there? Do you know what it is?
You and your stupid clappers.
I want to know what you did to Nishumbha.
I'll answer none of your questions.
You are stupid, you are nothing. I shall not answer.
Make way.'

With eyes that struck fear, arms raised, fists clenched,
Angry, right cheek contorted in pain, right eye pinched,
He stood among them.

The flying fox on the floor vomited, brought up blood.
Manas kicked it to its feet. He too felt like vomiting.
If he only could.

Horrible, horrible the black spring welling up within him,
Ghastly with its sand and mud,
That hideous desolate spring.
Among what monsters had he fallen, into what hell.
What did his tongue taste of,
How everything suddenly disgusted him, slid away from him.

And here the monkey-man still talking to him,
The elder with the long hands,
The Bhil priest and his greasy unguent.
If only it doesn't melt in the sun,
That layered heap of pasted muck, it really cannot hold together,
And will have to dribble down, a wet cowpat between his own two feet.
Maybe a hand should squeeze his head,
Crack the shell and let the muck run off.

The black mandrill with the sacrificial gear was still addressing him,
Boring deeper into him, dared bore into him,
As if the black spring were not flowing fast enough already,
The dog the dung-beetle.
The priest whispered, eyes averted:

> 'I will tell you, stranger, unknown man,
> Straight out how it is with you.
> Maybe you cannot form the words: your brain is closed to it.
> From one birth to another we have no memory,
> But I know it for you.
> You Rajput prince must have been a cruel man.
> For your rebirth after you were dead,
> One single person was not enough.
> They had to chase you from the Field of the Dead
> And back to Earth accompanied by demons.
> The demons, three of them, and this Rajput prince:
> All together these make you!

> Shiva shattered you to make you gentler,
> Then he could not tolerate you on his Field.
> You will have spent but seconds flying on the Field
> Before it spat you out.
> Although the Field of the Dead is rife with crimes and sins,
> You it could not contain.
> The sins you have committed must be truly vile.'

And Manas heard this.
He clapped hands to his ears, his mouth hung open.
And the spring gushed black within him,
It surged into his throat, his jaws, his mouth,
Stormed, raged through him, ebbed and flowed.
And Manas felt: I was on the Field of the Dead.
I am that Manas who stood at the window,
By a pool, and I would not look outside.
How long long long must I stand,
How long long long, endlessly long must I stand at the window,
At the window standing and waiting, awful waiting for what, for
    what?
For dying, it was for dying.
Fluttering in the wind, over ice.
Dreaming, gasping in the wind.
Nanda Devi, Nanda Devi looming through the storm.

From tears came trembling,
From tremble-trembling came a fainting
And blindness. Blindness locking in.
He groaned, groaned as he stood up,
Both eyes squeezed shut, lips thrust out,
Ears closed, mouth slack.
He rocked and swayed. The black spring was washing him away.

He screamed, encircled by the Bhils.
Spittle ran along the runnel of his lips.
A terrible roaring from his wide-open mouth: *Oh, oh!*

Beat his breast, his eyes stayed closed.

The priests thought the moment opportune.
They paced around the giant with tympani and hand drums.
They flicked his legs, his belly, with little ropes and sticks,
Blew incense smoke at him.

The dread mariner noticed nothing of it,
He had lost all ballast from his vessel
And the sea was bearing him away.
The sea roared, and the storm,
And Manas roared in rage, turned round in circles,
Brandished fists before his dumbfounded mouth.

His groans woke the two Kalongs in the forest.
They trembled horribly:
Manas is running here, means to slay us.
And their fearful cries, they were still tied up,
Penetrated to the humans down below.

> 'Hear that, wicked man, Rajput prince,
> The others up there, your companions, are raging.
> Your soul is mortally hurt.
> We have seen the truth of you.
> They are breaking apart.
> Shiva is strong, Shiva helps!
> You shall creep under the earth, Rajput prince, to the beetles.'

But he heard nothing, not the roaring of the Kalongs
Nor the exorcising chant.
The ship was speeding on a sea of blackness,
Capsizing, coming aright,
The sailor on the ship swallowed cloying water, spat it out,
Grabbed at ropes, was blinded, swallowed water, chewed water,
As it dashed against his nose and mouth, and knew:
Atone, atone, I am a sinner,
I am cursed, I am cursed. I am not for saving!
This the punishment. How long yet.

Let it come.
My gullet. If I could only choke.

His stomach heaved: the Field there with him.
He closed his eyes to see it all.
Paused his circling.
Surging surging there below, the Earth to which he had been harried.
And saw, saw the black Bhils, the Kalong,
The big Kalong licking at the blood it had vomited up,
Manas scuffed some to it.
He staggered, stumbled closer.
Knocked down a priest. Then stood by Nishumbha,
Touched his head with a foot, breathed softly, breathed:
'Up, Nishumbha, here we are.
We're going away, away. Carry me away.'

And as the Kalong scratched and licked about him,
Manas shoved at him more roughly:
'Up, Nishumbha, away, we must away.'
Kicked him on the ears.
Nishumbha squealed, flew at him in anger, snapped.

This the Kalong that would not listen to him.
And Manas growled a low growl:
So, it thought him weak.
Kicked him in the throat, under the chin,
Laid a good one on his neck that woke the creature up.
It flapped up, fell back to the ground,
Crawled drooling on the ground.

Now Manas grabbed it by a hind leg,
Held on, grimly silent as the creature struggled,
Pressed down the wings.
He landed another blow on the monster's neck,
Then flung himself heavily onto its back,
And at once it knew who the rider was, felt Manas there.

And at once stretched out its wings.
At once snapped apart the ropes they had thrown around it,
And at once crept, Manas on the red-brown back,
Forward, swaying, snorting.
The black Bhils scattered hastily, with cries and howls.

At once Nishumbha, the Kalong, lurched across the ground,
Turned, flapped into the air a little,
Uttered his sharp bleating cry.
And he was gone, across the dry grey plain,
Gone with Manas high above the green riverbank.

Once more Manas saw the plain, the riverbank,
He groaned into Nishumbha's ear:
'We're flying away, Nishumbha. We must fly far away.
Fly, oh fly, Nishumbha.'

      'Yes.'

'Curse this land. How did I end up here.
I came to fetch you back, Nishumbha, you.
If they'd beaten you to death, it's no more than you deserve,
If they'd skinned you alive, the fat Bhils, the blacks,
If they'd dragged you into their temple.
You, and you'd have gone back to your Field all broken,
Ganesha with his elephant's trunk would have laughed,
And stuck you in an icy hole.'

Nishumbha as he flew:

      'Stop your growling, master.
      You won't send me back.
      I made a mistake.'

Manas groaned: 'On, on, fly on.'

THE FOREST was there.
The two Kalongs dangled in a cinnamon tree,
Not moving, overrun with big white ants.
They wheezed.
A panther lurked beneath Chanda's dangling snout
From time to time leaped up,
But did not bite, repelled by the demon's smell,
And would not leave, attracted by the yawns and wheezing.

Then it was scared off by the crack of branches, Nishumbha
 coming,
A frightful crash as Manas landed with Nishumbha.
Manas stood beneath the tree on his own two legs.
Two tugs and the ropes were pulled apart.
The demons flapped down, writhed on the ground,
Shook off ants.

Manas stood, leashes dangling in his hands.
Not a word from Manas.
Darkly he harnessed all three to one leash, as before,
Then stood like a rock beside them,
A long while.
The forest began to darken.
Silent and still as a rock was Manas.

He threw himself onto Chanda, beat his back.
Into the air again.
And crashed through branches, up and on.
Flew over treetops with the three of them.
Plains below, the riverbank, the river, huts,
Nary a downward glance.

The Kalongs flapped along at no great height.
A dust storm blew. Manas buried himself in Chanda's pelt.
Silent for long hours.
When it grew dark, Chanda heard him whispering on his back,
 and cursing,

Felt the man's hands clutching at his pelt
Pressing ever closer to him.

In the night Manas whispered: Hungry.
They swept low over a settlement.
Hungry, hungry, Manas groaned.
Moon shone fiery red.

Near a village in the plain they came down.
Manas drank from a well.
Then the giant, arriving like an errant Shade,
Knocked gates down, fences down.
The village was in uproar.

He grabbed jars from sheds.
Whatever he found he drank, shook it out,
Asked no leave, gave no thought to the Kalongs
As they harried the screaming people.
Went lipsmacking into a grove of cedars near the village,
Lay down.

When the sun rose he moved up higher,
To a deep limestone cave.
All four of them slept there in the dark,
Kalongs on the ceiling, Manas in a corner.

Stars came out, flashing flickering.
Now Manas crawled out of the cave. Doubting, whispering,
Chewed his lips. Am I a demon?
And chewed his lips: Hope the Kalongs don't see me.
His eyes glowed: Maybe I'll make a move on Kailash.
I'd like to tear Shiva apart.
And shook from the feet up,
Like a mountain about to split asunder.
'I don't know why I've been sent back,
What I'm supposed to do on Earth.'
Struggled with himself.

He rousted the Kalongs from the cave. Then dug himself in,
Dug himself into the damp soil in the corner,
Tried to bury himself deeper and deeper,
Groaned gasped: 'I shan't walk the Earth again.'

The three dreadful Kalongs blocked the entrance to the cave,
Their bodies stood tall.
Stuck their snouts in to see what Manas was up to.
But the cave had bends, with niches and protrusions.
They only heard him muttering and gasping at the back,
Shifting dirt and stones like a busy mole.

They bayed bleated. In there he groaned:
'Manas escaped from the Field of the Dead,
Manas with the hands of a lion, teeth of a tiger.'

    They squealed: 'Fists of stone.'

He toiled and roared: 'Manas stands in a cave,
Stands at the wall, digs in the corner at dirt that's damp.
And roars and roars: I don't know why I'm back.
Just to have wet hands from scrabbling at the rock!
Just to see nothing but desolate steppelands!
Nothing but stupid humans,
I, who once was human too.'

    They squealed: 'Come out, Manas.
    Come with us, come along now.'

He roared: 'I'll go with you to the Field of the Dead.
I must tear someone apart. I want to go into battle.'

And whole long days Manas dug, dug in the cave.
Finally no words emerged.
Only his low groans and the crack of thrown rocks
Told the Kalongs he was still alive.
They dared not go back in.

But one night without warning he crawled to the entrance,
Hollow-eyed, chin quivering,

Daubed from head to toe in mud.
They snarled in his direction.
Arms dangling, dull-eyed, he blew air from him:
'But can I actually die?'
Stood, scraped shoulders legs against the rockface.
Kept asking the same question.
They did not understand.

In the middle of the night his face changed.
He seemed to see the cave, the night, the Kalongs.
He summoned Nishumbha to him, petted him a long while,
Then lay on him, but would not let him fly.
He seemed to fall asleep there.

Then Nishumbha felt Manas growing heavy, heavier,
Manas squashing him in fury, in a spasm.
Nishumbha squawked and fidgeted. Manas wheezed.
His arms were made of iron. He beat at Nishumbha's throat.
'Up, up,' he cried, always 'up!'
The other Kalongs came flapping.
'Up, up,' constantly from Manas,
Though he was squashing Nishumbha to the ground
Until he almost choked.
It was one wild stretching motion.
Then he relaxed. 'Up, up,' in Nishumbha's ear.
He was lighter now, Nishumbha crawled.
The Kalongs spread their wings.
'I want to go into battle.'

>They whinnied: 'Where then.'

He breathed: 'Onward.'

They flew, cutting through the night.
From time to time they touched down. They were thirsty,
Drank and bayed, terrorising people.
They overflew rounded hills of trees.
Little flying foxes bobbed like butterflies alongside.

The air wafted streaks of flowery scent.
Treetrunks rose like columns in dark woods,
Green parrots, big monkeys, all asleep just now.
Giant black butterflies with bloody markings,
Flowers with a sulphur-yellow calyx, climbing lilies,
Everything down there alive.

And how terrible: it had still not let go of Manas.
Hot tears came to Manas' eyes
As black treetops rose and fell below them.
The moon did not want to rise.

This seething surging in him, urging him
Back to the Field.
Yes, that was it, he'd head back to the Field,
To sorrow, sorrow.
Now there it was before his eyes, dazzling him:
Danu and Daksha, he had lived with them.
The shepherd boy. To them,
It all came back again, came back, back. Go!
And tears burst from him.
And his roaring, his laments,
Whimpering full of yearning for them, and for himself.
And down below more rounded forest-covered hills,
A hundred kinds of creature in them,
Thorny plants palms and ants beetles lizards.

As if something stirred him from within,
As if he had been forced up from the bottom of the sea,
Thus did Manas lie, stretched out on Nishumbha's swaying back.

And now he felt, for the first time felt
That he was flying, and had no part of anything below.
He could feel Nishumbha, the air. Smelled flowers.
Lifted up his head, his breath heaved.
Looked up with a sob.
No stars to be seen. There were stones.

When a cluster of huts came below them, the Kalongs flapped
    down.
Manas wanted them to land.
His feet trod soft ground. He stretched out on the ground.

When he stepped into a hut, and without a word
Began shovelling in the cooked rice he found,
An old woman stood there with a torch of twigs.
A man, a child appeared as well,
Watched without fear, in disgust and anger, as Manas guzzled.

They raised a cry, they cursed. He kept guzzling.
He was glad, the noise pleased him.
The woman, ragged and ugly as she was,
Came up to Manas, grabbed the bowl from his hand,
Splashed water from a jug at him, with curses.
Manas gulped and gulped, was startled.

The woman flung spilled rice at his face.
He stepped back to the door, wiped his mouth, his legs.
The three of them, woman, man and child,
Scolding horribly, came at him with sticks and brooms.
Manas, still wiping his mouth, pushed his way out.
He had to scare away the woman
Who came after him with a stick and threw it at him.

He slipped behind the huts to find his Kalongs.
Every few steps he stood quite still.
Sobbing gulping were all past now: little jolts of laughter rose up
    in him.
How strange it all was: that fat woman, the child.
They grabbed the bowl from his hand as he was about to eat,
Took it from him. Splashed him.
He was still wet. He'd be ashamed to let the Kalongs see.

It was magical. He laughed laughed:
The fat woman who grabbed away the bowl

And cursed, cursed: it was a woman.
Sat laughing on the ground, felt his fingers:
Rice stuck to them, he hadn't managed to eat his fill.
Sucked at his fingers, lay down in the sand, was happy.
Full of love he was, full of love.

'I had nothing to eat, Chanda.
They gave me nothing. We'll find another place.'

And off they flew.
Stretched out, Manas stretched on Chanda.
His limbs felt warm. Little giggles kept erupting.

THEY flew along the flashing Indus.
The sturdy flying foxes flapped low in reeds,
Among purple herons, snow-white egrets.
Now and then, steered by Manas, they flew low over water.
Dark humps reared from the surging river,
A big beast, a crocodile, leaped, plunged back, splashed.
Fish leaped high: fish eagles already diving on them.

Over white sand flats, windswept, Manas flew out across the sea,
Out to the source of all the rolling thundering endless rumbling,
Where white foam sprayed tower-high,
Out over the endless radiant sea.

Brown-black, silent under him the flying foxes.
The radiant heaving blue.
The sun a thousand torches on his back.
Light breeze over coastal dunes.
Flying foxes on gliding wings, the breeze lifted them, tossed them.

Wave-mountains assault the beach, line after line,
Heave up, curl over, roll onto the beach.
And their rolling rushing sweeping in,
Rolling cold-exhaling gliding,

Then speeding flying,
And crashing, drumming,
And they are shattered, smashed to pieces, dragged away.

Out of the blue a green, a white, towering like clouds,
White overwhelming the shore, the coconut palms, the
 mangroves.
A mighty sea out there,
The source of every wave, watery mass on watery mass,
Huge expansive outsized sea,
Overlain by the sun's heat,
Loaded up with fires, not steaming,
Heaped-up store of gathered waters,
Steel-blue sea that fearless held the sun's reflection,
And crashed and breathed.

The Kalongs were nervous when they heard the crashing
 down below.
Chanda, the demon, groaned.

'Don't shake, don't tremble, Chanda,
Fly steady, great hound.
You've been in Himavat, have clambered in rocky gullies,
You've seen the panther and the tiger.
Down there lies a being, no other like it on the Earth.
It's godlike or a god, Chanda, a great god.
Breathe in its breath, Chanda, listen to its voice.
Did you ever hear a voice like that? You lose your soul.'

 'Is it a great dead thing, Manas? What is the god called?'

'The greatest there is.
Shiva and the lightning may perhaps be greater.
No need to see it, you can feel it with your eyes closed.
It's sumptuous, bluer than the sky:
We're flying over it, Chanda.'

On Chanda's back Manas twirled around,

His hand let go of Chanda's pelt,
And he rolled.
The flying fox lurched trembled, groaned out:

    'Such a great god, watch out, master, watch out for it.'

Manas screamed for joy into the hot air,
Arms stretched out above him.
He gave a kick, and with every swelling wave he grunted: *Ah, oah, oh, oah.*
And rigid with delight, taut with delight,
He let himself, let himself
Fall from Chanda's back
And roll across his wings
Down into the windy air
From up high, through the swaying fissured air
Into the crashing water.

It closed gurgling over him, gave him up again,
Held the brown strong stretched-out body.
Up above, the flying foxes bayed and cast about.
Manas dived dug kicked and trod: *Oh, oah.* Wash, wash.
He kicked and spat.
The sea rolled past in gentle waves.
A voice came from the sea, contented rumbling:

    'Now I have you, have you, have you.'

Manas spat: 'Have who?'

    'I have you.'

'I have who?'

    'Manas. From the Field of the Dead.
    Him. I have you.'

'That's right. You know me.'

    'I have you. Manas from the Field of the Dead.
    I'm glad to take you in.

> I know you from Milam glacier, when the water burst through,
> You slipped away from me, hid behind a rock.
> I am water, strong water,
> Water that once failed to swallow you.
> Now here I am!'

Manas swung his arms, started swimming:
'You couldn't hold me. Didn't knock me down.'

> 'I have you, have you.'

And Manas lay beneath the fingers of the sea
That spun lifted carried him away.
He spat, was joyful: 'Wash, wash.'

The sea roared *hurr-hah, hurr-hah!*
As avid and voracious as Lal Gulam
When Savitri came along the mountain path.

> 'No need to praise me, I have you, have you.
> You can praise me afterwards.'

'What comes after, you don't know and I don't know.
Washing, washing, rolling, turning.
Water, salty sea, you are divine.
You spring from Shiva's head, you're of his blood.'

The waves beat down on Manas in his ecstasy,
The sea's cries grew more fervent, its colours sparkled:

> 'Wrong song. Your mouth is stupid.
> Your stupid mouth. Into your mouth.
> I have you, *hurr-hah*, you just don't know it yet,
> I have you, I'm already gnawing at you.
> Crumpling you.
> First I flay your skin.
> Then I tear your ears to ribbons.
> Then down your throat I pour, *hurr-hah*,
> You'll see.

I'll grab your tongue, wind it about my hand,
And then I'll stuff it down your throat,
Squash it down into your gullet.'

Manas swam on.

'You don't know what I'm saying, *hurr-hah*,
I shall choke you. I have you, have you,
And I'm glad.'

'Nonsense, nonsense. *Hurr-hah*.'

How the sea roared. Up it reared.
Manas was tumbled in the roaring sea.
Lay on his back, sank, was carried high, tipped over.
He summoned the Kalongs from a wave-crest with a
    primal scream:
'Chanda, hear me, the sea is roaring.
See where I am.
Wash, wash, washing, here!
Wash away the cave, wash away the black Bhils!
Washerwoman, roar. Scrub me, scour me!'

'Tear you apart, swallow you.'

How the sea hurled itself on him,
Manas trumpeting whooping.
Called: 'Kalongs!' Whooped: 'Kalongs!'
A mountainous wave carried him away to bury him.
So Manas pulled himself higher.
Like a fish he sped high out of the rushing wave-mountain,
Straight up to where Chanda flapped, bending his neck down,
    snuffling.

Manas shot up through hot shimmering air,
Spume flicked uselessly at his heels.
His wet arms clung to Chanda's neck.
He was about to fall,
But Chanda sensed his move, and slowed.

And then there was Manas, lying on fur, catching his breath.
Catching his breath.

Below them lay the rushing roaring sea.
Manas rode quite passive over the blue baying scolding sea,
Spat water, and dried off.
Half in a daze he shifted from Kalong to Kalong,
Steered them half asleep.
They crowed, glad to have him back.
He looked down with sleepy eyes, smiled, enjoyed the sun.
And for hours and hours the hot flaming greenblue sea.

Until Chanda felt the pressure of Manas' hand
And they swept round towards the east.
They flew in golden yellow air inland from the sea,
Over the coastal stilt-forests, mangrove and pandanus.
Kingfishers and purple herons whirled up from thickets.
Hupp-hupp said the jungle crows.

THIS was the country Manas had entered once with a great
    army,
Royal elephants battle-chariots axe-whirlers archers swordsmen.
Where he had leaned down from his horse
To one who lay there, twisted face, glassy eyes:
And that one day will be me, that is me.
And on the Field a Shade had risen over the path in front of
    him.
They looked lovingly on one another,
The Shade received a swordthrust in its tender young breast.

Manas stormed over the wide empty landscape.
Thought about everything, thought about nothing.
Day and night, day and night.
They marauded through the landscape, fattened themselves up.

But Ganesha, the elephant-headed god,
Was unwilling to leave the Kalongs to him.
Over mighty Himavat, the craggy peaks of Himalaya, Ganesha streaked,
With howls and trumpet blasts from his trunk.
Streaked over Kailash, Nanda Devi,
Urged on by his mother, the awful Kali, Durga.

Three demons had broken out,
He had sniffed intently for a trace of them on every dreadful peak.
Were they nearby,
Was it his fearful trumpeting that made them flee?

Human souls came by, lamenting,
Fresh ones, blood-wet.
No tiger had mauled them, no snake attacked them.
They wailed of flying foxes that had knocked them down
And drunk their blood.
Of gigantic flying foxes that flew blind by day
And targeted them by smell alone.
Three Kalongs there were. A brown man with them,
A man strong as iron, looked like a Rajput,
He held them on a leash. Went quite naked,
Nothing even to cover his loins.

These were the three, Ganesha knew it.
They must have broken out from the Field of the Dead.
Maybe Puto had defeated them, carried them off as booty,
Maybe they had felled Puto, that old man,
And abused his body.

These dead had come up from the Punjab plain,
So far had the demons advanced already.
Ganesha bent down at the Milam glacier,
Whistled with the voice that rings out across the mountains,
That finds its target,

Whipped his trunk on ice, showed his words the way:

    'Thief, dog, give back the demons.'

Manas heard it speaking. It was night.
He lay in a hollow in the wastes of Thar, scrub all around,
Heard Ganesha in his sleep.
The demons lay around him, crept about, whining.

Manas sat up in the gloom, hit at a claw, a foot:
'I thought you were dangling from a branch.'
They tried to jump away, scratched the ground, squealed.
Manas came alert at once, held them: the leash was broken.

    'Oh great master, we did not break it.'

'Why are you whining?'

They paced restlessly about the hollow, spread their wings:

    'Master, lord, we'll stay with you, believe us.'

'Stop babbling.'

    'Master, lord, take care.'

'I'm taking care, I've tied your leash again.'

    'I don't mean us, master, lord. Protect us.'

Manas roared. The night was cloudy,
He had no clear view of the Kalongs.
Roared: 'Are there tigers lions snakes in here?
Are you demons scared of tigers and snakes?'

    'It's not those, master, lord.
    We're not afraid of those.
    And you don't need to be afraid of us.'

'No!' raged Manas.

    'Master, someone's coming. Lord, he's on the way.'

'Who?'

    'From the Field, from Shiva's mountain.

>Someone's coming. He'll fetch us back.
>Watch out, great lord. Protect us.'

Horribly they whined, burrowed into the earth,
Dug holes at Manas' side. Then they lay quite still:

>'He's sure to find us. Great lord, watch out.'

Manas stretched out in the dark, went back to sleep
Full of anger at the demons.
He had tied the leash around his chest,
The end was wound about the muscles of his right arm.

And sulphur-yellow light, dazzling.
And the demons baying.
And sawing tugging at the leash.

Manas leaped to his feet. He had to look away.
Had to close his eyes.
Clouds of sand billowed towards him.
A low imperious voice called:

>'Chanda, Nishumbha, Munda, here!'

Manas braced himself in the hollow,
Head tucked in, feared he would choke,
Held tight to the leash.
The demons snarled out from their holes:

>'He's here, great master, he won't show himself.'

The low voice:

>'Into how many lives have I harried you already.'

And the terrible haughty summons:

>'Here Chanda, Munda, here Nishumbha.'

Yellow flashes. Pricked ears of the demons, their fur bristling.
Their heads lolled out of the holes, they snapped at air.
Great clouds of sand, as if a giant dog were scratching just in
    front of them,

Billowed towards them and Manas.
They strained forward, in their fear dropped dung.
The voice was silent a long while.
The demons kept their ears pricked, lay flat,
Whispered: 'He hasn't gone away, master.'

Suddenly something tugged at Manas' leash, something that breathed cold.
A terrible blow on his arm, it turned to ice up to the shoulder.
Manas beat about him with his left arm.
Stumbled from the hollow, the demons at his heels:
'I can't see him, Chanda. Can you lot?'

They let him lead them on in silence.
Manas roared out into the night: 'Can you lot see him?'

    'Great master.'

'I can't see in the dark. Catch him!'

    'Ganesha's here.'

Manas furious: 'Catch him.'
He kicked them, laboured his left fist on their heads.

    They yelped: 'Don't hit, master.'

'I'll throttle you. Stay by me.
You think I feed you and let you fly, just so you can hide away.'

They followed whimpering.
Suddenly Chanda barked: 'He hit me.'
In the dark, invisible Ganesha had hit Chanda with his trunk,
Had lifted Chanda and flung him from on high over the other two.
They growled. But Manas called out:
'Catch him. Tear his eyes out. He dares not show himself.'

And in the sand in deepest darkness the battle started
Between the four of them and Ganesha.
A furious raging battle, Manas and Ganesha fearless,

Fear and fury only among the demons.
Manas panting recovered quickly from Ganesha's icy blows,
Leaped to the side.
As soon as a blow landed, between two leaps he was already
    over it.
Ganesha had an elephant's head, and the body of a grey rat.
Manas caught the rat's tail, the long whiplike twitching tail
And did not let go, despite the lashing trunk.

He wrapped it around his arm,
Beneath the ends of the leash by which he led the demons.
The demons fearful cries – 'Watch out, Manas,
It's Ganesha, he's a god' – put Manas in a rage.
If he weren't busy struggling with Ganesha,
He'd have torn the demons to pieces for those words.

Now he knew for sure this was Ganesha,
A god, one who thought to conquer him in battle,
One he had to kill and bury in the sand.
I'll not leash *you* to my hips, he panted.
You'll count for less than my Kalongs.
You'll be dead, Ganesha, torn to pieces,
You'll have to search in the sand for your trunk, your tail,
Your entrails, this I tell you.

Ganesha sprayed gouts of ice.
He tugged, he tugged, he reared up over Manas' head,
But Manas did not let go.
With Ganesha's every heave, up overhead,
He fell back onto sand.
Ganesha tried to lift Manas in the air,
But they spun only for a moment off the ground.
Then Manas, as if he were an entire continent, held firm.
The demons dug in beside him in the sand.
The rat lay scrabbling under Manas' chest, he had thrown
    himself onto it.

Now Ganesha came free,
Darted out from under Manas' neck with such a wrench
That the end of his tail tore off, was left hanging under Manas'
    leash.

Ganesha uttered not a sound.
He snapped towards his tail.
Sulphur-yellow dazzling blood spurted from him,
Rose from Manas' arm a pillar of light, mountain high,
Then went out.
A streaking comet shot through the air, vanished,
In a hissing of light Ganesha vanished,
Maddened with pain.
Into the great blackness of the night, to the north and east,
Over yonder, to great Himavat,
Ganesha vanished.

THEY stayed close, silent and not moving,
These four, Manas and the demons.
The demons stiff as corpses in the sand,
Manas upright, straddled legs, chin thrust forward.

Until light came up in the east, purple-red,
A flame of light, the sun, and everything could be seen,
The churned-up ground, stiff demons crawling
And he himself, the leash about his swollen bloody arm,
And the booty too, the long grey drooping rat-tail.

When Manas tried to move he noticed
That he himself was stiff, had to strain a long long time,
Let the sun's heat penetrate deep within him
Before he could take his hand from the leash-end,
Bend a knee, free the muscles of his pelvis, open his mouth,
And breathe more deeply, turn his head.

For more long hours, well into the middle of the day,
He tugged at the flying foxes, threw them about
Until they crawled by themselves, flapped their wings
And could let droop the heads they had upraised,
Until their bristling fur lay sleek and smooth.

Towards evening they set off again in flight.
Manas wore no clothing on his body,
Only Ganesha's rat-tail, that he had wound about his hips.

And thus attired he swept for many days through Rajputana,
Sought out the villages and towns where he had lived before.
The Kalongs fed on people and wild game.
He broke into houses, leaned over wells.

There was great lamenting in the land.
He fell on human settlements as if still on the warpath,
He, Manas, who in this country once dismounted from his horse,
The victor, walked up to a dying man,
Twisted mouth, blind eyes:
'My brother, it is my brother
And this what I shall be one day, this is me.'

Weeks passed before he quietened down.
Then he grew merry and unrestrained.
Scattered hearth fires when he broke in,
Left burning huts behind him.
Was like a glutton who pays no mind
If the table should collapse beneath him.
Watched the demons, the three dreadful creatures,
That flew with him like clouds,
The three who, sated, now bayed no more,
From one drunken binge went straight into another.

Rumours of this Manas,
Who raged like a whole pack of tigers,
Who here and there enticed people to him,
Talked to them and then let them go,

Whose companions were beasts from Hell,
These rumours had already spread
Across the whole radiant horror-stricken plain.

In radiant Punjab, from Indus to the Ganges
Prayers went up hourly from a thousand temples, aimed at
    Shiva.
But he, the occasion of these prayers, continued on his menacing
    way,
Disappeared for weeks,
Waiting for Ganesha or whoever else might come.
When he came down to earth he had Ganesha's rat-tail with him.
When Manas came down to earth,
He held Ganesha's rat-tail in his hand.
In his hand he swung Ganesha's rat-tail,
It was five arms long,
And swung the tail and cracked it.
Flying in the air he cracked it over rooftops,
Down on the ground he cracked it against huts.
Huts burst and shattered when he cracked the tail.
This made Manas happy.

[2] AMONG HUMANS

THE Victory Tower of Chittor, nine storeys high.
Broad mountain ridge beneath it.
Once a Pathan Emperor rode up to Chittor: Alla Ud-din,
Camped outside the gate.
Out rode the Rajah with beautiful Lady Kinnari
To a banquet with the Emperor.
For a moment during the meal she raised her veil,
The foreigner saw her in the mirror.

And then the dastardly ambush of the homeward Rajah,
Kinnari slipping away,
Kinnari the ransom demanded by the Emperor for the Rajah.

From Chittor, from the castle, her palanquin emerged once more,
Alla Ud-din had awaited her with longing.
He had not forgotten her reflection in the mirror.
Seven hundred virgins came from Chittor with the palanquin.
Alla Ud-din rode out to meet them,
Dismounted from his horse.

The virgins were knights, a warrior sat in the palanquin.
Swords flashed, arrows.
The foreigner was driven back, the Rajah freed,
The Emperor's tents now in his hands.

But Alla Ud-din was the Pathan Emperor,
He assembled an army of thousands, stormed Chittor.
A spear caught the Rajah.

And the ending:
The women had been left back in the castle,
Kinnari with them, she who cast her reflection in the Emperor's
    mirror.
They did not sit quietly awaiting his arrival,
Flutes heralding the eager hedonist, man of many victories.
Kinnari's victory was greater.
She did not wait around.
She had the strength. She won:
She set fire to the castle,
The castle burnt! The women burnt!
Kinnari with Chittor and the women burnt! –

Manas went down from the heath towards the ruined pile.
A procession was heading his way
Over the stony ground,
Between candles of cactus and thorny hedges.
They meant to petition him.

Stupid people. As if he meant to harm them.
He had no desire to deal with them.

In front of all the people, an old man fell prostrate,
And began to address him:
'I knew it was you.
And because I knew it, I dared come and meet you.'

This man had some knowledge of him.
And when he stood up, Manas realised:
I know this long black beard, little bells in it, this figure.
It's Puto, from the Himavat scree slope, Puto.

    'Look here, Kalongs! Who's this. Back again!'

But they just lay there tawny in the hot sun,
Blinking, they were blind.
Only Nishumbha sniffed the air.
And not uttering the slightest sound, the sleek monster
    suddenly flapped high,
At first towards the people by mistake, who fled away,
Then straight for Puto, now on his feet again,
Who took just one small surprised step back,
And then held his ground against the sleek blind beast.
He grabbed it grimly by the throat, twisted aside the slavering
    muzzle.
The monster did not snort, could not snort,
Was close to choking. Puto snorted.
And spitting his disgust, flung the limp choking creature
At Manas' feet, gasped: 'It didn't bite me!'

Manas laughed, his eyes aflame: 'No, so it seems.'
And his foot nudged to check that Nishumbha was still living.
The Kalong wheezed, biting the air and slavering.

    'You should give the others the same treatment, Puto.
    They deserve it. They drink and guzzle overmuch.
    They should be drowned in water.'

He kicked Nishumbha in the chest, until he yelped and flew
Whining back to lie beside the others.

> 'And what do you want, Puto and these others?
> Why are you here? Are you not afraid?
> You think I'm just a puny little manikin?'

'Manas, this is the Tower of Chittor.
You are in Udaipur.
Jayanta, king of Udaipur, still lives, he is your father.
You and your demons are laying waste his land.
He wants to see: what is it that comes like this.
He does not believe it is his son.'

> 'He's right.'

'You're laying waste his land. He is the King.
He wants to call you to account.
You must give him an accounting.'

> 'Here, talk to Nishumbha.
> He'll give the accounting. But not Munda
> Or Chanda.
> You'll never lay hands on those. And I....'

Manas, winding in Ganesha's tail, laughed and stretched arms
out to Puto.

> 'Puto, who told this Jayanta that I'm his son?'

'Murderer, land-destroyer!
I know: this strength you now possess
Is not of human origin, and neither is its origin divine.'

> 'Do you really need to talk so much?'

And Puto, softly: 'I saw you on the scree in Himavat.
You subdued the demons that once tricked me.
There they are now. You are Manas.
And go marauding with them, to our shame,
To the shame of everything that is human.

I carried you to the Field of the Dead,
And now you have returned. So. So.'

Hid his face.

'You weep for me?'

'You were my beloved child.
I cannot understand, not I,
Why Shiva released you from his Field and sent you back like
    this,
Like this, having first let you be killed, you,
Along with these three accursed things.
I took you to the Field of the Dead.
And now you have returned,
Returned in such terrible guise.'

'Returned, returned! I haven't returned.
I was never here.
I lay in the sea and washed myself.
I know none of you, not you, and not the natives of this
    country,
And not your Jayanta.
All of you, all, I see here for the first time.'

'The vileness must have sat in you already
When I carried you to the Field.
I should have known you better.
Whoever you may be, go no further.
Accept a sacrifice. I am one of Shiva's men of powers.
Whoever you are, tear me limb from limb.
Take me in place of all the others.'

Silent, silent, silent Manas.
No breath, no breath, no breath from Manas.
The one called Manas stood,
Silent, not breathing. Then his eyes moved,
His eyes rolled.

Then toneless from his throat: 'Out of my way.'
Then more urgently rasping from his throat:

>'Out of my way.'

Then he stood silent, silent, silent,
Chewed at his mouth.
His head drooped to his chest.

And Puto softly: 'You don't want to know yourself.
Don't want to know who you are.'

And Manas stood there. Not a sound from him.

'You're afraid to know who you are, Manas, Manas.'

Now the head lifted, the head stood straight and firm.
The face was turned towards Puto,
And slowly the lips moved,
The mouth slowly, slowly
Slowly drew itself, the face's mouth, into a broad grin,
And whispered:

>'You are right, I know nothing.
>But, but: I do not fear myself.'

Manas let his shoulders drop.
He stood there loose and mellow, rocking on his legs,
The hips swayed gently as if he would now move off.
He turned around, looked about him:

>'So this is Chittor. Blessed Kinnari! Blessed Kinnari!'

And tugged the demons forward, walked away:

>'Don't just stand there, Puto. What are you waiting for?
>Let's go to Jayanta.
>I want to be off. Lead the way.
>I want to see Udaipur, which once gave birth to me.'

The look he gave the man of powers was friendly, happy.
Puto saw: 'This is the look
That drew men and women to him, caressed them,
They told enraptured stories of him.'

AND the people surging on ahead.
The flying foxes waddled at the end of Manas' leash.
'No. Not the demons, Manas, to Udaipur.'
> 'They are my Kalongs. They go where I go. I like them.
> If you had killed one, you'd have gone the same way
> soon enough.'

The people in a rushing stream ahead,
Behind them, on his own, alone and naked, strong Manas,
Ganesha's grey frayed tail about his hips.
They all knew, those rushing on, what battle he had fought
to win it.
All went in fear of him.
All knew the god would not take it lying down. He would
come, and soon.

There he went, naked, the elephant-headed god's tail at his hips,
A votary of Hell.
The block of ice that fell on him was still in Ganesha's hands.
Now he would attack, now, now.

Slowly over the heath they went, past cornfields.
At the rear the demons waddling, clumsy, crowing,
Up bushy rounded hills and slopes.

And now the mighty gate, palaces gleaming white:
Udaipur, Jayanta's city and once that of a general
Who looked like this man, Manas.
His body invaded by this monster that was now approaching.
People flooded through the gate, and vanished.
Puto was the last one standing in the opening.
And before Manas could pass through it, demons tugging at
the leash,
Puto turned to face him,

Touched his forehead to the ground, whispered a protecting
>   prayer:
'Above this city are Heaven and the Sun.
Nothing happens in the city which He of many names has
>   not decreed.
No speck of dust, no flower's scent comes without Him to
>   this city.
The ocean of our suffering is immense.
Into it not one drop falls without his knowing.
Now is hot day:
Thanks be to the Flower-footed, the Red-eyed Lord
For sunlight. How many thanks to Him.
Thanks be for those things by which he brings us grief and
>   weeping.
The burning stars above, burning, burn because he set them
>   there.
O Dancer, O Three-eyed one, Blue-throated,
Keep firm hold of your lamps,
Let nothing destroy – do not let gutter –
Those things by which you give light to the world.
Everyone desires to see you.'

And lay there, whispered, until Manas shouted: 'Up, move on.'

Puto clambered to his feet, his hands down from his forehead:
'Yes, go now.
What I have placed in your path, you must thrust aside.'

And hastened through the gate.
And Manas, Manas calmly put his best foot forward, went,
Tugging at the demons, went calmly through the gate,
Nothing hindered him, nothing cast him down.

And Puto watched him calmly walking,
Puto trembled as he watched him striding through the gate
And into the city.

Puto trembling: 'O Blue-throated one,

Your light! Let not your light be doused.'

But Manas put an arm around his shoulders,
Shoulder to shoulder he and Puto entered Udaipur.
They walked the long streets side by side, the empty streets,
Puto filled now with fear, now with horror, and–
He could not help himself – with indescribable bliss.

These the streets that had seen dead Manas,
The cart that clattered under white shrouding cloths.
Now a savage walked the streets, through the bazaars,
Puto stumbling beneath his arm.
At his heels bloody demons waddled,
Horrible things, enemies of humankind, of gods,
Fit only to be trampled down.

Muffled prayers and tomtoms from the temples.
And he was not felled, the savage, by the prayers.
Strolled calmly, beamed about him,
Gazed at houses, trees, looked out for people.

On the path where he had received the corpse,
Carpets had been laid out for Jayanta.
White palaces shimmered through the mango trees,
Pools glinted.
Deep blue sky, steps leading down to the water.
A frightful cawing piping in the trees,
The pillared halls.

Doves whirred up. People shouting.
Jayanta stood tall.
Servants with fly-whisks fell prostrate on the carpets.
The brown monsters came flapping down the avenue,
Behind them a giant naked man
Who ran, let them pull him, held them on a leash.

> 'Don't be afraid, I'll keep hold of them.
> Nishumbha, Chanda, down. Munda, down.'

He laughed towards the King, the demons pulled him backwards:

> 'You are Jayanta. Don't be afraid.
> They don't like crawling. They only like to fly.
> You'll see later how they fly.
> Nishumbha. Down Chanda, Munda.'

And stood before Jayanta, not stepping on the carpet.
The old king, long white beard, coat of chain-mail,
On his head a round helmet with a plume, he groaned:

> 'Why will you not sit with me?
> Why will you not step onto the carpet?'

'I don't step on carpets. I don't enter houses.'

The old man, fingering his chain of pearls, stood up,
Looked hard at him, looked hard at him.

> 'Just speak out whatever's on your lips, King Jayanta,
> Say "demon" or "evil spirit", I've heard it all before.'

The old man stammered: 'My son.'
Then hands held out to him:

> 'Manas, my son, my child. My beloved child.'

'Have too many of your people been mauled by those things there?'

> 'Manas, my beloved child, it is you. You are here again.'

'I was never here, Jayanta.'

> 'You had to go to the Realm of Death.
> You have returned.
> You were stronger than them all.
> Sorrow has not defeated you.
> It was not your body that we burned. Was not you.'

The old man wept tears of longing, held out his hands.
His long beard bobbed across his shoulder.
The white sleeves emerging from the armour

Swelled like balloons.
Manas stepped nearer. His right hand held the leash,
His left arm held Jayanta in an embrace.

> A sob: 'What happened when you were there.
> I am still alive, but for how long.
> You sought sorrow in the Realm of Death.
> What is in the Realm of Death?
> What did they do there to you?
> Did you conquer it?
> O how strong you are.'

'The Realm of Death is no Realm of Death, Jayanta.
Don't be afraid of the Realm of Death.
Whatever is there is also here.'

> 'What are you saying, Manas my child?
> Tell me more.
> How long shall I still live.'

'Don't be afraid, Jayanta.
I tell you: nothing will become of you.
Nothing will happen to you there that does not happen here.
All of you are already… dead.'

> 'Manas my child.'

'I don't mean to upset you, old man, but you did ask.
You have a long straight sword, you're wearing armour.
What are these toys you carry,
Just look at yourself.
Tenuous, feeble, you'll all be blown about.
That's how it is up there.
They tumble across the ice, and moan.
I could believe the Earth is made of mud,
Of soft wet mud,
And you are all heavy, you are stones,

Sinking into it.'

> 'You were once here with us, Manas,
> You were like us, you were my son.
> You were our general, saviour of Rajputana.'

A laugh from Manas:

> 'Saviour of Rajputana! What did I save?
> Leaving, for me, was the wiser course.
> Saving Shades, smiting some and saving others.'

And stepped back again to his three beasts.

> 'Don't be afraid, Jayanta, of the Realm of Death.
> The Realm of Death and the Earth are one and the same!
> All of you – now I say it plainly – all of you here are not real.
> It's possible you only dream yourselves.
> Someone prevents you from waking up.
> I want to move on.'

> 'Stay with us, Manas.'

As Jayanta stepped off the carpet, he stumbled over his long sword.

Manas grabbed him, held him up.

> 'What use is your long sword, Jayanta?
> You almost fell over it. Throw it away.'

Jatyanta clung to Manas' arm:

> 'It gives me a good but very anxious feeling
> When you hold me, my beloved child.
> The gods have made us and our life this way.
> So, who are we then.
> But you, my child, who are you?
> How did you come back from the Realm of Death?'

'With three Kalongs.'

> 'With three demons. Then who are you, Manas.
> Anyway you are my child, you have found your way back here.
> Are you not my child,
> Are you a god, have you just assumed my Manas' shape?'

The demons were already dragging Manas on,
He went leaping stumbling down the avenue to hold them back.
To Jayanta, bending to retrieve his sword, he called:

> 'Honour your gods in your temples. You have temples enough.
> Set out flowers, pour hot fat.
> They'll guzzle it, and grow sleek!
> Don't bother me with them.
> Feed your gods, Jayanta, to keep them well
> So they can harry you across the ice and tumble you about.
> See how they leap, my Kalongs that I took from them.'

Jayanta hid his face.

> 'Look, Jayanta! These are mine!
> Ganesha tried to steal them back, but I defeated him.
> He paid for it!'

He cracked the long grey rat-tail.
Jayanta lay face-down:

> 'Don't make that sound. Ganesha will hear you.'

'I'm waiting!'

And from far off, already in the trees, Manas called:

> 'You think me a demon.
> I am no demon. I am just... not dead.'

And cracked and drove the demons on.
He tied them to a sturdy palm tree.
To Puto, ash-smeared man, he turned his face:

> 'There's something I must say to you,

You'll understand, or fail to understand.
Tell it to the King, Puto.
He asked me about Life, troubles himself about Life.
Look up at the night sky, tonight.
Up there is a sleigh. Someone pulls the sleigh behind him.
It flings out dust, such dust.
The stars are this dust,
And the Earth and flowers and people,
And the gods and what you will.
Such a pulling, such a sleigh is moving up there through the blackness!
Wonderful pulling and sparkling.
I... can feel the one who pulls the sleigh, Puto.
Although I too tumble in the dust, I feel him.'

Manas looked up at the open sky.
The Kalongs panted at his side,
Flapped high up the palm trunk, clawed into it.

'I don't know if you understand. But tell it to Jayanta.'

Puto sought his eyes: 'And you, Manas, you so strong,
You are more than dust,
You are... the one who pulls the sleigh?'

Manas knelt beneath the palm tree:

'Lead me not into temptation,
Oh lead me not into temptation.'

HE SAID not one word more to Puto,
But walked exploring down the paths
That he as Manas, jewel of his people, had so often walked.
A boat carried him across the pools, past the Jag Newas steps.
He was heading for the little houses,
The garden houses, in which he had sometimes dwelled.

In his ear a constant quiet calling.
He did not know if he was hearing it or thinking it.
And what it called he did not understand.
Here now were the women's quarters.
He went directly to a tree, huge ancient tree,
That stood outside a door,
And moved its branches in such a lovely way.
None following behind him, and no one before.

All was silence at the pools and on the island.

A peacock strutted slowly across his path, dragged its tail behind it.
Then Manas tripped on the tree's root.
The tree would not let him pass. The roots reared up so tall.
The call came louder. And Manas stood still.
Now the tree bent down its branches,
And shivered, as if they were the little leaves of a mimosa.

It was a Bo-tree. It whispered: Savitri, Savitri.
Why do you call me Savitri? thought Manas,
The Kiru too called me Savitri.

'Savitri, is it two days or ten, or even a year, since you went away?'

Once Manas' wife was Savitri, favourite of his consorts,
He had not seen her since the wastes of Thar.

    'Why did I go away, Bo-tree?'

'Do you not know, Savitri?'

    'No, it was so long ago, more than a year.'

'Longer, much longer. All I do is stand and wait.
As long as I live I shall wait for you.'

    'Why did I go away, dear Bo-tree?'

'You don't remember?'

    'Just tell me what I had to do.'

'You had to look for Manas, yes! And found him.'

And the branches beat down low and dense:

'Ah, I am blind, Savitri, but I'm happy
To breathe your scent.
What has happened your shoulders, Savitri?'

> 'But Manas was already dead.
> Why would I go to look for him?'

'He was not dead, you yourself said so.
They carried him on a cart.
A false Manas lay there in the hall.
You went to look for him, he was calling out, no one else
    could hear him.
Ah Savitri, your shoulders are so strong.'

Manas kept quiet, branches like arms around him.

'You had soft narrow shoulders. Give me your mouth.
Makes me so happy to have you back again.
Don't be embarrassed.'

And before Manas, trembling Manas could avert his face,
Branches brushed across it,
And jumped shook started wildly back.

'Who are you, are you!
You are not Savitri,' the tree rustled, wailed.

> 'I am Manas.' And sobbed.

'Who, who?' – 'Manas.'

'Ah, ah.' And the tree's crown swayed,
And branches felt their way down again:

'You are Manas, and she's not here.
She fetched you back, and she stayed there.'

> 'I have come from Himavat. Was on the Field of the Dead,
> I am that Manas who was laid low.'

'Savitri has not returned.
And yet you are she, I can breathe it.
Savitri, not Manas.'

'I am Manas.'

'These his strong shoulders, and his face.
And it is Savitri too, I breathe her.
So she found you,
So... she lies embedded in you, that you could return.
Savitri in your body.
Be tender to me, Manas.'

And again Manas was embraced.
And as the tree embraced him
And he stood dreaming, in confusion,
Sobbing, feeling, before his eyes an image rose,
And he was floating over the Field, a bundle
And arms received him.
He swarmed about the woman, he must encompass her
And grew towards her, grew into her.
Hot ecstasy surged, through him and her.

And then a thunderclap: It was Savitri!
And sobbing in his mouth,
And whimpering, endless whimpering.
Manas flung himself down: 'How can I live.'
The tree could not reach him.

'She's not here. She didn't come back.
She's not with me.'

'She is here.'

'Not with me. Stayed on the Field of the Dead.
She gave her life for mine. Sent me back alone.'

'You are not alone.'

'I am alone. Savitri is not here.'

And to his sobs were added the Bo-tree's whispers
And consoling, comforting, cajoling,
Embracing, rocking.

WHY DO you turn and turn, Manas, among the pools?
Many are the skiffs that skim across the round pool
With their pale blue awnings, past the fan palms.
Calling out from one skiff to another: *aai, aai.*

The coiled tresses of those with tender limbs attract you,
The high-pointed breasts of those with the gazelle eyes,
Who come out from the little garden houses.
Just as the sea can never find water enough
To fill it up, so you can never have enough
Of longing,
And sorrow and sweetness,
Of all that is spread forth in the heavens, in the trees,
On the waters, underneath your feet.
All of it, the longing, twining.

The God of Death is never sated with the living,
The world is never sated with what is loved,
What loves itself, loves back and forth,
Rocks back and forth, and raises itself up.

The dark eyes of the women have long lashes,
Slender their bodies, their bottoms rounded,
Their toes shine as they step through grass,
Some keep their heads down, some raise them like proud mares.
Strong rows of teeth.
How languidly they move.

Which one do you look at first, Manas,
Lifting your head, lowering it like these women?
Or do you glance at her who leans against a tree,

Short plump one with the broad brow, her neck is strong,
She gazes at the water, her eyes red,
She's heavy as a female elephant.
What voice will be hers? Deep-throated.
She's sick for love, for love that she has relished,
And love that has eluded her.

Ah, where is Savitri?
When was the last time, Manas, that a woman,
Any woman, placed her feet upon your toes,
And laid her tender tendril arms about your neck?

The skiffs, the skiffs so many,
Skimming over the round pool.
Aai, aai from boat to boat.
You temptresses with shining hair, do not flit past,
Do not float past like leaves.
Pause a while to bring Manas peace.
Calm his eyes, his hands, and help him catch his breath,
There outside the hall, the Victory Theatre where they sang:
'Manas our jewel, we rejoiced when you rode out,
Now you are here again.'

How they dance, the women. They have no fear of Manas.
The men have run away.
The women – whose work is this? - have come out from their houses
And stand and try out steps and sing, and move their arms.
Such grace in their shoulders.
Their bracelets tinkle, and some spin around.

How they throw out ribbons, spin around,
Throw out ribbons, wave the ribbons up and down,
Wave red ribbons, wave blue ribbons.
Dance, fling their slender legs,
Stretch out their ring-decked toes,
And spin, sway, wave ribbons.

His soul, it was not calmed,
Was filled, his soul, with a longing deeper yet
Than the longing of some dead thing for life.
No dead thing can be so filled with yearning, such deep
    yearning,
Enormous thirst for life, can be so filled with love
As a living thing, as he himself for love.
His breast was seized by it, arms seized,
So deluged was he by the founts of love.

His eyes stayed open, the lashes forgot to blink.
The women danced, waved ribbons.
Manas' breath fled.
He was a sigh amid the waving ribbons,
A delight.

– And where is Savitri, are you thinking of Savitri?
Is she not here, – and everywhere here,
And not here -
She who wore the wedding mark on the Field,
And approached over the Field, the mountains?
Everything came whirring from the gorges,
Shades demons fallen gods,
Trembling in the scented mist the wind brought to them.
Penitents lured from their caves.
Savitri's face wild and bristling,
Her hair billowed smoke and flames.

Savitri is here, not here,
Here, not here.
A wafting breeze is here, the wind's breath.
Winding branches, tendril arms,
Crinkling lips, striding legs,
Savitri, here and not here.
Who else if not Savitri is everywhere here, tender, entwining.
The gods came storming up, scented the blood-mark on her
    forehead.

This was when you lay in Death's grip, Manas,
Drifted as a Shade without a body,
Everything taken from you,
And everything flowed to you from her.

– And must I not hunger and thirst,
And be filled with longing and weep and plead,
After I have gone through all this,
And Savitri is no longer with me? –

And for nothing, this I say to you, does Manas have such thirst,
Always and always and always,
And must turn towards what strolls beneath the trees,
What presses toes to the ground,
Sails a skiff out on the pool,
And lets scarves flutter –
Towards distant women who crouch down
And lower their arms, or lie and sleep and groan,
And for men who walk away with serious faces,
Children jumping: – such thirst for it all.

My blood, my flesh, away. Slip the flesh from my hands
And from my face.
My flesh, quake with theirs, with all of theirs,
A single tremor.
My flesh, blood, my senses, be not stilled!
The air, the light, the smiling faces,
The feet that step, the boats that flit,
Sink into me. Storm into me,
All of it.
We take flight together, fly fly all together.

HE STROLLED around the pools.
The women brought him flowers from the boats,

As if he drew them, they came near and swarmed about him,
As clouds approach the moon
And the moon draws white clouds close.
They brushed against him, sleek, light-bodied, those with dainty feet.
Women with their perfumed breath
Stood on his toes.
They fell on him like gentle dew,
In the groves he and they a single twining.
Like little scraps of silk they glided from him,
His hands still reaching for them as they tripped away; he sighed:

'It makes me happy when I look at you.'

GANESHA came to Manas in the night.
Manas, full of longing, asleep by the pools,
Woke up beside the demons.
The elephant-headed god struck out, but could not reach him.
He sat up unconcerned in the tall grass.
The poolside reeds bent down, behind them trees soughed crackled.
But over and around him, despite Ganesha's onslaught,
All stayed calm, left just a whisper.
Was warm and gentle, the air over Manas,
And was not rent asunder.
The ice-mist flung out by the trunk melted.
The trunk flailed icily, frosted in the air.
Dripped soft as melting butter, drooped.
Ganesha the rat struggled to withdraw it,
Retract it from the mild strong air, swing it high.

Another surge of ice-breath.
And again the hissing melting, the trunk drooping impotently down.

And outraged he leaped back,
Braced himself, the giant rat Ganesha,
Stood on his two hind legs and dragged the trunk up high,
To keep it clear of Manas, so that Manas would not tear it off
As he had torn off his tail,
To his shame.
Ganesha howled up through the air, over dark Udaipur,
In sorrow, in rage.
The gods must come and kill this one!
He had to fly away north and east, to the Field of the Dead,
To Kailash, to Shiva.
He sped away to seek Shiva's help!

JOYFUL seductive music!
Manas at ease outside his garden hall.
Across the glittering lake the Rose Palace,
Its dome, its oriels and pillared halls,
Built by long-dead people for their pleasure.
Were they dead? Their faces were there still.

Manas' gaze lighted on papayas, plantains, coconut palms,
Storks in the azure sky so close above.
How the musicians blow honk tootle clapper.

The Kalongs hung tied up, black in the tamarinds,
Sated on the meat and blood that people threw to them.
The musicians played.
Over in the open plaza they were praying
To Lakshmi, goddess of love.
Manas had requested it.

Puto the only one who dared approach him –
Brought him bowls of fruit, salads dressed with honey and
      vinegar,

Brown pancakes,
Big bowls of berries, coconut milk, olive oil.

> 'Will you stay with us, Manas, great Manas,
> Or what path will you take?'

'I won't let you call me "great", Puto,
Because it seems you are excusing your own smallness.
I've no idea where I shall go.
Listen to the music, Puto, and as you listen, tell me
If *you* know what you want, where *you* want to go.'

> 'They worship Lakshmi, to make you happy.'

'Hear the music, the notes, how they climb
And move around, invert themselves,
How they stretch and fade and resonate.
They are as filled with truth as this nut is of milk.
Puto, trust me, music is true,
I feel it, it's the magical,
The compelling, compelling truth.'

> 'Do you worship the gods, Manas,
> Do you pray to the Three-eyed Blue-throated One?'

Manas rolled a coconut on the floor, smiled at Puto:
'I'm sure I do pray to him.
I've never given it much thought.
So many marvellous things on this Earth come my way,
I never have time for contemplation.
Maybe I do worship Shiva the Blue-throated One.
Must be a powerful god, Shiva,
Don't you think, Puto?'

Who touched his forehead to the dirt, kept silent.

'What say you, Puto? Is he so powerful?'

> Puto whispering, hesitant: 'Don't ask, O Manas.'

Manas nonchalant, coconut-ball now in his hands,

Pulling at the tufts:
'Then I don't know if I do worship Shiva,
He being so powerful.'

Puto breathing, as if to himself:

>'The highest He, the Mightiest, the One.'

Manas irritated: 'Then I don't know
If I worship him. I... shall have to see.'

And suddenly he threw the ball, the brown hairy coconut,
Away over bowed Puto's back,
Threw it with a giant's strength onto the shining surface of the pool.
The musicians kept up their joyful playing.

'I told you they're worshiping Lakshmi, goddess of love.
Shiva – I never mentioned him!
And what's more, Puto, I am here.
You say it's I who once stood at the window,
And I've returned.
Puto, are you sure?'

The black-bearded man stood up, stepped back:

>'I see it, Manas, great Manas.
>I cannot say I know it.'

'See it, see clearly and know it, know it very well.
You are cleverer and older than I.
So how is it you don't know?
I am, I live.
I won't let you call me "great".
I already see that you are small.'

>'You saw me when I fought the demons,
>Manas, I am not nothing.'

'Then know it well. Still better.
Then you won't touch your forehead to the sand

And scratch welts in your skin.
Welts for whom?
For a thing that beats you down? Are you mad?
You, I cannot listen to you. I won't eat your food.'

    'Don't lose your temper, Manas.
    I didn't mean to make you angry.'

'I sit here listening to you.
I will not be humiliated by such questioning.
Your kneeling, lying in the dust disgusts me.'

    'Oh you were in the Realm of the Dead.
    You have seen Shiva's might,
    I felt it when you tugged at the chain, you can't deny it.'

'Keep talking. Say what you like.
Listen to the music, don't talk, it'll do you good.
And are you still alive as you listen to it?
And does it not soothe you as you listen to it?
See how little you exist, how you do not yet exist!
Listen to the singing, Puto.
They sing to Lakshmi, goddess of love.
They sing of her bathing, how the elephants spray water over her.
You see how you are nothing, how unreal you are.
You see how you're all ghosts,
You are nothing more than rumour.'

And as the music soared and droned and cooed,
Manas stood.
His arms and shoulders moved in time to the music,
His lips were pursed.
Puto watched him as he danced and sang,
Not following the music that they played in Lakshmi's honour:

'What is the Highest I do not say.
What is the Greatest I do not say.
I do not envy the doves and storks,
I have wings, wings,

I have longing, joy,
Have peace, endless peace.

'Puto, on Himavat there blooms a flower,
They call it Modest, Layalu, Layalu.
At night it hangs there like a dried-up weed,
In the morning comes the sun,
The mountains thunder,
The mountains boom what they have to boom,
The stars have wheeled away.

'In the morning when the sun comes back,
Layalu spreads big roses, white as snow.
By midday they are red, turn ever deeper red,
Under the sun's relentless wooing.

'And in the evening she sits there deepest red,
Layalu, and gazes after the blazing sun
With all her opened blooms, Layalu.

'I… do not close my blooms at night,
I am not pale when the sun comes up,
Do not turn red beneath its rays,
Am not dismayed when it goes down.

'I… am Light,
I swim in the flood, like the sun!
I hold the line, I know it, the line
By which the world is drawn along!
It gives me peace and endless joy,
To hold the line by which the rock is drawn along.
Not I the rock, the cliff.
I… am the line.'

AND SO Manas danced away from the lawn outside his garden
   house,
Danced for a long time among the ponds and flowerbeds.

Towards evening he glanced dreamily across at the old Bo-tree,
Which shook and rocked its branches wildly.
Always Manas wore a kindly, tender smile
And his lips moved.
They were conversing at a distance.

Then – Puto following well behind –
He went among the trees, mango, banana,
Past pillared halls, away from the pools and ponds
Across into town.
He walked the bright streets of Udaipur alone,
Strong naked Manas, Ganesha's grey rat-tail about his hips.
Women in bright clothes scooped water at wells.
They were as if enchanted: just a few fled away
When Manas came along.
The bazaars, the leafy avenues heaved with people,
And carts drawn by zebu,
Dogs chasing, coppersmiths hammering.
Manas walked on with his tender dreaming smile,
Beyond range now of the Bo-tree's whispering.

None fled when he appeared, his brown slow bulk,
Amid the throng,
Often with cooing doves above his head.

They sat in silence, stood silent and profoundly moved
And jolted to the heart, those on whom his gaze fell.
He strolled past many-storeyed temples, stone elephants at the
    gate,
His wide eyes taking it all in.
When the streets grew narrower, he stood still.

Here was a muddy square,
And a rich man had placed an overseer here
To watch over slaves outside a simple hut.
They squatted on wide boards, wove garish rugs,
Women and children face to face, knotting cotton tufts.

The overseer patrolled among the dye-vats, bamboo cane in
 either hand,
At his belt a wirebound whip.
He went among the vats, his back to Manas.
The slaves, men women children, had already noticed Manas,
The hunchbacked overseer still shouting, hitting out at shoulders,
 arms.

The slaves dropped to their knees,
Showed Manas anguished faces.
When the overseer turned to see what they were looking at,
The strong naked figure was standing at the exit to the street,
At his back a nervous swarm of people.

The overseer's mulish face, his eyes downcast.
And the smiling figure called out: 'What kind of face is that?'

> The reply, defiant bitter: 'These are our slaves.
> Their work is bad. If not for the whip and bamboo canes,
> They would do nothing.'

The figure, smiling still: 'They would do nothing.'

The other thrust his chin out:

> 'They'd just lounge in the sun, beside the water,
> Stuff themselves, or bill and coo at one another.'

Manas laughed aloud: 'And why not lounge in the sun?'

> 'They are our slaves, my master's slaves.'

Manas laughed more loudly: 'All right then.
I won't disturb you. I was only passing.
So, hit away.'

Blows rained down.
Wailing, screeching. Manas looked on calmly.
He went across the square through the mud,
Passed close by the boards.
The wailing was right by him, furtive hands stretched out.

His eyelids lifted, menacing: 'Touch me, you, you wretches.'

And after he had passed across the square,
He held them once more in his gaze,
His terrible jolting penetrating gaze,
Shattering gaze.
He shouted to the overseer: 'Go on! Make them do their duty!
Grant no respite! Beat them!'
And spat in their direction,
With knitted brow, mouth pursed in disgust.
He chased away the swarm of people following him.

But then, the muddy square behind him,
He had to turn around once more
To fling sand by the handful at the slaves,
Had to stop himself from running back to them,
And beating them himself.

When he moved on from the square,
High white walls showed behind a row of trees.
A prison. Manas saw the windows and their bars.

The gate was ajar; he stepped through into the yard.
Guards with whips and spears fled from him.
The prisoners in heavy chains and wooden collars shrank back,
Lay down, face and hands in dust, groaning, whimpering.

One screamed when Manas grasped his shoulder,
As if touched by red hot iron. But Manas whispered:
'Why are you in here, with iron fetters on your legs?'

He screamed again, blinked sideways.

'Why are you in here?'

> 'I'm innocent, I'm not a thief,
> They caught me in the neighbourhood.'

'You're ashamed to be a thief?'

> 'I'm innocent.'

'Stop whimpering. Stand up. Run away.
Do you want to stay in here? You're not ashamed to stay here?'

>He whined: 'They sentenced me unjustly.
>You, set me free.'

'I asked: aren't you ashamed to stay here?'

>'I can't escape. You see my chains.'
>And brightened eagerly: 'You set me free!'

'I, you? And what have you done, yourself,
To free yourself? You lie here whining.'

>'Help me.'

'They should whip you more, dumb beast, let you go hungry,
To wake you up.'

Another lying near the thief heard this,
Called out to Manas: 'Come to me.'

'And what do you want?'

>'Set me free. That one's a rascal, a beginner,
>They caught him at his first attempt.'

'And you?'

>'Thanks be that you have come.
>I was steward to a prince, a relative of great Jayanta of
>   Udaipur.
>I often stole from him, by intent, you.
>I was no beginner. I'm an old man, as you see.
>Then he was on to me, my master.
>I already had my lands, and children and a palace.
>Then I lost it all. He had me locked away.'

'I hear you. So what is it you want?'

>'They're all afraid of you.
>You set me free, that's what I want.'

'And?'

'I won't reclaim my castle,
I don't want the gold that's mine by rights.
Even though all of them are thieves,
Even though the prince I serve is a cheat and a despoiler,
I want nothing back. I want my freedom.'

'So break your chains!'

'Can I?'

'You still have teeth, a skull.
I don't see that they are broken.'

'I'm supposed to kill myself?'

'Then you are already dead!
You have it too easy still.
Why call to me, why not stir the others up?
Why not help each other? You all want to leave.'

'They're all cowards.'

'And you?'

'I'm in despair. Who are you actually? Why talk to me?'

'Better you tell me, old man,
If I should free you, what would you do then?'

'Yes, free me!
I shan't lay a finger on any gold,
I'll walk right past my castle.
I shan't avenge myself on any of them.
I shall – go into the forest, and end my life, atone!
That's all.'

Manas was already on his feet, a weary glance, a yawn: 'Uh huh.'
Scratched his arms, ambled slowly on,
Sat down in the women's yard.
It was one big screeching whining.
Only a few lay in chains.

Manas studied his hands. He listened as the old hags cawed.

Truly, he muttered to himself, this is no different from the
    Realm of the Dead.
A to and fro. Like throwing sand from one hand to the other.

A female hand clutched his leg as he strolled out.
Manas bent down, prised loose the fingers:
'You want my help, yes I see.
Don't tell me your story.
You know, when you go to market and buy some cloth,
You must pay for it.
If I should set you free, what payment would you give?'

    The woman looked up: 'Give myself to you? I'm old.'

Her laugh was coarse.

'It's not the point, that you are old. You have to pay.'

    'So take what you want.'

'Your teeth, your eyes, your head.' – 'What?'

'Your head, your eyes.'

    'You – you – you're –'

Manas pushed her hand away:
'It doesn't matter what I am. Leave me alone.'

As he crossed the men's yard, arrows came at him,
Guards' ranging shots from behind barred windows.
He stood still, looked around as the sharp darts flew.
His smile was happy, his breath easy when he saw:
They're shooting at me!
He scooped a fallen arrow as a forfeit,
Carried it from the screeching prison.

It was already dark.
The enormous starry firmament came wheeling out.
He turned towards the torchlight in the streets.
Breathing, breathing calmly, in the dark lane beside the prison
He saw a light, a light that charmed him.

He crept nearer, looked into the hut.
An oil lamp burned within.
A man was seated on a mat, alone,
Head lowered, at his knees a scroll.
Manas stayed a while in silence, in the darkness of the open door.
The man within made no move, just now and then looked up
As if perhaps his neck hurt.

Manas, waiting, grew more and more enchanted.
Chirping in the trees. Glow-worms, fireflies flew about.
The tree outside the hut, a fig, was filled with them.

After a long while Manas stepped through the doorway,
Stood at the threshold to the hut.
And the man made no move.
He had a fine brush in his hand, gazed straight ahead,
Wrote on his scroll.

Manas called: 'You!'

> He, not looking up: 'Yes.'

'You! There's someone here!'

> 'Be welcome, sit yourself down.'

'Will you not look at me?'

> 'My little lamp does not reach so far.
> What is there to look at?
> Please, be welcome, and keep quiet.'

'Perhaps indeed you see me, my good host.'

> 'Please be patient, dear guest.'

And after he had spent some time in writing
The man himself spoke up:

> 'I do not look at you. I see other things.'

'Tell me.'

'Noor Begum, wondrous beauty
Who lived in Kashmir, Noor Begum with the swan's hand.'

'She's in the hut? I don't see her.'

'That's not what I said, dear guest.
Two men fought for Noor Begum's favour,
Jahangir, soon to be Emperor in Delhi,
And a nobleman.
She was betrothed to the nobleman and had to marry him.
But in the end she did become the Empress,
The Emperor's Empress.'

'This is what you're writing, host?'

'I see it, then I write it down.
It stands before me, in my hut.'

'Your clothes are ragged, your hut lets in the rain,
Your jug is broken, your mat is falling apart:
Why do you write this?'

The man did not turn his head to Manas.

'Your main hope is that I should look at you,
If I looked at you, I'd pay you no more heed
Than I pay the jug.
But Noor Begum and Jahangir, these I see,
And how Afgham, the nobleman, fought the tiger with his bare hands
And tore its jaws apart.
And yet he had to yield,
And cede the wondrous beauty to the other man.
This I see – my previous life.
It is my previous life, my previous births.'

Manas silent.
The man on the mat turned his slow gaze on him:

'Now you keep silent, dear guest.

> Your silence pleases me.'

And Manas softly: 'So that's why you don't see the jug,
Don't feel the rain, and how the mat is rotting under you,
And how lean you are.'

> 'That's why.'

'But this… is your present birth.'

> 'It is so. You're right, dear guest.
> But the old life lives on into this.
> In what way?
> As if a man once went swimming in a raging flood,
> And now sits calmly on the shore.
> Or: I have dismounted from my horse,
> And now I lean my back against a wall.'

Manas stepped back across the threshold, left,
Stood outside in the dark, glanced in:
'Fare well, dear host.'
Bowed, raised one hand to his forehead:
'I'm glad that I have been your guest.
May your breath be calm in your present life.'

Their glances met.
Such joy in the proud man on the mat.
Once more they bowed to one another,
Exchanged greetings with their glances, as if old friends.

Manas strode on into town, cheerful, blessed.
Sometimes he moved his arms as if in swimming,
Swimming in the green-blue sea,
In the green-blue sea, swimming as it thundered under him,
Tossed him,
Held him, yes, held him up.

[3] MANAS AND SHIVA

ONCE again Udaipur heard the demons' dreadful yowling.
Manas bid no farewell to his father or to Puto,
Their happiness suffused with longing.
He steered south on his Kalongs,
In Udaipur left joy and terror in his wake.

In many places demons came up in his path,
Sent by Ganesha.
Not yet at Amber, one night among palms and towering
    gopuram,
A demon emerged from the coconut palm
Where the Kalongs were hanging.
Their yelps woke Manas up.
Once again they were first to spot the fearsome enemy.

On it came with its pig's head, nostrils flaring,
The forehead lay flat. Its ears pointed forwards like handles.
Out it climbed on short fat legs, trotted on tiptoe like a pig,
Little stubs of arms, flabby chest with teats, belly swaying.
It took hardly five steps towards Manas
And he was already up from the sandy ground.

The pig-demon snarled and grunted and bared its tusks,
Thinking to strike terror into Manas,
Intent on stealing back Ganesha's rat-tail.
Manas gave the three Kalongs a whipping with the tail,
Drove them and the pig-demon in a heap together.

The Kalongs, now fat and lazy, grew livelier under the lashing.
They covered the opening in the palm with their enormous
    wings
To stop the demon from retreating under Manas' blows.
The demon tried to crawl into the sand.
It almost choked. The Kalongs dug it out.

It tried to bat away their claws.
Then Manas laid hands on the demon's yacking chest,
And tied the Kalongs' leash around it:
'By what name do they call you?'

    'Namuchi.' Tried to pull itself free.

'Ganesha sent you.' – 'Yes.'

It whimpered as the Kalongs leaped about it.

'You'll stay with me.'

Namuchi, surrounded by the Kalongs, grunted horribly:

    'You'll starve me.'

'You'll find enough to eat.'

The pig-demon danced for joy.
The Kalongs crowed with pride, flew up,
Munda with Manas on his back.

And this was the final demon targeted at Manas.
He had made short work of it.
Went on into the town of Amber
Where Ganesha would not dare to follow him in person.

But there he met –
There strong Manas, stealer of demons,
Defeater of the elephant-headed god –
There he, who had come away from the Realm of Death,
There he met his hardest challenge.

A CASTLE on a cliff loomed over Amber.
The land below was stony.
A big lake stretched away beneath the castle.
And once again, attracted by the gleam of water, Manas went
Along the shore beneath feathery acacias.

He climbed up to the temple courtyard.
The drums still beat ceaselessly.
In a corner Kali stood, six-armed,
The dreadful Goddess.
They had hung pearls on her
And hung on her a chain of bloody human skulls.
No one was praying in the courtyard when Manas entered.

Three priests lay prostrate before Kali's statue,
The fourth beat on the drum, eyes tight shut.
And when they made no move as Manas stood there, looked about,
He went up to ghastly Kali's statue,
And removed the chain of human skulls.

And when the priests still made no move,
He hurled a skull with a mighty crash onto the drum,
So that the priests, whitehaired, started up,
Twisted and turned there on the floor.

They cried out softly, could not even cry out loud.
Lay paralysed where they had been lying,
One on his back, another on his side,
Made no sound, hardly breathing.

Manas spat as he wound the chain of skulls around his arm.
The Kalongs, smelling blood, flew at it snapping.
But Manas whirled the chain about his head
And with a heave flung it far out over the lake.
The drum already beat again from the hill behind him.

Manas lay two days in a grove outside Amber.
Then went into Amber, into the town,
Through the deep verdant valley below the castle hill.
Elephants on the cliffside path turned away
When he came up towards the gate,
Dragging the three demons along behind him.

In the town he spent the night near the ramparts
In the broad gardens of a palace, beneath pomegranates and
    oleanders,
Among tuberoses and mango trees.
That night beneath the moon
The battlements gleamed harsh yellow.
Manas slept. His demons patrolled.
In the dawn twilight they flew back to the garden,
Hung by their claws in branches.

He saw them hanging in the purple light, dribbling wheezing in
    their sleep.
Then he walked alone through the sunlit streets.
And here too the people in their bright clothes did not run
    from him,
Were drawn to him.

The domes of the town, snow-white marble palaces,
Clattering of zebu-carts, bells ringing, hammering, street cries.
Tangle of wretched alleys, little houses blue green pink.

Manas headed for the skirling tootling
That came from a secluded square ringed by banyans.
First he had to go down a narrow lane,
Where they were beating tomtoms, strumming mandolins.

In the little painted houses
The air was heady with the scent of musk and henna,
Silken girls sat on balconies, at windows,
They sang and never left the windows.
Scented candles burned in their rooms.

Girls with lovely eyes came stepping out to Manas.
They kissed him, he pressed them close.
Behind him was a calling, cooing, craving,
As he left the narrow street and walked down into the square.

A swarm of people thronged about him in the square,

A heaving surging crowd.
Where did it come from, that skirling tootling?
From the temple with its triple dome.
The temple towers soared like skittles, the roofs gleamed gold.
Little bells hung down on iron chains.
To one side was an open hut,
And a brass ox glinting on a stone plinth.

Manas went on past deserted market stalls, with their pots,
Their flowers for offerings, past cows lowing in their pens,
Up to the temple's silver door.
Sitting there all alone, sitting on the step, a priest,
Had on his knees an ancient book, he reading, murmuring.

Manas studied the temple frieze,
The heavenly devadasis carved in stone.
Grey doves flew down to Manas from the roofs,
Longtailed monkeys swung onto the roofs from trees.

Now the priest stood up.
He was naked, the triple mark of Shiva on his forehead,
Body ash-smeared.
He saw giant naked Manas, rat-tail around his hips,
At his back a nervous crowd.
Recognised who this was.
Rumours of this one, his marauding like a pack of tigers,
Had raced across radiant Punjab.
This was the one. Standing right in front of him. This one.

He laid the book aside,
Made an averting gesture, was unafraid.
'Begone from here. You! Begone from here.'

The huge dreamy figure turned his gaze
From the heavenly dancing girls.

'Do not stand there, you. You cannot stay here.'

    'What's that you're whispering, priest?'

'You hear me. Be on your way.
Dog, the sight of you is loathsome, loathsome!
You – who could say your name.'

    Manas dreamy, looking at him: 'Yes.'

'Shiva sent you back here, to our shame.
Now you are among us. It has come to us.
We are to suffer like all the others.
Let me look at you.
What did Shiva have in mind for you, you scourge.
We are meant to see: that we are you,
As wicked as you are, a horror just like you!
Shiva now does so, and then does so.
Now he sends us spirits that should save us,
And then sends beasts, evildoers, mirrors.'

    'Go on.'

'Go on! Still you stand there in my sight, you sinful creature.
I already know myself. Have long known it.
That's why I sit here.
I know your father, Jayanta of Udaipur, and your mother.
You were on the Field of the Dead,
You for sure are not the same one who went away,
Our jewel who kept us safe from slaughter by the enemy.
Then your eyes were not so big and wild.
Who now would want to gaze into them.
Those lips: how you thrust them out, how you smack them.
This moist entry to your mouth:
Worse than the Field of the Dead.'

    'Go on.'

'It is enough already.
I can keep watching you, watch how you bloom,
You sleek monster, standing there.
I must look at you, for I am pious, and the Gods sent you here.

You don't know, d'you hear, what I have long known,
You do not know extinction.
Do you know, you, you,
What it is to be extinguished?
And what it is, the sea of birth and death?'

The holy man, the priest, coughed, had swallowed the wrong way,
Stood up.
Ash-smeared, he stepped down close to Manas,
Leaving the ancient book behind him on the step.

'Revulsion and delusion, you hear me,
Revulsion and delusion, nothing else!
Repeat it after me!
Wash your mouth out as you say it.
Extinction, you,' he pressed close to Manas,
'The world must be extinguished, we with it, you with it!
All must be extinguished, so that calm may come!
You do not know this, you with your beast-face.'

    'No.'

'No. You rampage, and you know nothing.
You run around like a Shade
And do not know whose Shade you are.
And turn up here, you,
You feel your fat thighs, your beast-face,
Squeeze your plump cheeks, twirl your moustache.
Now it is thick and black.
Once you had none, and soon it will be grey,
Grey and bristly like a cat's.
Why do you stare at me? I am telling you the truth.
Clutch your loins, your genitals that give you so much pleasure.
Some time something else will spurt from them:
Bitterness revulsion misery,
Just what I feel when I see you.
Then everything turns bad. Then you gasp and groan.

But your belly brings you no more pleasure.
You are withering, Manas, as everything must wither,
People, animals, plants, all of it,
All the stars and suns.
Better to be extinguished, to make an end.
For there must come an end, d'you see, Manas?
Perhaps you are still human enough to see it.
There comes a time to spit out this life of ours,
Like a rotten fruit, a mushroom
That is poison to us.
A slug lies at our feet, decaying.
We must kick it aside.
The decay is in your belly,
You understand me, hey? You understand?'

Manas stood silent.
People had drawn nearer,
Men with little top-knots, women in dazzling clothes.
Manas turned to them. Held a hand up to his eyes against the sun.
Spoke softly: 'What is he saying? What is this?'

Some among the men gathered courage.
A vulture flew low across the market.
They murmured to Manas:

> 'Listen to him! He is a wise man.
> Have pity on yourself.
> A holy man, he follows the path of holiness.'

Manas rasping: 'I never spoke to this man.'

> 'He is a holy man, you.'

Manas rasping to the priest, who had squatted down again:

> 'I'd rather listen to the monkeys screaming.
> I did not encourage you to speak to me.
> So we're to be extinguished.
> And why then was I born, you?'

'You gave birth to yourself.
Because you are evil.
You will always be born that way.
So that is why. That's why.'

Manas bit his lips, tugged at his moustache: 'So what should I do?'

'Go away from us.
We have looked enough into your mirror.
Go away.'

Chewing his lips, Manas: 'I asked what I should do.'

The holy man snuffled over his book.
He read and read.
After a long while he raised his head:
'Do not disturb my peace. I have seen enough of you.
You are behind me now.
I know what Shiva wants with you.'

Manas came one step closer:

> 'You, you, I tell you:
> Do not take that name into your mouth.'

'What?'

> 'Leave that name alone, the one you just said.
> You see, I don't say it either.
> Also: I am not your enemy.
> You are wise. You should instruct me.'

'Begone. I have nothing more to say to you.'

> 'One who possesses wisdom should not keep it back.
> It's granted to him so that all can share. Me too.
> Explain to me what you just said. Because I, I –'

And Manas spoke in confidence, bent down to the priest:

> 'I shall not be extinguished, you pious man.
> I… cannot be extinguished.'

'I know, you have returned a thousand times,
As tiger, dog, a pig.'

> 'As dog, pig, yes.
> Leave it. It's all the same to me.
> I shall not be extinguished!
> You may be extinguished.
> Savitri came to me, Savitri took me to herself,
> And removed all doubts from me,
> So that I no longer want to be extinguished
> And cannot be extinguished.
> You don't know this.'

And suddenly he took one step back and then another:

> 'Pooh, pooh. Now I have to spit it out from me.
> I'd like –'

He flexed his arms:

> 'I'd like… a sword, holy man!
> To cut you down, send you to your death.
> Yes, you, holy man.
> Let those who stand there hear it.
> Yes, that's what I would like to do.
> I'd like to think my thoughts through to the end.'

Silent over his book, the priest: 'So do it.'

Lips trembling, Manas: 'You… have insulted me.'
He trembled violently.
As his knees shook, he seemed to collapse.
But controlled himself,
Made ready to leave, walk away on stiff legs,
Run away across the marketplace,
But unsteady, on the point of falling,
Past the flower stalls.
He ran down streets he did not recognise.
There was calling out around him as he ran,
But no cry came from him.

HE OVERTOOK all the carts and people.
Past the palace, the garden where his Kalongs hung.
Traversed in endless headlong fury
The whole green valley in which the town of Amber lay.
His legs were always near to cramping.
The boggy lake below the castle hill came in his way.
There he sank down after his wind-swift flight, Manas.
He lay rigid, his body now at last a rigid stretched-out thing.

'He… he insulted Savitri! I can't go on.
He… insulted Savitri!'

By the lake Manas burst out weeping: 'Savitri insulted! I can't bear it.
What, what, what is meant to happen?
She who bore me, she that I held,
She is no longer with me,
Has abandoned me, sweet woman.
She showered me with everything, my life,
I long for her with all my being.
Tear down the temple that he keeps!
No matter whose it is, the temple has to go.
I must purify the town.'

He was suffering, suffering.
But his legs released him. He set off, he ran,
In through the gate in unstoppable fury,
Through the streets, calling to men and women.

'Come, come with me! Purify the town!
Don't hold back. Everyone come!'

Young and old, men, women surged around him,
That cry in the street was his. They pleaded:

>'It is Shiva's temple!'

He trembled: 'Come, come with me. No matter whose it is!
Quickly, axes, fire, it must all be gone by nightfall.
Then at night –
At night Savitri will come, and look at me,
The sweetest life, the Earth's boon, and see
What I have done.'

A ghastly squealing crowing rang out behind him.
The three demons had heard him running, shouting,
Had woken, were tangled in the leash.
Manas stormed to them in the garden,
Lips always moving, every limb in agitation,
Eyes shifting uneasily, hands cold,
Whispered to them as he untied them:

'Cleanse the place where he insulted her.
You understand, Nishumbha, you all understand?
And if you don't,
And if it does not happen, then – I am extinguished!
Manas… really is extinguished!'

They flapped, the Kalongs, across the garden with Manas,
Flew over the town.
So dark and menacing his mood that he forgot
To steer them, and they zigzagged blindly to and fro
Until he roused himself and forced them down
And tied the leash and tugged them.

Manas swept down into the empty square with his wheezing
    cawing demons.
They overturned the market stalls, devoured the offering-
    flowers,
A holy calf that lay sleek there was lifted up by Chanda
And dropped to smash onto cobbles.
They all three licked its blood, grew even greedier.
Monkeys swung from trees down to the temple.

In the empty square, on the steps,

The priest sat alone.
He sat on the steps, in the sun,
With the threefold mark of Shiva, his wizened body ash-smeared,
Reading, reading, legs tucked under him, book on his knees.
The uproar did not draw his eyes up from the book.
The holy man, he thought and knew:

> 'The world is full of uproar.
> Deception is cocksure, deception is alluring.
> Deception is the hallmark of this world.
> What helps against it? Nothing helps, but insight.
> No seeking and grubbing in the world can help,
> Just as it's no help against a noise to speak softly and more softly,
> But only deafness.
> Who can help against this force that bursts in so murderously,
> Swinging its clubs, shooting arrows, hurling firebrands?
> Not an army! One army is just like any other.
> But fire melts wax.
> Everything that moves is wax, wax made solid
> In a multitude of shapes, fantastic shapes. They make a noise,
> Are proud of their shapes.
> But a hot wind comes, and they collapse.
> Where then is their pride? Their pride is useless then.
> Look on, look on, gain insight
> Into everything that moves and sits!
> It is no cause for tears that someone suffers.
> And if he be oppressed by the strongest power,
> It is no cause for tears!
> All paths in the world are smoothed for one who wants to know.
> Suffering leads along the path.
> Sorrow: how can one give a name to sorrow?
> One who possesses knowledge can give a name:
> He is the torchbearer at the dark crossroads.

He chirps within us from morn till night like a little
 bird.
Care is taken to feed the little bird
Day by day, year by year.
At last it chirps no more, now it rings out its song,
Screams like a vulture in the mountains, spreads its
 mighty wings,
Soars over the ravines.
The vulture sees everything, knows everything.
What is sorrow in this world?
It starts as a spider's web, yet cannot be torn,
Can only be observed, now and then.
Then it becomes a hawser,
And the boat that it tows,
The boat must follow and will run onto rocks
And be shattered, unless the hawser is held fast.
The hawser must be held in the hand.
Hands may be soft: they will harden
As the hawser chafes them.
Knowledge exists, truth exists.
I can know it
Just as mighty Ganges springs from the head of the only
 God
Because the only God wills it:
I can go to the river,
Plunge into it and be cleansed, to my blessing!
They cry: sorrow is in the world.
Once there was a young woman.
She was alone, living with her relatives,
And sat and knew not what to do.
An old feeble man came to the house, and begged for alms.
She gave him some, fed him,
And when he came again she fed him again.
Her greedy relatives saw this.
And when the old man came a third time,

They chased him away, the relatives,
And they drove the young woman from the house.
Oh how she cried, the young woman in the wilderness.
All alone she was, suffered hunger, misery.
The old man appeared again.
She comforted him, hid her tears from him.
But then, at the crossroads, he sat her on an ox.
It was Shiva himself,
He carried her and rode with her, rode away
To where the Blessèd dwell.'

And the priest, eyes closed, chanted out over the book:

> 'Extinguished. Not be born.
An end to deception. An end to suffering.'

THE FIGURE with glowing eyes came running leaping across
    the square,
In his hands were torches of blazing pitch.
The wooden market stalls went up in flames.
Overhead, blotting out the sun,
The three Kalongs flew in close formation,
Demons from the Field of the Dead.
They were to attack Shiva's temple.

There, triple-domed gold-glittering,
Stood the temple of the Three-eyed One
Who once had subjugated them.
But he could not hold them in the icy mountains.
Secluded on his throne in Himavat he had no way
To stop them flapping free across the landscape,
Over flowers rivers creatures, sating themselves.
Behind them was a stronger power.

Now they would attack Shiva's temple
Where he was worshipped, the over-mighty God, the Dancer –

Where he preened himself.
Golden roofs: they crashed headfirst into them!
With their claws they tore tiles loose.
They squinted at the garish friezes:
Down with them, down onto the marketplace!
God-statues, ten arms, twenty arms, with peacocks and snakes:
Topple them!
The statues lurched,
Crashed down onto the steps,
And were shattered.

'Priest,' cried Manas from the foot of the steps,
Sweat dripping from his mad twitching face,
'Priest, have a care! Take your book, go away from here.'

Even as the statues crashed he still read on, pondering.
Now he looked up at Manas, wild twitching monster, torches in his fists.
Stood up in horror: 'You're going to burn down Shiva's temple!'

'Leave, no more questions, you.
The market, the temple have to go.'

The priest cast a glance at Manas, hid his face: 'I shall go.'
Picked up his book, ran from the temple,
In the burning marketplace pressed forehead to the ground
To beg the god's forgiveness –
To appease Shiva.

People piling up in the side streets
Were a single wailing, calling to Shiva:
That he show mercy, mercy, that he be merciful.

> 'Three-eyed One, Blue-throated One, it is not we who transgress.
> Blue-throated One, do not blame us for what another,
> A ghost from Hell, has done.
> Do not forget, do not dismiss all that we have done,
> What we have built for you,

How we humbled ourselves before you.
Do not drag us down along with him,
Do not trample us.
Come, come in mercy, Blue-throated, Terrible,
   Lion-eyed One,
Soft heart, sweet song.'

Fire swept hungrily across the marketplace.
Flames consumed the temple.
Smoke and murderous flames rose through the damaged roofs.
Between the pillars Manas stood with empty hands,
Trembling still, near the steps,
Now lit up harshly by the flames, now hidden in smoke.
The Kalongs yowled with joy in the black clouds.

RESPLENDENT, Kailash high in icy Himavat.
There the black icebound mountains lay,
Ponderous mighty mountains, age-old embedded beings.
In the blue above them, shimmering green,
Flew the World-shaker, Penitent,
With him the curly-headed youths, the Rudras with their
      moon-horns.
The humming cooing of the mountains
Was amplified by the tenthousandfold swelling hovering
      overhead.

The World-shaker flew over snowfields,
Cho Mafam came, the lake where he had burned,
Nanda Devi, Trisul, all the endless soaring peaks flown over
      in the blue.
Then the mountains sank, plummeted away,
Became forest swampland level plains.
People lived down there, tended fields.
Flown over in the blue, the cities Meerut and great Delhi.

And humans and beasts became conscious of a sweetness
As he flew over, though they could not see him.
For just a moment they were freed from cares,
Everything around them simple, fluid, within hand's reach.
The people seemed to hear a ringing in their ears:
Who was thinking of them at that moment?
But it was the humming of the ground, that hummed
As it sensed the Three-eyed One and his company of Rudras,
And now wanted to stammer
No more distinctly
Than when one says *ah*.

The waters in the many little rivers danced,
Their currents mingled. What lay below strove higher.
Stands of bamboo rang with a hundred voices.

But beyond Delhi with its ramparts forts towers triumphal arches
Lay Amber, mountains on each side.
In broad daylight fires were burning, dense palls of smoke.
A jumbled flood of cries prayers menaces rose up.

The one who wore Ganesha's rat-tail at his hips
Lifted a toppled horse of stone up from the step,
Stepped forward with it in his arms, flung it to the flames.
A questioning voice in him as he came out from the smoke:

> 'And what have you achieved, what's happened, Manas,
> When you set fire to the marketplace, and burn the horse,
>   burn the temple?
> The Earth has a hundred thousand marketplaces.
> In the Soul, in yours and those of all the others, nothing
>   has changed.'

'You're bluffing,' Manas stood there calmly,
'Don't think you can bluff me, voice.
This is a place,
And a place is more or less a piece of Soul.'

'This little corner?' asked the voice again.

> He murmured: 'More or less a piece of Soul.
> Just wait, just wait. The flames will make it better.'

And as the flames licked over the three domes,
With every billow the people in the ring of streets about the marketplace
Saw Manas as he stood, chest swelling *ah*,
Breathing out contented *ah*,
Tracking the flames with a hungry gaze.
And when a fiery finger flared and seized another timber,
They saw him groan in lust, and swell, eyes glazed and avid:
'It's not for my sake, after all.'

And twitched and cramped in anger,
When he heard the cries to Shiva from the street,
In disgust:

> 'Good there's such a thing as fire. Let fire devour them all.
> My Kalongs should crow, and drown out their cries.'
> And spat in black rage: 'Yes, come on, Shiva, come.
> Protect them. Help them.'

And yelled into the smoke, called through cupped hands:

> 'So summon him! Just let him see you.
> Who you are. What you are.
> He's missing from me, I've already dumped him.
> Fetch him, you dogs, it's all the same to me.
> He sits on crystal Kailash, sirens and youths on every side,
> Has little bells and slings and chains, daggers and skulls.
> Sits there on Kailash.
> That's your Field of the Dead.'

As they prayed and lay prostrate, they heard Manas roar.

> 'Fetch him! Call him!

> I'd like to see him, your protector,
> Let him come, it'll be fun for me,
> Endless fun, fun ten miles long, to watch him gobble
>   you up,
> The shepherd his flock, the wolf the sheep!
> Call him, the old goat-guzzler!
> Baa baa, goat-guzzler, on you come!
> Baa baa. The little lambs are calling you!'

The temple burned. Flames devoured the trees all around.

AND HIGH up in the blue, which had a greenish shimmer,
There suddenly rose up, steep and straight,
Sheaves of red and white.
As if a wind had risen, all the black swirling clouds of smoke
Vanished all at once.

The marketplace lay white and spotless in the sun.
Pale red flames played on, almost invisible,
Transparent fingers in the air.
A deep silence on the marketplace, the whole town.
Deep silence.
No crackle of burning timbers, no crash of statues toppling.

And in the deep silence of the market, over by the steps,
As tall as the central dome,
Stood Shiva, in his tigerskin.

He stood there, flames licking crooning at him.
Stood without a sound,
As if he had stood since time began,
The feet with all their rings and buckles
On ground that heaved and rippled and pulled and slid away,
And caressed the feet.

On the Three-eyed God's blue neck sat the head,

Its black locks dangled across his brow.
He stood silent on the marketplace, Shiva,
And though he himself stood still, on him everything was moving.
The cobras played across his fleshy cheeks,
His eyes, green as Cho Mafam lake, shimmered and turned.
The pearlstring quivered on the sleek bare chest.
His expression changed from one moment to the next.
The muscles of his feet, his legs rippled gently.

Manas saw all this,
His eyes saw saw,
His limbs felt it all, all all.

He stood up, stammered, lay on the heaving ground:
'I love you so. I, I, I love you so.'
He quite dazed, submissive, urgent:
'O I love you so.
All that I am, all that I am, all, I love you so,
So, so endlessly.'

The Kalongs stayed well behind him in the marketplace.
When the air's humming blew across the plain,
They knew who was on the way.
The demons dug in under charred stalls, played dead.
Manas still had hold of them by the leash about his arm.

Shiva's voice came softly, enclosing like a bubble those who heard it:

    'Give me my Kalongs, Manas.'

'O I love you so, O you of giant's strength,
You who are Delight, Devourer, Chain-hurler.
That I should be alive and you are too.
And I am at your side.
You more lovely than the sea,
More wonderful than women and forests and mountains.

That I should live when you live. Oh am I still alive.'

The head of snakes, tongues flickering, bent down:

'The Kalongs, Manas.'

A giant hand hovered over Manas, seemed to grasp towards the leash.

Manas groaned:

'Do not do that.

O Shiva, down what paths have I already followed you.

I love you endlessly, love you so.

Now I know it all, what I am, what I have done.

That I am still alive, and breathe, and can love you.'

The giant hand came lower.

Slowly, as if bending in a wind, Shiva leaned down over the marketplace

Where all the ground was heaving.

The burned hulk of the temple came crashing down.

'O do not do it, Shiva.

Do not touch me, do not touch my chain.

Here I am on my knees.

As the ground heaves and lifts itself towards you,

I follow only you.

Down to the very core you are mine.

Now I am no longer alone,

For a long time now I have not been alone.

I feel you, you are here, you Delight, you Blessed One.'

The darting tongues and whistling of the snakes lay close on the marketplace.

The cobras, their golden eyes, slid down from Shiva's shoulders.

As Shiva leaned down he cast no shadow,

The marketplace did not darken,

Sunlight still glared.

Only a humming twitching started up across all the ground.

Everything he neared acquired a voice, spoke to him,
The wooden bench under which the demons lay
Began to croak like one deaf and dumb.
Ashes blew about. In the air such a sharpsweet breath.
It caused the demons suddenly to rear up
As if they choked, or had been bitten.
They too felt an urging to call out.
They flung themselves high, whined.

In the marketplace Manas went down on his knees,
Still stammering: 'Do not do that. I love you so.'
Wept, tears flooded from him.
Then, the cobras playing over him already,
He stammered, trembled, stood: 'It must be. It is your will.'
Darted away, leash about his arm, across the market, rasped into
    the lanes:
'Go away, little people! Nothing will happen to you.
Go far away.'

Dreadful dreadful:
He dragged the drooling whining demons out from the ashes,
Into the blinding light, into the sweet air: 'Here they are.'
Dragged them behind him,
Flung them into the middle of the marketplace:
'There they are. Try it. Take them from me.'

AMBER was ringed around by craggy hills.
These were covered in scrub and forest,
The ground threw up stones and hedges in between.

Shiva stepped back behind the temple, was already in the plain.

'I did not want this, you Delight, our Blessing,' sobbed Manas
    from below,

The Kalongs' leash still wound around his arm, his body, neck.
Two snakes lunged at him from Shiva's shoulders, mobbed him.
Shiva retreated to a line of hills.

'What will you do with me, Shiva?'

    'You must show remorse. Hand over the Kalongs.'

'You could drag them from me.'

    'You must hand them to me.'

'Drag them from me, you're the stronger.'

    'You must show humility. You must submit.'

Manas cried and wept,
Swung high over the ground gripped by the two snake bodies.

'This to me. Shaming me. Saying this to me.
Now it's all over between us.
Now I shall listen to nothing that you say.'

Shiva stepped onto a rounded hill, masonry trickled down.
And with Manas swinging from his shoulder
Shiva started his first dance around the bounds of Amber.
From rounded hill to rounded hill he set his feet.
Houses underneath were crushed.
People poured out from the valley.
They lay helpless when his flowery foot rose over them,
Then they hurried away: no one was harmed.

And the only sound across the town and in the hills
Was the sighing and soughing of the air.
Visible in the sky were the rose-red clouds
On which the Rudras lay, the curly-heads,
And the Earth heaved, hill and valley heaved in harmony like a sea.

'It will happen,' Manas muttered as he flew along on Shiva's
    shoulder.
'It will happen, I shall tumble down.
Maybe I shall die.

I shall not die. I won't allow it.'

Shiva twirled leaping over rounded hills.
Pink clouds hung motionless above the valley.
Shiva twirled and twirled from hill to hill.
A crashing, clattering of stones.
The cobras rearing writhing all about him,
And in the clattering rumble of the stones was mixed another
    sound:
In harmony with the stamp of Shiva's feet, hands clapped.
It was the sirens in the rosy clouds, their hands were clapping:

> 'A thousand doctors, - twirl, king, twirl –
> A thousand herbs, a thousand doctors, thousand potions!
> There are trees that heal, there are sufferings that heal.
> A thousand herbs, a thousand potions, thousand doctors!
> Let them see you, king,
> Show how you sway and never stumble.
> The air is full of threads for you.
> Tread, foot – roll, stones – twirl, toes – stamp.
> The one who swings and sways
> Is our king of kings, Blue-throated,
> Victor of all victors.
> He treads the hills and stands.
> There is none who heals like you,
> Who gives release like you.
> A thousand herbs, a thousand doctors, thousand potions!'

Manas flew along on Shiva's shoulder.
He was conscious.
He heard them clapping singing from within the rosy clouds.
They sing my death. It will happen that I die.
It is his mercy.
And it went through him:

This is how I flew once, on the Field.
Ice below me, snow flurries at my back.

I flew, I flew. The wind picked me, spun me.
I couldn't reach the ground.
Only on the ground, where the air was gentle, could I hold on.
Now I'm flying just like that.

The singing-girls clapped. Shiva leaped his next leap.

This is me, held fast by snakes.
They'll stupefy me, strangle me.
And what will they do to my Kalongs.
For this I endured the Field of the Dead,
For this did Shiva fetch me back.
For this the Bo-tree spoke to me.

He ceased his roaring, wept in his closed mouth:
I shall not weep. It was not for this I endured the Field.
It was not for this, not for this, that Savitri gave me my rebirth.
I must not, shall not let them strangle me, the snakes.
I must not, shall not.

He gasped. No matter how the flight, the twirling, dazed him,
His senses did not leave him.
He gasped: I must not, shall not.
And there came to him the words he had spoken on the Field
To Puto, who held him by the chain:
Puto, my death is mine.
And even if you are Puto, the mighty man,
And can shift bolts,
I am Manas, I am Sorrow,
Crushing frantic Sorrow, terrible Sorrow,
I am dreadful Sorrow.
I am as strong as you, stronger than anything there is.
I am the water that blasts away the mountain.

And pulled himself together, and no longer muttered
And walled himself in.

MANAS, borne aloft by the great Blue-throated One,
Spoke not another word.
As a hand pulls the bowstring
To speed the arrow so terribly, most terribly on its way,
So he pulled himself quite taut.
No longer heard the singing of the heavenly women,
The stamp of Shiva's dancing steps,
The humming of the air around Shiva,
And of the yearning loving plants and mountains beneath his heels.

Though terribly taut he still could feel his skin,
And knew the snakes had him pinned.
Felt his knees, his toes, the water in his mouth,
And kept his eyes unopened.
These were his mouth, his forehead, his knees.
Were mouth forehead knees still there?
He pulled back from his eyes, his ears.
The legs were there, squeezed by the snakes,
Arms pressed to his chest:
He withdrew the feeling from arms and legs,
Let them go from him, away from him,
No longer felt them.
They dropped from him like leaves.
Likewise the mouth, the forehead, chin, the trussed up twisted body.

As a player knocks a ball away with his fist,
He pushed them from him into the void.
Onward he pressed, Manas, tautened himself onward,
Terribly most terribly.
Where to? To himself, along a path.

'I'm still breathing. I don't want to breathe.'

An eddy of light within him, silent lightning.

The one who flew on Shiva's shoulder, Manas,
Did not release his breath.
He swung along, did not yield to the urge to breathe,
Took the urge into himself,
Took from his heart the urge to beat.

And so burdened, Manas made himself quite taut,
And like an attic cat that leaps this way and that,
Up the ladder, down the ladder, bumps her head on rafters,
She finds the window, it lifts up,
Rain beats in, she slips through, into open air,
So Manas, walled in on himself, slipped suddenly away from Shiva,
From the lovely furious Dancer, Strangler, Snake-swinger
And ran ran, to fetch the strength of iron
And evade his death.

Ran along a path, an endless distant path
On his own legs, stormed along.
How he raced past everything, stormed straight ahead.
His right arm stretched out straight, tore clear the path ahead of him,
Nothing but will, and anger.
Then he stormed up to a building, a mighty castle.
The door stood closed. He shouted to it: 'Open up.'

'Who are you?' cried the door.

'Manas.' It did not open.
He kicked it, then calmed down, and stroked it.

It called out: 'Who are you?'

'I… am…you.'

The door still would not open, began to shake, to bulge.
Manas stood and waited, gathered himself up.
It creaked, shook, would not open.
He did not touch it, he turned away.
Turning away, chin on his chest, he murmured:

'Open up!' – 'Why should I open up?'

'Because I,' Manas murmured, and felt fully what he murmured, 'I am not Manas, I am not you, I am… .'

He could not say it, his tongue would not produce the word. He stammered: 'I am… the Third.'

   'The Third, what is it?'

And Manas, with no sense of horror, in calm assurance:
'Open up, door. You know what is the Third.
I can't name it, you can't name it.
I am not the Third… yet am.
Don't speak, say nothing.
Open up, door, because you know what I am saying.'

And the door silently opened.
And Manas crept into his limbs,
As he swung on Shiva's shoulders.
He surged out through the pores of his skin.
Went, trussed up by Shiva's cobras, to seek help for himself.
A huff of breath, a smoke seethed about his body,
He was too heavy for the snakes that held him.
They were rendered helpless by the smoke
That smouldered from him.

Shiva had completed his third circuit, ten whirlings for each circuit,
Stood on tiptoe behind the burnt-out temple
At the start of the fourth circuit.
The cobras dangled like wet hair from his head and shoulders.
At first two had carried Manas,
Then four had had to wind themselves around him, then ten.
Once they had him in their grasp, they reared up,
Then had to brace themselves, then bend,
Then sank back, writhing limply, and their bodies cramped.

But for the cramps, they would have let Manas fall

Down over the hills, onto the ravaged town.
For Manas, swaying across Shiva's shoulders,
Manas called out to the Ego,
That makes lips of lips, tongue of tongue, and makes hands of hands.
Manas oh Manas, Savitri's beloved child,
Called out to the Soul of the Soul, the secret hidden Ego,
Which is as hidden as the air is to the eyes
And lifts up everything as the air lifts birds.

And proudly he lay in the snakes' clutches, and let them lift him.
Manas called out to the Ego, which the mountains –
They were still at rest, and silent –
Once had summoned up and put in place,
And which had made the gift of fire, its glow and flare.
Manas, Manas in the strangling grip of snakes
And the entrancing clip-clap of the heavenly women,
Manas called out to the Sun and knew it once again,
And claimed it for himself, his eyes closed.
It knew him too, they knew each other,
The Sun that shone so radiantly over Amber,
That sailed aloof across the mountain peaks so far away
And basted the sea.

Manas, Manas, half throttled by the snakes,
Manas called out to the distant sea,
The blessed bluegreen sea that foamed, that rose up foaming,
And hid whole living species in its deeps.
And they were to come to his side, and he had command of them.

Manas called out to the myriad humans on the shores,
People on the plains and in the mountains.
And even if they died like nothing,
What he called out did not die with them.
When fire spits sparks, the spark extinguished falls back in the fire,
The fire keeps burning.

He called out to the people,
With the frail enormous shattering explosive Ego,
And saw them give a start, stand upright,
Saw their eyes open, and they knew themselves again.
And Manas hung enraptured from the snake bodies.
The heavy writhing bodies covered his mouth.
He pressed his mouth to them:
'Should I not kiss you? Am I not Savitri's child?'

NOW the Earth beneath Shiva's feet ceased its quaking,
Its tender rippling.
The rocks, the craggy peaks did not stay put,
The water summoned did not stay put,
The gusting wind did not keep its place.
The call of Manas came,
Not at all uncanny, not menacing horribly from a cave,
Called to their heart of hearts that they could not stay forever
  rock and crag,
Or lie in the watery mirror of a lake, or float as wind, or sway in
  treetops.
They were loosened, drawn along,
Yearned to follow the call.
For those that were called were themselves the call's voice.

Amber was encircled by hills upon hills.
They brushed Shiva's feet,
Brushed them no more.
His heels slid down from hillcrests.
The ground surged.
But Shiva did not notice,
And the singing-girls did not notice,
Still clapping with the beat, though Shiva breathed a little
  heavily

And something in him strayed far from the song.
The ground beneath him giving way, gathering like a closing
    hand.
Still Shiva twirled.

The landscape had grown dark.
Thick clouds had come up from the west,
The sea had breathed them out
To veil the singing-girls, so they would not look on Shiva
And be torn away from him.

The ground was a furrowed face, a boiling menacing breast,
Was a body, a giant, at rest,
It had no eyes and wanted grimly to stand up,
Terrible with arms and legs so it could grab at things around it.
It rose around Shiva like a corrie.

It was no longer a lake that lay there, thick with lotus flowers
    and reeds.
The water foamed when the call came,
Flung waves and sand over Shiva's feet.
It swelled in harmony with the ground, swept crags against
    Shiva's legs.

The ground itself, in Shiva's footsteps,
Ground rose up round him, closed in on him,
Like a garment pulled up ever higher
Which Shiva, dancing slower ever slower, tore with each step,
Until it reached his navel, squeezed tight,
Up over his tigerskin, clung tight to it.

Shiva was wading through crags, deep muddy ground,
His arms flailed down, head still unaware.
Shiva merely wondered wondered, with a twinge of anger,
Where the darkness came from,
What was that booming from black clouds,
What was the blackness blackness, far beyond where eye could see,
Covering the ground on which he danced
And rearing up around him.

Then it came to pass: lightning flashed from the clouds,
Thunder crashed down, lightning and thunder not hurled by
    Shiva,
But by whom?
And the singing-girls all flighty, screaming – what had seized
    them –
And the howling of the Rudras, scattered by the storm to
    south and west,
Across the plains to the sea that now pulled back its clouds.

Down below the lovely Behemoth was barricaded,
His breast hemmed in by boulders, rocky strata,
Walled in.
Darknesses around him, floods to drown in,
Waters pelting down on him.
The god could dance no more. He pulled his feet together.
Rocky strata heaved in time against his shoulders.
As drivers on a battue
From every side with their long bamboo staves
Break through the grass and thickets with their nets and slings
    and spears,
So the strata heaped up on all sides around Shiva,
Allowed huts and forests on their backs to slump and sink away.
Whole landscapes were in motion.
Rivers and hills rolled towards him.
The Earth's ground sent them
To cover Shiva up
And raise a giant mountain here,
Black, with a crater cradling the fires that would break out
    beneath him.
A volcano, the god buried under it.

And as Three-eyed Shiva stood stood, he thought *Ah,*
And *Who's crippling me? Who's crushing my limbs?*
Now at last there came to him
The huge outcry of rivers mountains, and the myriad people.

'Shiva, Flower-footed, Sea of Mercy,
Shiva the Terrible, our Lord,
Who is cooled by the fanning of areca palms,
Who scatters flowers all through the chanpaku forest,
Shiva, how the bells on your feet jingle!
Because you are strong, a giant,
Whirl snakes, gaze out from three eyes,
Are you not almighty!
You are not alone. Something lives that can kill you.
Something lives that gave birth to you!
Shiva, you are a created being, progeny,
Like us.
There's a place called Kailash beyond the mountains,
There's a Heaven above the Earth,
There's something above you.
Have a care, Shiva!'

Waters gurgled boiled, clouds bubbled up:

> 'Stay still, quite still, Manas. Have no fear.
> We are water. Do not regard us lightly,
> Our vapours permeate the air
> And sail like smoke across the sky,
> We douse the fire, choke the breath.
> Have no fear, Manas.'

On the hill's crest, the trees:

> 'We drink you in, take you into our sap.
> Slip into our roots!
> The mountain buries us, and we shall keep you safe.'

And the grumbling hills, the quaking ground,
As strata heaved one over the other:

> 'No need, no need for shouting. I am coming.'

And with a forward thrust he swam, swung back, lunged forward.
Forward thrust, backward swing.

The dense muttering, dense muttering of people
Like flocks of birds:

> 'Manas, we are with you, people,
> Wretched beings, wretched as you.
> Manas, you are suffering; do not suffer!
> It is we who call out.
> What are we?
> Ashes that the fire has left behind, or will leave behind,
> Bodies thrown here and there by inward and outward causes.
> Manas, what are we?
> Fish in water placed over fire.
> Still we swim, the water heats up,
> We snap at air, must leap out, and cannot help ourselves.
> If we boil we're dead.
> Manas, what are we if you don't resist?
> Feel us, do not die, do not give up.'

'I'm resisting, I shall resist,' murmured Manas.

AND WHILE Shiva was held down among the hills –
Who was crippling him, who poisoning his snakes? –
On sharp crags he wanted to stamp smooth because they cut his heels,
But he could not lift a foot,
Water foaming past his neck –
He noticed that his right shoulder drooped, and he could not lift it.

He felt over it in anger and in fear.
Lying there, the weight crushing, crushing,
Was the man he meant to kill, kill kindly for Savitri's sake.
A trivial being, a robber, who would not bow to him.

And the snakes could not support the man.
All his weight lay heavy on Shiva's shoulder,
Could not be shifted, not shifted from the shoulder,
The shoulders drooped beneath the load,
Shiva was being pushed into the foaming flood.

And only now, hand on his drooping shoulder,
Did Shiva sense that he was hemmed in, spellbound.
And saw it all,
The land that sought to spread itself on top of him,
Black water flooding, clouds hurtling down,
And heard – his hand dropped from the shoulder –
Heard the call that came from Manas. From this man, the call.
Terrible unprecedented call!
That he could stand as this cry rang out!
That he was not toppled long ago,
Not tripped and tumbled in his twirling dance!
The call that came from mountains, rivers, people!

'Manas, Manas,' Shiva cried.
But he paid no heed, continued calling.
'Manas!' A tremor in Shiva's knees.

This was why the crags dug into him, the sea roared up against him,
Shades would storm down from the Field of the Dead,
Kailash would be cast adrift from Himavat with all its gods ghosts demons,
Because he would not cease his calling.

'Stop now, Manas, everything can hear you,
I can hear you.
Do not destroy the world.
I release you.
Tame yourself, Manas, and cease your calling.'

But Manas would not be silenced yet.

'Leave the rocks alone, Manas, the sea alone, the people.
Don't stir them up against me.
Let them go back to be what they are, comforted.'

But Manas was caught up in a kind of web,
Could not free himself.
And since he would not let go, Shiva struggled with the walls of
    rock:
'I did not summon you, I did not conjure you,
Move back from me.'

Shiva's ghastly roar of pain when the walls stayed put:
'If you won't move back, then I shall stay here for you.
Take me. Swallow me. Inter me.
Shiva, who defeated the Asuras,
Here I am!'

And in the onrush of the landscapes that still stormed towards him,
Billowing thrusting ever denser high about him,
He let himself drop, his four arms over him,
Into the corrie, head first like a fish.
The tigerskin was torn from him,
The belt with the snakes and slingshots lay beneath his breast.

The dreadful weight of the great three-eyed god,
Despairing,
Was too much for the heaving ground.
It was squeezed down, bulged sideways, cracked,
Billowed like a cloud.

He lay face down, chin buried in the ground,
Mouth open, Shiva, on his body,
Knees, the golden feet rammed into the ground.
Manas falling with him, dangling from the rope of snakes,
Collided with a mountain that reared up.

The deadly impact shocked Manas from his trance.
Almost shattered, near to death, he came back to himself,

Entered his body again, which had been looking for him.
The smoke, the glare around Manas began to dissipate.
And Manas' call, too, receded.
And all at once, all at once the land sank back.
The plain the plain lay calm,
The lake the lake rippled in a new bed.
The sky grew bright.
Through the warm air, now warm again,
The Rudras came swooping down to Shiva.
And the Rudras' wailing, the musicians' weeping,
Imploring of the blessed spirits, sirens.

SHIVA'S roars rang out day after day,
His chin still buried in the ground, fists pummelling the Earth.
But the earth, now quaking happily again around him,
Had already opened up a cosy hollow for the lovely Three-eyed
    God,
Had gathered grasses, scented orchids all about his face.
Buzz and chirp of crickets. Goldgreen jumping spiders hopped.
The blessed spirits sat distraught beside him,
Tried to pour soma into him, the intoxicating potion of the
    heavenly beings,
Dared not let him see their agitation.

Then four days later Shiva felt a huffing huffing at his throat.
Tried to brush it away.
He thought his snakes were puffing, or his dancing-girls were
    clinging to him.
And still the steady huffing, something breathing.
Shiva stumbled slowly to his feet, heavy heavy,
Face sombre, deathly stiff, lumps of mud on his chin,
An entire sweet-scented orchid meadow on his arm, up past
    the elbow.

And as he sat, one hand feeling at his throat,
There were the strong cobras playing, a warm huffing wafting
    over them.
This was not their breathing.
They were rocking a body.
They let the breathing being slide onto his hand, down his arm.

It was a human, loose-limbed,
And when Shiva stretched out his open hand
It was a human, warm, asleep, all bloody, curled up tight,
Its back all scratched,
Legs deformed and swollen, lips puffy, ears,
Eyes popping out like orbs, rope-marks on its body,
Almost suffocated, squeezed breathless by the snakes.
In its sleep it covered Shiva's hand with kisses,
Slid torn and tattered over Shiva's fingertips,
As it slept and slid held tight to them,
Clung to the fingertips with mouth and hands,
But sank down to the ground moaning, reeling, dazed.

Shiva's great sleek breast heaved,
His face relaxed and brightened, a smile:
'Savitri's child, Savitri's child.'

He pulled his feet out from the heavy ground,
Felt for his tigerskin, found it, tied the belt.
The blessed spirits swarmed about him.
He knew them, drank down what they gave him.
Life flowed back into him,
The Three-eyed One was standing
At the craggy mountain's foot by the big sun-glittering lake.

For a long long time Shiva stood below the castle,
Not moving, still enchanted by the call, as if spellbound.
The eleven Rudras, howlers, youths, gathered in a white cloud
    about his head,
Swirled in a knot, fearful, confused, as were the sirens.

But the big snakes in Shiva's hair and on his shoulders
Reared their bodies calmly.

And now there came a rippling in Shiva, and he began to jiggle.
And calm and steadfast, like a transparent wall,
He lowered himself in his tigerskin to the ground.
The Earth, so long unenchanted,
The ground trembled tongued towards him
In long gentle waves, wheedling, tender.
But he took no notice.
Had to bend down.
On his head among the black locks the cobras played,
The third eye on his forehead stared intently.

Slowly, when his torso rested on the ground,
Shiva bowed, could not resist the urge
To bow his head down to the ground,
To the source from which had come that terrible call.
Manas sat up by the glittering lake,
Saw the wonderful head sink low,
Saw how Shiva bowed to him with head and torso.
He had no idea what Shiva was doing.

Just as star and star greet one another,
So did Shiva, bowing down, greet him:

'Blessed be the Earth, blessed the sky,
Blessed be every world,
Blessed be Manas.'

Then Shiva swept off with the Rudras
Who had come to fetch him, to Cho Mafam.
He did not go to Kailash.
At Cho Mafam he hung himself in flames,
Purified himself, atoned, glowed, to gain himself new strength.

BESIDE the glittering lake Manas sat straight.
Sat as once there on the Field, in the meadow
When the Shade of the shepherd boy left him,
Hours and hours.
The big yellow sun moved silent overhead, began to set.
But he sat there in a rapture,
His innermost being imbibed the mighty rapture
That the Three-eyed One in the tigerskin had bequeathed to him.
The choking rapture of his near gaze,
As he bowed down with his snakes and clinking chains
By the lake.

And in the morning Manas still sat there by the lake,
Sat there in the hot noontime.
Crickets buzzed and chirped, goldgreen spiders jumped.
The rapture was in him and did not fade,
So he wondered if he should not, must not die,
Leave now, die to follow Shiva.

Towards midday he was woken by snarls and wheezes
That did not stop.
The Kalongs lay behind him by the lake.
His gaze swept over them, and then he bowed his head:
'Shiva, here are my Kalongs.
They are yours, they don't belong to me.
Take them.'

And again: 'Shiva, I am no murderer.
I was never one.
You are filled with strength and sweetness.
If you will take the Kalongs, Shiva,
If you will give them to Ganesha, I give you them.'

He waited whispered: 'I have never stained my hands with
    murder,
I have always venerated you.
I know sorrow, the Field of the Dead has witnessed me.

If you want the Kalongs, I give them to you.'

No movement. Just louder coughs and wheezes,
And then growls that brought Manas to his feet.
What was growling?
Those things there.
Not Kalongs, rather ochre-yellow beasts
That stretched out giant wings just like the Kalongs,
But the soft supple arching bodies were those of panthers.
Yellow-white the throats, the bellies,
Flecked black, striped black the pelts,
Bright cats with fearsome claws, strong tails whipping.

They leaped high at Manas, pinned his body down.
He wrestled them off, two with his hands,
The third clawed at his chest.
Manas flung himself about, squeezed it to the ground.
Then let them go. They crawled around him,
Crept around him, batted him in play.
Spattered sand on him, dug growling.

'Yellow pelts, yellow eyes, why do you growl?
Are you Nishumbha, Munda?'

They rolled their springy bodies, whipped sand with their tails,
Turned yellow eyes on him, and growled.
Manas could not understand what they were saying,
Grasped them by the neck, tenderly, most tenderly,
Blessedness in him:
'Shiva's gift! He's given them to me!
The lovely god has bestowed on me a gift: you.
He has blessed me. And you shall stay with me.'

In the lake below the cliff Manas washed himself clean of blood.
He lay all day long below the castle hill,
The dream surged once again up through him.
He had to lie down, burrow in the sand, arms around a panther:
'I clung to his neck,

He lowered me over his fingers, the Flower-footed One,
I slid down his arms,
He held me like a pearl, let me slide down.'

The stupefaction that came over him!
He could not tear himself away from Amber.
The dreadful wounds on his back soon healed.
Then the panthers stretched their yellow wings.

'I'm coming, Nishumbha, Chanda.
I don't know if I have a home,
But if I do, then it is Amber.
It's so hard, so hard to leave.'

They growled, and swung blithely up into the blue air.

NOW Manas flew with the panthers away from Amber,
Swung with them across the wide land,
Swooped over hills steppes thickets.
Where doves and parrots flew through blue air, there he sailed.
On the dusty plain between Jelum and Satlej,
He descended into reeds, lush grass.
These were no night-beasts, the ones he flew with.
Did not waddle, or hang themselves in trees.
Ran springy and silent, bright bodies weaving this way and that.
They leaped with iron strength, brought down jackals antelopes.

But Manas thought of Amber, always of Amber.
Loud cities, wilderness, forests.
The great mountain range of Himavat.
Phoenix and palms grew there, the shala tree, acacias,
The forest rose in steps, fringed with reeds and grasses,
Reeds invaded the river valleys.

Manas, who never forgot Amber, tucked himself away on
      Himavat,

Scrabbled around with beasts and trees.
For a long time there was no sighting of him,
That dreamy being who sang out joyfully.

He went wandering with his panthers.
Ice-crowned mountains shimmered in the background.
He crossed the boundary of the Field of the Dead –
Demons could not withstand him –
And stole away souls wailing for a return,
That craved a return to Earth, to Earth's delights.
There were delights enough, enough plants beasts and people there,
In which they could live, those that no longer wished to live,
And needed new souls.

He came down to the land of Sindh along the Indus,
Had to fly through rain over fields of rice and millet,
Far across steppes hills and deserts.
He was not the sambu deer that devastates the crops.
He left his panthers in the bush,
And like Shiva in the fires of Cho Mafam,
Hung himself in the woes of people,
Of the poor, the peasants, the oppressed,
And suffered suffered.

As he had discovered ecstasy, so now he suffered suffered,
So that nothing should be forgotten.
How he turned his face away, sobbing, this deadful Manas,
How he crouched down at their side.

And with heavy heavy heart flew with his panthers,
Appeared over Delhi, Lucknow,
Dropped into towns, the strong naked brown man,
Terrible his gaze, burning flashing penetrating,
His shattering gaze.
In the squares, elephants in purple blankets stamped their feet.
Jains went by, mouths covered by a veil so no fly would be swallowed.

In the streets they cried out: 'Fear the Lord thy God!'
A procession to the burning ground.
They touched torches to the corpse's lips.
His glowing shattering gaze!
They flung themselves down, wailed hopelessly:

> 'What is left of one who gives his soul to the fire,
> His breath to the wind, his eyes to the sun,
> His blood to the water?'

His shattering gaze! Manas' shattering gaze!
Shiva had bestowed bright bodies on these demons.
They had been freed from the Realm of Death,
Could see by day without squinting.
They were Manas' servants.
They swooped on those immersed in misery, Manas on their
    backs,
By night, with snarls and growls that only those immersed could
    hear.
Swooped on them, invisible to others,
Appeared out of Nothing, tore it open,
Dug claws into their hearts.
Manas' menacing scourging call!
In the morning they lay dead, those who had been visited,
No wounds on them,
Or stumbled about in the light, seared, their gaze strange.

In white clouds flashing yellow,
Manas flew above the villages and towns of Punjab,
The terrible call always in his mouth, enticing compelling
    luring,
Savitri's call, blissful, searing, from his mouth:
'Up, up, lift yourselves! Lift your arms! You have arms!
Power! Power!'

Wails and sobs mingled with his call,
His call broken by weeping.

Then again an organ-roar, a gaur-ox in the forest underbrush:
'You! You! Do not immerse yourselves in misery!
Do not give in!
Shiva lives!
You are not alive! Not yet! None of you is yet alive!'

And lay with them in Shiva's temple,
Embraced them overflowing with love,
And flew on his panthers from Kashmir to Bhopal,
Full of joyful longing from Tarashi to Bharatpur.
A glow in him like a light that waits in a house
For one who is not there,
Someone longed-for, who will return.

In what far distant heights now was Savitri,
Loving child of sunshine, healing herb,
Who plunges into every world?

He is not extinguished. Not extinguished.
Manas is not extinguished.

THE END

Alfred Döblin

Born 1878 in Stettin, fourth of five children of a master tailor. When the father absconded in 1888 the family had to move to Berlin, reliant on the charity of relatives. The family was Jewish by background, but non-practising.

Döblin began writing while still at school, but qualified as a medical doctor specialising in psychology and neurology. Even as his fame as a writer grew, he regarded his clinical practice in a poor district of Berlin as his primary profession.

Before the First World War he befriended the Modernists Herwarth Walden and Else Lasker-Schüler, and in 1910 helped found the Futurist journal *Der Sturm*. Döblin's first great epic novel, The *Three Leaps of Wang Lun*, completed in 1913 and published in 1916, led to a breach with the Modernists: 'You tend your Futurism, I'll tend my Döblinism!' Through the Weimar period Döblin was a prolific polemicist and critic, and wrote insightful essays on the craft of fiction.

Wallenstein, a 900-page epic begun during the First World War about an earlier disastrous episode in German history, the Thirty Years War (1618-48), was published in 1920. It was followed by an epic of the far future, *Berge Meere und Giganten* (*Mountains Oceans Giants*) in 1924, and in 1927 by the verse epic *Manas*, a dramatic intriguing narrative blending Hindu mythology and Existentialism.

The success of *Berlin Alexanderplatz* (1929), his only best seller and subject of an acclaimed 1980 TV miniseries by Rainer Werner Fassbinder, eclipsed the rest of Döblin's large oeuvre. In the Anglophone world almost nothing is known of his other works.

In 1933 Döblin fled from the Nazis, settling first in Zurich and then in Paris, where he acquired French citizenship. In

Paris he wrote the South American trilogy *Land without Death* (a.k.a. *Amazonas*), an engrossing and wide-ranging critique of the Eurocentric view of the Americas.

Forced to flee again in 1940, Döblin spent the war years in Los Angeles, working like many other exiles on the fringes of Hollywood. Returning to Germany in 1945, he had little success in connecting with a traumatised postwar public. His last major works were *November 1918* and *Hamlet: Tales of a Long Night*.

Since his death in 1957, Döblin's reputation in German-speaking lands has risen steadily, and new critical editions of his works appear every decade or two. But publishers in the U.K. and North America are reluctant to take on his other works– because he is "unknown".